Quoth The Raven

Jim Roper

AmErica House
Baltimore

First printing

ISBN: 1-59129-051-1
PUBLISHED BY AMERICA HOUSE BOOK PUBLISHERS
www.publishamerica.com
Baltimore

Printed in the United States of America

Quoth the Raven is dedicated to the memory of Raven FAC D. Craig Morrison II (1945-1994). Craig enjoyed life the easy way--one day at a time.

Acknowledgements

Special thanks to Jimmie H. Butler, John Clark Pratt, Charlie Pocock, John Plaster, and Keith Rosenkranz, warrior-authors who encouraged me through the minefields. Jimmie suggested the title. Thanks to Jimmie Butler's Critique Group: Charlie Rush, John Becker, Dave Claytor, Drue DeBerry, Beth Groundwater, Debby Lince, Keith McGinley, Susan Rust, and Ann Black, who ripped me to shreds, twenty pages at a time.

Thanks to all the Ravens, and especially Big Al Galante, Larry Sanborn, Ernie Anderson, Carl Goembel, Chad Swedberg, Jim Hix, Lew Hatch, Frank Kricker, Lloyd Duncan, and Fred "Magnet Ass" Platt.

Other special people who contributed are: General Ed Eberhart; Dr. Jim Titus at the Air Force Center for Aerospace Doctrine, Research and Education; Bill Forsyth of Project Full Accounting; Don Brown, Dick Anderson, Larry "Chance" Hughes and Paul Smith of the Thailand Laos Cambodia Brotherhood; Chuck McGrath and the others on the crew of Jolly 54; the staffs of the Air University Library and Airpower Research Institute; Tim "Captain Skinny" Eby, who supplied his dialogue with Major Major; and "Uncle" Al Dyer, Jack "Spider" Webb, Larry Hauser.

And I thank my wife, Liz.

Chapter 1
Plan B

June 2, 1968

"I won't do it. No way," I told John Hudson, my Beta Theta Pi roommate. We walked in the shade of hardwood trees and red brick buildings of the small central Indiana campus.

John had been accepted at Indiana University Medical School. "All you have to do is write a letter."

"Yeah, a letter saying my four years at Wabash College were the most wonderful times of my life. No way. I won't lie for the dean or anybody." My Ph.D. fellowship in chemistry had been negated--no, annihilated--by my local draft board.

"The Dean of the College sounded serious the last time I took his call for you."

"I'm serious, too. I won't compromise my integrity, while the federal government cancels my dreams. My very existence becomes a question when they send me to Vietnam."

"The Army may have your number, but Vietnam's only one possibility."

"I took my draft physical two days after the Tet offensive in January. Have you ever heard of supply and demand?" I ducked behind a tree, adjusting the baccalaureate cap that stuck to my sweaty forehead. The black gown covered me like a shroud.

"What are you doing?"

"I'm waiting for that group of faculty ahead of us to pass. All I want is a diploma--not a confrontation with the dean. Without a sheepskin, the Air Force won't accept me for pilot training--my plan B. I'll carry a rifle for sure."

John laughed. "Why don't you just lay back and enjoy it?"

"After you're a doctor, do you plan to use those words on rape victims?"

John shook his head.

"How can I say I've enjoyed Wabash? Sometimes I enjoyed wrestling and playing football. But I paid the price by groveling for my grades. Life here was four years of sleep-deprived, last-minute intellectual chaos."

John smiled. "So?"

"First, I won't compromise my integrity and say my experience was anything else. Second, the whole effort means nothing."

"I don't know." With his future secure, I surmised, John couldn't understand the turbulence that had taken over my life like a fatal disease.

"Also, I'm in a major war of words with my parents--my stepfather hates me. And Elaine has backed away from the man with no future. Emotionally, I've got nothing more to lose."

"She'll wait."

"Nah. I don't want her to wait."

We approached a line of capped-and-gowned students that wound from an outdoor stage along the sidewalk beside Baxter Hall.

"Let's talk later." John turned away.

"Get in line, soldier," a football pal yelled. He had attended Marine bootcamp the previous summer. "Alphabetical order by height."

I saluted and found my place.

The short gray Dean of the College came down the line, shaking the hand of each graduate.

When he arrived before me, he stopped, folded his arms and scowled. "I need a letter from you. The Baker Foundation is dividing the scholarship fund among individual colleges. Each Baker Scholar owes them a good letter so Wabash can receive its share of scholarship money."

"No, sir. I won't lie."

"If you don't write the letter, you can't graduate."

I turned toward the fraternity house and stepped from the line.

"We all have to do things we don't enjoy," he shouted. "I don't care for neckties on hot days, but here I am, wearing one."

I stopped about twenty feet away. "I finished four hard years the draft board renders irrelevant. At this moment, I feel no joy about Wabash College. But our disagreement isn't about joy. It's about truth."

My peers in the line grumbled.

I sensed their empathy, but I stopped short of advising the dean that Vietnam was his war, not ours.

"You can graduate." The dean compromised. "Give me a letter before you leave town."

"I have bills to pay, sir. Tomorrow morning I start laying sewer pipe in front of Munster High School. You win. Keep your diploma." I walked.

"Come on and get back in line, mister." The dean had to yell. "Promise me you'll write a letter thanking them for the scholarship. Be honest. I know you won't be rude."

"Fine, sir. I'll thank them." I marched slowly to my place in line.

May 1970

Turquoise breakers crashed without a care onto the pure white sand of Fort Walton Beach, Florida. Ray Stevens sang Everything is Beautiful from a radio lying on a carpet of colorful beach towels. My red cooler attracted a half-dozen thirsty Air Force compadres from pilot training and officer training school.

Two dark A-1 Skyraiders approached in close formation. On their way to bombing ranges on the Eglin Military Reservation, the huge single-seat fighters thundered overhead like armored knights. Deep throbbing of 2700 horsepower radial engines carried me back in time.

Maybe I was born one war too late.

"Are you ready for class tomorrow?" Dugan asked.

"I'm not finished with today." I took a long sip of cold beer. "I won't quote Shakespeare, but one of these tomorrows will find all of us in Vietnam."

"I picked up a schedule at the Q." With a heavy New York brogue Dugan referred to the Visiting Officers Quarters where we had checked in earlier. "We begin with a week of counterinsurgency training, then Air-Ground Operations School for three weeks, and finally a ten-week upgrade in the O-Two for us. Don't know how long the O-One and O.V.-Ten courses last."

Dugan was six feet tall with blue eyes and brown hair. His upper lip sported red fuzz--a mustache begun a month ago when he entered basic survival school. We'd spent a year together at Vance Air Force Base in Oklahoma, where we competed intensely throughout Undergraduate Pilot Training. Of ninety-eight graduates, he finished fourteenth and I ranked thirteenth.

"Looks like three weeks of training crammed into three months," John Browning added. "I only have a short time left."

Since graduating from Officer Training School, I hadn't seen Brownie in more than a year. We had completed Undergraduate Pilot Training at different bases. A Harvard graduate, Brownie had large brown eyes, a crew cut, and an olive complexion. He took no leave since being sworn in and entered the FAC class a month ahead of me.

"One of your U.P.T. buddies told me you finally found an aircraft you could handle in the O-Two."

The group laughed at my jab.

"After flying the supersonic T-Thirty-eight, you'll be hard-pressed to call the Oscar Deuce an upgrade."

My mind flashed a picture of him at O.T.S. on all fours using tape to collect lint balls before a room inspection. "Beats chasing woolies with scotch tape."

Brownie smiled. "You almost got tossed out of that place--more than once. Still pushing limits, aren't you?"

"Tell us more," Dugan and others chimed.

"He got into a fight in a flickerball game."

"Self-defense," I said. "Some guy named Les slugged me."

"Then," Brownie said, "he continued the fight in the penalty box."

"They put us both in the same penalty box. What do you expect?"

Rowrowrowrow. Unsynchronized front and rear propellers produced the distinctive, unpleasant drone of an O-2 over the white-capped gulf. The gray aircraft banked toward the beach. Twin-booms and white wing-tops flashed briefly when what we called the Duck made a low pass over the officers club.

Several friends raised beers in salute.

"A classmate flew one of those things into the ground yesterday," Brownie said. "He probably got target fixation on a rocket pass. Never pulled out."

"Geez," I said. "Good guy?"

"Yeah."

Crashing breakers filled the pause in conversation.

"Losing a friend hurts," I said. "Last summer I opened Life Magazine featuring two-hundred and forty-two faces of one week's dead in Vietnam. I saw my next-door neighbor, John Abbott, staring at me. Before him, the war took my pal, Mike Hall, captain of the Wabash football team. His nickname was Campus Leader. What a damned waste."

"Feels like a part of your soul has been ripped away," Brownie said. "Sorry I mentioned the accident."

"Where are you guys from?" I changed the subject and pushed the cooler at two newcomers who sat with our group of fledgling Forward Air Controllers.

"I'm Pete Landry." A tall man with angular features pulled out two beers. "I hail from Boston and lately from pilot school at Big Spring, Texas. My big friend here is Jerry--Jerry Bevan, from Minnesoter."

Dugan asked, "Baaston? Are you a Haavard type like Browning?"

"No." Pete boomed a deep bass note. His brown hair was longer than average, and he combed it straight back. "Prior enlisted service. Worked nights for my degree, earned my commission, then my wings. And are you making fun of my accent, Mister Bad Mustache?"

Dugan's cheeks turned red. "No offense. Before graduation day, you'll envy my handlebar." He flattened the tiny red hairs on his top lip outward with his index fingers.

Jerry's boyish face reflected the humor his friends exchanged. Tall and muscular, he had short brown hair that defied a comb.

I asked, "Did you play football in college?"

"Tight end at Northwestern."

"Linebacker at Wabash." We clinked beer cans.

Jerry asked, "Indiana, right?"

"Wabash is a Division Three school in Crawfordsville, near Naptown. We play for the fun of the game."

"Did you volunteer for this fracas?"

"If you mean the Air Force, I guess I joined to avoid the infantry, like everyone here. Barely escaped hauling a rifle."

Jerry nodded. "Me, too."

"My late father, Jesse, served as an Air Corps crew chief in World War Two. I have pictures of him standing beside P-47s--probably planted the idea."

Several friends nodded and spoke of fathers in the forces.

Jerry smiled. "The Selective Service came after me like a pack of wild dogs."

The Selective Service makes the Internal Revenue Service look good," Brownie said. "After all, the I.R.S. only wants your money."

Two F-4 fighters roared over us headed out to sea. "The sound of freedom," I said. "Lord knows, it ain't free."

My friends shared my feelings. We had signed Air Force paperwork, happily trading the hard life of foot soldiers for the hope of becoming pilots. Under the shadow of Vietnam, law-abiding members of our generation no longer controlled our lives.

When I pinned on my wings, I decided I would go to Vietnam. My class standing qualified me for a stateside instructor job, but I felt attracted to the idea of combat. Since the military was inevitable, then I wanted to go be where the action was. I had studied enough history that my curiosity had evolved into fascination with warfare. But the books never answered the real question for me: Why did men stand and risk it all? I had no intention of dying, but like many soldiers I felt attracted--irrationally perhaps--to the sound of cannon.

The next morning I sat with Pete and thirty others in a small auditorium at the Special Operations School on Hurlburt Air Force Base. As the curtains opened, the house lights fell. On stage, a makeshift lean-to sat among infantry gear and leafy bushes. Inside the tent two pretend-Viet Cong insurgents lit candles. They wore drab clothing and carried the same austere equipment as real Cong.

One soldier began, "The U.S. aggressors cannot prevail against the dedicated soldiers of the Vietnamese people."

"Uncle Ho teaches patience," the second said. "In time the Americans must leave."

Our class sat in silent awe as the soldiers ate rice with their fingers and planned an ambush. Finally they stood, picked up A.K.-47 rifles and wandered menacingly into the audience, inviting questions from the Yankee imperialist students.

Eventually we rose above their intimidation and learned about a typical day in the life of our enemy, how he fought, and his vulnerabilities.

After class, Pete said, "These people are hard-core. Can you imagine trying to win their hearts and minds?"

"No," I said. "I think the war has passed into the annihilation phase."

"I learned more today than I ever knew about Vietnam."

"The entire faculty has been to Southeast Asia," I said. "They tell it like it is."

Tall pine trees shaded the concrete balcony of our two-story red-brick quarters. Pete, Jerry, Dugan and I relaxed in chairs against the aluminum railing near the building's second-floor breeze way.

I asked, "You guys up for a night out?"

"Not in my plans," Pete said. "I'll eat here and call home." He held out a picture of his wife and three little girls, each smiling under thick blond hair.

"Picture time?" Jerry asked. He showed me a photograph of a gorgeous brunette. "My girlfriend's coming to visit in a few weeks. I'll save my social energy for then. Don't you have a photo to show us?"

"I can't match the All-American family and Miss Universe. I dated a girl named Elaine in college. You'll have to take my word for it. She was a pretty blond--a math major at Purdue, thirty miles north of Wabash."

Pete asked, "Where is she now?"

"Grad school at Cincinnati."

Pete persisted. "Did you guys ever get serious?"

"We got hilarious a few times." I smiled, holding back a flood of memories and maybe a tear. "In my senior year, I asked her to wear my Beta pin."

"And . . .," Pete said.

"And she said no."

"Why?"

"I don't have the slightest idea. Haven't seen her since."

"You should call her."

Just in time, a short lieutenant with blue eyes and curly brown hair approached. "What's that thing on your lip, Dugan?"

I recognized the speaker as Ferret, an easy-going lad who finished dead last in our pilot training class in Oklahoma.

"Ferret," Dugan said. "What ill wind blew you into town?"

"I'm here for FAC school. I got the O-One assignment nobody wanted because most O-One slots are being changed to trash-hauler jobs."

I shook his hand. A copilot job on a cargo aircraft would suit Ferret perfectly. With no natural flying talent, he needed years of direct supervision. "You still have the O-One?"

"No. It's being phased out," he said. "The system changed me to an O-Two."

I saw Dugan roll his eyes. "Jerry and Pete, meet Ferret of Oklahoma fame."

Ferret smiled and shook his head. "More like infamy. I'd embellish that comment, but I got to unpack the car." He waved and departed.

"Be careful of him," Dugan warned Pete and Jerry. "He flunked every checkride at least once. Great personality but lousy hands."

"He must be tough," Pete said. "He kept coming back, and he made it here."

"I guess I'm bitter," Dugan said. "Our pilot class at Vance offered no fighters. You had to finish high to get a FAC job. Ferret finished last."

"I flew my T-Thirty-eight four-ship formation checkride with Ferret," I said. "He busted without even leaving the ground."

"Huh?" Pete said.

"All four of us had check pilots in the back seats. Ferret started as the leader. I was number three, leading the second element. We lined up on the runway behind the first element. Their blue afterburners flamed, they rolled, then Ferret aborted."

"Did he say anything on the radio?" Pete asked.

"No. But I had to wait for him to clear the runway before I could roll. Meanwhile, two, the new leader, became a dot on the windscreen. When we finally launched, I took a shortcut on the standard departure course to join on the new leader." I waved my hands to illustrate. "My check pilot grumbled. I asked him if I was taking an instrument check or a formation check."

Pete asked, "What was Ferret's problem?"

"One of his afterburners blew out," I said. "He never noticed. The aircraft slowed and drifted toward his wingman. The instructor took control and aborted."

"Ferret didn't recognize the problem?"

"No. Fortunately, the rest of us passed. Ferret passed his re-make. You guys need to know. I heard that during the flying phase, the FAC program requires us to fly every day. When our names are not on the schedule, we're to jump into any empty seat. I'd avoid being Ferret's co-pilot."

Air-Ground Operations School began with a lecture on the Forward Air Controller situation in Vietnam. The speaker, a major and recent Southeast Asia returnee, held our rapt attention in spite of the auditorium's nickname of Blue Bedroom. "I'll bet you didn't plan to start your jet-age flying career in a propeller-driven bug-smasher."

We laughed.

"You've chosen a most exciting and powerful mission. Almost every airstrike in Vietnam is controlled by an airborne FAC. He is the de facto local air commander."

I nodded to my pals seated nearby.

"You can recognize the FAC by his large Seiko watch, low-slung revolver, and a Philippine bola knife that drags the ground. Binoculars and a huge bag of maps are his stock and trade. FACs fly long missions searching for signs of the enemy. Some have described the mission as hours of boredom, interspersed with moments of stark terror."

His stale joke drew a small laugh.

"Nothing has been more rewarding for me than a thank-you from the ground commander after I pounded bad guys attacking his position."

"Yeah." The crowd made enthusiastic noises.

"Each of the four military regions in Vietnam has an assigned Air Force Tactical Air Support Squadron," the lecturer continued. "Airplanes and pilots are dispersed to small strips throughout each region. The Twenty-third TASS in Thailand shares the Ho Chi Min Trail interdiction responsibility with Twentieth TASS units in Vietnam."

The major showed some combat action footage from the war, then put up slides of various FAC aircraft. "The O-One is being turned over to the Vietnamese. A limited number of O.V.-Ten Bronco aircraft, specifically designed for the mission, have been delivered to Vietnam. The workhorse of the FAC fleet remains the Cessna O-Two Super Skymaster."

"We're finally gettin' to the good stuff," Pete said.

I nodded.

Jerry, an O.V.-10 pilot, smiled.

"Modified with more windows, auxiliary fuel tanks and extra radios, the O-Two has a two-hundred-horsepower engine in front and another in back, between twin booms. The Air Force also installed four wing pylons that can haul a variety of weapons. The O-Two can even carry a mini-gun pod--just enough ordnance to get you into trouble."

Over the next three weeks we learned the fundamentals of airstrike control. Spending a week in the woods, we used map and compass to direct flights of T-33s onto ground targets. When possible, we enjoyed afternoons at the beach and acquainted ourselves with warrior hangouts like the Seagull Lounge and Bacon's-by-the-Sea.

During an afternoon bull session on the balcony at the Q, Colonel Andrew Iosue stopped by to sip some fine Cold Duck with our group. The short, handsome colonel said he enjoyed his accelerated checkout in all three FAC aircraft, anticipating his next job as commander of the 504th Tac Air Support Group in Vietnam.

"I guess we'll all work for you over there," I said.

"Right," he said. "I already have a vested interest in your careers. I just came from the Military Personnel Center where I signed the aeronautical orders officially making you pilots when you graduated from U.P.T." He took time to meet and talk personally with each of us.

After Colonel Andy departed, Pete said, "The guy is obviously headed for stars."

I nodded. "Kinda makes you eager to get into the fight."

We boarded a blue bus in the parking lot near our quarters. Our destination was a small paved airstrip called Holley Field, about forty miles west. Time to fly had arrived.

I took a seat next to Pete. "Where's Jerry?"

O.V.-Ten pilots train here at Hurlburt."

"Oh. Are you ready to log some first pilot time?"

"Can't wait. My girls are excited, too. They want me to finish early and spend a few weeks with them before my portcall."

As the bus pulled onto the main street between the pines, palms, and low frame buildings of Hurlburt, Pete asked, "Did you call Elaine yet?"

"No. I've thought about it. I don't want to start something I can't finish."

"Just do it. Tonight, after your first beer, call her."

"My sister's getting married in Chicago in July. I might ask Elaine to go."

We turned west onto the divided highway. Pete slapped my back and smiled.

After half an hour the bus turned north onto a narrow road. Soon, we headed west into a clearing and saw scattered Quonset huts and trailers. Eight or ten O-2s sat in a row with three O-1s. The bus squeaked to a halt.

I followed the crowd into the operations shack. A major gave words of welcome and read instructor assignments. I walked over to a small table and reported to Captain Dave McKay. He sat with Tom Duckett, a tall blond lieutenant who looked like a surfer.

"Nice to meet you." McKay had dark hair and eyes. His smile came quickly. He explained daily procedures and showed me where to find charts and study materials.

I sat with them and asked Duckett, "Are you in the class ahead?"

"Two classes, actually." He showed a huge smile. "Broke my ankle playing basketball two months ago. I only need a few rides, then I'm on my way."

I nodded and asked McKay, "May I ask your background, sir?"

"We don't worry about that sir stuff. Just stay prepared and work hard. I spent a tour at Pleiku with the callsign Covey."

"He flew over the Ho Chi Minh Trail," Duckett said. He turned to McKay. "Tell him about the red tennis balls."

"A huge war is underway in Laos," McKay said. "The North Vietnamese move supplies down the panhandle. They're fighting Laotian forces in the rest of the country."

"Laos? I haven't heard much about that place."

"After a large attack in sixty-five on a Special Forces Camp at Plei Me, near the Lao border, a Tigerhound Covey FAC unit was organized at Pleiku. The mission was to interdict movement of supplies and prevent surprises on that flank of the war in Vietnam."

"What about the tennis balls?" I had to ask.

"Triple-A. Anti-aircraft artillery. Twenty-three and thirty-seven millimeter shells fired from five-round magazines. They fly up like strings of red tennis balls."

I asked, "What kind of problem is triple-A? How accurate?"

"It's optically aimed and not a big deal, really. Even for the Oscar Deuce."

I didn't take his word for gospel truth. I opened a red tennis ball file in part of my brain near my active imagination.

"Grab a map," McKay said. "We'll brief your first ride."

An hour later we were taxiing out with McKay very laid back in the right seat, and me, slightly tense and sweating in the left. I told him, "My cross-check looks easy enough, but I'm not sure what to do with the six levers on the console."

"When we get to the runway, push 'em all forward."

I did. Shoving mixture, propeller, and throttle levers to the firewall in two or three handfuls got us rolling, slowly at first. I expected to feel mashed into the seat, however the airplane's predominant characteristic was not thrust, but noise.

Rudders became effective early, and I used them to stay in the middle of the narrow runway. Approaching a hundred knots, I pulled the nose up, and we lifted off.

"Gear and flaps comin' up," I said.

McKay nodded. "The airplane's easy to fly. The mission will challenge you."

After some perfunctory stalls and falls over the Gulf, we returned to Holley for about thirty practice landings--touch-and-go's.

"Make the next one a full stop," McKay said. "Next time we'll practice tactics."

I fumbled with long distance information and finally learned Elaine's number. I may as well dial it, I thought. I felt as if I were climbing on an express train to nowhere. With no control and no future, a stop in Cincinnati didn't make a lot of sense. Besides, the thought of being emotionally shot down scared me more than red tennis balls.

"Elaine?"

She recognized my voice. Her voice sounded soft--comfortable.

After some dumb small talk to fill in the missing years, I nervously asked her to go with me to my sister's wedding in northern Indiana. "Uh . . . we'll slip off to Chicago later."

"Sounds like fun. Let's do it."

"Great. I'll call later with details."

If she had a new relationship, she hid it well.

Returning from a solo navigation mission a few weeks later, I overflew Holley Field and saw fresh black skid marks leading off the runway. The trail led to a damaged Oscar Deuce surrounded by blue trucks. I noticed a missing nose wheel and a mangled propeller.

Home at the Q with beer in hand, Dugan seemed to be feeling no pain at all. His red handlebar mustache, now mature and carefully waxed, added to the sense of animation as he told his story to the usual crowd.

As I came closer, Pete told me I was hearing version number four.

"I'm doin' touch-and-go's, you know, on that solo ride where all you do is traffic patterns. I touch down on number seventeen--really grease it on the runway--and push the power in for the go-around part."

I saw Dugan's flushed face. He shook my hand with both of his and grinned.

"Then, something goes wrong, see? I hear the front engine surging, like 'Wa Wa Wa,' so I yank back the throttles to abort." Dugan flailed his hands wildly, acting out his tale. "But I look out front and there's no fuckin' way I can stop now. So I push the power in. Now, I hear this sound, like 'Wa Wa Wa Wa,' that tells me both engines might be surging. So I pull the power back again."

"Dugan, you're a sight," I said.

He smiled, shrugged, and continued. "I lock the brakes and go off into the boonies. I'm bouncin' and bangin', and all kinds of shit is happening. Finally, I stop. Crunch. I crawl out of the plane, feeling pretty glad to be alive, you know, and I see the fire truck comin'. Soon as it leaves the runway, it bogs down in the swamp. And--I swear this is the truth--a guy gets out of each door, and they run into each other in front of the truck. Just like the Keystone Cops, see?"

By now I had joined the laughter. Dugan was alive, and I felt glad.

"The first guy reaches me, picks up the broken nosewheel, and starts yelling, 'Look at this, look at this.' I say, 'I've seen it, I've seen it.'"

The crowd screamed with laughter.

"Now the next guy shows up and says, 'I need a urine sample.'"

"I say, 'You're too late.'"

The next afternoon I visited Dugan in his room. "How are you doing, my friend?"

"I'm okay," he said. "I have to meet the wing commander at three."

Later that evening, the old Dugan returned. "I spent one long hour with the commander. He talked about my crash for five minutes and my mustache for fifty-five."

I departed Holley field with McKay in the right seat. We were number two on the far-left edge of a loose four-ship formation. I maintained a position several thousand feet left of and behind the leader. Number three mirrored my position on the right side and, with number four, they formed the ring and pinkie digits of a right fingertip formation.

We purred along at three thousand feet, watching sparse beach flora give way to tall pines. I searched ahead for a huge clearing where old trucks and airplanes had been arrayed for aerial bombardment. One-at-a-time, we would act as FACs on the live range, while instructors in the other aircraft played fighter pilots.

As we approached the range from the south, McKay asked, "Have I shown you a stand-off rocket pass?"

"Not yet."

"In well-defended areas, you'll need to fire rockets from a safe distance. We're about five miles out. Set your switches."

"Roger." Turning a knob below my bombsight produced a faint orange aiming dot inside small concentric circles. On the long row of arming switches bolted above the instrument panel, I selected the Fire position on the Fire/Drop toggle. Leaning forward, I confirmed the pod of rockets on the right wing inner pylon matched my switch selection. I flipped the Master Armament Switch to the On position. The firing circuit awaited only my right thumb to mash a button on the yoke.

McKay asked, "Do you see the truck convoy in the middle of the range?"

"Affirmative. I count seven trucks about four miles ahead."

"Pull the nose up thirty degrees, then let it fall. When the bottom of the outer aiming circle touches the convoy, fire a rocket."

I complied.

Bam. Like the sound of a baseball hitting a tin roof, a six-foot long white tube almost three inches in diameter streaked forward from my right wing. Halfway to the target, the rocket appeared to go out of control.

"Shit," McKay muttered as the rocket turned hard left then dove into a pine forest.

"Not good," I said, floating the plane down to proper formation position.

"A fin or a nozzle failed. The bombing ranges in Laos are larger."

I figured he was joking as I watched white phosphorus smoke billow above the dark green trees. I wondered how much trouble this little anomaly would bring.

Number four peeled off and descended to assume the FAC role. I recognized Pete's voice. His hesitant first-ever target briefing brought an arrogant response from our leader. We spaced ourselves like fighters preparing to strike.

"When your turn comes, be crisp and confident on the radio," McKay said. "You're in charge. Don't let the fighters take over. Soldiers' lives will depend on you."

We twisted and dove at the ground over a fast, sweaty hour. I learned to keep the nose moving to present a difficult target for enemy gunners. My head moved as never before to track other airplanes and avoid a collision.

When I retarded the power in a dive, McKay said, "No, leave the throttles alone. The gunners hear the power change and shoot. Besides, if you change the mixture setting from eight-and-a-half gallons per hour, you'll never know how much gas remains."

The engines droned steadily, even as we jerked the airplane up and over the top. I saw attitudes and maneuvers I had never thought possible for a Cessna. Sweat pooled at the top of my helmet. During hard turns it poured into my eyes.

Halfway through the mission, wispy gray smoke rose in the southwest where our errant rocket had impacted. I asked McKay, "Do you think we started a fire?"

"Yeah. I'll make an anonymous call to Range Control."

That evening our group convened at the officers club for our standard celebration of being alive. McKay joined us for the dollar-a-dozen oyster special. Above the whiskey bottles, a small television set showed local news footage of a large forest fire.

I nudged McKay and nodded to the screen. I noticed Pete at the end of the bar, shaking his finger at me. Behind him, Jerry smiled.

The long Fourth of July weekend with my sister's wedding date finally arrived. As I walked from the airline gate in Cincinnati, I saw Elaine, slim, smiling, and more beautiful than I remembered. When I hugged her, all my nervousness melted.

"Can't believe I'm here," I said. "I thought I'd feel awkward, but I feel great."

"Me, too."

"I should never have let the years go by--"

She laughed and shook her head.

We flew on to Chicago and my sister's wedding.

On Saturday night I tried to slow the furious rush of time in a quiet Old Town restaurant where we sipped Lancer's Rosé by candlelight. Holding her hand, I focused on the present.

Trying to be first, Vietnam was the last thing on my mind.

"This moment is so special," I said. "I'll carry it around in my head for a year. Wish I could stop the clock."

"How long do you have?"

"One month. Why don't you come to California with me? Share my last weekend in the States. We'll do Fisherman's Wharf, Yosemite . . .."

"Let me think about it."

Chapter 2
Into the Pipeline

July 1970

"See you in San Francisco," I said to my FAC pals in various stages of pre-dawn packing. "All my worldly goods fit in this slightly pregnant B-Four bag. Color me gone."

The responses I heard reflected sarcasm and excitement that matched the moment. We had completed the program. We had absorbed our required quota of stateside theory. The Air Force loaned us our lives for two weeks, until a portcall would sweep us to Southeast Asia and the real thing--war.

As the sun appeared, I parked in the lot at the officers beach club. I ran to the top of a white sand dune and inhaled the ocean breeze. I felt alone, but I drew strength from thinking about rejoining my peers, the best and brightest Americans on my horizon. If all I ever knew about Vietnam was the high caliber of those men, that knowledge would be enough.

From a phone booth outside the club, I dialed Elaine, at home in Indianapolis for the summer. "I made plane reservations. Should I buy tickets?" Anticipating bad news, I had procrastinated making the call. I steeled myself for her answer.

"I've thought about this trip a lot. Finally, I asked Mom."

I sensed her solid Midwest conservatism. She sounded wary. "And . . .."

"Mom said I'd be crazy not to go with you."

Like the rising sun, a warm glow pushed aside my dark imaginings. We made plans, then I phoned my former Wabash College fraternity roommate, now a medical student in Indianapolis.

"Wake up, John. Or were you busy counting your money?"

"No way. I'm surely headed for the poorhouse. Dorothy crashed the Corvair yesterday. She and the kids are okay. The car's totaled."

"We have a match here. How would you like a slightly used sixty-five Mustang? Runs good. Just had a valve job."

“Boy, could I use a car.”

“Then, it’s yours. I won’t need one in ‘Nam. I’m passing through town next week to pick up Elaine. We’ll drink a beer, and I’ll sign over the title.”

“I always suspected you were crazy. Now you’ve confirmed it.”

“Seems simple enough to me, John. You need a car. I don’t.”

“I was talking about Elaine.”

“Fisherman’s Wharf’s a tourist trap,” I said, “but, after all, we’re tourists.”

“I can’t believe we’re in San Francisco.” Elaine had never traveled west of Indiana. Her blue eyes had sparkled since we boarded the jetliner that morning.

“Let’s just have fun. No serious subjects. I want to watch you smile for three more days.” I challenged myself to avoid falling off the edge of the earth.

We explored, clowned like school kids, and laughed from the bay to Yosemite. We honored our commitment to say and do only fun things. I held her tightly at times demanded by moonlight and to help me believe she was really with me.

After three days that passed like minutes, we were saying goodbye. Holding her at the departure gate, I saw her tears and felt my own rising.

“Don’t cry now,” I said. “Your trip’s a lot shorter than the one I take tonight. Nicer destination, too.” With no notion of what lay ahead, I searched for words.

“Promise me to be careful,” she said. “I can’t believe how fast our time flew by.”

“I promise.” I’d have promised her anything. I wondered what be careful meant. Would I have that option?

“Goodbye.” Smiling and crying, she disappeared through the gate.

Not knowing if I’d see her again, I watched her plane pull away.

After a tasteless lunch, I boarded a bus for Travis Air Force Base. San Francisco moved in a blur past the window. The Golden Gate Bridge looked brown in the fog. Stung by that simple word goodbye, I tried to focus beyond my consternation. What a time to feel vulnerable.

Early that evening I joined my Hurlburt FAC friends in the huge Military Airlift Command Terminal. I smiled with the happy ones and waxed sentimental with others. I wasn’t sure how to feel. I thought about calling someone, but I had assured relatives that no news would be good news for the next year.

Since I had given away my car and paid all my bills, everything I owned fit in the sage green bag at my feet. At the moment my only real valuables were memories. I hadn't packed the dreams sent into long-term storage by the draft board.

I thought about Elaine, now surely asleep. Nice image.

After two hours we boarded an airliner contracted by the government to haul passengers to Clark Air Base in the Philippine Islands, via Honolulu. In the large, crowded passenger compartment I sat next to Mike Thrower, an O-2 pilot. Ground delays caused the cabin temperature to rise to tropical discomfort level. After takeoff, the air-conditioning blasted us to polar frigidity.

I asked Mike, "How was your leave in Atlanta?"

"Wonderful. You met my wife at Hurlburt, didn't you?"

"Terrific lady. You done good."

Mike had spent most of his free time at Hurlburt with his wife. I knew him as an exceptional pilot and congenial friend.

"I've been meaning to tell you something," he said. "When you get to Vietnam, you need to look into a deal called the Steve Canyon Program. You're perfect for it."

"What's it about?"

"Classified. I have hard-nosed single friends there who love the mission."

"Where are they?"

"Laos, I think. Their callsign's Raven."

I put the information in the file with red tennis balls. Enter another dark mystery of this war, I thought, as I tried to doze.

On our second leg a power reduction changed the cabin pressure and woke me.

"We're descending into Clark Air Base," Mike said. "The Philippines. Are you ready for snake school?"

"Do I have a choice?" The lush jungle below burst in shades of green. "Looks like an ideal setting for Jungle Survival School."

"Some of the world's most poisonous reptiles are native to these islands," Mike said. "The bamboo viper's a one-step snake. After he bites, you take one step and die."

"Are you into herpetology?"

"No. My buddies ahead of me have kept me informed." Mike paused to smile. "Kraits are your basic two-steppers, and the cobra's a cigarette snake."

"Let me guess," I said. "A cobra bites you, and you have time for a smoke?"

"Right."

"Recently, someone accused me of being crazy."

After the cattle car landed, buses moved our herd to quarters. Year-round warmth and frequent rain nurtured plants larger than I knew existed. Huge tropical flora dwarfed buildings on the base. I wondered how big the animals grew.

Pete and I shared a small room. "Hope the wind stays calm. This building's a flimsy wood frame held together by screen," he said, pulling an alarm clock from his bag.

"And the bunks come with mosquito netting," I said. "This ain't Kansas."

"School starts tomorrow morning." Pete perused a brochure. "Club's walking distance away. We have three days of classroom training, then three days in the jungle."

"My survival mode starts with extra sleep," I said. "Goodnight."

After breakfast, Pete and I joined our group of about twenty friends and fifty other Asia newbies in a small flat auditorium. The entire right wall served as a billboard, listing a day-by-day history of search and rescue efforts in Southeast Asia.

Pete said, "The sheer size of this list serves as a reality check."

"Look," I said. "Some character named Fred Platt has been shot down and rescued nine times. He's still on the job."

"Probably one of those Steve Canyon guys," someone said.

Class began with a welcome from the commander. He supplied general information and warnings about the local area.

Then a flight surgeon lectured about tropical hazards. He emphasized that most medical maladies were preventable. "Malaria's common here. Transmitted by a mosquito bite, the disease causes severe chills and fever."

"Mosquitoes nailed me last night," someone whispered.

"Every American dining facility has a bottle of pills next to the salt and pepper shakers," the doctor said. "Take one pill per day to minimize chances of getting malaria."

At lunch, I noticed a large brown bottle full of large tablets on the table at the club. "Don't think I'll rush into this pill thing," I told Pete. "I avoid aspirin if I can."

"Me, too. I'll stick with cheeseburgers."

In class I sat in the center of the audience. Fifteen minutes into the afternoon session, my eye caught the swaying blond head of Paul, an O-1 driver. He sat in the row ahead, four seats to my right. I hardly knew the tiny, quiet lieutenant.

"Arrch." Paul stood and gagged. Then he vomited onto the neck of a large lieutenant colonel sitting in front of him.

Amid moans and gasps, Paul staggered to his right. Folding chairs clattered--parting like the Red Sea--as Paul raced to the front right corner of the stage, where he apparently expected to find toilet facilities.

"Arrch." Paul choked and vomited again.

"The latrine's over here." The instructor pointed to the other corner of the room.

Paul staggered to center stage, where his stomach erupted violently. "Arrch."

Large chunks splattered on the floor. A sour odor spread across the room like a toxic cloud.

Class dismissed itself.

"Little Paul has a huge stomach capacity," Pete said and smiled.

"He took a whole malaria pill at lunch," someone said. "You're supposed to break them and eat the pieces with all your meals."

I decided to take my chances with malaria.

I enjoyed the three-day field exercise. We found native sources of food and water and baked a true feast in a huge section of bamboo. A layer of rice with bananas, mangos, and pineapple qualified as a luau to our group of hungry campers. We learned to evade capture during hide-and-seek games in the jungle.

After returning by helicopter from a simulated rescue, I had time to have first lieutenant rank sewn on my uniforms. We kept the club open until leaving for Vietnam at four a.m.

The morning sun at Cam Ranh Bay felt blazing hot.

A crusty old sergeant drove up to the terminal in a blue pick-up truck. He opened the door and said, "Welcome to the five-oh-fourth. Pile in."

I almost said, "Glad to be here."

He helped us toss our belongings into the truck. When he saw the second lieutenant rank, he dropped Paul's bag and said, "Let's go."

Home for the next five days was a Quonset hut with four bunks per room. I shared quarters with Dugan, Pete, and an Undergraduate Pilot Training friend, Jim Latham.

"Let's take a tour of the base," Dugan said. "Theater Indoctrination School doesn't begin until tomorrow."

"Sounds good," I said. "Cam Ranh looks pretty, like the California coast--white sandy beaches and green mountains."

Pete laughed. "California doesn't have Cong."

"Nor the excessive heat and jet noise," Dugan added.

As we walked down a main road, we encountered Colonel Andy, who greeted us warmly. "Be careful. Take care of each other," he cautioned.

Next, we found the bay. From the white beach, a rock jetty pointed to an old French bunker. We swam until we discovered jellyfish under the beautiful blue surface. Latham found the first one with his right forearm. "My wound requires medicinal alcohol," he said. "Where's the club?"

Around five o'clock, we found the dark frame building housing the officers club. Inside we met more friends from the past. Their celebration sounded like New Years Eve.

"Ed Stevens, you old dog," I said. "You're a C-Seven pilot already?"

"Just a copilot," he said. "Ptui. How are my U.P.T. buds doing?" He seemed to envy our first-pilot status.

"We're just passing through," Dugan said. "What are these walls made of?"

"Paper. Black paper. You can put a finger through it. Can you smell the open sewage ditch that runs under the floor? Nothing but the best for the Caribou troops."

I was surprised the rowdy crowd didn't flatten the structure.

"Nice club," I said. "Who's your friend? He looks familiar."

"I'm Les." A stocky lieutenant extended his hand.

I laughed when I got a clear view of his face. "I remember you from O.T.S."

"Oh, yeah. Let me buy you a beer. I'm sorry about that flickerball thing."

"These C-Seven pilots are certifiable," Pete said.

"I love it," I said. "A trash-hauler squadron with spirit."

Three loud explosions cracked the five a.m. stillness.

"What the hell?" Dugan shouted.

"Rocket attack," I said. "Has to be."

Loosened by concussion, dust hung in the air like fog.

Pete and Latham rolled out of their bunks and huddled with us near our only window. A block away, the Security Police Squadron sprang to life. An armored personnel carrier slid screeching to a halt. An airman with a green metal box of ammunition climbed on top.

"Look at the kid trying to load that ammo belt," Dugan said.

"The barrel's pointed at our hooch," I said. "The kid's having trouble."

"He's pounding the ammo into the breach with his damn helmet," Pete said.

We slipped on our flak vests and helmets.

School began at eight. In a drab building similar to snake school, a bright major in a sharply tailored uniform gave us a review of the culture, climate, and history of Vietnam. During the next five days, other staffers spoke about their areas of expertise. We learned about more threats, including a particularly nasty session on venereal disease.

After viewing movies of various antiaircraft artillery pieces in action, Pete said, "Those twenty-three-millimeter rounds move like streaks across the sky."

"Faster than any tennis balls I've ever seen," I said.

The school staff circulated a preference sheet to collect our desired final duty locations. I wrote Pleiku on the form. McKay's stories had hooked me.

The major from day one taught the last session. "Mid-air collisions are a hot item. Always be aware of other aircraft in your vicinity."

"This guy seems pretty capable," I whispered. "I wonder why he isn't out in the field leading troops."

Pete rolled his eyes. "Are you kidding?"

"Sorry," I said. "He's exactly where he wants to be, isn't he?"

The major warned of the Army helicopter collision hazard. "They're everywhere. Most pilots are high school graduates. You'll understand the problem better when I tell you how they get their wings."

We listened closely.

"They have a program at Fort Rucker, like our U.P.T., only shorter. At graduation ceremonies, they receive diploma and wings, just like we do. But here's the big difference. The Army has an extra station on the stage. A guy with a rubber mallet beats their fucking brains out."

The class roared.

"Don't misunderstand me. Army aviators are brave and tough."

I asked the last question. "What can you say about the Steve Canyon Program?"

"I can say . . . the program exists. After you log five hundred combat hours, send us a volunteer letter with your commander's endorsement. If you have no more questions, good luck and good hunting. Your assignments are on the bulletin board in the hall."

We crowded around the list. Dugan, Pete, Jerry and I would fly to Danang that evening to join the 20th TASS, the parent unit and training base for Pleiku.

The flight to Danang took less than an hour. We walked along the dark ramp behind the C-130 into a surreal world. Artillery flares spiraled down in front of black mountains that seemed higher and closer than did those around

Cam Ranh. An eerie mist swirled around the peaks. Protective layers of green sandbags were stacked everywhere.

"I feel closer to the war," I said. "Sure is hot for nighttime."

Pete said, "Danang's awesome, in its own way."

A captain wearing a 20th TASS patch walked up to us. "The night belongs to Charlie. Drag your bags over to the pickup. I'll take you to the dorm."

Pete and I sat in front. We drove into a compound that held most of the wing support offices and barracks. "Welcome to Gunfighter Village," the captain said. "I'll drop you here in temporary quarters. Rooms are small, but you'll have your own bunk. The training officer will move you to better digs tomorrow."

After the four of us walked into our room and put down our bags, no walking space existed. A window opened to the outside world but offered no real ventilation.

"Latrine's at the end of the hall," Pete said. "I think I'll just crash. Even if I shower, I'll need another one in the morning."

Pete's plan sounded good. We crashed.

Boom. Boom. Boom.

We awoke to the rockets then heard a warning siren.

"Same welcome as Cam Ranh," Dugan said. "Must be a newbie thing."

"No," Pete said. "Mosquitoes are the newbie thing. I must have a hundred bites."

"Make sure you take your pill," I said.

Pete gave me a huge smile.

After showers and breakfast, we sat before a major in the training office. His disinterested tone gave me an immediate wishy-washy impression. "Sorry, guys," he said. "We run the program by rank, and we're working a bunch of field-graders now. Just hang loose. Your turns will come."

"We need quarters," Pete said. "We slept in a closet last night."

The major issued us keys. "These are for air conditioned two-man rooms."

I asked, "Any idea how long before your program reaches the lieutenants."

"Relax," he said. "Every day counts for your year tour here."

Pete and I found our room. A single window had boards where an air conditioner should have been. A sign indicated that a maintenance unit had taken the machine.

"Sorry for the inconvenience," I read aloud. "This should say sorry for the sauna they created. At least they left a phone number."

"I'll try to get us an air conditioner," Pete said. "You see the major about a fan."

As I left the building, Pete lifted the hall phone and put on his booming Bostonian voice.

In two hours I returned with the major's office fan.

Pete smiled from a chair under the humming window unit. "Welcome to our cool but filthy room. I found some cleaning supplies. Let's fix up this place."

We scrubbed and mopped, producing a spotless accommodation, although drab in gray and green. With bunk beds apart, we had room for a wall locker, table, and chair.

I showered and climbed in bed for the first comfortable rest in weeks.

"A rat," Pete screamed. "We have a rat in our damn clean room."

Pete cornered the critter, and I tossed him a boot to finish the job. He threw and missed. The rat ran across his bare feet.

"Aaaaeeeee!" Pete jumped onto his bed.

Laughing uncontrollably, I watched the animal scurry behind the wall locker.

"Kill it," Pete yelled.

I put knee and shoulder to the locker, crushing the pest. I disposed of the body.

Next morning, Pete placed on our small table a framed photo of his three daughters. "Let's go to the MARS station."

"Let's go where?"

"The Military Affiliate Radio Station. We'll try to hook up with a ham operator and a free phone patch home."

"No, thanks. I think I'll jog and pump some iron."

After a week of over-exercising all afternoon, over-drinking all night, then oversleeping, we grew bored. With forward progress stalled out, I felt imprisoned by the rice paddies and ugly shanties of Danang City that surrounded our compound. I tried to write letters, but with no job and no final address, all I managed was a note to Elaine.

One night at the bar I met Major Schillinberger, who commanded an Army helicopter unit. He claimed Vietnam had grayed his hair.

He asked me, "How are you helping the war effort?"

"I'm not, sir. I just sit around doing nothing."

"I could check you out as a door gunner," he said. "You could fly with us until the Air Force needs you."

"Wow. That sounds great."

"I have to go. I'll bring you details tomorrow evening."

When I told Pete I had found a mission, he said, "I think you're crazy."

Standing with our group of FACs, Dugan overheard. "Can I go, too?"

"Dunno. I'll ask."

Next morning, the hall phone rang, then someone pounded on my door. "Roper. Report to the major at the TASS."

"Maybe we're starting our checkout program," I told Pete.

"I doubt it. He told me yesterday we had another week to go."

I reported as ordered and stood at attention before the major's desk.

"What's this shit I hear about you flying with the Army?" His face turned red.

"Yes, sir. I start tomorrow as a door gunner. Only temporary."

The hell you say. No way you're going be a helicopter door gunner."

I remained at attention. "Sir, this won't interfere--"

"Lieutenant, have you lost your fucking mind? There's plenty of war here for everyone."

"May I inquire, sir, about the schedule?"

He looked at a list on the wall, then shuffled through some other papers. "Okay, go to the Life Support Shop. Collect your flight gear. Tomorrow morning report to the Standardization Section. Ask for a captain they call the Crazy Man."

"Yes, sir." I saluted, spun around, and marched out of his office--smiling.

Loaded with parachute, survival vest, pistol, and helmet, I reported to the Crazy Man. His name gave me only slight pause. I heard rumors that the TASS had reeled in the trim young captain after he had buzzed a Navy ship.

Crazy Man had light brown hair and a matching full mustache. His steel blue eyes seemed fiery. "Take a seat at this table," he said. "Let's look at a map and make a plan."

An hour later we launched from the long Danang runway. Flying again exhilarated me, in spite of the heavy load of equipment I wore and the instructor in the right seat.

"Fly northwest," the Crazy Man said. "Climb to three-thousand. We'll clear the artillery belt and do a touch-and-go on the P.S.P. airstrip at Quang Tri."

"P.S.P?" I asked.

"Pierced steel planks. Slippery as snot in the rain. You'll learn to love it." He grinned.

After dragging the wheels over an artillery tube at the end of the runway, I logged my first bounce-and-go on P.S.P. I added full power, and we crawled into the sky.

"Fly west," Crazy Man directed. "Follow that trail." He pointed to a brown line that twisted in and out of leafy cover.

We flew over triple-canopy jungle toward rugged mountain peaks. I had no idea of our location until Crazy Man pointed to an overgrown airstrip.

"This is the Ashau Valley," he said. "I used to fly here every day. Look northwest of the strip. You'll see pieces of the A-1 flown by Jump Meyers."

I saw what looked like brown and white wing sections. "Bernie Fisher landed here and pulled Meyers out, didn't he?"

"Earned the Medal of Honor for his trouble. Enough sightseeing. Go north. Climb to five thousand."

Crazy Man turned the F.M. radio selector switch to the homing mode. He set his old unit's frequency and called a friend by his callsign. He pointed to the F.M. homing needle, which locked forward when his friend answered. "Turn to keep the needle at the top. Search behind, ahead, and below for an O-Two."

While he chatted on the radio, I followed the needle. Finally, I spotted the O-2.

"Seen any MiGs lately?" Crazy Man took control. We closed to five hundred feet above and behind.

"Oh, the usual number," his friend answered. "Where are you?"

"I'm with a new guy. We were discussing how to check six in a combat zone . . ..."

Immediately, the O-2 ahead pulled straight up.

Crazy Man shoved the yoke forward, then pulled back. I saw four on the g-meter as we reached vertical, behind and slightly right of the target. I felt safe enough and tried to learn how he kept the Duck from stalling.

As if in slow motion, the O-2 ahead fell onto its left wing, passing about two hundred feet to our left.

Crazy Man unloaded to zero g and kicked the left rudder. We rotated left and dove in pursuit. "You're watching a poor man's vertical scissors," he said, then repeated the maneuver twice, mixing in rolls and flips I'd never seen.

The other O-2 pulled out near the treetops and called, "You win. Knock it off."

"Roger." Crazy Man smiled and turned to me. "I flew F-Four backseats in the States with that guy. I've been sneaking up behind him for years."

"How did you switch to the O-Two?"

"When my time came to upgrade to the F-Four front seat, no training slots were available. I put in resignation papers with a one-year commitment left. And here I am."

After the slow start, we zipped through our flying orientations. The last ride was a solo navigation sortie where all the checkpoints were wreckage of FAC aircraft. The accompanying syllabus described the crashes as unnecessary.

We reported to the major for final assignments. On the wall behind him I noticed a poster showing 20th TASS callsigns and supported units:

BARKY- 1st Brigade, 5th Infantry Division

BILK- 101st Airborne Division

HELIX- Americal Division

TRAIL- 1st ARVN Division (Army of the Republic of Vietnam)

JAKE- 2nd ARVN Division

LOPEZ- 51st ARVN Regiment

SPEEDY- (Developing interdiction mission)

COVEY- Laos- Visual Reconnaissance Sector 6 (Danang)

COVEY- Laos- Visual Reconnaissance Sector 7 (Pleiku)

The major issued callsigns reflecting our job assignments. "For the next eleven months," he told me, "you'll serve at Pleiku as Covey Five-nine-one."

Pete became a Trail FAC. Dugan got a Lopez FAC assignment. Jerry joined me as a Pleiku Covey FAC in the Central Highlands.

The end of the pipeline was at hand, but as I would learn, I now faced the beginning of the tunnel. With three-hundred-and-thirty-nine days to go, I saw no light.

Chapter 3
F.N.G.

August-September 1970

A first lieutenant in a worn flight suit with no unit patches walked to where I stood at the 20th TASS operations counter. He flashed a smile under his black-rimmed glasses as he signed flight orders. He looked like a thin Clark Kent with a trim mustache.

The main entrance to the squadron sat across an open area in front of the ops counter, which occupied one end of a long green building. A narrow gray hall led away with offices on both sides. On the other end of the ops area was a door to the flightline.

I asked, "Are you from Pleiku?"

"Yep. I drew the Danang run today. You need a ride?"

"Affirmative." I shook his hand and introduced myself.

"I'm Larry Meredith," he said. "I've hauled several F.N.G.s to Pleiku lately."

"F.N.G.s?"

"Fucking New Guys."

"I see."

"Drag your bag to the O-Two with tiger stripes on the tail while I get the official distribution and some aircraft parts. Don't let anyone touch the airplane. I'll be out in a few minutes." Meredith had a hard demeanor--a cold, tired look in his eyes.

Wondering how many red tennis balls I would have to see flying past my windscreen before my eyes took on Meredith's stare, I trudged out to the flight line and loaded my bag into the Tigerhound O-2.

Meredith arrived, walked around the aircraft, and climbed in. "I hate Danang. If you ever land here, guard your airplane. Troops steal parts to fix the local birds."

As I strapped into the right seat, I watched his hands fly around the cockpit. In only a few minutes we were climbing out on a southerly heading.

I asked, "How do you like Pleiku?"

"It's okay. Lieutenant Colonel McGraw's a great commander. Weather stays nice and cool most of the time. The base sits half a mile above sea level."

"You're happy there?"

"Sure. Even happier when I get home." He leveled off at eight thousand feet.

I thought about home as I watched the beautiful jungle pass below. I wondered what Elaine might be doing. On the instrument panel I noticed a red label taped on the pilot's side that read Acrobatics Prohibited.

Meredith pointed to the label. "Ya see that?"

I nodded.

Meredith pushed the nose down abruptly and reversed straight up into a loop. As the ground re-appeared on the back side of the maneuver, he rolled right, and pulled into a rivet-bending barrel roll. "Don't do that."

"Rog." I suspected he was testing me. After a pause, I said, "I've read some of the history of Pleiku. Attacks on the base in sixty-five resulted in retaliatory bombing of North Vietnam. The Covey FAC unit was formed about the same time."

"Yeah," Meredith said. "Biggest battle around Pleiku was the Seventh Cav fight out west in the Ia Drang valley. Same year. Nowadays, all we have is the occasional rocket attack."

"Do you fly a lot of night missions?"

"Yeah. We give round-the-clock coverage to the Trail in Laos. We added fifteen-thousand square miles of Cambodia in June. Gained eight more Oscar Ducks and ten pilots for that mission. Laos still has the best action. Lots of trucks and guns there."

The TACAN navigation indicator showed Pleiku straight ahead for ten miles. We approached a large lake. Beyond it I saw the eight-thousand-foot east-west runway. "Tally ho our destination," I said.

"Just this side of the strip, across the main road, is Pleiku Air Base. South of the runway you should see a ravine, then Camp Holloway, an Army chopper base."

"Roger," I said.

Meredith pointed to a huge radar antenna. "That's Peacock G.C.I., the ground-controlled-intercept site for this area. Call them for radar flight-following. Nearby, on the highest hill on the base, you can see the officers club."

I nodded.

Meredith pushed the power to maximum and lowered the nose. We zoomed down to about twenty feet above the ground. "We're coming up on the Covey hooches."

I spotted long parallel brown buildings with white roofs. We eased between two of them, then down some more. The airspeed needle flirted with two hundred knots. Holy shit.

Meredith lifted us over a power line then down and slightly left toward a volleyball net. "Damn. Usually I scatter a volleyball game with this Oscar Duck pattern entry procedure. Invented it myself." He pulled hard and rolled left.

I watched our airspeed drop by one-half as the ninety-degree climbing turn--a textbook chandelle maneuver--took us to a downwind leg of the traffic pattern.

Meredith lowered gear and flaps. He kicked right rudder and rolled into a steep descent. To the control tower he said, "Gear down, full stop."

"Cleared to land." Tower troops were loose, too. They didn't use his call sign.

On final approach, my driver lit a cigarette. He glided the Duck into the setting sun and touched down like a feather, then taxied to a refueling pump and shut down both engines.

I liked Meredith--good hands and probably too crazy to get killed.

Outside I enjoyed a panorama of distant green mountains. Generations of rice farmers had cleared rolling hills--tan in the soft early evening light--that extended out for miles. The temperature felt perfect. Two Army helicopters broke the stillness, passing overhead with their characteristic wop-wop noise.

"Grab a room key at the ops desk," Meredith said. "Someone will give you a ride to the hooches. A pretty good party was underway in the bar when I left."

A government-issued steel bunk, wall locker, and chair filled the tiny gray room I would call home for my foreseeable future. I donned the latest beach fashions--white bell-bottoms, red nylon shirt, floppy Budweiser hat--and cruised out in search of the party.

Darkness had arrived. Low clouds threatened rain.

I followed the sidewalk channeled between the hooch and a chest-high brick revetment wall. The wall's large gap at the middle of the building allowed passage from a bar to a concrete patio, crowded with a picnic table, chairs, and revelers.

I felt at home when I spotted Jerry on the patio. "You beat me here. Did I miss the party?"

"Don't think so. Beer's in the fridge inside. Enter at your own risk."

Through a screen door, I saw that the wide access to the other side of the building served as the hooch bar. The walls had an ugly shade of yellow paint, a backdrop for works of art former Coveys had deemed unsuitable to ship home. A large bar top that had once been a helicopter rotor blade was now nailed to the top of a homemade bookcase. Worn sofas and chairs sat in a half-inch of brown water.

Undeterred by the general disarray, I sloshed to the refrigerator, where I ran directly into two first lieutenants in smelly flightsuits. I introduced myself.

"I'm Ed Eberhart," the tall one said. From his large ring, square jaw, and muscular physique, I guessed that he once filled an Air Force Academy football uniform.

We shook hands.

"This is Kaiser," he slurred.

The smaller man had kinky blond hair and that hard look I had seen on Meredith's face. We shook hands.

"Excuse me." I stepped between them to the fridge. I took a beer and added my name to the tally sheet on front. Turning, I popped my beer top.

Kaiser said, "Look, Ed. The F.N.G. has some nice clothes." He took off my hat in mock admiration and dropped it in the muddy lake on the floor.

"Oops," Ed said. "Let me pick up newbie's hat." He stepped on it, ground it with his foot, then replaced it on my head.

Sipping my beer as filthy water poured down my face onto my shirt and trousers, I analyzed the situation. I had overdressed.

Ed stood like a huge oak tree swaying in the wind. Alcohol had not altered his confident linebacker pose. I'd tackle him first. If I took Ed down hard, his smaller friend might back off.

I had earned a wrestling letter at Wabash. A simple arm-drag put me behind Ed. I stood on his heels, pulled his left arm, and swung him neatly and firmly into the mud. I sat on top of him for less than a second.

Ed sprang up and turned hard. We rolled and tumbled out the screen door.

I threw him over the brick wall, but he pulled me with him onto grass slippery from steady rain.

As we rolled down the sloped grounds, I hung on for my life. Ed had no wrestling training, but he negated my advantage by ignoring N.C.A.A. restrictions on gouging, punching, and blocking air passages. He finally prevailed using brute force and a chokehold he had seen on T.V.

I gagged, then rolled over, exhausted.

As I shook Ed's hand, Jerry walked over. "Are you all right?"

I wiped blood from my mouth. "No permanent damage. These guys know how to throw a party, don't they?"

Jerry smiled. "Here's your beer."

Sitting on the brick revetment at the end of the hooch at dawn, I waited for a ride.

"Call me Uncle Al." Lieutenant Dyer, tall, with auburn-brown hair and freckles, extended a hand. "I'm an O-Two instructor. Today I have the jeep keys."

Two other FACs emerged from their rooms. We piled into the olive-drab convertible Ford jeep for the one-mile trip downhill to squadron operations.

"I love this quiet and cool morning," I said. "Seems almost peaceful."

"Pleiku has its moments," Uncle Al said. "Plan to finish all your paperwork and study today. Tomorrow we fly."

I nodded to a Vietnamese guard at the base gate. After a quarter mile we passed an empty guard-shack at the airfield entrance. "Is the airfield unguarded?"

"Someone's probably inside--just asleep on the floor." Al leaned on the horn and a green helmet appeared. We drove on. "The new guy program takes one hundred flying hours. Fifty will be spent riding with other FACs. Thirty will be solo hours, and I get you for twenty."

I nodded.

"Today in the squadron intel vault you'll study and take tests on Rules of Engagement, standard procedures, and threats in the area of operations."

"Okay," I said, as Al parked. I jumped from the jeep and walked toward the one-story, light green building with a huge sign that read 20th TASS, Operating Location 201, Home of the Highland Coveys. Tall steel revetments nearby hid the aircraft.

Following Uncle Al, I entered a hallway that ran the length of the building. The first office on the left had a blue shingle with the word Commander in white letters. On the right, a similar sign marked Life Support. The duty desk came next with a lieutenant sitting at the counter and behind him an airman facing a wall of radios.

More signs marked a conference room, a latrine, scheduling, administration, and other small offices. We entered the intelligence vault, and Al introduced me to the commander, who was leaving with a bag full of maps.

"Great to have you with us," Lieutenant Colonel McGraw said. "We'll talk more later. Right now the N.V.A.'s pressing my favorite good guys."

Inside a room with detailed maps covering all four walls, Al said,

"Operation Tailwind has everyone's attention now. A company-sized Army element is surrounded by several regiments of North Vietnamese Army troops."

I asked, "Where? How bad is it?"

"Here." Al pointed to a six-kilometer square in Laos, near the tri-border area. "The friendlies are Special Forces. They're reporting a target-rich environment."

I stared at red arrows penetrating all sides of the square marked Tailwind.

"Colonel McGraw takes the tough missions," Uncle Al continued. "He approves Ed's schedule each morning, then takes off. You met Ed last night, right?"

"Yeah." I rubbed my swollen bottom lip and observed several squares throughout the southern panhandle of Laos.

"Ed kinda runs things. These boxes are no-bomb-lines. Special Forces recon teams operate there." Uncle Al picked up a set of maps. "Gotta fly another newbie today. Hit the books. See you later."

At eight that evening Jerry and I rode the Covey van to the officers club. We had spent a full day in the books.

I asked, "Do you think we earned a hot meal and maybe a cold beer?"

Jerry nodded. "I've never been so bored in my life. I'm ready to fly."

From the parking lot we climbed the last hundred feet to the dark frame building. Two large groups of Coveys had gathered, one at each end of the long bar. I joined Uncle Al in the middle. Non-flyers sat at several tables in the large room.

"What's up, Uncle Al?"

"Culture wars. Have a beer and watch."

Suddenly the Coveys to my right yelled, "Who'll take the mail through Dead Man's Pass?" Their noise sounded like thunder.

The other group answered, "I'll take the mail through Dead Man's Pass."

"What about the lions?"

"Fuck the lions."

"You'd fuck a lion?"

"I'd fuck a lion's mother."

"You lion mother fucker."

Laughter from both groups drowned out shouts of derision from the non-flyers.

"The audience isn't impressed," I said.

"They've heard it before. Besides, support officers hate Coveys," Uncle Al said. "They accuse us of disrespect all the time. They're mostly captains, and they always want their asses kissed. Fuck 'em."

"Even in the States, I've seen rowdy nights at the club. What do they expect?"

"Many come here for the movie each night at nine. They think the club is some kind of holy shrine. If they had their way, we'd all be wearing ties. REMFs."

"What's that?"

"Rear Echelon Mother Fuckers. They don't realize that Vietnam's just a toilet, and they're turds--trapped here just like us."

"Does the entire base act this way?"

"No. Good guys from the support side come to the Covey bar all the time." Uncle Al handed me a card with Falcon Code written on top. "Here's another spin-off."

The card codified common Vietnam observations into a simple number system:

101 You've got to be shitting me.

102 Get off my fucking back.

103 Beats the shit out of me.

104 What the fuck, over?

105 It's so fucking bad, I can't believe this place.

106 I hate this fucking place.

107 This place sucks.

108 Fuck you very much.

109 Beautiful, just fucking beautiful.

110 That goddam O club.

111 Here comes another fucking Lieutenant Colonel.

112 Let me talk to that son-of-a-bitch.

113 Balls.

169 I love you so fucking much I could just shit.

An angry captain wearing fatigues walked by, muttering.

I heard "assholes." I asked Uncle Al, "Would a one-oh-eight apply here?"

Strapping into a cockpit every day made three weeks fly quickly.

Time stopped when I learned that Mike Vrablick, an O-2 pilot and friend from Officer Training School, was shot down and killed over Cambodia while rescuing an ambushed convoy. We heard the clouds were too low for fighters, so Mike rolled in with rockets. He had served as an O.T.Squadron commander.

One day as we followed the highway from Pleiku fifteen miles north to Kontum, Uncle Al said, "The Army calls this road the redball. Tanks in the trees on both sides provide daytime security. They roll home at night."

"We don't even try to own the night?"

"Only over the Trail," he said. "Take us down to the deck, as though you were leading a helicopter to a landing zone. Then, pull up and see how high we climb with this combat load of rockets and gas."

I eased the nose down and dove to treetop level.

"Stay over the road. Army tanks on the sides have tall fiberglass antennas. I bought one once."

I pulled straight up until the airspeed dropped below a hundred knots. The Duck had gained three hundred feet.

"You are now in the heart of the small arms envelope. If you have to go low, take stock of your fuel and pylon loads. Find a safe place to climb."

"Roger that."

Uncle Al's tactical lessons filled in the blanks reading hadn't taught me. Crossing the Lao border, I did a fence check, an acronym for firepower, emitters, nav, comm, electronics. I set the ordnance panel to a ready position, turned all lights off, and called the airborne command post. I learned to move the nose of the aircraft constantly and to keep my eyes searching. Setting the engine levers to burn eight-and-a-half gallons of fuel per hour, I left them that way for over four hours. On a one-to-fifty-thousand-scale chart I learned to read contour lines like fingerprints.

Uncle Al showed me likely hiding spots for trucks and guns along the Ho Chi Minh Trail. "We're near the end of the rainy season. Laos will heat up soon."

Some parts of the Trail looked like a dirt super-highway. Bomb craters made other areas look like the moon. We searched our entire segment and found nothing.

While cruising to a Trail mission one night, Uncle Al said, "Break left. I'm simulating that a gun has opened fire on my side."

I yanked on the yoke and kicked left rudder. The aircraft stalled, shuddered, and snapped over. My helmet hit the glare shield. "Shit, we're spinning."

"Upside down, too," Uncle Al said. "Pull back and roll out."

I recovered the airplane, but my bowels churned. "What happened?"

"Stall plus yaw equals spin." Uncle Al smiled at his successful demonstration. "You're right on the edge with this night ordnance load. A gentle evasive turn will usually suffice."

"What's the falcon code for holy shit?" I felt out of breath.

"The violent spin entry comes from tired, warped wings. Too many guys do acro in this aircraft." He pointed to the red warning label on the instrument panel.

I crossed into the turboprop subculture to fly an O.V.-10 backseat. Flying with other FACs counted toward my total time, regardless of aircraft type.

Designers had built the Bronco for the observation mission. With a huge canopy, internal machine guns, and excess thrust, this FAC platform seemed ideal, theoretically. But our primitive night vision scopes did not function through Plexiglas, so the O-2, with windows that opened in flight, kept all the night missions.

Even though Army troops called the O-2 a Ford and the O.V.-10 a Cadillac, they focused on the mission accomplishment, not flight performance. Extra seats in the Oscar Deuce allowed space for upgrading pilots and Army observers. So the O-2 hung onto the primary role in supporting the Special Forces.

The lesser-performing O-2 held better missions than the craft designed for the task, fueling another culture war. The teasing began as I climbed into the rear cockpit. My pilot was Bruce Lamping, a recently certified FAC and a friend from Officer Training School.

"Come to learn how the big boys do it?" He fired the first round.

"I need fifty hours with other FACs. I'm obviously not particular."

Lamping started engines and taxied. "How're you doing back there?"

"These Martin-Baker harness straps are cutting my shoulders. Engine vibrations make the canopy rails untouchable. The people who built this airplane never sat in back."

"Let's close canopies for take-off," Lamping said.

The sealed cockpit instantly became a greenhouse. Sweat drenched my uniform. "No wonder you guys fly so high. You're searching for cool air."

"Relax. Here we go." Lamping pushed the props and throttles full forward.

With a painfully loud humming roar, the Bronco leaped ahead and upward.

"Performance is great, but so is the noise level." I kept the kidding going.

Lamping shook his head. He found the Trail at the tri-border of Vietnam, Laos, and Cambodia, and began a mechanical search pattern, using sixty-degree-banked pulls across the road a mile below.

"I've never been airsick," I said, "but this seat has nausea written all over it."

"Here," he said. "Take the binoculars. Make yourself useful."

I scanned below, but the hard maneuvering made the Trail a blur.

Lamping said, "What's that flash?" He yanked hard on the control stick.

The sudden acceleration jerked the binoculars from my unenthusiastic grip.

Bam. They hit the cockpit floor.

"What the hell?" Lamping pulled and pushed and rolled the aircraft. "Are you okay?"

"Yeah. Just dropped the binoculars."

"Geez. Scared the shit outa me."

"I could tell. You don't have to maneuver so hard, you know. They're all asleep."

"Huh?"

"The gunners, the truck drivers, the road repair crews. They sleep in the daytime. They have to be alert at night when the real men show up in Oscar Deuces."

"Nuts to you and your puddle-jumper. A twenty-three-millimeter shell would pass through the wing of the Oscar Deuce, but it would explode on impact with the O.V."

"Not today, pal. We're too high."

"Takin' her solo, sir?" A smiling crew chief helped me load my gear into the O-2.

"Yep. I'll do visual reconnaissance over Cambodia way. Been here several weeks, but I'm not yet allowed to kill without adult supervision."

He smiled. "Be careful. Weather doesn't look too pure at the moment."

At the end of the runway, tower read my instrument clearance to climb through the gray overcast to Visual Meteorological Conditions above the clouds. "Covey Five-nine-one is cleared direct to the Papa Uniform radio beacon. If not Victor Mike Charlie by one-zero thousand, maintain and advise. Read back."

"Rog." Nobody read back clearances in Vietnam.

"Cleared for takeoff." Tower understood.

I climbed through the soup on a westerly heading and broke out at three thousand feet. For over an hour, I tried unsuccessfully to find a hole to view the ground below. Feeling thoroughly bored, I returned early to Pleiku.

Inside the ops building, I ran into Ed.

He asked, "Aren't you supposed to be flying?"

"Already did. Weather was dogshit. Couldn't see the ground."

Ed leaned into my face. "Do you want to complete your hundred-hour checkout? If you fly the four-point-five-hour sortie that I schedule, you'll finish in three weeks. Get it?"

"Got it."

I read the next day's schedule posted over the urinal in the hooch's communal latrine. Again, I had the fifteen-thirty takeoff for a solo Cambodia V.R. mission.

Weather over Cambodia had not changed. I flew and flew and flew. I skied on the clouds, dove into valleys, and rolled over hills and misty obstacles. I never saw Cambodia.

By nineteen-thirty hours, I turned east to return to base, or R.T.B., and log four-point-five hours for Ed. The sun had set, and the cloud cover below me sealed a dark sky.

I called Pleiku Approach Control. "Covey Five-nine-one, thirty west. Request G.C.A. full stop." A Ground Controlled Approach was the quickest way to descend below the clouds with radar help.

"Roger, Covey Five-nine one. Turn left to heading zero-four-five. Descend and maintain three thousand five hundred. Set altimeter two-niner-seven-eight." The controller sounded confident, steering me to, and then down, the glide slope.

I broke clear of clouds about a thousand feet above the ground, three miles from the runway threshold. "Covey Five-nine-one has the runway in sight."

"Roger, contact tower for landing clearance."

On tower frequency I said, "Covey Five-nine-one, two miles, gear down, full stop."

"Roger, Covey, you're taking fire from ten o'clock low."

I whipped the craft to the right, and the stream of green tracers stopped. The source seemed to be the airfield perimeter. I turned back on course, scanning the ground below.

"Cleared to land."

At the hooch bar, I picked up a newspaper.

News from home, in fact news from anywhere came to Pleiku via the Pacific *Stars and Stripes*, the authorized but unofficial newspaper at the scene of action. Often the headlines announced a new peace plan, and most Washington D.C. datelined articles sparked heated debates in the bar. Every issue included a personal story from the war.

I sipped a cold beer and told my indignant story of tracers during landing to the dozen FACs there.

Uncle Al brought the house down when he asked, "Were your lights on, Newbie?"

"Over the airfield perimeter? Our own guys?"

"The Vietnamese augment our Air Force security forces. Sometimes they get bored and shoot at airplanes. Welcome to the fuckin' war."

After three weeks I sat across the table from an evaluator from Danang.

"I'll need to see an airstrike to certify you're mission ready." The pudgy captain reminded me of some of my pilot training instructors--the ones without combat time.

"I have a plan here," I said. "We can cut the road in southern Laos at a point called sixty-nineteen, then look for trucks and guns at a place we call the Falls. I also have a report of an N.V.A. training base in northern Cambodia. We could look for---"

"No need to go into Laos. Nothing to prove there. Cambodia's fine. What kind of published approaches do you have here?"

"The TACAN is a straight-in," I said. "The A.D.F. has a teardrop penetration." The Automatic Direction Finder procedure showed an outbound course, then a wide turn inbound to the runway. Viewed from above, the track was tear-shaped. I hoped he was joking. I didn't feel enthusiastic about hours of sweating and staring at instruments.

"Great. Let's do both of them." The captain sounded excited.

As we stepped out the door, Ed slapped me on the back. "Relax. Have some fun."

Our O-2 droned northwest into Cambodia, and my evaluator did the same--about his office duties at Danang.

"Here's my fence check." I verbalized each switch change.

The captain pulled out his camera. "Brand new Minolta. Saved a bundle on it."

I unfolded my map where I had noted the suspected base camp with a black wax marker. "I'll follow this stream and look for these three small but distinctive hills."

The captain nodded. "I'll set the shutter speed on two-fifty."

I found the coordinates and noticed the corner of a building under heavy jungle. "I think I see something under the trees. I'll call for an airstrike."

The captain droned on. "I hope to land an assignment in training command."

His words were easy to ignore as I requested the strike and organized the information I needed to present a FAC-to-fighter briefing. Thirty minutes passed.

"Covey Five-nine-one, Litter Zero-one." The flight leader called me.

"Litter, Covey. Loud and clear."

"Litter's a flight of two Fox-One-hundreds. Mission number seven-one-four-one, six five-hundred-pounders apiece plus twenty mike-mike strafe. We're at base plus ten, five minutes from your rendezvous point. Twenty minutes of playtime."

My code card said base altitude for the day was eight thousand feet. The fighters were cruising at eighteen thousand.

I searched high for two F-100s. "I have a building under the trees. Supposed to be a base camp. Weather's no factor. Winds east at ten knots."

"Roger."

"Target elevation, twenty-seven hundred feet. Set altimeter two-niner-seven-seven."

"Copy, two-niner-seven-seven."

"High terrain goes to five thousand feet, eight miles north."

"Copy."

"Negative friendlies. Immediate bailout heading is east--sixty-five miles to Pleiku."

"Roger. Coming up on the rendezvous."

"Expect small arms ground fire." I spotted the swept-wing F-100s descending like darts in half-mile trail against high cirrus clouds. "I'm at your ten o'clock low in a left turn."

"Litter one, tally. Green 'em up." The leader's jargon meant that he saw me, and he directed his wingman to set his bombing switches.

"Two has the FAC. Switches set," his wingman acknowledged.

"Your target is in the clump of dark green trees a mile north of me. Call ready for a mark." I turned northeast, selected a right-wing rocket pod, and flipped on my guarded master armament switch. Mashing the pickle button would complete the circuit and fire a rocket from the pod of seven.

"Litter's ready."

I let the nose fall in a descending left turn. I glanced at the captain.

He smiled and said nothing.

I rolled the wings level in a twenty-degree dive. With the aiming dot just east of the target, I fired.

Bam.

A single smoke rocket blasted from under the wing. I watched the dot of fiery exhaust smash into trees near the target. I pulled up hard and turned right, then reversed left. White smoke billowed above green foliage. I thought I saw green flash past my left wing.

"Hit my smoke."

An F-100 rolled over and pulled its nose to the target.

"Lead's in."

"Cleared hot," I said. "Watch for green tracers."

The dark airplane swooped down and released bombs that looked tiny from my perspective. Two large red fireballs flashed on the target. Gray smoke boiled. I heard dull wumps, and one end of the target sparkled briefly.

"Two's in."

"Same place. Looks like small secondary explosions. Cleared hot."

Two explosions rose from the target. I saw more secondaries.

"Covey," Lead said, "We're taking fire from the ridge two hundred meters north."

"Roger. Make your next pass on the ridge."

"Lead's in."

"Cleared hot."

"Two, hold high while I mark a trail that runs east from the target." I watched the leader dive toward the jungle.

Two bombs exploded on the ridge as I rolled in and fired a rocket.

"Two's in, smoke in sight."

I moved to the east and saw the fighter's nose line up on target. "Cleared hot."

After three more passes, the leader said, "We're Winchester bombs." He confirmed they had expended all bombs.

"If you'd like to use your gun, I'll shoot two smokes to mark a trail segment that meanders under the trees."

"Sounds good."

I marked, and they strafed. From a high angle dive, their cannons left trails of dashes, like Morse code. Twenty-millimeter bullets exploded along the major escape route from the target area.

"Super job today, Litter flight. Standby for Bomb Damage Assessment." I used binoculars and made a pass across the target, still smoking from the assault.

"Roger. We're headed home. And the unit's headed home, too. Today's the last day for the Litter callsign in Vietnam."

"There's a piece of history for you," I told the captain beside me. "The Colorado Air National Guard returns."

Looking through his Minolta, he said nothing.

"Litter, you were on target at fifteen ten, off at fifteen twenty-five. A hundred percent of ordnance in the target area. Eighty percent within ten meters. One military structure destroyed. Twelve small secondary explosions. Eighty percent target coverage. Great way to finish a tour."

"Copy all. Enjoyed working with you, Covey. Litter, go channel five."

"Two." His wingman acknowledged.

"I've seen enough," the captain said. "Let's do some traffic patterns."

"If you have any film left, you could take a picture of Pussy Mountain."

"What's that?" The captain seemed to wake up.

"Twenty miles from here sits a mountain that looks exactly like . . . you know."

"I suppose we could check it out." He cleared his throat.

I orbited around the large hill whose south face resembled a female crotch.

The captain clicked and wound his camera like a machine. "Hang on while I reload." He exposed another long roll of film while I circled. Finally he said, "Take us home."

I turned toward Pleiku. "What type of approach would you like to see?"

The captain's eyes appeared glazed. "Your choice."

"Visual straight-in, full stop?"

"Fine."

The evening celebration of being alive featured several new steely-eyed, mission-ready FACs. Jerry and I had shaken off the cocoon of ignorance. Old heads let us strut and fret in the Covey bar for an hour or two.

"We've been students all our lives," I told Jerry. "Now, we're real people."

Jerry smiled, and we clinked beer cans.

A few days later, I entered the dirty little barbershop on base. Still gloating over my mission-ready warrior status, I treated myself to a razor cut, administered by a Vietnamese barber. I wondered what else the wrinkled little man might have done with a straight razor.

I paid my forty-five cents and opened the door to leave.

Brrap. Brrap.

I thought, what the hell was that? Bursts from automatic weapons? Could the Cong be attacking at two in the afternoon?

I ran down the steps and looked a half-mile west to a hill off the end of the runway. Amid swirling black smoke, the wing of an O.V.-10 stuck straight up from twisted gray metal. A landing gear strut and wheel extended from the wing.

Chapter 4
Old Guy Status

October 1970

"What happened?" I ran up a small embankment where a group of maintenance troops stood. "Anyone see what happened?"

"Yes, sir," a sergeant said. "We looked up when the O.V.-Ten came over with only one engine turning. He landed, but he bounced real high. Took off again but stayed low. Then the backseater ejected. I think the pilot did, too, but I never saw his parachute."

"Thanks." I ran the mile down to the squadron, mumbling to myself. The noises I had heard were ejections. Only one chute. Damn. I reached the building in about eight minutes.

Panting, I asked the duty officer, "Who was flying the downed O.V.?"

"A new guy--Jerry was his name. He called with an engine fire coming back from Danang. Crew chief in the backseat made it. Jerry's dead."

"Are you sure?"

"We just got confirmation."

"I fly tonight with Captain Ringstrom," I said. "When he shows up in an hour or so, tell him I'm in the lounge. I feel like shit."

I collapsed in an easy chair, sweating from my run and crushed by the news. I had never felt so helpless. I drifted back to the beach in Florida and evenings in the breezeway at the Hurlburt officers quarters. Strong, quiet and always there with support, Jerry had become like a brother. My life would always have a hole where my smiling friend used to be. God keep you, Jerry, I said to myself. I closed my eyes and tried to relax.

"Hi. I'm Ron Ringstrom." A captain with glasses and thinning hair walked in. I saw him through my fog. He had an average build and wore navigator wings.

I stood and shook his hand. "I've heard you're a real truck-killer."

"I've had some good missions. Covey navs have letter callsigns. Mine's double alpha. Call me Alfalfa."

"Okay. Paperwork's done for the flight. Let's talk about the Trail."

"Since you're flying your first night mission, I'll try to show you all I know."

We moved to a small table where my map bag sat.

I opened a chart of VR-7, a thirty-mile wide visual reconnaissance sector that covered the Ho Chi Minh Trail, north for fifty miles from the tri-border area.

"We can pick up the main road just inside Laos," Alfalfa said. "For every mile we can see, ten miles are probably under woven jungle cover. I usually find trucks jammed up at the choke points--the numbered I.D.P.s—where they can't hide as effectively."

"I.D.P.s?"

"Interdiction points. The afternoon O.V.-Ten drivers use fragged air--bombing sorties from the daily tasking order--to make craters along mountainside roads that can't be easily by-passed. Trucks have to stop there, and I've learned to see through hasty camouflage jobs."

"Sounds like a plan."

"Biggest I.D.P. is the Falls." Alfalfa pointed to the south end of the sector. "It's also the most heavily defended. The other big one is farther north where the river bends around to form a dog's head." He slid his finger two-thirds of the way up the sector.

"So, we can move from one to the other, depending on truck activity. Okay?"

Alfalfa nodded. "Intel will show us today's fragged road cuts. We'll start with those. Laos is heating up. The dry season begins next month."

"The muddy Trail dries up and the trucks roll. Right?"

"Exactly," Alfalfa said. "By December half the available daily fighter-bomber sorties in theater will attack targets along the Trail."

Thirty minutes later the sun disappeared while we walked to the aircraft.

Alfalfa said, "Right-seaters usually pre-flight the ordnance, comm and nav gear."

"Help yourself." I felt confident about my flying partner. For brief periods his easy-going explanations took my mind off Jerry's death.

The wings of our black O-2 bristled with ordnance. Red streamers with Remove Before Flight printed in white letters hung down from pins that disabled firing circuits. A long pod containing seven rockets hung from each outer pylon.

The inner pylons held racks of target markers designed to fall and burn like a star on the ground. Four silver tubes on the left wing pylon resembled flares, but they were magnesium target-marking logs. They'd burn for thirty minutes. Four dark cubes on the right resembled bricks. When the pilot pressed the Fire button, a burning brick would tumble to the ground and provide a bright reference that fighters used as an aiming reference.

Our friendly young crew chief greeted us. "She's loaded for bear, sirs."

I hustled through the inspection rituals. We boarded, started engines, and taxied. On the runway at seventeen-forty hours, I ran up the engines. "Ready to go?"

When Alfalfa nodded, I released brakes, and we rolled. And we rolled. Halfway down the eight-thousand-foot runway, we still did not have take-off speed. "No wind plus high drag from the night load make a difference, don't they?" I tried to sound calm.

"Yeah," Alfalfa, said, "Sometimes the Duck is really a Pig."

"Two thousand feet to go," I said. "Now or never." I pulled back on the controls.

After a small bounce, the airplane lifted off.

"I'm glad for the darkness," Alfalfa said. "We can't see how low we are. Make sure your lights are off."

I raised gear and flaps, then started a gentle left turn. "We're holding a hundred and fifty foot-per-minute climb rate."

"May need three circles over the field to clear Big Mama." Alfalfa referred to a mountain peak that rose almost four thousand feet from the surrounding terrain near the Lao border, which we called the fence. Climbing two thousand feet above Pleiku ensured ground clearance by the time we reached the peak.

After ten minutes of clawing for altitude, I called tower. "Covey Five-nine-one's departing your area and frequency."

"See you later, Five-nine-one."

In ten minutes we approached Big Mama, an eerie slab of rock that cruised by on my left like a dorsal fin in a dark ocean. "Time for a fence check." I turned on the shielded rotating beacon, visible only from above. Then, I began to fumble with the armament panel, a long series of switches bolted above the glare shield to the right of my bombsight.

Alfalfa assisted. "You turn all the cockpit lights off. I'll make sure the target markers--the logs and bricks--are set to the Fire position. If you select Drop, the whole rack falls off the wing. We already have enough rack-FACs in the squadron."

The logical switch position was not Fire, since the munitions dropped from the rack. Pilots who could not subdue their logical processes and select

Fire instead of Drop became rack-FACs. I heard rumors that this problem had strained the logistical system.

I called Covey Five-four-oh, the O.V.-10 pilot we were replacing. "Any updates?"

"Not much going on today. The last fragged mission had a good cut."

"Roger. Weather at home is clear. See ya."

Alfalfa pulled the two-foot-long black starlight scope from its case. "This baby amplifies starlight four-hundred-thousand times."

I watched him set up the scope. *A labor of love.*

He opened his window, and a cool breeze whipped his collar. "Put the road on my side. Let's kill something."

I unsynchronized my propellers. The steady drone changed to a dispersed *rowrowrow*, a more difficult target for the gunners. Every little bit helped.

Holding six thousand feet on my altimeter cleared all mountains in our area and kept us around four thousand feet above the guns. I saw moonlight reflect off the ribbon-like marks moving in and out of black jungle cover--the Ho Chi Minh Trail. I flew to the left side and turned to fly parallel to the road.

"Moonbeam," I called the Airborne Battlefield Command and Control Center, or A.B.-triple-C. "Covey Five-nine-one is on-station with Covey Double-alpha, Victor Romeo Seven." I pictured the dark C-130 flying racetracks for his twelve-hour orbit well above me. Moonbeam's cargo section held a control room with a colonel or general officer and staff. They could divert airstrikes like a fire hose to the moment's most lucrative target.

"Roger, Covey Five-nine-one. Use working frequency Golf."

Alfalfa set the U.H.F. radio according to the daily code card frequency for Golf.

Ironic, I thought, how the dark visual cues seemed ominous while the auditory sensations--steady engine purr and confident voices on the radio--felt so reassuring.

"Ten left," Alfalfa said.

I checked my heading and turned ten degrees to the left. I scanned everywhere. My body jerked whenever a star reflected off a water-filled bomb crater. Even the tiniest unexpected flash of light triggered an avoidance reflex.

Over the next half-hour I rolled my eyes across the engine instruments every fifteen seconds.

Alfalfa yelled, "Break left."

I jerked the nose left just ahead of five red balls moving in echelon, followed by two more strings of five.

"Thirty right." Alfalfa's call sounded businesslike.

I turned back. "What's going on?" I felt the adrenaline hit my spine. A chill climbed my backbone, and my hair tingled.

"Two movers at the Falls. Call for an airstrike if you like. Two is the minimum number of trucks for a strike. But it alerts Moonbeam that we're looking at something."

"Okay." My palms poured sweat. I cleared my dry throat. "I will."

"Look on the north horizon." Alfalfa pointed to a fireworks display. Forty or fifty tracers rose and exploded fiery red. Bombs flashed like strobe lights. "The Danang Coveys have a truck park burning. Our two trucks and a gun are small potatoes."

"I'll try anyway." I passed my request to Moonbeam.

"Having a request in the system is always a good idea," Alfalfa said, "in case the Navy turns a carrier into the wind and launches everything. Meanwhile, let's keep looking. Five left."

I turned. During the next hour I prepared a briefing as we wiggled up the Trail. On the map I found coordinates, target elevation and high terrain details. I referred to the Pleiku weather report for wind and altimeter setting information. I reviewed the standard briefing format to ensure I covered every detail.

"Gunfighter three-one, check." An F-4 flight leader checked in on our frequency.

"Two." His wingman acknowledged.

"Covey Five-nine-one, Gunfighter Three-one, five minutes out with twelve Mark eighty-twos apiece." The flight of two carried twenty-four five-hundred-pound bombs.

I launched into my briefing and moved south to the last known location of the trucks. Alfalfa saw nothing, but described a spot where our trucks might have parked.

My confidence fell. "We're probably going to waste taxpayers' dollars tonight."

"If they don't drop for us, they'll have to dump the bombs into the ocean."

"Rog." I turned north and let the nose fall to the target.

Bam.

My rocket flew straight and true. A fireball rose near the Trail.

"Hit my mark." The rocket made a fireball that glowed red for about ten seconds. Then a puff of white smoke blossomed in the darkness.

The Gunfighters made four passes apiece, none of their bombs hitting within five hundred meters of the target. No fire came from the gunners on the ground.

At ten o'clock, I turned for home. "I'm frustrated. We wasted time in the south end of the sector. The bombs may have had a psychological effect, but that's all."

"Don't worry about it. Gunfighters are usually lousy bombers. The Trail will be here tomorrow. You did a reasonable job--for a new guy." He smiled.

I ensured my exterior lights were off and called tower for landing instructions.

The Trail would be here tomorrow. Jerry wouldn't.

One afternoon I read a *Stars and Stripes* article suggesting the Selective Service should terminate draft deferments for college attendance. I passed the paper to some new-guy friends, O.K. Bryant and Jim Lee, who had joined me in the hooch bar.

"The story reminds me of a day on the beach at Hurlburt," I said. "Grad school deferments went into the toilet just when I was accepted for grad school. Now the government's after undergrads."

"The Air Force is a volunteer outfit," O.K. said, "but most volunteers are driven to join by the giant sucking sound of the Army infantry requirement."

"The Selective Service Director sounds pompous and arrogant to me," Lee said. "He has no appreciation for the disruption, chaos and death his organization brings."

"If he's having trouble finding enough bodies for Vietnam," I said, "perhaps he should figure out why. Who wants to fight with one hand tied behind them by politicians?"

Several days later, noise from a loudspeaker woke me. "This . . . is a test . . . of the Giant Voice Warning system." The monotone human voice tried to sound like a machine. A loud warbling came next, and finally, "Test . . . complete."

I grabbed a cup of thick black coffee from the bar and joined a group of Coveys on the patio. "What's with the public address system at ten in the morning?"

Meredith answered, "In eleven months, I've never heard that thing warn of an impending attack. They should change the words to, 'Those explosions you just heard were incoming rockets. You should have taken cover.' Totally useless."

Kaiser added, "The warbler is a REMF thing. Somebody will get an end-of-tour Silver Star for waking the night flyers each morning with that fucked-up test. Remember that day several months ago? The speaker said, 'This is a test of the Giant Voice Warning System . . . Test complete.' The warbles were missing."

Meredith added, "That same night we had the biggest rocket attack of the year."

I joined the laughter. "Announcing your warning system status to the world?"

"We told the warbler people. They blew us off. Pleiku is their war," Kaiser said, "The Trail is our war. Never the fucking twain meet . . .."

A black and tan dog lying on the corner of the patio raised her head. She had recently given birth to three pups. Short Round and Willie Pete slept nearby. The Prairie Fire pilots gave Stoner, named for a designer of Colt firearms, to the Fifth Special Forces Group at Kontum.

I asked, "Who named the mascot Warbler?"

"Don't know," Kaiser said. "Cockwarbler's been a Covey cuss word forever."

"That cockwarbler woke me up after only three hours' sleep," I said. "I landed at dawn. Alfalfa's been giving me the big picture of the Trail over the past few nights."

"He's a good one," Meredith said. "Double Alpha is fired-up and fearless."

"I start another night cycle tonight with Covey Whisky."

Kaiser and Meredith looked at each other and raised their eyebrows.

"What's the deal?" I asked.

"Irony," Meredith said. "The old fart major with a drinking problem happened to end up with the Whisky callsign. Be careful."

In the small squadron lounge Lieutenant Colonel McGraw conducted his monthly Commander's Call at four p.m. He praised everyone for their hard work and announced his pending departure. "I love you guys, but one year here is plenty. Don't know who my successor will be."

Everyone booed the announcement.

"Do you need an aide?" A voice came from the back of the room. "Someone to carry your briefcase?"

"Thanks, everyone." McGraw smiled. Seeming to pass on the opportunity to become sentimental, he said, "I've checked with the local Army units and several intel sources. Looks like a high probability of rocket attacks this week. Keep helmets and flak vests handy. Dismissed."

"We can relax," Meredith said, as the crowd moved down the hall. "He's been wrong with every one of these predictions. Take care when he forecasts all clear."

I stepped out of the herd into the intelligence vault to prepare for my mission. Within a few minutes my right-seater joined me.

"Call me Whisky." Major James stood six feet tall. He appeared to be near retirement age. His dark hair was oily and combed back in the style of a generation past. Whisky's most prominent features were a large red nose and a drinker's paunch.

We shook hands and entered the vault for an intelligence update. I noted several no-bomb-lines on the wall map, but none conflicted with our planned Trail mission. The lines formed six-kilometer squares where recon teams operated.

Our intelligence officer told of increased truck traffic. He gave the numbers and locations of the day's latest anti-aircraft artillery firings. "The fifteen-thirty Cambodia FAC has a storage area burning here." He moved his pointer due west from Pleiku.

An hour later, we approached the fence in a black Oscar Duck. "Moonbeam, Covey Five-nine-one, on station with Covey Whisky."

Whisky nodded and took a drink from his plastic water bottle.

"Roger, Covey Five-nine-one. Please contact Covey Five-six-four on Fox Mike."

"Roger." I moved the radio selector from V.H.F. to F.M.-1.

"Covey Five-six-four, this is Five-nine-one on Fox Mike."

"Roger. I have a great target here, but I'm out of gas. I have a set of F-Fours inbound. Can you please help me? I've cleared it with Moonbeam." I recognized the voice of another new Covey, Jim Lee.

Fifteen minutes later I spotted Lee's shielded beacon.

"You can see small secondaries sparkling occasionally on the hill below," Lee said.

"Roger." I noted the target's range and bearing from the Pleiku TACAN. "Pass coordinates and target elevation, please."

Lee obliged and turned his O-2 toward Pleiku.

I told Whisky, "Keep the target area in sight while I circle and build a briefing for the fighters."

"Shure." He drank more from his water bottle.

Five minutes later, Gunfighters checked in.

"Where's the target?" I asked Whisky.

"Issh over here shomewhere."

I mouthed the briefing while chasing the TACAN coordinates. Frantically, I scanned the ground. No target.

"Gunfighter's ready for a mark. We have your beacon in sight."

Finally I saw a small flash below. I pulled up hard. "I'm in with a mark."

Bam.

"Attack north to south, east pulls. I'll hold west of the target." I set the fighter attack pattern to ensure I would have clear holding space.

"We have flares, Covey. Stand by while I light two million candles."

A flare popped above me. In the artificial daylight I saw smoke on the ground from earlier strikes. "Secondary explosions popping on the west side. You're cleared hot."

The fighters began north-to-south bomb runs.

Whisky jerked suddenly, when five-hundred-pound bombs thudded below. "Lemme talk . . . uh . . . to th' fighters . . .I wanna . . . uh . . . talk--"

"We're too busy now," I told him. "Gunfighters, keep working the bombs west."

Ten minutes later the Gunfighters headed to Danang with a good bomb damage assessment from me.

Whiskey passed out.

Heading to Laos, I called Moonbeam and gave them the Gunfighter B.D.A.

Then I woke Whisky. "We're over Laos. Time to go to work."

"Uh . . . roger." He fumbled with the latch, then cranked the window open slowly.

"I see lights ahead on the Trail. Put the scope on it." I turned left then right.

A green glow from the starlight scope reflected off Whisky's leathery face. "I've got a bulldozer. He's running for the trees."

"Describe where he's going relative to the bend in the road." I circled.

"Just where the road turns west, he's going north into a valley. He's gone."

I called for an airstrike and began to circle left. In the moonlight I could see dark trees where Whisky said the dozer went. "We'll move north while we wait for fighters. Maybe the bulldozer will come out again."

An hour passed.

"Cobra, check-in."

"Covey Five-nine-one, Cobra One-one's inbound. Two Fox-fours. Hard bombs."

During my FAC-to-fighter briefing, I jinked left hard when Whisky lighted a cigarette without warning me. "Say something before you make flashes over there, please. And get ready. I plan to roll in with a mark in one minute."

Whisky cranked his window shut, stowed the starlight scope, and pulled out another water flask containing clear liquid. "I'm all set."

I rolled into a thirty-degree dive. With throttles at cruise power, the airspeed approached two hundred. I fired a rocket.

Bam.

Wham.

Whisky's window flew open and slammed into a receiver bracket on the wing. In that instant the crank made ten unexpected revolutions under his right arm.

"Ooow," Whisky screamed. He lunged across the console between us and clawed my back and shoulder. He wasn't hurt, but I had a wide-awake drunk on my hands.

Burning bits of rocket exhaust blew into the cockpit.

I smelled the strong burning odor, watched the rocket explode with a large round ball of flame in the target valley, then pulled back on the controls.

Fifteen fiery tennis balls passed under the nose. I loaded the airplane up to four g's in the pullout. I heard the rumble as the shells burst above and to my right.

Whisky groaned. He fell back into his seat.

I kept the hard turn going. "Hit my smoke. I'm holding to the south. Make east to west passes. Guns are north."

"Roger. Those rounds looked close."

"Yep. Dozer's in the dark trees, north of the road bend if you can see it. My smoke is in those trees."

Whisky rubbed his face. "That rocket shit burns. I thought we were hit."

"Cobra One-one is in."

"Cleared hot." On the intercom I said, "Close your window. While it's open, our speed limit is one-twenty. If the window comes off and hits the rear prop, we're fucked."

Whisky tugged and yanked and cursed.

Cobra's bombs hit the valley.

"Two, aim just north of lead's hit. You're cleared hot."

Whisky grunted and pulled. He couldn't budge his window. "The newer O-Twos don't have the crank."

I shook my head and lectured. "Both have locking latches, though. The window opened because you didn't latch it. Now I'll have to somehow stay under one-twenty when I fire rockets."

"Thought I was dead." Whisky swigged from his water flask. "The window is really stuck."

"If it comes off, you jump out and get it." I meant my angry words.

Cobra flight completed their last attack and turned for home base.

"Looks like you destroyed the target area." I said. "We'll look it over. Thanks."

"Roger. Nice working with you. Cobra, go button five."

"Two."

After directing two more strikes on the bulldozer target, I pointed the Duck home.

Whisky dozed, notwithstanding the noise and wind from his open window.

I picked up one of his empty water flasks and smelled it.

Vodka.

In the crowded hooch bar, I pulled aside a scheduler, Jack Muirhead. "Whisky needs help. He's gone over the edge with his drinking." I told Jack about the mission.

"He's a major, and I'm a lieutenant. What can I do?"

"Shoot him," I whispered. I put on an angry face. "Tell Ed. Schedule the commander to fly him to the nearest real hospital. I don't care, as long as you don't put him in my cockpit."

"Okay. I'll change the schedule. You've got the Danang run tomorrow."

At the ops counter I signed the daily flight orders for a ten a.m. takeoff.

One of our navigators, Captain Joe Dipietro, stepped up. "Put my name on the orders. And don't write Captain Abort." Small and energetic, Joe had a reputation for finding aircraft discrepancies that pilots missed during preflight.

"Business at Danang?" I had heard that if a pilot reached the Trail with the dark-haired Italian, he performed like a surgeon.

"Yeah." Dipietro had a large smile. "We can grab a hot lunch, too."

We walked toward the door when an airman from Life Support stepped in front of us, holding a helmet and O.V.-10 harness. "These items need to go to Danang."

I saw dirt and deep scratches across the helmet and blood on the torn harness.

"They're from the accident."

"No way." I shuddered at the gory image Jerry's smashed equipment caused my mind to conjure. "You seal that stuff in plastic, then box it. If you finish before I can take-off, tell the Danang people to pick it up at the airplane. C'mon, Captain. Let's hurry."

After a quick preflight inspection, Dipietro and I climbed in. I started both engines. Before I could taxi, the talented airman arrived at the right door with a cardboard box. Dipietro leaned forward while the airman put it on the bench seat behind us.

"Thanks, sir," he said. "I'll call Danang."

The Duck seemed strong.

"I have a civilian license. Mind if I fly?"

"You've got it." Leveling at six thousand feet, I shook the controls to signal the hand-off.

Weather deteriorated as we neared our destination.

At eleven o'clock I contacted Danang Approach Control. "Covey Five-nine-one requests G.C.A. full stop." I asked for a ground controlled approach.

"Covey Five-nine-one, G.C.A. is down. You're cleared to the TACAN holding pattern. Maintain one-two thousand. Altimeter two-niner-eight-zero. Expect approach clearance at eleven forty-five."

Dipietro added power for the climb. "Danang G.C.A. only works in clear weather."

"More irony," I said. "I still can't believe that Jerry's gone." I glanced at the cardboard box. "The ride back will be more comfortable for me."

"I heard the accident investigators are looking hard for a bullet hole. They want to get Danang maintenance off the hook. The bird had just come out of a phase inspection."

"If Danang screwed up, then somebody should be hooked, or maybe skinned. I guess a combat loss is easier to write off over here. Either way doesn't do Jerry any good."

I landed at noon, and parked near 20th TASS operations.

An airman slid yellow chocks in front and behind our tires.

I told him, "You may remove the cardboard box. Otherwise, please don't touch the airplane."

We checked our parachutes and weapons at Life Support, then went for lunch. Dipietro ran errands. I picked up a few parts and filled a pouch with official mail.

At three, we walked to Life Support. A sergeant told Dipietro, "Sir, these snub-nosed weapons are on a recall list. I have orders to send them to the states."

"Damn," Dipietro said. "I really like that gun."

The sergeant placed a box on the counter. "I'll trade you this brand new Smith and Wesson Combat Masterpiece."

"Fine." Dipietro shrugged. He wiped down the black thirty-eight caliber revolver.

As we approached the aircraft in a light drizzle, I said, "Something's wrong. The nose gear doors are closed. Someone either pumped a handle in the cockpit a hundred strokes or started the front engine. Why would they do that?"

"Dunno," Dipietro said. "We'd better look and see." He leaned inside and pumped a small lever between the seats.

The doors inched open.

I crawled under the plane, reached up, and removed the nose gear downlock pin.

Dipietro said, "You've got to be shitting me. What idiot would install the pin, then close the doors so we couldn't remove it or even see it?"

"The nose gear would not have come up when I raised the handle," I said. "No telling what the drag would have done during that critical phase of flight."

"Danang maintenance is famous for this kind of horseshit. If I catch some asshole in the act, I swear I'll shoot him in the nuts." An approaching sergeant overheard my loud expletives and did an about-face. I thought about Jerry. "These mother-fucking bastards are going to kill somebody," I yelled, "if they haven't already."

We pulled our own chocks, started engines, and joined a long line of airplanes on the wide parallel taxiway. I called Departure Control for my clearance.

"Roger, Covey Five-nine-one. Departure radar is down. You are number seventeen for departure. Expect clearance in one hour and twenty-five minutes."

"Gimme tower frequency," I told Dipietro. "I'll check the weather."

"Ceiling three hundred feet, visibility three miles," tower replied to my query.

"Roger. Covey Five-nine-one requests Special V.F.R. departure with an intersection takeoff." Technically, under a three-hundred-foot ceiling I could use visual flight rules to depart the airport. The runway intersection left plenty of room for my takeoff roll.

"You know the saying about runway behind you," Dipietro said.

"And field-grade navigators," I said. "Both useless." I laughed.

"Not how I heard it," my navigator friend said. "But I agree with your plan."

The O-2 rocked as two camouflage-painted F-4s roared by trailing bright orange afterburner flames. The wingman moved up and down like a porpoise as they rose into the soup.

"Covey Five-nine-one, cleared for takeoff, six thousand feet remaining."

"Roger." I pushed the levers forward and launched. After raising the gear and flaps, I turned hard right and flew over the TASS ramp at two hundred feet. "Wish I had a bag of shit to drop on those jerks down there."

Dipietro nodded.

I headed out to sea and thanked the tower troops when I cleared the airdrome. I turned south just below the clouds and two hundred feet over the deep blue white-capped ocean. "We'll have to cruise about thirty miles to clear the Danang artillery fan before I can call for traffic advisories from Waterboy or Panama radar sites."

"Fine," Dipietro said. "Mind if I put a few rounds through my new pistol?"

"Don't kill any whales."

He loaded six cartridges and opened the window. Bang. Bang. Bang. "The pistol seems to have a nice balance." Bang. Bang. "Oh shit."

I leaned to the right, afraid that Dipietro had put a hole in the strut--and my career.

"Look," he pointed down to the ocean.

I banked right and saw another O-2 over the waves headed north toward Danang.

"He flew right into my sights when I fired."

I turned and followed the other craft for a few miles. "He's not trailing smoke."

"That's a relief. I think I hit him. He'll have some explaining to do."

I turned to the south. "What's his altitude--maybe ten feet? He's probably a guy they call the Crazy Man. He's good with explanations."

We reached Pleiku and landed without further crisis. As we walked from the aircraft, our crewchief asked, "What's this?"

He held a handful of thirty-eight-caliber brass he had taken from our ashtray.

I pointed to Dipietro. "The captain can explain."

After another night cycle with Alfalfa, I found my name on the schedule beside a new navigator, Major Bill Simpson. I met the crewcut former football player in the intel vault before our ten p.m. launch.

"I've been here a few weeks," he said, "and I've noticed that you guys always go to Laos by the same route. Why don't we try something new?"

"Sure."

"If we go due west over Cambodia, then turn north, we'll intercept the Trail at the what you call the Western Ford." Major Simpson pointed to lines he had drawn on a map. "Then we turn east and follow highway one-ten here along the Kong River. Brings us to the Falls at a different time from a different direction."

"I'm a great believer in tactical surprise, Major."

We took off on heading two-eight-five and leveled at four thousand feet over dark northern Cambodia. No lights came from the jungle below, and scattered clouds above blocked starlight. Following Simpson's plan, we turned north after about an hour.

Thirty minutes later I asked, "Where's the river?" I began a slow circle.

Simpson took out the starlight scope and opened his window. "We should be crossing it now. Don't know what the winds are doing."

I resumed the northerly heading. "We can drive on until we see the

Bolovens Plateau. It rises a thousand feet straight up."

Thirty minutes later, the major scanned again. "No Bolovens."

"We haven't crossed the Mekong, but the winds may have blown us west. I'm turning northeast."

"Roger," Simpson said. "I'll keep searching. Nothing but jungle below us now."

We droned in silence for an hour-and-a-half.

"Major, we've been out here for three and a half hours. If you have the slightest clue as to where we are, I'd love to hear it."

"I'm disoriented at the moment."

"Disoriented?" I smiled. "If you saw a truck right now, who's to say it wouldn't have Pennsylvania plates?"

Simpson nodded.

"Let's find Pleiku and live to fight another day. We've used three-and-a-half of our six-hour fuel load. Tonight's wasted."

"Roger." Simpson sounded discouraged.

I turned southeast. "I'm holding one-five-zero, unless you have a better heading. Climbing to ten thousand feet to save gas." I leaned the mixtures until the cylinder head temperatures inched toward the redline.

After an hour, I could feel sweat soaking my uniform. "We should be on the ground at Pleiku now. Fuel is low. All I have going for me is the Orion constellation over here." Three bright stars of Orion's belt lined up just behind my left shoulder, as I remembered from the previous night. "I suggest you tighten your parachute harness."

I called Peacock, the ground-controlled intercept site at Pleiku.

"Covey Five-nine-one, this is Peacock." The transmission was scratchy and weak.

"Pigeons to Pleiku, please." I requested vectors home.

"Covey Five-nine-one, Peacock is radar-unable. Radio flight-following only. Say TACAN radial and D.M.E." He asked my position from a TACAN station I couldn't receive. If I had that information, I wouldn't have called.

"Shit." I looked at Simpson and shrugged. I subdued an impulse to say, "We're ten degrees off Orion."

Simpson said, "I'm afraid to say anything. This nightmare shouldn't be happening."

I called the incoming Covey FAC.

"Roger, Five-nine-one. I have you lima-chuck." He heard us loud and clear.

"Please give us a hold-down on Fox Mike." I turned the F.M. radio selector to the Home position. The homing needle made clockwise circles in its small case. On any other night, the needle would have pointed to the transmitter on the other O-2.

Another hour passed. We called every radar site in range and tuned every TACAN station with no results. My body ached after five-and-a-half hours in the seat. Still, we did not know our location. Now the information we did have became unsettling. Not more than thirty minutes of fuel remained.

I spotted a glow on the horizon straight ahead. The TACAN indicator locked onto Pleiku at twelve o'clock for nineteen miles.

"Look at the TACAN," I told Simpson. "Everything at Pleiku is intermittent--hot showers, mail, TACAN signals."

I called tower. "Covey Five-nine-one, landing instructions, please."

"Roger, Covey. Pleiku is closed. Say intentions."

After a long pause, during which I could not think of any intentions other than landing, I asked, "Why is Pleiku closed?"

"Zero ceiling, zero visibility in fog. Say intentions."

The needles of both fuel gauges rested on E. However, in my mind they screamed, "Empty."

I turned to Simpson. "Why do they keep asking about intentions? Seems a bit personal at the moment. We're passing Kontum on the left. Airfield's buried in fog. Bailout just became a high probability."

Simpson squirmed in his seat. "I have no idea what went wrong. Fog was not in the weather forecast." He looked down and shook his head.

"Tower, we intend to call RAPCON." I asked Simpson to change the radio frequency to Radar Approach Control.

"Pleiku Approach Control, this is Covey Five-nine-one. We're in a heap of trouble. I figure we have enough fuel for one short precision approach."

A calm voice came back. "Roger, Five-nine-one, squawk ident, radar contact. Set altimeter two-niner-eight-one. Fly heading one-seven-zero. Five-mile base leg. Descend and maintain three-thousand two-hundred feet . . . Report cockpit checks complete . . . Gear should be down . . . Weather at Pleiku is zero-zero. Winds are calm."

"Two-niner-eight-one. One seven zero. Three-thousand two-hundred." I read back the required numbers. Bad-smelling sweat poured down my neck. The dark cockpit felt cramped like a coffin. Stress took a viselike grip on my chest.

We turned onto final approach. "Covey Five-nine-one, gear down, full stop." I made tiny moves in response to the controller.

"Do not acknowledge further transmissions. Begin descent . . . on course . . . slightly above glideslope."

Moving the throttles back just a hair, I watched the vertical velocity move from six hundred feet per minute to eight hundred. Then, I eased the power forward again.

"On course, on glideslope."

We entered the fog. I saw nothing but white ahead.

"Yell if you see the runway," I told Simpson. "I'm ready to spike us on."

He nodded.

"On course, on glideslope," the calm controller's voice continued.

My right-seater scanned ahead like the captain of the Titanic should have. "I'll level off over the runway. Look hard. We're betting everything on this approach."

"At decision height. On course, on glideslope." The legal and proper move was to add power and go around, since the runway was not visible from one hundred feet up and a quarter of a mile out from the touchdown area.

"Keep talking." I added a skosh of power. The vertical velocity moved from six hundred to five, then four.

"On course, crossing runway threshold."

I added more power. Three hundred feet per minute became two hundred.

Squeak. Squeak. My wheels touched the runway.

I chopped power and stood on the brakes until we stopped. The white runway center stripe hid in the fog four feet below my window. Sweat poured down my face like tears. I turned to Major Simpson. "Are we there yet?"

Chapter 5
Prairie Fire

November 1970

O.K. Bryant sat at the Covey hooch bar. “You didn’t land in this fog, did you?” His average build seemed small beside big Jim Lee. Another lieutenant pilot, Jim had arrived with O.K. a month before I did. They owned the bar at four a.m.

“Shhh,” I said. “We don’t need to tell the world.”

Major Simpson, who had had entered with me, bragged. “My pilot did well. We’re living proof.”

“Just between us chickens,” I said, “I never saw the runway until it hit the wheels. Didn’t have a lot of options after five hours and forty-seven minutes in the air.”

“Holy shit,” Bryant said. “Thirteen minutes of gas left. Maybe.”

“We made conservative decisions,” Major Simpson said. “Started home after only three and a half hours.”

I pulled out four beers. “The only help we had all night was the belt of Orion.”

“My mission was weather-canceled,” Bryant said. “Tower’s calling ceiling and visibility zero-zero.” His large brown eyes shone with both amusement and amazement. “What did they say when you landed?”

“We didn’t talk to tower. I followed the runway centerline until I found a yellow stripe. Followed it to the taxiway. Ground control asked for a Pilot Weather Report.”

“What did you tell them?”

“I figured they were recording a statement for my court martial. I told them I didn’t recommend that any pilot do what I just did. Honest but vague.”

Jim Lee asked, “How did you find the fuel pit?”

“We didn’t on the first attempt,” I said. “Went right past it. So I shut down the front engine, and the major took his flashlight and searched ahead. Finally guided me in."

Simpson finished his beer. "Tonight changed my life. We made good decisions and nearly bought the farm anyway. I don't know . . .." He walked out.

I stayed. "I'm buying."

"We were talking about Prairie Fire," Bryant said. "Three slots open this month."

"Prairie Fire?" I asked.

"You know. Supporting Special Forces reconnaissance teams. Old FACs in the program vote on replacements. The three of us are in the running."

Lee nodded. "Killing N.V.A. seems more thrilling than hunting trucks. Helping ground troops brings more satisfaction than interdiction, too."

"If they ask," I said, "I'm in."

Feeling drained, I slept all day. Besides, my profile needed lowering after breaking weather minimums--a strict Air Force no-no.

At four-thirty the mail flag rose to the top of the staff and drew me to the post office where I found my box empty. My mail exchange with Elaine had been sporadic. The postal system moved slowly, and I couldn't find much to write about that she would understand.

Our new commander probably had not yet tuned into the grapevine, so I didn't expect any questions from him about my long mission. He seemed much more tuned into the flow of paper through his office than the flow of his people across Laos.

I went for an early dinner at the club. Nobody said anything to me about my lengthy sortie and busting minimums. My guilt dissolved into conversations about increased gun activity in the dry season.

The schedule named me as the duty officer from six p.m. until six a.m. By ten o'clock, I had posted all notices and safety messages and briefed crews for night missions.

Then, jungle crud struck.

Severe intestinal cramps and diarrhea took over, as though the phantom I had cheated on the previous night had come back with a vengeance. Lying on the floor, I called Ed at the hooch bar. "By the time you find a replacement, I'll be incapacitated."

I stayed in bed for three days. I couldn't move. All I could do was groan, and groaning made me vomit.

O.K. Bryant stopped by my room every morning. On the third day he asked, "Are you well enough to travel to the flight surgeon?"

"I still can't keep water down. I suppose I should go. Looks like the alternative is death. He'll want to ground me for two weeks."

"Let's go. If he grounds you, we'll lose the paperwork. Fly when you're ready."

Not ready to fly the next day, I worked on my non-volunteer additional duties of supply and budget management. Everyone contributed to the squadron operation with jobs like mine. The secret to my success was seeking help from experienced non-commissioned officers.

The supply N.C.O. led me on a complete inventory of the squadron. "No sweat, sir," he said. "We'll make everything balance if we have to change tables into lamps and beds into footlockers."

"Can we produce an accurate report, too?" I asked.

He smiled and told me not to worry.

My budget N.C.O. used a simple rule. "Take last year's budget and add ten percent."

"Okay," I said. "Let me play with it." I visited everyone impacted by the budget and came away happy enough. Then I secured Ed's blessing.

The next day I was scheduled for an easy V.R. mission over Cambodia. As I trudged out the door of the squadron, the new commander, Lieutenant Colonel Timmons, called to me. Laden with parachute, survival vest, weapons, radios, binoculars, M-16 with ten-clip bandoleer, and ten pounds of maps, I clanked into his office. "Yes, sir?"

"I have a question about the budget."

"Sir, I have a fence time to meet. Could we talk tonight or tomorrow?"

"This won't take long. Where did you get the figures for the x-ray delta account?"

"We expect growth and inflation to run at four percent, so if we ask for ten and get five, we're covered. If we ask for the four that we need and only get two, we can't do the mission." I spent ten minutes going over dollars that made little sense. "We have to play a silly game to get what we need, sir."

"You're going to have to write this information in more detail."

"Sir, I'd be happy to do so, anytime but now. If I don't check in within twenty minutes, an angry colonel at Seventh Air Force will call you. Sergeant Ramsey can make you feel really comfortable with all this budgeting stuff."

"Go."

I sprinted to my Oscar Deuce thinking about our former commander who was probably arriving home in the U.S.A. Things are going to change around here, my intuition told me. And not for the better.

In the intelligence vault after landing, I wrote a list of suspected enemy activity.

Ed stepped up with another old-head pilot, Ken Blutt. "Ever heard of Prairie Fire?"

"Not in detail," I said. "I have some vague ideas."

"Supporting Green Beret recon teams who run into all kinds of trouble in the extreme western D.M.Z. If you think you're tough enough to stomp out prairie fires, Ken will train you on the specifics." Ed could challenge and motivate with just his facial expression. He gave me that look.

I nodded enthusiastically to Ed before he departed.

"Since sixty-five, the Army Special Forces have watched the Ho Chi Minh Trail." Blutt swept his hand upward along the Lao border on the wall map. "Laos forms the war's western flank." Blutt had dark shiny eyes and brown hair chopped off in a flattop.

"They just watch?"

"Theoretically. Fifth Special Forces--Green Berets--have a forward operating base at Kontum. More than twenty teams are available to run missions of about four days' duration. Most teams have two Americans and eight Montagnards, recruited from the hill tribes in Vietnam. Holding ten teams in place requires only twenty Americans. But twenty thousand N.V.A. have the mission of hunting them down."

"I'm impressed. A thousand-to-one odds."

"Nine times out of ten, teams make contact. That's where we come in." Blutt smiled a lot.

"Close air support?"

"Right," Blutt said. "Lots of it. Many strikes are near heavily defended interdiction points—I.D.Ps. You could find yourself dodging ten helicopters, four A-Ones, F-Fours stacked up to the ionosphere, and triple-A, too. The mission is to save the troops on the ground. And you're in charge."

"When do we start?"

"Flying starts tomorrow. Top secrecy starts now."

"Why the secrecy? The North Vietnamese know exactly what we're doing. They have a thousand times more troops violating Laotian neutrality than we do."

"Our government openly honors the nineteen-sixty-two Geneva Accords. Leave politics to the politicians. We just do the dirty work and keep our mouths shut." Blutt shook his head. "We launch at five-thirty."

I went to bed early but didn't sleep much. Directing strikes close to friendly troops was an incredibly rewarding proposition. Doing close air support--O.K. called it hair, tooth and eyeball extraction--would take me where I'd never been.

I took off at dawn in Blutt's right seat.

"Today I fly, you watch. Tomorrow you fly, I watch." After raising gear and flaps, Blutt seemed pleased to show me his piloting skills. "We'll pick up a Rider at Kontum, then go to the area of operations. We'll do what we have to do, then, if we need gas, we'll drop into Dak To, about thirty miles northwest of Kontum. An O.V.-Ten will show up this afternoon and relieve us or work alongside."

A million questions surged through my brain. I knew most answers would come not in words but in the action ahead of us.

"Always call the F.O.B.--the Forward Operating Base--at Kontum before you land. Check your secure radio and remind them to send the rider out to the runway."

"Tell me about the Riders."

"Green Berets, mostly N.C.O.s. They're excellent--great guys. Totally fearless. As individuals, they're all different but hard as steel. Riders got here by doing well as one-zeroes--team leaders--on the ground."

I nodded.

"The F.O.B. is about a mile south of the airstrip." Blutt made his call. When the voice answered, he said, "Go green."

"Roger."

Blutt pushed a button on the radio encryption device. After some whirring, the machine illuminated a bright green light.

"Covey, radio check green." Blutt's voice sounded distorted.

"Roger, loud and clear." The answer came from the bottom of a barrel.

"Roger, Covey out."

Blutt landed with minimum ground roll on the three-thousand-foot east-west strip at Kontum. He stopped, turned around, and taxied back. South of the runway he parked on a small ramp and shut down both engines. I noticed a few vacant buildings nearby and revetments for helicopters on the north side.

As we climbed out, a jeep delivered our passenger.

"I'm Sixpack." A tough-looking soldier in crisp green fatigues extended his hand. He showed a quick smile under a ruddy complexion and close-cropped, curly blond hair. He looked like a broad-shouldered Ned Beatty.

I shook his strong hand. "I'm the new guy."

Holding his flight helmet and a green map case, Sixpack said, "Covey Rider at your service. I speak Army."

"Now that the amenities are over, let's go," Blutt said.

I climbed into the backseat.

Blutt taxied onto the packed dirt a hundred feet short of the approach end of the runway and started his takeoff roll. We lifted off at the far end of the pavement. He raised gear and flaps and glanced over his shoulder at me.

I didn't say what I was thinking. Holy shit. He's gonna kill us. The full fuel load and extra passenger had made the Duck a ground-lovin' Hog.

Sixpack brought out maps and an array of colored markers from his case. He noted names of states and other data in neat rows on his window. When he saw me watching, he said, "Helps me stay organized. The colors represent priorities."

"And the states are . . ."

"The unclassified names of recon teams. The no-bomb-lines in your vault at Pleiku name the operations. Today, Team Mississippi will activate Operation Zulu Dancer." He handed me a six-kilometer square map, cut from a one-to-fifty-thousand scale chart and sealed in plastic. "That is the only paper these teams carry."

As he took the map, Sixpack pointed to primary, secondary, and tertiary landing zones. "This area has so many N.V.A. per square foot, we expect to use at least two zones."

Blutt flew around high and well north of the no-bomb-lines. "We don't routinely overfly a team or a proposed landing zone. Good guys check-in with an okay or a message each morning and evening." He pointed to his map. "Today's infil is far enough from the big guns that we'll just use the A-Ones--the Spads. If in doubt, call for F-Fours, too."

I asked, "Do you request specific ordnance loads?"

"No. Spads carry soft stuff--cluster bombs, strafe, and nape--that you can drop close to friendlies. F-Fours usually haul hard bombs. The book says keep hard bombs a half-mile from friendlies. I add another half-mile because we don't normally tell the F-Four crews that our troops are down there. Spad pilots listen on their F.M. radios. They know."

Sixpack studied the ground through powerful binoculars. "Primary L.Z. is a sit-down. Others are probably low-hovers."

"Okay. Let's go to Dak To." Blutt turned southeast.

I checked my watch. Four hours had passed in what seemed like twenty minutes. We had checked landing zones for future operations, taken messages from teams in place, and searched the Trail when we crossed that highway.

Blutt made a few radio calls then planted the Duck firmly on a tiny, once-paved airstrip, barely inside Vietnam. Helicopters--Hueys and Cobras--lined the north edge of the runway. Blutt taxied back to the west end and parked near large black fuel bladders.

Sixpack headed for a large bunker made of sandbags.

Blutt walked to a fuel pump where a blond, suntanned teenager sat, smiling. "How's my favorite draftee?"

"Great, sir. Check the oil?" The kid pulled a rope starter on the pump.

"Sure." Blutt dragged a thick black hose over to the O-2, stepped up on an old ammo crate, and filled the right wing tanks. "Sometimes you just pump enough to get home."

I filled the left tanks. Home, I thought. Where the hell is home? My friends here formed a closer family than I had ever known.

We walked a hundred yards down the runway to the big bunker. Graders had scraped away the jungle for three hundred yards around the strip. This clearing would increase the vulnerability of V.C. or N.V.A. troops who might try to overrun the base. Green mountains dominated the western horizon. Terrain to the east fell off into a huge rice-growing plain.

The sandbag structure had a shaded porch below ground level. Ten soldiers in black uniforms relaxed before huge piles of ammunition, grenades, and claymore mines. Sixpack introduced me to the leader--the one-zero--of Team Mississippi.

We shook hands. A dark, camouflaged face smiled slightly.

"We're all set," Sixpack said. "We'll call for launch when the Spads show up."

We would take-off and advise the choppers to bring the team over when the A-1 Skyraiders--air cover with a Spad callsign--arrived.

Blutt pushed power to maximum while still short of the runway.

From my tight quarters between a wall of radios and the front seats, I saw dust swirling as we bounced across the holes and patches that covered the runway. What a shitty place to die, I thought. I reminded myself the rear seat was a one-time deal. And normally only two of us would be aboard.

We lifted off with zero feet remaining. Wheels and flaps came up.

Blutt checked-in with Hillsboro. "Request a Spad launch." He used a special callsign that told the controller the rest of the story.

"Roger."

"The one-zero doesn't want a prep on the L.Z.," Sixpack said. He turned to me and said, "Normally we prepare the Huey landing zone. You know, sanitize the area with bombs. Today, we'll only use the Cobras. They fire flechette rockets--nails--that keep the bad guys' heads down pretty good."

Blutt droned north until the Spads called on U.H.F. He told them, "Hold high and listen. First target's on a sixteen-hundred-foot hillside. Altimeter three-zero-zero-one."

"Roger."

At the same time, Sixpack used his F.M. radio. "We have a sycamore." He turned and said, "Any tree is code for launch. Don't use words like launch or L.Z. in the clear."

Nodding, I visualized the black-clad one-zero in the bunker strapping on his gear, muttering, "Let's rock and roll."

After ten minutes, Sixpack said, "Tally on a string of five Hueys, with two Cobras out in front." He pointed to the east.

Sixpack had eyes like binoculars.

I searched the ocean of green mountains below for three minutes before I spotted motion. The Hueys were circling to increase their spacing behind the Cobras. "Tally on the cavalry."

Blutt fed headings and ranges to the Cobra leader. "Five degrees right. Four miles."

I felt a minor adrenaline event.

"Two miles." Blutt looked back and forth between choppers and L.Z.

The Hueys followed one mile behind the gunships.

"Five right. One mile. Call tally."

"Tally." The first Cobra pulled up, rotated right, rolled out and fired.

Blutt pointed. "See the puff of orange smoke over the L.Z? That's the packing material for the flechettes. Confirms the warhead has opened and released thousands of darts."

"Roger."

I watched five more orange clouds appear. Then the first Huey approached the landing zone. Both Cobras continued to circle the craft on the ground. The other Hueys climbed and circled wider.

"Taking fire from the treeline on top." The Huey on the L.Z. lifted and turned.

Blutt rolled in on the hilltop.

Bam.

A rocket blasted from the right wing.

"Head south," Blutt said. "I'll take the lead." He switched from the helicopters' V.H.F. to the fighters' U.H.F. radio. "Spad Zero-one, hit my smoke when the Cobras are clear. We're moving out."

He turned to me. "We're going to the secondary L.Z. Too much fire for the helicopters on this one."

"Spad one is in on the hilltop."

"Cleared hot." Blutt had pulled up only slightly from his rocket pass. Now he descended in front of the first Huey. He switched back to V.H.F. "Follow me."

I saw the airspeed indicator peg at two-twelve--maximum warp for the Duck.

Blutt leveled off on the trees. He slammed the O-2 around like a mad carpenter would employ a wrecking bar. We jerked and bounced over the jungle. "Spads, make two passes, then hold high."

Airspeed fell to one-sixty. We were losing energy.

"Twelve o'clock, one mile." Blutt told the Hueys behind us to prepare for the secondary landing zone. He lifted us over a ridgeline. I became light in my seat as he shoved the aircraft controls forward and drove the nose down into a valley.

I saw one-twenty go to one-forty on the airspeed indicator.

Over a small clearing, Blutt rolled ninety degrees left and pulled hard. "Bingo, bingo, bingo. My wing is a pointer." Blutt rolled out heading west.

The helicopter armada approached as we cleared the zone.

"We'll climb up again in this valley," Blutt said. He kept the nose of the aircraft moving from side to side as we climbed up.

I caught glimpses of helicopters landing and depositing Team Mississippi onto the secondary zone.

Back-up Hueys flew a wide circle a few thousand feet up. Cobras cut tight circles on the deck. Spads orbited above, ready and waiting for a signal. Radios were silent. Now, seconds seemed like minutes. Suddenly the string of helicopters headed east.

All this effort, I thought, to put people on the ground in Laos. I had been trained to spend every penny getting people out.

"Tell me when the team calls," Blutt told Sixpack and continued to climb.

Sixpack nodded. He was busy with his pens, preparing for tomorrow.

On the Army F.M. frequency, I heard a whisper. "Team okay."

Sixpack gave Blutt a thumbs-up signal.

Blutt fired a smoke rocket north of the original L.Z. "Spads, hit my smoke. Drop everything." On intercom, he said. "If we can't have it, neither can they."

We completed our climb and explosions danced over the enemy position.

Blutt and Sixpack spoke to counterparts on an arriving O.V.-10. We turned east.

"The O-Two launches at dawn for Prairie Fire primary," Blutt said. "You'll almost always refuel at Dak To. Try to finish around one o'clock. That's when the secondary aircraft, the O.V.-Ten, shows up."

"How long does the O.V.-Ten stay?"

"As long as necessary. But, normally, they don't like to refuel at Dak To."

As we approached Kontum, I had a better look at the place. My mind had been fully occupied earlier. A small river formed a natural barrier around the west end of the runway and the village on the north edge of the airfield. Bunkers covered the east, and the F.O.B. was south. Grass had recovered from the original plowing of the jungle around the perimeter.

We landed at two p.m., climbed aboard a jeep, and bounced down the mile of bad road to the F.O.B.

"Our living quarters are here." Sixpack pointed to low, screened buildings.

I saw C.C.C. on a sign at one end. "Command and Control, Central?"

"Covey Country Club. Sometimes." He and Blutt smiled.

"Here's the bunker."

We pulled up to a large square mound of dirt. A concrete slab protruded from the top. Stairs led down to offices in a heavy vault.

I met several other Covey Riders and team leaders.

Sixpack introduced me to Major Greenberg. "He's our S-three, or what you call the Operations Officer."

The burly Army major offered after a firm handshake. "Have a seat." He began a briefing. "Each of our missions has a specific objective, such as counting trucks, plotting gun positions, or destroying a facility. Three to five days is normal for these operations."

I took in the whole scene. All around me, soldiers studied maps, photographs and other documents with absolute intensity. Most wore starched uniforms with rolled-up sleeves that revealed heavy muscles. Younger troops moved stacks of paper from tables to files. A FAC named Marshall Harrison would later describe this atmosphere as "full of excess testosterone."

"Of course a prisoner snatch is a bonus on every mission," Greenberg said. "We love to chat with the enemy when we can."

Behind him, a large flat cardboard box lay on the floor, just outside the door. Pouch, Human, was printed on the end in black letters beside a federal stock number.

Body bags. Damn.

"The words Prairie Fire Emergency mean 'I'm in deep trouble, and I'm in the wrong country.' The system is set up to divert every available tactical airplane to your control."

I nodded.

"We expect you'll work airstrikes closer than other FACs do. If a one-zero says put it on top of his position, you do it." Greenberg rose to leave. "I'm sure you'll enjoy working with the Fifth Group. Welcome aboard."

I came to my feet as the major did. "Sir, I'll do my best." No doubt in my mind. If I screwed up, these guys would kill me.

Captain Bob Howard passed by and handed me a stack of photographs.

Sixpack said, "The team leader of Iowa did a recce mission yesterday in one of our O-Ones. Took pictures of four hundred North Vietnamese soldiers in his six-klick square."

I scanned the glossy eight-by-tens and stopped to study a formation of over a hundred enemy soldiers marching on a wide road. "Maybe we should send B-Fifty-twos there instead of a recon team."

That night at Pleiku, I enjoyed a hot meal, a shower, and clean sheets--three items that clearly distinguished me from Team Mississippi. I didn't sleep well.

I took off at five-thirty the next morning with Blutt in the right seat.

"I brought my movie camera," he said. "I'll stay out of your way. Remember to be flexible." He smiled.

I overcame my psychological barrier to risky maneuvers such as using the entire paved surface on takeoff roll and survived minimum runway operations at Kontum. With Sixpack aboard, we approached the fence, trying to appear innocuous at four thousand feet. I asked, "Where's the team that's coming out?"

"Just over the border. I'll ask for a shiny."

"A shiny?"

"A signal mirror." He made several radio calls, then pointed to the jungle less than a kilometer east of the Falls interdiction point.

I saw the blinking mirror flashes that seemed to say, "Take us home, Covey."

"Those guys are easily within range of dozens of antiaircraft guns," I said. "Can they move east?"

"No food and water." Sixpack had checked. "They have to come out today."

I thought about the problem as we cruised around the area, collecting routine reports from other teams. "I'll request F-Fours and Spads for an eleven o'clock operation. Can your boys behave themselves until then?"

"Sure." Sixpack smiled and made notes on the window.

At nine-thirty I turned southeast and called Hillsboro. "Request four Fox-fours and four Alpha-ones for an eleven o'clock time-on-target." Adding rendezvous details, I started a descent.

I set an F.M. radio to the uncontrolled runway frequency and called, "Covey Five-nine-one is a single Oscar Deuce approaching Dak To from the north." Noting a couple of Cobras parked near the strip, I made the standard traffic pattern calls and landed.

Blutt and his draftee pal began the refueling process. Sixpack and I went to the large bunker. Noticing a swarm of Vietnamese children around the helicopters, I asked, "What are those kids doing?"

"Waxing," Sixpack said. "The chopper guys give them cans of C-rations to wash and wax their flyin' machines."

"Why?"

"To justify giving food to the kids. And because they're nuts. You'll see."

I found the Cobra pilots. "Where is everybody?"

"The slicks," slang for Hueys without armament, "should be here any minute. They're hauling a team up from Kontum."

"Don't stray to the west of the landing zone." I explained my plan. "I'll distract the Falls gunners with five-hundred pound bombs. You'll be operating on the edge of the Mark eighty-two fragmentation envelope. Do you need a shiny to find the team?"

"Sure. Every little bit helps. We inserted them near the same spot where you saw them this morning, so the N.V.A. will be looking for an extraction."

The Cobra pilots seemed calm. They had obviously internalized their apprehension, as I was trying to do.

Blutt appeared and gave me a thumbs-up. "We should minimize our ground time, especially when choppers are parked here, too. We make a good mortar target."

We scrambled aboard. I used all the narrow roughly patched runway to lift off the ground. One survival instinct overrode another. Not having a safety pad of room to stop in case of engine problems seemed less significant than witnessing a mortar attack up-close. I flew north and climbed. I asked, "Who's responsible for perimeter security at Dak To?"

"The Army of the Republic of Vietnam," Sixpack said. "The ARVN have taken over this sector. They seem a bit scarce most of the time."

Blutt added, "They handle the big stuff fairly well, but they're not very good with details. The program is called Vietnamization."

When the F-4s and A-1s checked in, I told Sixpack to call for the recovery helicopter launch.

"Ready for the maple," he said on his radio.

I briefed the F-4 pilots by the book. "Friendlies will be one klick east. Attack on a north-south axis with west pulls. I'll keep smoke on your target."

To the A-1 pilots, I said, "Keep your orbit to the east and watch the F-Fours. Stay below their pull-out altitude, if you can, and respond to emergencies." I didn't have to tell them that lives would depend on their performance.

Sixpack showed me the inbound stream of helicopters.

When I estimated them to be two minutes out, I rolled in from the north and fired two rockets.

Bam. Bam.

I pulled off east and located the choppers. "Hit my smoke."

"Roger," the F-4 leader said. "One is in. From the green jungle canopy, two marks a kilometer apart rose like cottonballs. I knew that several anti-aircraft batteries were hidden on the ridge between my smokes. The quasi-diversionary target was west of a cleared red oval where previous bombs had left holes on top of holes. The clean and smooth Ho Chi Minh Trail snaked around the craters.

"Your target is between the smokes. Start north and work south. Expect groundfire." Other than smoke I had no visual clues to help the fighters aim. I moved southeast and ducked under the orbiting A-1s.

Helicopters chugged in from the east. Cobras closed to within a mile of the L.Z.

I heard the wumps from the first three bombs.

"Two's in." The second F-4 rolled on its back and cued me for a correction.

"Cleared hot," I said. "South of lead's hit. Keep your spacing tight. Don't leave big time gaps. Let's keep their heads down."

"Choppers are taking fifty-cal fire from the south," the team leader called.

I told Sixpack, "Have them circle north once, while I mark for the Spads. Tell the Cobras to stay with the slicks." I swung down hard and fired a rocket on a prominent hill. "Get a correction from the team if you can."

Sixpack directed the Army show with calm indifference. He relayed, "Hit a hundred meters north."

"Three's in." The F-4 attack continued.

"Cleared hot. Work it south. I'll mark again after three's attack." The angry jet trailed a whisper of black exhaust as it rolled and pointed downward.

"Spad-One is in." Much lower and to my south a propeller-driven A-1 rolled and dove at the jungle.

"Spad, you're cleared hot, a hundred meters north of my smoke. The hillside's yours."

Airbursts appeared in the F-4 orbit to the west. The fighter pilots debated the caliber. Twenty-three and thirty-seven millimeter fire looked similar.

I fired another smoke on the west target. "Leader's correct. The gun's a twenty-three millimeter. Hit my new smoke."

"Four's in."

"Cleared hot."

The Spads covered their target with fire as the first Huey landed. No one could threaten the choppers under the A-1s' strafing and bombing attacks.

Cobras set up a tight orbit over the top of the landing zone. They streamed fire on the perimeter.

F-4's dove like frenzied sharks on their jungle-covered prey.

Hell itself unfolded under the A-1 deluge of strafe and cluster bombs.

A second Huey replaced the first and collected the remaining team members.

The Cobras fired on the treeline atop a nearby mountain ridge. I saw orange clouds burst from flechette warheads.

"Spads, watch for choppers. Keep the pressure up."

"Roger. We're doin' fine." The A-1 leader sounded calm.

For two minutes after the helicopters cleared out, the ground shook under a storm of fire and steel. Then, as quickly as it had begun, the action ended.

I climbed eastward, sat back and relaxed. I rolled my shoulders to relieve tension that was trying to immobilize my neck. Sweat flowed from my helmet onto a soaked flightsuit. Damn. The last half-hour wasn't easy. But everyone came out okay. I felt pretty good about myself for an instant.

I turned to Blutt, whom I had forgotten. "How about a critique?"

"Cleared solo." He smiled.

O.K. Bryant greeted me at the bar. "How's the checkout coming along?"

"No big deal," I said. "Nine hours of sweaty heart attacks."

"I have the Danang run tomorrow. A day off."

"Do me a favor. At the ops desk, I heard an O-Two--Trail Two-five--went down this afternoon. Get the pilot's name, please."

"Sure."

When I landed at Kontum at five forty-five the next morning, Sixpack was waiting.

He climbed in. "We've got trouble."

Two minutes later I pushed the throttles, pulled back the controls, and we were airborne. "What's up?"

"Last night, a team of one American lieutenant and four 'Yards parachuted from a Huey. We think the lieutenant broke his leg. One soldier's dead, and one's missing." Sixpack held up his map. "The coordinates are here in no man's land. No trails, no guns."

I surveyed the ocean of rolling jungle. "No real military value here. And one nasty drop zone."

I asked Hillsboro to put the Spads on ground alert.

Sixpack talked to the team. "Our first report's confirmed. The lieutenant played John Wayne--strapped his rifle to his leg. The leg couldn't bend on landing, so it broke. One Montagnard fell from a tree and died. The good news is they found the missing guy."

"No enemy to deal with?"

"Not for several hours, I'd say. I'll call for a Huey with a winch."

Thirty minutes later the chopper arrived. "We think our F.M. radio is broken. Can you relay on V.H.F?"

"Okay," I said to the helicopter pilot. "Sixpack, this looks like an Army problem."

"Roger, sir." Sixpack relayed F.M. information from below the jungle cover on V.H.F. to the helicopter above. After several minutes of hit and miss activity that Sixpack called a goat-fuck, the chopper hovered above the team. "Casualties are coming up first."

The slick hovered over a sea of trees, unable to talk to the people below. We relayed as best we could. I circled. Because of the dispersed team and our awkward communications arrangements, the rescue took hours instead of minutes.

After the injured and dead were loaded by the Huey crew, they had to go to Dak To for fuel. We followed and topped off our tanks. Thirty minutes later, we all went back.

An hour passed, and the helicopter lifted the three remaining soldiers away.

"Sir, I have another team in trouble," Sixpack said. "N.V.A. platoon is chasing them."

"Hillsboro, launch the Spads," I said on my V.H.F. frequency.

I turned southwest and descended so the team could hear my engine noise. I turned and crisscrossed to pinpoint the friendlies' location while Sixpack collected an update.

The Spads checked in, and I briefed them. "The good guys have separated from the N.V.A. platoon. We want to put a strike between the forces."

"We're ready."

"This should be easy," I told Sixpack. "All I have to do is fire a rocket less than one klick west of the point of loudest engine noise. No surgical strikes today."

"Sir, that's why they pay you all that money."

"Oh, yeah." I rolled in and fired a rocket.

Bam.

"I hate this wait--to learn if I've killed or hurt somebody. These few seconds are the longest hours of the FAC mission."

Sixpack nodded while he listened to the ground team's report. "They heard the rocket. Barely. Bad guys are closer than that."

Bam.

I fired again, closer to the friendlies.

"Two hundred meters north," Sixpack said.

"Okay," I said. "Get a reading on the next one. When the smoke rises above the treetops, I'm bringing in the Spads."

Bam.

"You're on the bad guys."

"Spad one, hit my last smoke. Work north-south, east breaks. You know why."

"We're in."

"Cleared hot."

"Dump everything but twenty-mike-mike." I wanted them to save strafing in case any of the N.V.A. force escaped.

Away from the bigger guns, the straight-winged beasts laid their carpet of fire.

"The team's loving it, sir," Sixpack said. "They're in the clear."

The O.V.-10 arrived on station. We handed the war over and flew south.

After landing at Kontum I jumped into the jeep to help Sixpack with the enormous volume of paperwork required by the Studies and Observations Group--SOG--in Saigon.

A corporal at the F.O.B. gate offered us quarts of chocolate ice cream. "A Chinook from Na Trang brought over more than we can store here."

"I haven't seen ice cream for months," I said. "The Pleiku club has no ice cream concept."

That evening at Pleiku I met O.K. in the hooch bar. "Well?"

"Sorry to have to tell you. Pete's dead."

Chapter 6
Cast of Caricatures

December 1970

During a crew meeting, our commander announced the impending arrival of Major Stillbern. "I have a message from the Pentagon saying the major is a real fast-burner. I expect your full cooperation."

"What the hell does he mean?" O.K. Bryant whispered. "Full cooperation?"

Another voice added, "Does the colonel seem more aquiver than usual?"

Adjourning to the officers club, I stood with O.K. in a circle of seasoned FACs at one end of the bar. We discussed the influx of strange and wonderful F.N.G.s.

"Sometimes I feel like Alice, tumbling into Wonderland," I said. "I can't believe some of these new guys are real."

"Yeah," another FAC said. "Meanwhile we lose rock-solid family men like Pete Landry, my pilot training buddy."

I raised a glass of scotch. "Somebody once said a man isn't dead until he's forgotten. Here's to Pete."

"And Jerry," O.K. added.

Toasting with us was Captain Tim Eby, an O.V.-10 instructor, and a tough little Texan who seemed to stay above the day-to-day friction. Eby had received the nickname of Captain Skinny, from a hooch maid. He had returned, lighter by a few pounds, from a Rest and Recuperation trip, meeting his wife in Hawaii.

I asked, "What's Major Boubek going to do about the new fast-moving major? One operations officer is plenty."

"Boubek can use some help," Captain Skinny said. "A group of angry lieutenants is screwing with his jeep. They added a gallon of gas every night for the last month. Boubek is clueless. Thinks he has some kind of karma."

"I heard him bragging about his jeep mileage," I said.

"Last night they drained the tank. They plan to keep it close to dry for a month."

"Why?" I asked. "Boubek seems like a nice enough guy."

"He pulled rank and took a jeep from the pool. Several guys have had to walk to the squadron. Now they're after him. Next month--tires." Captain Skinny had light wispy hair, large brown eyes and a perpetual smile.

I greeted Al Dyer, whom I hadn't seen for weeks. "Are you surviving the new guys, Uncle Al?"

He shook his head. "I'm working with two new lieutenants. Both are great guys--huge personalities--but they can't fly for shit."

"What do you mean?"

"I call the first guy the Plumber. You know, the tall goofy guy with longish black hair? He can't hit his ass with a smoke rocket. He kicks rudders and spews the things all over the place."

"Accuracy's a problem for the fighters," O.K. said. He was technically correct. The FAC only needed a reference on the ground to direct pilot's eyes to a specific spot. Fighters had to hit close enough to destroy the target.

"The plumber's marks defy description." Uncle Al shook his head. "Half the time he can't even find the smoke he's fired. And his F.N.G. buddy--Baby Huey with freckles--isn't far behind."

Captain Skinny added a nickname. "Does that make him the Plumber's Helper?"

I flew a three-night cycle with Captain Joe Dipietro, also known as Captain Abort. I'd heard he was an excellent truck-finder if you got his body over the Trail.

As we stepped out the door for our first mission, I took the issue head-on. "What's the deal with you and airplanes?"

"Flying these little Cessnas over heavily defended areas is a dangerous detour from my path to law school," he said. "If I can find a legitimate reason to abort a plane, I won't go."

I probed further, but never got an answer I could understand. As I placed my maps and weapons on the left seat, I heard duct tape ripping.

Captain Abort was sealing the air vent door on the right side of the aircraft. "Sometimes these things stick open. I get cold at altitude."

"Let me know if you're cold. I'll descend to warmer air." I began my walk-around inspection.

Captain Abort moved the seat through its full range of travel. He told the crew chief, "This seat hangs up in the middle. Change it." He caught up with me at the right boom. "I see dirt in these pitot-static ports."

"Something's wrong with your flashlight, Captain."

When I moved the elevator, it squeaked. Captain Abort whined.

"The elevator's supposed to squeak," I assured him. "All elevators squeak."

He reached up and confirmed I had tightened the rear engine oil cap, then challenged me on the condition of the left brake.

"The pads are half an inch thick," I said. "We're good for at least a thousand landings."

He inspected the ordnance, then climbed into his brand-new seat as I started engines. "The TACAN distance measuring equipment seems inoperative."

I moved the TACAN function switch from its warm-up position. The D.M.E. locked on to the Pleiku TACAN at half a mile.

At the end of the runway, I moved levers and switches as fast as I could during run-up checks. "Covey Five-nine-one is ready for takeoff." I wanted to launch before he found something else to grouse about.

"Cleared for take-off."

"What was the r.p.m. drop on the right magneto on the rear engine?"

"Seventy-five." I pushed in the power. We rolled.

"What's that smell? What's that smell?"

"You've got to be shitting me, Captain."

We lifted off, and Captain Abort became silent.

We found trucks at the pock-marked Falls interdiction point. Moonbeam sent us two F-4s.

During the strike, Captain Abort yelled, "Break left."

I dipped the wings slightly. Fifteen red tennis balls streaked by, directly in front of the propeller, closer than I'd ever seen them. "Sorry," I told him. "I don't know when to believe you."

Near the end of our watch, we found movers south of the Dog's Head, a series of river bends that looked like a Snoopy profile. Moonbeam sent Yellowbird, a single B-57.

After I briefed him, the B-57 pilot said, "I'm locked onto several trucks here."

"Roger. Attack south to north. I'll hold west."

"Yellowbird is in."

I flew west and descended. "Cleared hot."

"Yellowbird is off, switches safe, departing."

Three large explosions blossomed north of the river.

I flew in that direction. "Let's see what's burning."

Captain Abort panned the area with the night scope. "Three trucks are cooking just behind the dog's neck."

"I'll circle once. See if you can find the movers you saw earlier." Our station time had expired. I teased my right-seater by hanging around.

"Sure. I see something. They're putting the clip in the gun. They're aiming."

"Okay. Let's go home." I turned southeast. "Here, you can fly if you wish." I turned up the instrument panel lights.

"I have the aircraft." Captain Abort moved his seat forward. He wrinkled his brow and focused on the instruments.

I slid my seat back and stretched my legs. "Wake me when we get there." Just for fun, I moved my thumb a half-inch from the intercom toggle to the electric trim switch. I gave it two-seconds of forward pressure. The manual trim wheel down on the center console spun forward as I leaned back.

Slowly the nose came down. The night sky offered my pilot no horizon reference. Soon we dove at thirty degrees, and the altimeter began to spin.

"Damn." Captain Abort jerked the controls with both hands and fumbled with the trim wheel.

I slid forward in mock surprise. "What the hell?"

"The thing just went for the ground. I don't know."

Suppressing a huge laugh, I watched him climb back to cruise altitude. "Just trim this baby up and let her take us home, old sport."

"Rog. I had it trimmed."

"Wake me at Pleiku." This time my thumb pulled the trim switch backward. I leaned back again.

As the nose came up and up, stars sank below the glare shield. I felt slight tremors as the airflow began to separate from the wings.

Captain Abort tried to hold the wings level as the vibrations increased to heavy buffeting. "Damn. This thing is fighting me."

I watched the textbook power-on stall. We could no longer read the shuddering instruments. Wings rocked us like a bumpy road.

Aaaee. The stall-warning horn screeched.

Captain Abort's eyes opened wide. Apparently unaware of the nose high condition, he fought to keep the wings level. When the nose fell abruptly, his mouth opened wide. He banged the momentarily useless controls against the stops as we fell straight down. Then, he panicked. "We're out-of-control."

He looked at me and saw convulsions of laughter. "You sonovabitch." His look of terror changed to one of disgust.

Tears streamed down my face. I nodded.

"Okay. You're still pissed about the preflight." He regained level flight. "I'll make a deal to behave, if you will. But what did you do?"

"Electric trim." I pointed to the tiny switch.

He shook a fist at me and began to smile.

I was still laughing when I entered the hooch bar with Captain Abort. "I thought your eyes were going to pop out of your head."

"My two-year-old son could do a better triple-A break."

We entertained a room full of O.V.-10 drivers with our story. Afterward, I asked Captain Skinny, "Why did you guys look so glum when we arrived?"

"Look at this letter from our O-Two-driving commander, prohibiting O.V.-Ten hot-refueling at Dak To." He handed me a single sheet of paper. "He's completely out of touch."

Our commander spent most of his time in his quarters or in his office. We rarely saw him. But we saw his letters.

You guys have to leave one engine running when you refuel there. Dak To's a bare airstrip--no external power units to supply air and electricity."

Captain Abort jumped in. "Even I know most battery starts in the O.V. don't generate the necessary r.p.m. Am I right? You'll melt engines if you obey the letter."

Angry voices muttered agreement.

"You're exactly right," one pilot said. "The commander's never been to Dak To. He doesn't fly the O.V.-Ten. He knows zero about Prairie Fire. What the fuck is going on?"

Captain Abort and I enjoyed our beers while we listened to the tirade spilling from the bar full of Bronco pilots.

"What's the worst thing that could happen during hot-refueling?"

"The refueling hose could get sucked into the turning propeller."

"Then, what would happen?"

"We would have to bring the airplane back to Pleiku."

"Then what?"

"The colonel would run up to the pilot and ask what happened."

"We could tell him we got hosed." Captain Skinny nailed the bottom line. "He'd think the N.V.A. did it."

In spite of the jokes, the O.V. pilots seemed troubled. One grumbled, "Fuck him. We'll do what we have to do to support the Green Berets."

Another said, "The only time he flew over Laos was on his checkout. He wanted to go to Cambodia, but Ed was his instructor and refused." He implied the boss wanted to avoid the concentrations of antiaircraft weapons along the Trail in Laos. Threats in Cambodia were smaller and easier to avoid.

I shook my head. "Maybe we should send him a letter. Or a postcard that says: Having a great time. Wish you were here."

Tall, dark and ramrod straight, Major Stillbern arrived as if he had stepped from a recruiting poster. "Hello." His deep booming command voice matched the visual impression.

I was standing at a map with our intel officer and turned to watch him stride into the secure vault.

"How do you do?" He greeted everyone in the room.

Our small gray commander was guiding the major on a tour of Pleiku. "I've located a car for you, a Chevy sedan. Hope it helps you get around the base."

After they left, I asked, "Where do you find a Chevy sedan in Vietnam?"

The intel officer answered with a question. "Where do you drive it besides the hooch and here?"

As I walked to the front of the squadron, I overheard a loud conversation behind the closed door to Life Support. The lieutenant-in-charge complained of being passed over for an O.V.-10 Prairie Fire slot.

"I'm as good a pilot as anybody," he yelled.

"Nobody questions your flying ability," a calmer voice said. "But you have to stay unruffled in the worst possible situations. Do you know what your nickname is around here? Lieutenant Ecstatic."

"What?" The word was squealed. "Ec-static?"

Wow, I thought. This officer was a super friend and one of the brightest people I knew. But his voice reflected his temperament like the needle on a Richter scale. I left the building before the shaking started.

Elf and Dego scuffled in the hooch bar. Athletic, with thinning blond hair, Mike Cryer's huge ears gained him the Elf nickname. George Degovanni was a small Italian-American O.V.-10 pilot who proclaimed himself Dego.

"Gimme the tape, damnit." Dego hung onto Elf's back.

"You promised to burn the thing." Elf was laughing.

Other FACs shouted Elf down, and he relented.

Dego placed the tape into a player. "We recorded this in our cockpit a few weeks ago. After a great Thanksgiving dinner at Ubon, we flew a mission on the way back."

"Real fine, guys," I said. "Here at Papa Kilo, we had canned turkey and powdered potatoes. Both were lumpy."

They ignored me.

"I was in the front seat on the flight back," Dego said. "We reported trucks crossing the river at the Dogs Head. Hillsboro responded right away with two A-Sixes."

Elf added, "You probably heard the gunners fired sixty or eighty rounds per pass for eight bomb runs. And they put another hundred rounds behind a recce bird that blew through the strike." Those numbers were double the norm.

Dego pressed the Play button.

"Two-one is in from the north, FAC in sight."

"Cleared hot. First truck is in the water now."

"Two-one's off. They're shooting."

The intercom sounded clearer: "Holy shit, Dego. I count sixty rounds comin'up."

"Two-one flight. I can keep you in sight throughout your pattern. If you see me, don't call in. No need to help the gunners' timing." The enemy listened on our frequencies.

"Roger."

"Move your bombs to the north edge of the river now. Guns are active at your two o'clock."

On intercom: "Hey, Elf. Look at our one o'clock low. Comin' down the road. Here's an RF-Four who never checked in with us. Tracers are crossing right behind his ass. He just lit burners."

"Two-one is . . . say, recce . . .you're takin' a little fire, sport."

Dego hit Fast-Forward. "Here comes the best part. I gave the A-Sixes credit for four trucks destroyed. We didn't try for the guns. Listen as I ask Elf about further Bomb Damage Assessment." He pushed another button.

"Say, Elf. Want to go down for a B.D.A. pass?"

"Uh . . . uhhh . . .."

A low pass to assess damage offered far more danger than potential benefit. We rarely used the tactic near the Trail. Dego's facetious remark caught Elf's ego off guard.

Elf shook his head and grinned. "I didn't know he was joking."

Most of the amused crowd left the hooch bar in favor of dinner at the club.

O.K. Bryant stayed behind. "Have you met the new lieutenant colonel? Tall, gray, balding. Name is Earl."

"No," I said. "What's he like?"

"Academic type. Everything strictly by-the-book."

"Another field-grader. What job will he have?"

"I heard the commander put him in charge of Prairie Fire." O.K. smiled.

"Perfect." I chuckled. "Nothing goes by the book in Prairie Fire."

Late the next morning, I waited for choppers to appear in response to my rider, Plastic Man, who had requested a launch.

Elf called me on the squadron F.M. frequency. "Five-nine-one, I'm at your three o'clock high, flying Colonel Earl around. Do you mind if we watch the ballgame? We'll stay clear."

"Not a problem." I looked up at the O.V.-10.

The lead Cobra didn't take my corrections and pointed for the guns.

I dove to the deck and led the string of choppers to the L.Z., crossing the Trail at ten feet. I found a steep limestone karst formation to hide my climb and spiraled up to a safe altitude. In the busy heat of the extraction, I forgot I was being watched. We pulled another team from southern Laos, then returned to Pleiku, via Kontum.

Elf and other O.V.-Ten drivers were in the hooch bar when I entered. Then, I remembered that the new colonel had watched me fly well below the textbook altitude for operating around twenty-three millimeter guns. "What did he say? Am I fired?

Elf laughed and told Captain Skinny about my maneuvers. "The colonel didn't see a thing. He focused on cockpit details. Missed the entire concept."

I asked, "Am I losing my mind, or are we surrounded by crazy people?"

"I agree. They're everywhere," Captain Skinny said. "I gave the new Major his first checkout ride."

"Major Major?" Elf said. He used our nickname for Stillbern.

"Exactly. I briefed him thoroughly. He assured me he had total recall. My first hint of trouble was when he didn't grasp the concept of flying higher than the terrain while in a cloud layer. I finally assigned Major Major an altitude, as a radar controller would."

"Sounds dangerous," I said.

"Second clue. I gave him the full tour of the Area of Operations. On the way back, I asked enough questions to learn he didn't remember any of it. But, listen to this. He wrote a lengthy combat after-action report. He sent it to the Pentagon through his own channels. By-passed normal intelligence routing."

"A combat report to the Pentagon?" I asked. "After one training mission?"

"He showed me a copy. The prose and syntax would water your eyes. Of course the subject matter was pure imagination. He has a strange fascination with cluster bombs, and he's totally disconnected from reality."

Over the next few weeks I flew extra Prairie Fire cycles. On a typical December afternoon, I slid onto a barstool after eight hours in the air. On good days I'd read a letter from Elaine for the fifth and sixth time. After great days, I savor a delicious photograph of my smiling blond dream near the Golden Gate Bridge or a Yosemite waterfall.

Elaine's world seemed a millennium away from the sweaty, crazy violence over Laos. Sometimes when I pondered her photographs, I wondered if I liked my job a little too much. I enjoyed long hot days of dodging and diving and found deep rewards from helping troops on the ground. I directed bombs onto people who were trying to kill me every day. I would never feel that adrenaline rush hourly or even daily back home. I couldn't even write about it. My letters to Elaine only told how good I felt when I read her words.

I felt older and more tired than a month earlier.

After dinner one evening, I walked into the middle of a raging debate in the hooch bar. Small Lieutenant Daniels from Approach Control stood on a chair to present his case. "This war's a conspiracy by the military-industrial-complex to line the pockets of the fat cats."

His statement brought a vigorous response from Covey Whiskey, who wanted to take the lieutenant outside for a history lesson. "Lemme at that sonovabitch."

Captain Skinny stepped in to mediate. "You each have ten minutes to prepare your remarks. Your subject is the relationship of the G.N.P. to the war in Vietnam. Give a five-minute speech, then a three-minute rebuttal. We'll judge."

The bar became quiet for about two minutes, when Daniels asked, "Will we be graded on grammar or loquatiousness?"

Whiskey had passed out on the couch.

I nudged Captain Skinny.

He nodded. "He's going to Cam Ranh next week for an alcohol program. He'll probably finish his tour on the staff there."

"How's your favorite major doing?"

"Major Major? I gave him ride number two yesterday. Started all over again."

I smiled. My simple question had fired up my Texas friend.

"He was unable to put in an airstrike or even brief one. The only rocket pass he could do was by-the-book, you know, wings level for ten seconds tracking time."

"Somewhat predictable, or should I say dangerous?"

"Dangerous. I spent thousands of dollars worth of rockets trying to teach him to fire from a split-s, a turn, anything but wings-level. Couldn't do it." Captain Skinny swigged his beer.

"Is he a could if he would but he won't or a would if he could but he can't type?"

"He's a combination of both. He said he understood perfectly the survival significance of random rocket passes. Couldn't do it. But that was yesterday."

"You flew him today?" I asked.

"Ride number three. Normally that's all experienced pilots need for orientation. We're going again tomorrow."

"What's his problem?"

"When I asked about his flying experience, he told me stories of funny things that happened to him in the F-One-oh-two and T-Thirty-three. I realized his adventures were the result of his stupidity. He thought things just happened that way. Totally clueless."

I couldn't help my friend with his problem. I shook my head.

Captain Skinny raised his eyebrows. "Tomorrow I'll try to be respectful."

After a full day of Prairie Fire, I met O.K. Bryant as I hung my parachute and helmet on a long rack in Life Support. I opened my locker and stored my M-16 and maps.

"You've collected some nice toys from the boys at Kontum," O.K. remarked.

"You can't have too much personal survival equipment. My first principle."

"Let's see." O.K. seemed curious, if not envious.

"Here's a Swedish K--nine-millimeter grease gun." The short machine gun had a folding stock. "Kaiser gave it to me before he left. This leather pouch holds twenty magazines of thirty rounds each." I cleared the chamber and handed it to O.K.

"Neat." O.K. clicked the trigger and re-cocked.

"And this M-seventy-nine has been cut down to pistol size. Fires forty-millimeter grenades--high-explosive, buckshot, and star-cluster flares." I pulled a handful of cartridges from my flightsuit's leg pocket.

O.K. helped me store the goodies in my locker.

"Look at this." I pulled out a brown plastic ball with a small string attached. "C.S. gas grenade. And this is C.S. powder, for their damn dogs." I held up a small bottle of the tear gas derivative.

O.K. shook his head.

"Here's my piece d'resistance. Sixpack gave me a pocket full of concussion grenades." I held out a dozen golf ball-sized hand grenades. Each had a pin that held a curved spoon close to the dark green body. "These mini-grenades have the same overpressure kill radius as the fragmentation kind. Want a couple?"

"Sure. You know, our life support officer would have a cow if he knew you stored this junk in his domain."

"Lieutenant Ecstatic has a cow when I walk in here. Let's go to the club."

Two tall captains from Phan Rang dominated the sparsely crowded bar.

Just for fun, I stepped into their space and ordered a scotch. "How you doin?" I noted F-100 patches, Jim and Lou on nametags, and grinning faces.

They each took an arm and a leg and stood me on my head. Lou tore off the knife pocket on the left thigh of my flightsuit. "Only trash-haulers wear these things," he said and tossed it over his shoulder.

Then, they threw me over the bar. Everything happened too quickly for me to generate much resistance. I went inverted, then airborne, then onto the floor.

Tradition required me--in the flightsuit behind the bar--to buy a round. "Drinks for my friends and water for these two horses."

"Real men wear those knives on g-suits." Lou referred to nylon-covered bladders sewn into chaps fighter jocks wore. The g-suit inflated under high g forces to keep blood from pooling the lower extremities. Lou laughed and shook my hand.

"Welcome to Pleiku," I said.

"We're interviewing for jobs at Two DASC--the Direct Air Support Center for Two Corps."

"In-country phenomenon. I deal with Hillsboro and Moonbeam. Your enthusiasm should fit right in."

I could hear Captain Skinny when I approached within fifty feet of the hooch bar. Uncharacteristically, he spewed a string of expletives.

I walked in the door. "Could we keep it clean, please."

Everyone laughed.

The ranting Texan turned and shook his head. "I signed him off. Training complete. It's murder."

"Major Major?"

"Yep. We worked four F-One-hundreds at the Dog's head. Guns were active."

"Sounds believable so far," I said.

"I told him a thousand times. Random attacks. Don't call in."

"Doesn't he know they listen to our radios?" I asked.

"He said, 'FAC is in from the west to mark.' I couldn't believe it. He told the gunners where to aim. Then, he pulled his textbook roll-in. Wings level, down we go." He swooped down his hand.

"How many rounds did that bring?"

"About a hundred. Above, below, both sides. Fucking everywhere. The F-One-hundred flight leader yelled, 'Break left, no, break right, no, oh shit.' His exact words."

"Were you pissed?"

"Almost pulled out my thirty-eight and shot the dumb bastard in the back of the head. I took the airplane and got us the hell out of there. Don't remember how. I told him not to touch anything, not to say anything. Just shut the fuck up."

"You cussed out the future Chief of Staff?"

"From the Dog's Head to the revetments. I told him I was signing him off, an act of premeditated murder. The only bad part was that he would take an airplane with him."

"How did he react?"

"Put on that stupid smile. Didn't say anything. Went off to write his combat report, I guess. I've ordered every lieutenant in the squadron not to fly with him."

"Maybe he'll just go away."

Major Boubek entered the room. He looked like an angry Richard Widmark. He surveyed the occupants, then cocked his head. "I don't know yet who is doing what, but I'm gonna find out. Yeah, and there's gonna be hell to pay. Hell to pay." Waving his arms, he scanned the room without making eye contact with anyone. He crossed the bar and departed.

I looked at Captain Skinny. "Tires?"

He nodded.

Chapter 7
Ho Ho Ho Chi Minh Trail

December 1970

"Covey Five-nine-one, Moonbeam." The airborne command post called me. "Move to grid Yankee Bravo six-nine-four-one. Call Sundown on New High frequency. He's declared a Prairie Fire Emergency."

"Roger." By four a.m., Alfalfa and I had bombed four trucks and were chasing two more. I turned east from the Falls and switched both F.M. radios to recon team frequencies on the daily code card.

"Sundown, Covey Five-nine-one." I called several times.

"Covey, this is Sundown. We're overrun." The voice panted, breathless. "N.V.A. are everywhere." Rifles cracked in the background.

"Can you hear my engines?" I descended. "Where are you from my airplane?"

"Roger, turn south. We're--"

The transmission stopped.

"Sundown, Covey . . . Sundown, this is Covey Five-nine-one." I circled. My heart pounded. Sweat poured down my neck and back in rivulets.

No answer from the black jungle below.

For two hours I called Sundown every five minutes. "Maybe his radio is out."

"Yeah," Alfalfa said. "He's probably on the run."

I sweated and prayed. Come on, Sundown.

Still no answer.

This felt too close, as if the cold hand of death had just slapped my face.

When I glanced at Alfalfa, he said nothing--just shrugged and shook his head. I felt my denial slowly melt into sadness as dawn nudged us to reality.

I handed the search to the Prairie Fire FAC, O.K. Bryant, and flew home.

"In ten months over the Trail," Alfalfa said, "I've never felt this bad."

"I'll fly your right seat if you want to spend a day in Thailand," Uncle Al said the next evening. "You're the only person in the bar who's never done a practice weather diversion."

"A what?"

"We tell higher headquarters we're practicing instrument approaches at our primary weather divert base. Actually we shop and screw off in Thailand for a day."

"When do we leave?" I hadn't paid much attention to Ubon trips.

"We have the six p.m. take-off tomorrow. We'll recover at Ubon Royal Thai Air Force Base. Then, we'll fly the ten p.m. mission home the following night."

Uncle Al continued his fine instruction in Ubon, which could have been ten thousand miles from the conflict. Happy faces replaced the hard looks I had seen on Vietnamese faces before they turned away. Marketplaces were full of busy people, smiling as if unaware or uncaring of the war a few hundred miles east.

"The Thai have a phrase," Al said. "Mai Pen Rai." He rolled the r sound. "Means nevermind--which describes how I feel when I visit. The war just goes away."

Uncle Al arranged a tour in samlars, bicycle-powered taxis, along muddy streets past temples and crowded shops. He said, "The huge contrast with Vietnam invigorates me."

I ordered suits at Maharajah John's Tailor Shop and custom shoes at Dan Thong's place. Paul, the jeweler, sold me a couple of Seiko watches.

On the evening of our return trip, we enjoyed a relatively terrific meal at the Ubon Officers Club. A big hunk of steak--probably water buffalo--was tender and tasty. Although not a Texas T-bone, the filet beat the standard mushy offerings at Pleiku.

We moved to the bar for soft drinks, served by pretty waitresses in traditional Thai dresses. Al noted, "I've always wondered how clothing that covers neck-to-toe can be so alluring."

We chatted briefly with Tai, a delicate beauty in a tight yellow sarong. She said, "I want to have ten baby-san, five boy and five girl."

After she wiggled away, Al said, "No doubt she'll find the required assistance."

We had to arm our own ordnance at the end of the runway, so I held the brakes while Uncle Al pulled pins and turned switches that set up the firing sequence of our rocket pods. Wind from the propeller whipped the red Remove Before Flight ribbons as he collected them from the pylons.

"All set." He climbed aboard. "The damned B.K.-Thirty-seven rack requires surgical skill to thread a ring from each of the four bricks through a tight clip. Next time you can handle that chore."

"Love to." Pulling pins would be a small price to pay for another night in Thailand.

I pushed the power in, and we launched. "I don't plan to spin inverted tonight." I motioned to the back seat, piled high with silk suits, boots, stuffed cobras, and brass candleholders ordered by Coveys on previous trips.

Al nodded and raised his eyebrows.

Five hours and three burning trucks later, we landed. I called the duty officer. "Covey Alpha, this is Five-nine-one. Please bring the van out to pick up Ubon goodies."

O.K. Bryant parked nearby and welcomed us home.

I asked him, "What happened with the Sundown operation?"

"We put in another team for a ground search. They recovered the bodies."

I winced. "When we go inside, show me the spot. I'll use it as a dumping ground for unexpended ordnance after each ballgame. If we can't have it, neither can they."

"Sure," he said. "You'll get your first chance tomorrow morning."

"Ken Carpenter." The stocky Army staff sergeant had dark hair and eyes.

On the small parking ramp at Kontum we shook hands.

"Shoebox is my real name." His deadpan expression didn't move.

I nodded. "Ready to go?"

"All set, sir."

As we cruised toward Laos, I asked, "What's your Green Beret specialty?"

"I'm a medic. Secondary is heavy weapons." Special Forces teams normally consisted of ten men. Each mastered two job specialties, so a team could be split further and still retain expertise in operations, communications, medicine, weapons and engineering.

All morning Shoebox directed teams like a field marshall. His demeanor never changed. At one point he pulled out a long heavy knife and sharpened his pencil.

"That knife is a beauty."

Shoebox handed it to me. "Guy in Florida named Randall made it custom."

"What's this groove scratched down one side?"

"I once had to fire my forty-five alongside the blade to pull it out of an N.V.A. soldier's skull. Damn thing stuck, and I wasn't going to leave it."

"I see." I returned his weapon, very carefully.

After refueling at Dak To, we flew north to where a team had contacted the N.V.A.

"We should pull 'em out," Shoebox said. "They're in a clearing."

"Hillsboro, launch the Spads for troops-in-contact," I called.

"These mountainside clearings come from years of slashing and burning by farmers making room for crops." Shoebox educated me and monitored the team.

I noticed similar cleared squares on gentler slopes in the area.

"Do you see the finger of trees coming from the northeast corner of this one?" He pointed to a ridge on his side of the plane.

"Got it."

"The enemy's in those trees. See where the tree-finger is pointed?"

"Yep. I see pink panels in the southwest corner a hundred meters from the trees."

"Those are the good guys. They're pinned down behind those nylon signal panels. Can we lay some smoke between the forces until the Spads arrive?"

"Sure." I dove onto the trees and fired a white phosphorous--willie pete--rocket.

Bam. The rocket flew straight and true. A smoke cloud covered the fingertip.

"One-zero says thanks. Firing has stopped."

I made three more passes, then four Spads called.

"Team says the N.V.A. are shooting again." Shoebox directed choppers to launch.

"Covey," Spad One said, "I have willie-pete. Let me mark the target." The A-1s sometimes carried one-hundred-pound bombs with white phosphorous for this purpose.

"Roger. Confirm friendly location."

"One hundred meters southwest of the finger. Pink panels."

"Cleared hot for the mark." I rolled in behind the attacking A-1 and watched the tiny bomb leave his wing, wobble a bit, then arc into the trees.

"Damn," I said to Shoebox. "Look at that huge fireball."

Red and orange flames blossomed across the entire finger. Journalist Bernard Fall used a term to describe a French firebase at Dien Bien Phu, but we, too, had created hell in a very small place.

"Spad Two is in with cluster bombs."

"Cleared hot."

After four passes, the choppers approached.

"Spad, can you make dry passes until the choppers are clear?"

"Roger."

They did.

After the team was up and away, I said, "The trees are yours. Dump everything."

"Spad One's in. Daisy chain. Keep it tight."

I circled and watched in fascination. As one A-1 pulled up, another dove down. For five minutes the trees sparkled under constant pounding.

"Spad's winchester, R.T.B." Out of ammunition, the Spads returned to base.

We passed words to the incoming O.V.-10 and landed at Kontum. A soldier climbed from a waiting jeep, signaled me to hold, and spoke briefly with Shoebox.

I recognized Plastic Man's thin brown hair and large mustache.

He climbed into my airplane. "We have to go back. The coordinates Shoebox reported are screwed up. I need the right numbers for the report."

I sighed. My body ached after eight hours in the seat. I wanted to go south, not north. "Okay. But we have to stop for fuel at Dak To."

As we approached the tiny airstrip, I switched to the frequency for the uncontrolled runway to report my intentions in a blind broadcast to any aircraft that might be in the area. "Attention aircraft at Dak To. Covey Five-nine-one is an O-Two on forty-five to left downwind for landing to the east." I turned hard right to parallel the runway.

As I rolled wings level, another O-2 passed us belly-up from left to right, about thirty feet out in front. He had come up from below the nose of my craft.

Holy shit.

"Where the hell did he come from?" Plastic Man was now wide awake.

"Probably made a pass down the runway and pulled up." With no time to react I ended up in left echelon formation with the O-2. I crossed under to his right.

When he lowered his landing gear, I lowered mine. I matched his flap settings.

When he turned left to land, I turned right and circled while he landed and cleared the runway.

Finally, I turned back. Unlike the other FAC, I announced my intentions. "Attention aircraft at Dak To. Covey Five-nine-one, left base, gear down, full stop." Thirty seconds on final approach were uneventful.

I touched firmly and applied maximum braking, committing the aircraft to stopping in the remaining distance.

Suddenly, a green two-and-a-half-ton truck pulled onto the runway ahead of me. A hundred feet ahead, he moved across from right to left. Collision seemed certain.

"We're gonna hit." Anger and dread swelled up inside me like a bad meal.

Hueys blocked the left side, so I veered off the right side of the runway. My brakes screeched. I saw a terrified Vietnamese face in the truck driver's window.

"Son-of-a-bitch," Plastic Man said.

My left wingtip cleared the truck by about a foot. Then, we stopped.

"I'll get that ARVN bastard." Plastic Man jumped out of the aircraft and drew his forty-five. He ran after the truck, now pouring out black smoke and accelerating away.

I turned around and taxied to the fuel bladders, stopped, and jumped out.

A tall lieutenant with curly blond hair was refueling his O-2. He smiled as if nothing was wrong. "Hi."

"Do you know how close you came to hitting us during your little airshow?" My anger peaked. I wanted to hit somebody.

"No." The lieutenant knew nothing or pretended to know nothing.

"Thirty feet, asshole. What's your home base? Do you know the uncontrolled radio frequency?"

"I'm a Herb FAC at Pleiku. I don't know the frequency." He climbed down from the ammo box he was using to reach the fuel tank openings on top of the wing.

I prepared to kick his crotch. "Make all the normal traffic pattern calls on six-eight-point-three. If the choppers know you're coming, they'll flatten their blades. Would you like me to carve that number on your forehead?" I yelled, "Sixty-eight-three."

"Gee, I'm sorry." He stepped backward. His naiveté appeared genuine.

To cut through any act, I made my face look livid and stepped forward. "If you're here when that Green Beret gets back, he'll break your arms and legs. And I'll help him."

His eyes widened. I could now see they were blue. Then, he squinted at Plastic Man, who trudged, pistol still drawn, from a quarter mile away. "I'm really sorry." The lieutenant put down the hose, started engines, and departed.

I pumped about thirty seconds of avgas from the large hose into each wing.

Plastic Man holstered his weapon. "The truck got away."

"The lieutenant played dumb. Let's finish this mission as quickly as possible."

In the sky again, we crossed into Laotian airspace, and I armed a rocket pod. "The clearing six or seven miles ahead has a finger of trees in the northeast corner. I'll fire a stand-off rocket." I pulled the nose up thirty degrees and mashed the red button.

Bam.

Miraculously, a ball of white smoke appeared on the correct clearing.

"Nice shot," Plastic Man said. "Yeah, these numbers are wrong." He studied the terrain and made notes on his map.

I descended along a high ridge near a friendly outpost called Leghorn. The listening post sat on a mountain peak near the border. Protected by mine fields, the site complemented the Coveys' twenty-four-hour listening watch over recon teams.

"Here's a low-threat rocket pass to mark where we found the team." I pulled the nose up and rolled right, to inverted. Then, I waited for the nose to fall to the target.

Pop-Pop-Pop-Pop-Pop.

Plastic Man turned to me with wide eyes. "Is that what I think it is?"

"Fifty caliber machine gun. Right behind us on the ridge." I moved the controls, but they were not effective at forty knots.

The popping continued.

"Damn." I pushed power to maximum and cranked in full elevator and left aileron. When the controls became effective, they were set to pull us away from the bullet stream. As the nose fell, I sliced down into the deep valley. "See the pink panels?"

"Tally the friendly location."

"Seen enough?"

The beer tasted awful, but it was cold. "I wonder how many months this cheap stuff sits in the tropical sun before distribution." I sat on the couch in the hooch bar with O.K. Bryant and some new guys.

"They sell the pallets with the most rust." O.K. scratched some brown flakes from his can. "Where have you been?"

"My post flight inspection took half an hour. I felt certain I'd find big holes today."

"What rules were you breaking?"

"I did something stupid. Ran out of airspeed close to a fifty-cal. My stupidity started last night. I hadn't heard from Elaine in several weeks, so I sent a nasty letter."

"And today you got a nice letter from her?"

"Exactly. I just wrote fifteen letters saying I was sorry. I doubt if any of them'll pass the bad one, but I had to try."

"Is she worth the trouble?" O.K. was probably kidding.

"I hope so. She's brilliant, but she'd never understand any of the shit we do over here. Letters are hard to write. Feels like a lot more than the Pacific Ocean's between us."

"Did you fly Prairie Fire today?"

"Yeah." I told him about my flight with Plastic Man and our close calls. "Two beers should be enough. I think I'll go over and talk to those damn Herb FACs."

The in-country FACs' hooches mirrored ours. Their small squadron operations area filled the far end of a long barracks.

I approached their operations desk where a lieutenant monitored radios. "Are you in charge here?"

"Yep. The major's flying. I'm Rhip Worrell. What can I do for you?"

I introduced myself and told my near-miss story. "If your boy had been talking or listening on the frequency, we could have prevented the problem."

"He's a dumbshit." Rhip looked like a boxer. I thought I noticed a twitch. "We'll put the word out. Trust me."

"Do I have a choice?"

"No." Rhip smiled like a cat in a cartoon.

"Log a beer against my name across the street sometime."

After my four-day Prairie Fire cycle with Shoebox, I took the milk run to Danang.

Dugan hailed me in the officers club lunch line. "Hey, ol' sport. Great to see you. "Did you hear about Brownie?"

"I don't need any bad news."

"How about good news? Several nights ago Brownie found the mother lode of truck parks. His target near a place called Ban Bak has produced over three thousand secondary explosions--the most ever seen on the Trail."

I laughed. "Are you talking about little Johnnie Browning from Haaavard?"

"The same. He got a Distinguished Flying Cross on the spot."

"I fly the Trail mission. The navigator finds trucks, which turn off their lights and hide. You mark a spot in the vast darkness where you think your nav said they might have disappeared. Then, fighters drop bombs somewhere within five hundred meters of your miscellaneous mark. Nothin' is precise out there."

"Even a blind squirrel finds the occasional acorn. I heard the brass was going to intervene in Brownie's next assignment as a B-Fifty-two copilot."

When I returned from the first mission of the next night cycle, all the Coveys were awake and loitering around the hooches with M-16s on their shoulders. I asked O.K. Bryant, "Have we suffered an attack?"

"Yes, but not by the Vietnamese enemy. The Security Police shot our dogs."

"No."

"Warbler, Willie Pete, and Short Round. The dogs weren't bothering anybody. Assholes killed 'em right here beside the patio. Then, the fucking cops told us to disperse. That's when we armed up."

More police arrived and joined a shouting match. "Return to your quarters" was answered with "Fuck you."

The Base Commander arrived. "Everyone calm down." The old fart appeared to be about eighty. "Return to your quarters."

"What are you going to do? Shoot us? We are at our quarters." Several angry voices answered the tired-looking colonel. No one moved.

"You must disperse." The wrinkled old face persisted.

"We are within our rights." This voice sounded like Elf. "Your cowboys are trespassing. Firing weapons near living quarters is illegal. We're filing charges."

Captain Skinny joined the tirade. "Colonel, you're out-gunned. Take your cops out of here before someone gets hurt. I suggest you give them all drug tests."

Our own commander arrived and spoke to the base commander. Then, he turned to us. "Let's break it up, guys. The base commander will conduct a full investigation."

The crowd groaned and mumbled. "Cops investigating cops. What a load of shit," someone said. Slowly, a few guys drifted back inside the building.

Someone else shouted, "What's to investigate? Those turds killed our dogs."

"I understand. He apologized to me. We can't solve this problem tonight."

I felt numbed by shock and disbelief. I told O.K., "I've seen bad behavior by the REMFs. Killing puppies represents a new low, even for them."

I awoke one morning thinking it was Saturday, but it was Tuesday. All days at Pleiku were alike, but I wondered if I'd gained four days or lost three. I made a note to buy a watch with the date feature on my next Ubon trip.

Similarly, Christmas arrived without warning or fanfare.

From my sister I received a box of cookies, but when I opened them in the bar, they disappeared in a feeding frenzy. The Red Cross provided a package of candy and small games. I swatted a rubber ball attached to a paddle, until I realized what I was doing. The toy I did enjoy was a laugh box that said, when pressed, "Ho Ho Ho Ho Ho. And a Merry Christmas to One and All. Ho Ho Ho Ho Ho." The voice boomed like Santa's.

At four a.m. on Christmas morning I carried the laugh box to the chow hall. “Ho Ho Ho Ho Ho.”

The droopy-eyed cooks were not impressed.

I played it for Tower after I took off at five-thirty. Next, I gave Peacock a blast. Then, I played the song for the boys at the F.O.B. “Ho Ho Ho Ho Ho.”

“Water buffalo’s on the way, Covey. Ho Ho to you, too.”

I landed at Kontum.

The jeep arrived with a Green Beret captain for a passenger. “Hi. Call me King Arthur.”

I introduced myself.

“Ohio is in contact,” he said. “The O.V.-Ten driver who put the team in yesterday came out and found them in the middle of the night. Let’s relieve him on scene.”

“Roger.” I said. “So much for the cease-fire.” We took off.

“The little cease-fire arrangement only covers Vietnam. Since Laos is neutral, and we have no troops there, how could politicians possibly declare a cease-fire?”

“You’re right.” I played the Christmas message to Hillsboro. After a decent interval--enough time for plausible denial--I checked-in.

“Roger. Covey Five-four-oh is expecting you. Ho Ho, yourself.”

“That’s Tim Eby’s callsign,” I told King Arthur. “Captain Skinny.”

He nodded and pointed to a valley ahead.

An O.V.-10 rolled inverted and dove straight down at the jungle. The aircraft left a tiny smoke trail. He was firing his guns. A line of helicopters approached from the east. We listened to the action on the radio.

“You killed two of ‘em. Bring in the choppers before their buddies arrive.”

“Roger. Stand by for a low hover.”

On another radio, Captain Skinny said, “Slicks, friendlies are in the clearing fifty meters south of my smoke. Cobras, follow me. Let’s hit my smoke again.”

While the O.V.-10 attacked nearby, the first Huey landed. “We got half of ‘em. Comin’out now. Takin’ fire.”

Cobras pressed their attacks while a second Huey landed. “We’re takin’ fire.” The Huey lifted into the valley and turned south. “I’ll try to make Leghorn. Took a round in the transmission.”

“Covey five-four-oh is outa gas. R.T.B.”

“Nice work, five-four-oh.” I stayed with the wounded Huey. He made a perfect landing on the P.S.P. chopper pad, one level below and beside the large bunker at Leghorn.

Someone had strung a huge sign around the west side of the peak. Three-foot-letters proclaimed, "Merry Fucking Christmas."

King Arthur discussed the situation on secure radio with the F.O.B. Then he said, "Three choppers took hits on this morning's operation. We have to wait for a decision from higher headquarters whether the remaining assets will suffice for more ballgames."

I nodded. While cruising around the Trail, I recognized the voice of the O.V.-10 sector FAC, Bruce Lamping. I climbed high and moved toward Leghorn, where he had been invited to make a low pass. The damaged Huey still sat on the pad.

As Lamping rolled into his dive, I followed, three hundred feet behind him. We crossed the bunker when Leghorn called, "Two for the price of one."

Lamping pulled straight up.

I followed.

He turned, sliced, and twisted, but I hung on. I could track him most of the time, using the pause at the top of his climbs to recover my own energy. Then, I'd jump him as he came down again.

"I don't feel so good." King Arthur didn't look so good either.

"We'll be done in a second." Holding the nose up too long, I stalled the O-2. I felt light in the seat as the nose fell to vertical. The close proximity of large trees in the windscreen surprised me. We had lost several thousand feet of altitude.

In a steep dive, I pulled hard. The aircraft buffeted. "Damn. Secondary stall."

While all my senses said, "Pull harder," I released back pressure.

When the airflow reattached to the wing, I pulled level just at the treetops.

"Let's knock it off," Lamping said on the radio. "I just had a big secondary stall."

"Roger." I looked at my passenger. If my expression matched my feelings, then I looked goofy but glad-to-be-alive.

He stared at me in sheer terror. Then, his face went into an airsick bag.

"Sorry, Captain," I said.

He shook his head. "Let's go home. We're done for the day."

I apologized again as King Arthur deplaned at Kontum.

He was a good sport. "We'll send a Huey to Pleiku in an hour. You're having dinner with us, right?" The Green Berets included Prairie Fire Coveys in their holiday festivities.

"I wouldn't miss it."

I landed at Pleiku around ten a.m. Loaded with weapons and maps, I found a Santa-bou parked in front of the squadron building. The C-7 Caribou had St. Nick's face painted on the nose and elaborate peppermint-striped propellers. The crew had lowered the ramp in back to reveal a bar. Smiling American Red Cross female volunteers--Donut Dollies--served strong eggnog.

I asked, "Am I dreaming?"

Leaning on the bar, O.K. Bryant raised a toast. "Here's to peace on earth. And you'd better change clothes like now."

O.K. wore a party-suit, a dark blue flightsuit replica, covered in bawdy and cynical patches. Proclaiming themes like Laos Highway Patrol, Southeast Asia Wargames Participant, and Cessna Suck-and-Blow Driver, patches told each Covey's own story. Individuals designed the patches for tailor shops in Thailand. Free enterprise did the rest.

"Don't leave without me." I sprinted inside the squadron building, secured my gear, and grabbed jeep keys. After a quick shower, I joined Captain Skinny in the hooch bar, wearing my party suit with patches that said, "Yankee Air Pirate," "Death Brings Peace," and "20th TASS--One Good Deal After Another."

"Ho Ho Ho." He seemed to have the spirit.

"Two K.B.A. Merry Christmas." I toasted his killed-by-air report.

Several new guys raised their eyebrows.

"We gotta go," I said. "I hope the club heats the canned turkey for you mere mortals. I don't think they bothered at Thanksgiving."

"Not that I recall." Captain Skinny bowed to the crowd as we departed.

I sped toward the flightline. Remembering the Security Police incident, I said, "I'd better slow down. I don't have a gun."

"I was ready to resign the other day--so pissed about those idiot cops. I had my rank and wings in hand when I kicked open the commander's door."

"Wow. What d' he say?"

"He wasn't in."

I parked near the Santa-bou where ten more animated guys in party suits waited with cups of eggnog in hand. All Prairie Fire pilots--O-2 and O.V.-10--gathered for this big event. Overhead, a Huey descended in a wide arc. The wop wop grew loud enough for some of us to cover our ears. He landed twenty feet in front of the Santa-bou.

We strapped in for the ten-minute hop to Kontum. I watched the scenery through the open sides of the chopper full of lively FACs.

At the F.O.B. we first stopped at the Covey Riders' screened hooch. Sixpack, Shoebox, and Plastic Man managed a five-gallon olive drab bucket of strawberries, a gallon of rum, ice, and a blender. A crunch and a hum signaled the production of another batch of excellent daiquiris. A brown and white dog watched from the corner.

I asked, "Is that Stoner?"

"Yep." Sixpack whistled and the dog ran to him.

"He's twice as big as his departed siblings at Pleiku."

"We feed him long-range-recon-patrol rations. LRRPs. Lots of nutrition and shit."

A huge SOG patch with the letters C.C.C., for Command and Control Central, hung at one end of the porch. Bullet holes covered the plywood sign.

I asked, "What happened to the Covey County Club sign?"

"Shoebox dropped his forty-five the other night," Sixpack said. "Accidentally went off . . . seventeen times." He smiled and raised a toast. "Merry Christmas."

"Hear, hear." We laughed and cheered.

I sensed the effects of the alcohol but stayed in control. Alert and happy, I rose above a feeling of deep fatigue inside me. Someday I'd sleep for thirty days and be fine.

Elf said, "How long has the Pleiku club been without fresh fruit? I'll bet you guys had these strawberries flown in from Na Trang today for the party."

"Sorry, sir, but the Army takes better care of its troops than the Air Force."

"You're right, Sixpack," I said. "The Army has to focus on troops that someday might have to be herded through the gates of hell."

"Yeah," O.K. added. "Most Air Force warriors are officers who can find their own way to hell."

During another round, we toasted Captain Skinny's two K.B.A. achievement from a morning that seemed farther from reality with each sweet sip. "Hear, hear."

Then, we moved to the chow hall where I apologized again to King Arthur. He smiled and shook my hand.

We joined about fifty men, some bandaged, but all in good cheer. Long tables covered in linen held turkeys, dressing, cranberries, pumpkin pie, and fresh green vegetables. The aroma took me to my grandmother's house.

I saw a few tears on faces that also remembered home and hearth.

Standing between Shoebox and O.K. Bryant, I looked out over a huge, succulent turkey. The drab room had enough garlands and colored lights to make me forget the war.

Someone read the biblical story of Christmas from a King James Bible. The atmosphere felt cozy and subdued. All our troubles seemed banished with the real denizens out in the jungle. A senior officer prayed for fallen brothers.

The true meaning of the season became clear in this setting--this family of warriors. Whether drawn together by the common danger or lifted by the opportunity to express the joy of Christmas, we were brothers.

Then, we feasted.

I told Shoebox, "I haven't seen food like this in five months."

He refilled my eggnog and nodded. He passed the pitcher to O.K., then carved off juicy slabs of white meat with his Randall knife. "Don't worry. I washed it this morning."

Hours passed like minutes. We stumbled to the chopper pad for the return trip. O.K. and I climbed aboard one of two Hueys, idling in the late afternoon sun.

"What are those guys doing?" I pointed to the O.V.-10 Prairie Fire pilots, who seemed to chase each other with ropes near the second chopper.

"They're hooking onto a rope. A string extraction. They're going home in style."

I watched the nearby Huey lift straight up with half-a-dozen screaming Coveys attached at intervals to a dangling rope. "I don't know if I'm too drunk or not drunk enough." I shook my head.

"I think we're on the right bird." O.K. sat beside me in the left door. Our feet dangled outside.

Wiser Coveys strapped into seats as we lifted off and turned hard to the east.

"Here we go." The pilot looked familiar. He and I had chatted at the nog bowl.

The chopper tipped forward. We sped toward a wall of trees.

The door gunner sat behind us on a bench with his M-60 machine gun across his lap. He explained our route. "Over the years, guys have cut a path under the jungle canopy. We'll come out near the redball highway."

I pulled an orange from my pocket and tossed peelings as the jungle flew past. We snaked and jerked at high speed with nothing around us but a green blur. When we broke clear of trees, our chopper began a maximum rate climb.

"We call this a swoop." My eggnog-buddy pushed the collective lever to the floor and dumped the pitch forward.

From two thousand feet we fell like a rock.

Grabbing a seat post, I told O.K., "Maybe we should've taken the string. I'll bet King Arthur whispered in this pilot's ear."

The wop wop changed to a slower grinding wop as the pilot pulled up on the collective lever and the blades began to bite into the humid air. We bottomed out near the ground, then flew on toward Pleiku.

Popopopopop. The M-60 machine gun exploded a foot above my left ear.

Holy shit. I nearly jumped out.

A line of red tracers curved down to the left and sparkled on a large white rock.

I saw the gunner and O.K. laughing at me.

I joined them.

The string-riders had landed before us. Some were tussling on the ground. I learned several celebrants lost the wonderful holiday meal, and the wind had formed a strange vomit path. It left their mouths and came back across their feet and the head of the Covey below.

I staggered to the bar with O.K. "I suppose I should write some letters."

"You have friends and relatives who would understand all this?"

"Hell, I don't understand all this. That big sign around Leghorn said it all for me."

Chapter 8
Cynicism

January 1971

To ensure 1971 began with a bang, I volunteered for the ten p.m. takeoff on New Year's Eve. I flew with my friend, Elf, an O.V.-10 pilot and scheduler. Weary of complaints from inspired revelers in the navigator corps, he took the mission himself.

At eleven, as a huge party developed at Pleiku, we cruised over the Dog's Head.

Elf leaned out the right window and peered through his scope. "I've got movers."

"Moonbeam," I called. "Covey Five-nine-one has trucks near Delta-forty."

Fifty minutes later, Gunfighter checked in as two F-4s from Danang.

"Four trucks are starting down the Straight-away," Elf said.

I gave the Gunfighters a thorough briefing, accomplished a visual rendezvous, and rolled in to mark at eleven-fifty-nine.

Bam.

"Tally the smoke, Covey," Gunfighter leader said. "We've got delayed effects on these cluster bombs. They'll be cooking off for a while."

"Roger. Trucks are on the Trail north of my smoke. Cleared hot."

"One's in."

Thirty seconds later the Trail sparkled. Random explosions covered a quarter-mile area. From the Dog's Head a stream of anti-aircraft tracers came up and exploded well short of our orbit. A similar display came up from the Falls. Hundreds of rounds flew straight up and burst like fireworks lighting the skies back home at midnight.

"The gunners are celebrating, too," I told Elf. "Happy New Year."

"Two's in."

"Start yours where leader's bombs stopped. Two, cleared hot."

Gunfighter followed my directions well.

"Great job. Keep working north."

The F-4's departed after dropping thousands of bomblets. Several actually found our trucks. We cheered as the Trail continued to explode. I passed decent bomb damage assessment. "I'd like to fire a few grenade rounds at the Falls gunners."

"Sure," Elf said.

I pulled out my M-79, broke down the barrel, and inserted a high explosive round. "Here." Snapping the breach shut, I handed the weapon to Elf. "You know where to aim."

He stuck the barrel out the window and pulled the trigger.

Click.

"A misfire. Cock it and try again."

Click.

"Why don't I just lose the whole thing?" Elf wanted to toss the weapon out into the darkness.

"No way. Pull the round out and throw it clear of the rear prop."

The wind whipped Elf's heavy mustache and howled across the barrel. Elf drew out the forty-millimeter grenade and tossed it clear. He handed me the M-79.

"Here's a mini-grenade with a rubber band wrapped around the spoon," I said. "Pull the pin and toss it. The band should come off when the grenade hits the ground."

Elf nodded. "These things are small. No iron casing for fragmentation."

"Concussion grenades," I said. "Not much frag, but a large overpressure kill radius. They're set with a two-second delay."

Elf threw the grenade out the window. "I think the rubber band--"

Boom.

We flipped inverted. I rolled right-side-up a thousand feet lower.

"--came off when I threw it." Elf shook his head.

"Shit." I felt lucky to be alive. My stomach gurgled.

"Let's go home and hope we don't have any holes to explain." Elf laughed.

I felt dumb. Like the government's Vietnam policy, I had become my own worst enemy.

Our commander brought in more field grade characters--chair warriors who shared his philosophy that war was a dangerous distraction from the business of seeking promotions. Each new arrival took his place in charge of a specific area of operations.

Major Baldacci tried to control squadron training. He stood at a Friday crew meeting in the squadron lounge. “You’re not logging enough precision approaches.”

Aircrews packed the drab twenty-five-foot square room.

Elf spoke up for the grumbling crowd. “Major, are not all approach requirements waived here?”

“Yes, but--“

”Are we not in a combat zone, Major?”

“Yes, but--“

”Why do you expect us to fly practice approaches over the gunners here?”

The crowd joined Elf in denouncing Baldacci’s attempt to impose his stupid ideas. Quiet rage grew toward explosion.

Baldacci held up both hands, trying to regain control. All he could manage to say was, “Log ‘em now and fly ‘em later.” He departed the room as though propelled by the angry buzz he had created.

The meeting soon adjourned.

“Who are these assholes?” O.K. asked. He and I shared a jeep returning to the hooches. “New field-graders are everywhere but in the sky.”

“Did Baldacci just tell us to falsify government records?” I asked.

“The hell with them,” O.K. said.

“He could have said we need to stay proficient in all piloting skills. He could have asked us to please emphasize precision approaches. I agree with you. Screw him.”

I would raise my concerns with Major Reed, with whom I would fly late that night. Reed was a handsome father-figure with silver temples and a trim mustache. He flew frequently, and thus had my respect.

Reed had spotted six trucks crossing the river at the Dog’s Head.

I made the call. “Moonbeam, this is Covey Five-nine-one. We have six trucks. Rendezvous point Delta forty.”

“Roger, Covey. Not much air available right now.”

I asked Reed, “What’s the deal with the new field-grade help?”

“I don’t bother them, and they don’t bother me.” He turned from his scope and shook his head. “As dumb as they seem, they’re a tight clique.”

“Intellectually, they’re easy to ignore.” I wondered what happened to the brains of people who were promoted beyond the rank of captain. “How are our trucks doing?”

Reed returned to the scope. “Right four. Prepare for a turn south. First truck is approaching the spot where the road forms the Little Dog’s Head. Turn right.”

After half an hour I called Moonbeam again, but still no fighters were available.

"Left three. Lead truck is approaching the Interchange."

"Let's head south, then turn and shoot rockets at them when they're on the Straight-away. Maybe we can slow the convoy." A sparsely defended, straight flat segment led ten miles south to a series of river bends called the Bra.

"Roger." Reed pulled in the scope while we droned south.

I armed the right wing rocket pod and turned west so Reed could search the Trail. "Are they all on the Straight-away yet?"

"All in the first mile. Six trucks, movin' fast." Reed closed and latched his window.

I could see the sliver of road but no vehicles. Rolling right allowed the nose to fall gently. Lined up precisely with the Trail, I fired five rockets.

Bam. Bam. Bam. Bam. Bam.

My hard pull up and roll to the left allowed Reed to check for results during the gentle right turn to parallel the road. We flew offset by half a mile. "How'd we do?"

"Right five. No effect. You hit close to a couple, but they're haulin' ass. Maybe they know something we don't about the airstrike situation."

"I'll hit 'em again at the Bra."

"Break left. Fifty cal."

Yanking the controls hard, I watched a hundred small red tracers arc away and burn out into nothingness. This left turn took us south, and we climbed to avoid the bigger guns at the Falls. "Let's search from the Bra to the Falls, then go north and attack our convoy again."

"Okay." Reed stuck the scope out the window. "Not much to see. Left four."

We turned north, and Reed scoped the Bra. "Our trucks are cruising into the ford on the left cup. First one is in the river."

North of the Bra I armed the left wing rocket pod. "I'll fire two from each pod directly at the ford." Sixty degrees of bank allowed the nose to drop to the target.

Bam. Bam.

Rockets streaked from each wing and seemed to converge on the Bra's left cup. I started to pull up and turn left.

"Break hard. We're taking fire," Reed yelled.

I pulled a nose low four-g left turn and rolled the wings level.

Bright airbursts began a few hundred feet above us. Eerie red light beams flashed through plastic windows on top of the cockpit. Thirty or forty explosions crackled above the drone of the engines.

"I think they know we're here." I pulled up level, moving my finger to the radio switch. "Moonbeam, Covey Five-nine-one, still chasing trucks. Got some guns, too."

"Roger, Covey. We're doing our best."

I climbed. "We have less than an hour before these guys reach the border."

"Roger, Covey."

Reed shook his head. "Let's watch from a distance. No need to die for nothin'."

"Okay." For forty minutes I flew a high orbit over the convoy. A hint of dawn softened the darkness. "Time to go home. Might as well spend these rockets."

"Rog." Reed closed and latched his window and put the scope away.

I armed everything, lined up with the Trail, and rolled in again.

Bam. Bam. Bam. Bam. Bam.

Five rockets, four logs, and four bricks fell earthward.

"Breaking left." I saw the tracers coming as I pulled. Airbursts flashed behind us. "Did we hit anything?"

"Nah. They're sill moving."

"Moonbeam, Covey Five-nine-one is R.T.B."

"Roger. We'll pass your target to Hillsboro."

"Moonbeam. Raven Four-one. I need snake-and-nape for a T.I.C. Now."

We rarely heard the Raven callsign at night. He had troops in contact and asked for napalm and high drag bombs with retarding fins.

"Roger, Raven Four-one. You'll have Cobra, two F-Fours, in ten minutes."

I pointed the nose to the right of the sunrise. "Unlike us, that Raven got everything he asked for."

Reed nodded and passed his details to the incoming O.V.-10 pilot.

After landing, I debriefed George, our intelligence officer. George was heavy-set with thick black-rimmed glasses. "We escorted six enemy trucks safely through our area."

"Don't write that down," George cautioned. "Somebody already did."

"Really?"

"A Danang Covey had to go to Saigon for a personal reprimand from a general officer. Just last week."

I mumbled to Reed, "If the truth begets reprimands, then the leadership problem extends beyond the FAC squadron at Pleiku."

George lectured us. "Most ordnance goes into boxes near the North Vietnamese border. They drop without a FAC in response to sensor strings. Blind and random."

"Blindly?" I asked. "I've seen fighters hit a tenth of the trucks they were aiming at on a good night. But I guess level bombing from fifteen-thousand feet is safer."

"Minimizes losses," Reed said. "But only until the defenses show up."

I looked at George. "Why don't we just dump everything on Hanoi, day and night? We might discover whether the North Vietnamese hold anything dear."

"Sorry. That's the President's call to make."

Walking out the door, I asked Reed, "Do you remember seeing L.B.J. on television a few years ago? He said something like, 'those boys don't bomb an outhouse in North Vietnam unless I say so.' Now I see the connection. We're in the middle of a leadership cancer that has spread from the White House through Saigon to this very building."

Reed laughed. "I hate to think of anybody dying for an outhouse."

I arrived at the hooch bar as the rising sun chased night fighters to bed.

Captain Skinny was busy behind the bar. "Coffee?"

"No, thanks. I'll have a post-mission beer, then take my nap."

"Good mission?"

I amused him with my escort mission story. "Moonbeam's positive response to that Raven FAC sticks out in my mind."

"I hear the Ravens fight a real war," he said. "They usually get what they need."

"I'll have five-hundred hours soon. May look into applying for that outfit."

He raised his coffee cup. "Here's to a better war. One worth fighting."

I raised my rusty can of bad brew, then finished it. "I'm looking into the Ravens. Good night."

"Good morning."

I slept well, then met Major Reed in the dinner line at the club. We slid trays along--cafeteria style--for all our meals. Surveying the mush on my plate, I assumed the cook had considered nutrition--he had obviously compromised taste and presentation.

Reed asked, "Ready for another try?"

"Sure." I followed him to the dining room. "Maybe Moonbeam will let us kill something tonight."

Reed nodded, and we filled the food square in silence.

"The food is so bland around here," I complained, sipping coffee from a heavy white mug. "What was that stuff, anyway? Roast beef or meatloaf?"

Two hours later we droned in the dark. I became impatient. "Any activity at all?"

"No movement on the Trail. They're hiding."

Ten miles ahead I noticed multi-colored flares popping, then spiraling downward. "What are those lights to the northwest?"

"They're not on the Trail," Reed said. "That's a strip on the Bolovens Plateau. P.S.-two two." Reed referred to his map. "And here's the frequency. Sixty-seven-five."

I remembered. "We had to monitor them day and night a few weeks ago. They anticipated an attack, but nothing happened."

"Something's happening now."

I turned toward the flares and called the site. "P.S.-two-two, this is Covey Five-nine-one. Do you have a problem?"

"Covey, this is site two-two. We have big problem. Big T.I.C." Fear, approaching panic, came through the heavily accented reply.

I asked Reed, "Troops in contact? Whose troops? In contact with whom?"

Reed shrugged.

I reported the situation to Moonbeam.

"Roger, Covey Five-nine-one. We'll send you some gunships."

We circled. Judging from flashes on the ground, the friendlies were outnumbered. A dirt airstrip came into view under a red flare. Then, a green flare burst open.

"Two-two, this is Covey. I see enemy southwest. They're shooting rifles, mortars, and recoilless rifles." Recoilless weapons flashed from both ends of the launch tube, then impacted beyond the friendly lines near the airstrip. "Do you have illumination rounds?"

"Affirmative. Big T.I.C. Maybe three battalions, N.V.A. Only have red and green left. No more illume."

"Two-two, confirm enemy are southwest, and all friendlies are near the runway."

"Affirmative. Please make airstrike southwest."

"Okay. Stand-by."

When an A.C.-119 Shadow called, I detected a Texas accent. I passed him the situation. "My altitude is base minus three. Request you operate at base minus two or higher." My code card showed the daily base altitude as nine thousand.

"Roguh, Covey. Why don't you climb t' base minus two. Let us work under y'all."

Reed sorted the altitude confusion for me. "Target elevation is three thousand. High terrain is forty-five hundred, northeast of the runway. Base minus two puts us at four thousand feet above the ground."

"Sounds good," I said. "As long as somebody is tracking the higher terrain. Confirm you have the friendly position, and you're cleared hot."

"Roguh. I have th' airstrip and th' friendlies around it. Lots o' muzzle flashes a couple hundred meters southwest in a lahge semi-circle."

"Affirmative," I said. "Shoot southwest, away from the friendlies."

"Roguh. We'll shoot 'em up fer ya."

"Site two-two, Covey. Put your heads down. We shoot now."

"Okay, Covey. You shoot now."

Major Reed surveyed with his scope and helped me understand the situation.

Shadow fired his miniguns. Every fifth round of his seven-point-six-two millimeter ammunition was a tracer. A red finger reached down and extinguished the N.V.A. muzzle flashes, like water on a fire. The deadly red stream cut an arc across the southwest quadrant of the eerie scene.

"Covey, this is site two-two. Thank you very much."

"Mah sensors have movemunt within fifty meters of the fence."

"Site two-two. Do you have friendlies outside the fence?"

"Negative. Outside fence all bad guys."

"Get down. We have to shoot close. Many enemy near the fence."

"Okay. Shoot close."

"Shadow, cleared hot."

"Roguh." The lethal red finger reached down again and wiggled near the fence.

"Stop attack now. Covey, stop now." Two-two sounded frantic.

"Is everybody okay?" I probably sounded slightly excited myself.

After a pause, the voice said, "All okay. You shoot very close. Scare soldiers."

"Good work, Shadow. Friendlies thank you for saving their asses tonight."

"Roguh. Anything else we can do fer ya?"

"I saw a mortar position earlier. Let me mark the spot with smoke." I warned two-two we would hit the N.V.A. again.

"Okay. You hit three hundred meters southwest."

I rolled in and marked a small depression where I had seen flashes.

"Let me tun on my flashlight." Like magic, a hundred-meter circle shone bright as daytime. "Yeah. We have movemunt. We'll shoot 'em up."

"Cleared hot."

The red line smashed down and cut away swatches of jungle. Two silvery explosions flashed under the fiery finger.

"Shadow's winchestuh. R.T.B."

"Thanks, Shadow. You saved some lives tonight." My fuel status was low.

"Site two-two, this is Covey. We have to go now. Another FAC is coming."

"Roger, Covey. Thank you very much."

"Moonbeam, Covey Five-nine-one is R.T.B. Thanks for the help."

"Roger. We have a Raven airborne now. Also a Spooky gunship's enroute. Good catch on the flares. Sounds like you saved the day for site two-two."

"Thanks." I turned to Major Reed, who had captured details of the strike for our report. "Kind of a nail-biter. A thank-you from the ground makes the effort worthwhile."

"Like a million bucks," he said.

Close air support brought a certain camaraderie to the war that was missing from the lonely interdiction mission.

A few days later I read a *Stars and Stripes* article about fighting on the Bolovens Plateau. Government forces, the article said, killed two hundred N.V.A. in fierce fighting around P.S.-22.

I showed the paper to Major Reed in the hooch bar. "Shadow should get K.B.A. credit for at least a hundred and ninety-nine of the enemy dead. We both know they were killed-by-air."

"Laos." He shook his head. "Nobody knows what really goes on over there."

"A few months ago, I'd have been irate. Now I laugh it off. Truth appears to change in proportion to the speaker's distance from the fighting." I scanned the room for field-grade slackers.

"I'm reaching the twilight of my mediocre career," he said. "At this point I don't care to go to Saigon and pick up a truth reprimand."

"Sounds like something that happens on the N.V.A. side, not ours."

I entered the hooch bar late one evening. "Do I smell real pizza?"

Several Coveys busied themselves near the small oven next to the fridge. Elf smiled and pointed to Tim Eby. "Captain Skinny brought all the fixin's from Ubon."

"Captain Skinny for President," someone yelled.

"I've seen guys bring those homemade pizza mixes in here at six in the morning," Captain Skinny said, "just so they can beat the crowd and eat more than one piece. Usually all they put on top are M&Ms. So, for ten bucks I can treat the whole warrior gang to the real thing."

"Smells delicious." I inhaled. My mind flashed briefly to Shakey's Pizza Parlor in Calumet City, Illinois. "Do I smell real Italian sausage?"

"You bet. The idea started with Robin Olds." Captain Skinny took some pride in his offering a slice of home to Pleiku. "When he commanded the

Eighth Fighter Wing, he financed a pizza joint in Ubon town called Tippy's. I stopped by and picked up the ingredients."

"This oven takes forever, but the pizza is worth the wait." Elf smiled and held up a piece of paper from the afternoon Danang run. "Have you seen this message? Our chain of command wants ideas on how to end the war."

"Does it say end or win?" I asked. "End--send us home. Win--destroy Hanoi."

"End," Elf said. He wrote my comment on the page. "Anything else?"

"Yeah. Let's go home," O.K. Bryant said. "Let the inmates run the asylum."

"I suggest we drop millions of bowling balls with no finger holes all along the Trail," Captain Skinny said. "First, we cover them in grease, so the N.V.A. can't pick them up. N.V.A.'d have to use gunners, drivers and coolie labor to clean up the mess."

"Maybe they would reach the same level of frustration with the war as the American people," O.K. said.

"Your idea might not choke the war to a halt," I said, "but it makes as much sense as those stupid blind-bombing boxes. Speaking of stupid, I haven't seen your pal, Major Major in a while."

"He finagled a big trip to the Nail FAC base in Thailand--Nakon Phanom. Nails call it N.K.P. Spent the holidays in Thailand. I heard he was trying to land a job there."

Around eleven Major Reed entered the bar with Jim Lee. Both appeared pallid, and Reed carried a bottle of bourbon.

I asked, "How's it going? You had the first night mission, right?"

Reed turned to Lee. "Do you want to tell them, or should I?"

"Go ahead." Lee shook his head and looked at the floor.

"We get to the area, see." Reed poured a slug of booze into a coffee mug. "After about an hour we turn west at the Bra and follow the Sihanouk Trail along the Kong River."

"I forgot to switch the tanks," Lee said quietly.

"For you O.V.-Ten types, you have to switch the O-Two from aux to main fuel tanks after about the first hour of flight." Reed's wide eyes and loud voice indicated more excitement lay ahead. "We're coming up south of the eastern fishhook when I see about a hundred tracers coming straight at us. Probably a Z.P.U.--quad-barrel fifty cal. I call a break."

"Yeah," Lee said. "I break hard left, just as the front aux tank runs dry. I switch both tanks to main, and a ton of tracers come up on my side. So I break to the right."

"The front engine doesn't catch, and the airplane stalls." Reed shook his head.

"The airplane bucks real hard--twice," Lee said. "Then, we snap into an inverted spin. I reach for the boost pump for the front engine but hit the rear by mistake. Now the rear engine floods. It quits."

"Fucking N.V.A. have to know what's going on because they keep shooting."

"We're spinning upside-down in absolute silence," Lee said. "I'm totally disoriented and scared shitless. Red tracers everywhere. Damn. Finally, I roll out of the spin. Both engines catch, and we're outa there."

"N.V.A. are still shooting," Reed added. "We lost three of our original four thousand feet of altitude."

After the laughter died down, someone asked, "Did you go back for the guns?"

"Fuck no." Reed's forehead bristled with sweat from recounting the adventure. "Another of those Trail heart attacks that ends before you know what started it."

"I aged about seventeen years," Lee said. "Sorry, Major."

The next evening Paul Curs, a new pilot, walked out the door to fly Captain Abort's last mission. Known to everyone in the squadron except Captain Abort, our maintenance troops had disconnected a lead from the rear engine magneto. Another crew went in secret to a spare airplane to fly the mission. Captain Abort was set up.

Curs told the full story later in the bar. "Preflight was normal but kind of a pain. Captain Abort complained about everything, and of course I ignored him."

The crowd began to snicker.

"At the end of the runway, I ran up both engines. When I checked the rear mag, the engine coughed and backfired. It nearly quit. I pretended nothing had happened and requested takeoff clearance."

Captain Abort smiled sheepishly, torn between the joy of completing his tour and the embarrassment of being the butt of a joke. "The son-of-a-bitch was going to take off with a bad mag. I went nuts."

"Yeah," Curs said. "He was cussin' and yellin' as we rolled onto the runway. Finally, he told me he was gettin' out of the airplane. I let him go on a while, then I taxied to the revetment."

"When I saw the fire hose and all the guys with champagne, I knew I'd been had."

Captain Abort referred to the tradition of a hose-down after the last combat mission. At Pleiku the fire department sometimes used foam, composed of liquefied animal protein. Foam residue had an odor of putrefied meat that resisted soap.

"Congratulations, Joe," I said. "Here's to your last abort."

I heard yelling when I walked through the squadron doorway. The shouts grew louder as I approached the intelligence vault. I opened the door. Tall Nick Lederle, an O-2 instructor pilot, put his scraggly mustache in the face of Major Major, who was sitting on a desk. Five or six O-2 pilots stood behind their fearless spokesman. Nick's hair grew in all directions, but his mind was a razor. And he had grit.

When they all looked at me, I asked, "What's up?"

"The major wants us to carry only flares at nighttime."

"My theory is," Major Major said, "we use a laser-guided bomb to cut the road at sundown. Then, we orbit the roadcut, dropping flares. When the bulldozer comes to make repairs, we spike the bulldozer with another precision bomb. The road stays closed."

"Nice-sounding, but impractical," Nick said. "How'll we mark any targets without logs, bricks, or rockets? We need a ground reference to direct strikes."

"The O-Twos at N.K.P. carry only flares."

"Wrong, sir." Nick kept his cool, but just barely. "They carry no flares. They carry target marker logs in silver tubes that look like flares. Logs fall to the ground and burn for thirty minutes."

Major Major gave his trademark goofy smile.

Nick asked, "What happens in the other fourteen hundred square miles while the FAC orbits one spot?"

Major Major stared back blankly.

I asked, "What about the defenses? How long before every gun in the sector and probably some missiles arrive at the single FAC orbit point?"

When the major said nothing, Nick rejoined his tirade. "How do we mark an important target like a bulldozer without rockets or log markers? And so what if we kill the bulldozer? The N.V.A. use manual labor to fill craters. At Dien Bien Phu the French paid the price for underestimating the Viet Minh."

Major Major sat in silence, smiling.

"If I were the N.V.A. Trail honcho," Nick said, "I'd let the Americans think they had stopped me cold while I ran everything around them under the trees."

Eventually, Major Major said, "I may have to re-think this one."

After I turned in my mission information, I walked to the Covey van with Nick.

He still seethed. "Dumb bastard doesn't fly the O-Two. He's never flown a night mission. He doesn't know a flare from his asshole. Lord, help us."

"We should talk to the maintenance superintendent in case the Major tries to change ordnance loads in spite of truth and logic."

"Let's do it."

Over the Trail at eight p.m. with Major Reed, I briefed Yellowjacket, a flight of F-100s. Four trucks had just crossed the Dog's head. I told Reed, "I've never seen this type of aircraft operate at night. Normally, these guys do close air support in the daytime."

"Tally your beacon, Covey. Ready for a mark."

"Roger." I rolled in from the east and fired. "Trucks are north of my smoke."

"Which mark? The first or the second?"

I looked at Reed. "I'm sure I fired only one rocket." To Yellowjacket, I said, "Let me move around to the south, and I'll fire another rocket." I did.

Again, the fighter leader asked, "First mark or second?"

I shined a flashlight on my rocket pod to confirm five rockets remaining. I had fired only one rocket each time. "Say your altitude, please."

"Base plus ten."

I told Reed, "He's up at eighteen thousand feet. He sees one flash when the rocket motor ignites on the wing and another when the rocket hits. I think I'll invite him down to the war." Trying not to laugh, I explained the situation to Yellowjacket leader.

After a pause, he said, "Look, Covey. We've never done this shit before."

"They probably have a Major Major in their outfit," I said on intercom. "Added the night mission with no training, no consideration of impact on other missions, and no added personnel."

Eventually, the Yellowjackets stung the trucks.

I landed around ten behind a C-130. When I called ground control, they said, "Roger. Follow the C-One-thirty to parking."

"Rog, behind the trash hauler," I said.

"Covey, this trash hauler is bringing fifteen-thousand pounds of mail to your location. Did we hear a disparaging remark?"

"Oh, no, sir. This Covey is honored to be led to parking by a magnificent craft such as your mighty Hercules."

Reed laughed out loud.

I asked him, "What kind of obstruction would hold up one-ounce letters until the load weighed fifteen-thousand pounds?"

Late the next morning, I flew to Danang.

Before I left my airplane, I told the crew chief, "I have right and back seats and two empty rocket pods. I expect the same to be on my airplane when I return."

"Yes, sir. We have a large load of parts to send to Plieku."

"Fine." I hitch-hiked to the club for lunch. When I returned, I found my aircraft stuffed. Cardboard boxes pressed against the back seat, wedged by a propeller whose tip extended out the right window.

As I pulled from my parking space, a colonel stopped me. He leaned to the partially open right window. "Got a full load?"

"Colonel, if you can fit it in here, this airplane'll take off."

He shook his head and walked away.

I wondered if I had offended the guy, as I sailed the Duck home.

At Pleiku the duty officer said, "Did you hear N.K.P. lost an O-Two last night?"

"No. How?"

"Midair collision with a B-Fifty-seven. The O-Two pilot was killed."

"Do you have the name?"

"Tom Duckett."

My surfer pal from Hurlburt. Damn. A hundred Vietnams weren't worth feeling like this.

Chapter 9
Hat in the Ring

February 1971

At the officers club I spied two bottles of Lancer's wine in a cooling tray in the cafeteria line. Normally the icy water held rusty cans of Falstaff Beer. My memory flashed back to Fisherman's Wharf, candlelight, and Elaine.

I looked over my shoulder like a burgular, bought both bottles, and took them to an isolated table. Part of me knew I was dreaming, but that part didn't deter me from a cozy escape.

Finishing the first bottle, I drifted to that special time. I saw every smile, felt every hope that accompanied the last soft taste of the rosé. I opened the second bottle.

"Wine connoisseur, are we?" Elf plopped his tray on my table with a bang.

O.K. Bryant had followed Elf down the hall from the bar. "The ceramic bottle has more value than the liquid inside."

"I shared this wine in San Francisco with a special lady."

"Would that be Elaine?" O.K. asked. "The one who never writes?"

"I just got a nice letter from her. And the last of our pictures from Yosemite."

"Emphasis on last," Elf said. "Long range romances fade away over here. They become war casualties--like Jerry and Pete and Tom."

"Yep," O.K. said. "She dumped all the pictures on you. Emphasis on dumped. You'd better write this one off."

"You guys don't undershtand." My tongue felt numb. When I stood, the room swayed. I staggered, then crumpled in the metal folding chair. "You're screwing up some perfectly good ambiance."

"You need reality, boy, not ambiance." O.K. laid on the southern drawl, thick as molasses. He nodded to Elf, then grabbed a plastic mustard dispenser and squirted me in the chest.

I turned O.K.'s beer glass over in his lap and nailed Elf with a huge squirt of ketchup before he could react.

Then I retreated.

Elf and O.K. pursued.

Near the door, I ran into a table and knocked a dozen glasses to the floor with a loud crash.

REMFs yelled.

Mustard and ketchup flew back and forth in long arcs.

I fought a losing condiment campaign down the hill and across the road. We stumbled through the hooch bar, then down the sidewalk between the hooch and the revetment. At the end of the sidewalk I didn't see the old bed frame. My shins found it, and I fell hard.

"You're gonna hurt in the morning." Elf shook his head and finished emptying the mustard container on my flightsuit.

At eight a.m. my breakfast included aspirins and extra water. While my hangover subsided, I found a desk with a telephone to call about a Raven FAC application. In-country phone systems were unreliable, and I used an hour to get through to FAC headquarters at Cam Ranh. I had to fly the Danang run at ten.

An airman at Cam Ranh Air Base answered. "Five-oh-fourth group."

I identified myself. "I need the format for a Steve Canyon application."

"Stand-by, sir. I'm not the regular crewchief."

A major identified himself. "May I help you, lieutenant?"

"Yes, sir. I'm approaching five hundred combat hours, and I want to volunteer for the Steve Canyon Program. Can you please tell me how to do that?"

"Sure. Put your volunteer statement in writing. Have your commander endorse the letter. Mail it to us." He passed an address.

"Thank you very much." I hung up and typed my letter with an endorsement below. I reported to the commander across the hall. The boss didn't say a word--just signed the letter and shook his head.

I mailed it and took off at ten. My passenger was another young airman facing disciplinary action for drug use. I recognized him as one of our radio operators. I asked him, "Why would anyone screw themselves up with drugs?"

"I don't know, sir."

"What if I used drugs right now? How do you think I'd do my job?" I unloaded, swerved, and rolled the airplane, sending the airman's arms and legs flailing.

His eyes opened wide. "I quit, sir. I'm clean now."

When I entered the clouds for a radar approach into Danang, he seemed terrified again--curled up into a fetal position. Small thunderstorms lined the coast. Turbulence shook and bounced us during descent, and we landed in a light rain.

The squadron first sergeant met the airplane and took the airman away.

I shook my head and went to the club for lunch. The food was hot, and I met several old friends. "I mailed in a Steve Canyon application this morning."

No one spoke at first. I expected a reaction of some kind.

Finally, Dugan asked, "Are you sure you know what you're doing?"

"Of course I do." Of course I didn't. I knew almost nothing about the program. Silence from my peers made me think I might have leaped when I should have looked. To them and to myself, I said, "I'm not turning back now."

At the TASS operations counter, I met three Pleiku Coveys returning from leave and R and R. "I guess the O-Two driver gets a front seat, and you O.V. guys can have the back."

They shrugged, and we walked to the airplane under cloudy skies.

I found clear air at eight thousand feet over the South China Sea. We flew down the coast parallel to a line of towering storms. Puffy white cells reached as high and as far south as I could see.

"Panama G.C.I., Covey Five-nine-one. How far south do these storms go?"

"Sir, my scope only goes to Saigon." Saigon was hundreds of miles out of the way.

"Funny guy," I told my passengers. On the radio I said, "We're trying to reach Pleiku. Do you see a hole in the wall of cumulonimbus?"

"No, sir. Looks pretty solid."

"If you see a soft spot, please give me a right turn."

"Roger, turn right."

I turned, thinking what a dumb thing I was doing. "We either poke through this wall or return to Danang," I said.

My passengers said nothing, so I pressed on.

I couldn't believe a cloud so white on the outside could be so black inside. The airplane shook and jerked like a wild mustang. The altimeter spun and became unreadable.

Fighting to keep the wings level, I watched the vertical velocity needle peg at the top, then the bottom of the case.

Then, the rain came. My side window leaked. Water flowed onto my left shoulder like a cold mountain stream. A puddle formed at my feet.

"We're going to die in an O-Two," a backseat passenger said. "Damn. I'd rather die in a gay bar than an O-Two."

"We have to be past the worst stuff," I said.

But nothing changed. The dark cockpit shook and rattled. Our altitude varied within a one-mile range. The radios fell silent.

I became concerned about the weight of the water we were taking aboard.

The O.V.-10 pilots continued to pass disparaging remarks from the backseat.

Suddenly the storm spit us out--wet but undamaged--into bright sunshine. Turning to the backseat passengers, I asked, "Now, where's that gay bar? I'll drop you off."

I spent the next day flying with Shoebox over Laos where our first two infiltration missions had each been shot out of three landing zones. Helicopter pilots had faced heavy fire again and again. We went zero for six in a long sweaty battle of wills.

"We'll never know, but I wonder how many N.V.A. we killed today." My flight suit was drenched in spite of cooling air. I felt beat up after seven hours. "We bombed the hell out of those places, and still, a bad guy stands up and shoots the helicopters."

"Target-rich environment."

"Yeah, but those guys pay a human price we'd never endure. They always come back for more. We're talking about Laos, not their homeland."

Shoebox held up his hand as he received a radio message from his commander, a colonel who had one bushy eyebrow that spanned across both eyes. "Brows wants us to cover a water resupply. The team is on the border."

"We've used every A-One in Asia twice today. No time to cycle more out here."

"Roger." Shoebox relayed my concerns to his colonel. "He said the resupply choppers would have Cobra escorts, and no enemy units are known to be within miles of the area."

"I feel like Spiderman. I can sense trouble."

Shoebox laughed. "Sir, the boys need a little water. We may as well help."

"Okay." I requested fighters just in case.

After Shoebox showed me where to look, I spotted the team moving through sparse jungle on top of a thirty-five-hundred-foot ridge. My map indicated they were in South Vietnam.

I pointed the border out to Shoebox. "Wrong country. Another bad indicator."

The team approached a clearing, and I saw the cavalry coming. Two

Hueys and two Cobras motored in at low altitude.

When the first Huey sat down, heavy firing began from the west side of the ridge.

"We're in," a Cobra said. Fire spewed from the diving helicopter's nose. Gray smoke billowed and swirled from the steep hillside.

A second bird dove in with more fire. The target sparkled.

"Troops are going hand-to-hand," Shoebox said. "The resupply choppers just became evacuation birds."

I called Hillsboro again, but they had no assets for immediate use.

The first Huey departed, and the second landed under the daisy chain of Cobra attacks. Finally, all the choppers moved southeast.

"The zone is clear of friendlies," Shoebox said, "if you wish to unload rockets."

"Oh yeah." I climbed up. "Everybody okay?"

"A couple of injuries. One troop took hot shrapnel from the chopper attack."

I rolled inverted and pulled down to the vertical. In one steep pass I fired eight rockets into the jungle. I spoke on the intercom over the banging of departing rockets. "Here you go, Nguyen. If you want this hill, pay for it."

"Feel better now?" Shoebox asked as I pulled level and pointed for Kontum.

"Yes."

A mile from the end of the Kontum runway, I lowered the landing gear.

"Look," Shoebox said. "A Cadillac driver on the ramp. Why don't you show him what this Ford can do?"

I saw the O.V.-10 and recognized the new Prairie Fire pilot with his preflight checklist. "I'll do a minimum-run landing and turn off at the first taxiway." Low on fuel and out of rockets, my O-2 had a minimal gross weight. All I needed was a reasonable headwind to stop in three hundred feet.

Shoebox smiled. He obviously enjoyed living on the edge.

I lowered full flaps and brought the nose up as we slowed to a few knots above a stall. An occasional squeak from the stall warning horn reminded me of the risk. I used full power to stay in the sky.

The O.V.-10 pilot put his hands on his hips.

My wheels touched with a screech on the first few feet of runway. Raising flaps, I stood on the brakes hard enough to lever my lower body against the loose lapbelt.

Wheeee. Brake rotors screamed in protest and sent up sprays of sparks like rooster tails. The aircraft shook, jerked, and halted.

I turned off at the point where O.V.-10s normally touched down. Taxiing past my O.V.-10 friend with his jaw lowered and hands still on his hips, I said, "I wish those Cadillac drivers could understand the FAC business is not about machines."

Feeling exactly like those old heads looked when I had first arrived five months earlier, I stood in the background of the boisterous hooch bar scene. My back ached from eight hours in the pilot's seat, and my flight suit had dried, stiff after its third complete drenching. I felt tired. The usual suspects surrounded me like cozy insulation from the rowdy newbies.

O.K. Bryant said, "I heard you put in a letter for the Ravens."

"Yeah. Rumors say they're fighting a real war." I wondered what my sisters would think. I sipped my beer and brought Elaine's fair image from a compartment in my brain. No help there. "Nothing better on my horizon. I hear you get the assignment of choice when you leave."

"If you survive." O.K. shook his head. "When do--"

"Damn. What a fucked up night!" Major Reed entered with Major Boubek. His loud expletive seemed out of character.

I asked, "Are you okay?"

"Short round. We hit friendlies tonight." Reed's comment silenced the bar.

Beside Reed, Boubek stood in silent study and sipped a beer. His eyes moved around the room. Earlier in the day he had found his office window boarded up. I knew a group of lieutenants were pushing his sanity to the limit.

"Where?" I thought about my recon team friends.

"P.S.-seven. Indigenous troops. Down south near the Kong River. The TACAN gave us a forty-degree lock-on error. The bend in the river was identical to the one where the TACAN said we were. We killed some good guys."

"I know you always do your best," someone broke the silence.

The background buzz returned.

"My best wasn't good enough tonight," Reed said. "I've had a lot of luck lately--all of it bad."

"Has anybody had any luck with Spectre?" O.K. changed the subject. "An A.C.-one-thirty nearly shot me last night."

"Yeah," I said. "They don't answer the radio, and they don't stay where they agree to patrol. Otherwise, they have a great system."

"Most Spectre pilots are field-graders," someone added. "They know most of us are lieutenants. They resent the fact that we're the boss in the sector."

"At least their field-graders fly," O.K. said, "but why are they so arrogant?"

Another Covey added, "Arrogance is a major problem. I hear they've claimed seven thousand truck kills--two thousand more than the N.V.A. operates on the Trail."

"I haven't had any problems working with Stinger and Shadow." I referred to the A.C.-119 converted from flying boxcars of Korean War vintage.

"Nor have I," O.K. said. "They fly below me. No way they could be a threat. They ask me to call when I find movers. And they come over and blast 'em for me."

"Speaking of blasting," I said, "once in daylight, and once at night, I've been caught in B-Fifty-two strikes. Like flying over a sea of flashbulbs."

"Did you have guard channel turned off?" someone asked.

"Attention all aircraft. Avoid the following coordinates within one-zero nautical miles for the next one-zero minutes." I mimicked the standard B-52 strike warning. "Then, the cockpit map-fight begins."

OK laughed. "I've been there. Finding the map takes five minutes. Unfolding it and finding coordinates takes five minutes. Plus, the O-Two can barely cover ten miles in five minutes anyway. Catch-twenty-two."

"You have to depend on luck or the big sky theory to be safe," a voice added.

"The BUFFs are controlled by Strategic Air Command," a new captain said.

"The what?" I asked.

"Big Ugly Fat Fuckers. Omaha, Nebraska, runs their war."

"BUFFs," I said. "Another system that ought to run across Hanoi day and night. They won't threaten any Cessnas there. Who knows? May adjust a few attitudes."

"Hand me another beer, please," Reed said. "I need to adjust my attitude."

Captain Skinny walked in and plopped his *Stars and Stripes* on the bar. "Anybody want to learn about Vietnamization? It's today's big story."

"Getting our boys out and their boys in has always been Nixon's policy. What else is new?" O.K. popped another beer.

"Just more wisdom and logic from Washington." Captain Skinny didn't withhold any of his strong Texas accent. "Like telling us to cut losses when the mission and threat haven't changed."

"If we can go home, I'm for it," I said. "But the Vietnamese have always been in this war. If they can't win with our help, then God help 'em without it."

"The South Vietnamese soldiers are well-equipped, O.K. said, "but they don't have the dedication of the N.V.A. I've encountered in Prairie Fire. Those guys don't quit."

I recalled my morning adventures. "I know."

At six a.m. the next morning I flew across the Lao border with Shoebox in my right seat. Our mission included locating a ten-man team and bringing them home. We'd scout and plan for several hours, then refuel. Missions near the larger guns required several four-ships of strike aircraft for suppression, and I'd have to give Hillsboro several hours to organize those resources.

"Fly straight ahead," Shoebox said. "I'll ask the team to put a shiny on us. I'm not sure where these guys are." He held up his map.

I noticed the upper left corner of the no-bomb-line--actually a six-kilometer square--cut the Trail below the heavily defended Falls interdiction area. "They know better than to press the guns along the road. They have all this other area to work with. Right?"

Shoebox smiled. "The one-zero's name is Walker. His brother's a one-zero in Command and Control North--C.C.N.--out of Danang. They have a contest going. Our man leads--seventy-six missions without enemy contact."

"No contact?" My experience had taught me teams always found bad guys.

"You know by now that most of these guys try to start World War Three when they find a lucrative target. But the best recon missions don't involve any contact."

"Quite a feat considering the number of N.V.A. units who know they're out there."

"The mission is reconnaissance. And our Walker's the best. He may be too fearless." Into his radio he said, "Go Green."

I spotted the shiny, winking from a bomb crater next to the Trail. "Can he move? He's camped in range of the nastiest bunch of gunners in southern Laos. This shit is hard enough to do without having to run helicopters over triple-A emplacements."

"No, sir. He's undetected but quite surrounded."

"Can he behave himself until noon?" Feeling frustrated and angry, I turned north and called Hillsboro. I faced several bad options. To suppress the guns here would require a lot of airplanes and some luck.

I told Shoebox, "Collect your status reports, then we'll talk to the helicopter pilots at Dak To."

He asked, "Are you pissed off, sir?"

"I know thirty big guns defend this piece of the Trail. But I won't know exactly where they're hiding until they start shooting. Someone could get hurt."

Shoebox supervised the refueling while I met with the chopper drivers. I recognized the faces of the Camp Holloway-based pilots who frequented the

Covey FAC hooch bar from across the runway at Pleiku. "The five-man team is hiding in a bomb crater inside the triple-A ring at the Falls. You'll be in range of at least a dozen twenty-three and thirty-seven millimeter weapons."

I didn't perceive a reaction from the group.

One pilot said, "I'll go in alone."

"You're Brillo, right?"

"Yeah." A short warrant officer with an olive complexion shook my hand. "I'll sneak in for a five-second sit down. We can snatch the team before the gunners react."

Brillo had volunteered for what could be a suicide mission, and yet he looked calm. The Huey pilot was probably nineteen. His innocent blue eyes and smooth chin made him appear even younger. His name came from the curly hair that pushed a bit beyond regulation length around his ears.

"I'll use airstrikes to cover your exit."

Everyone gathered around close when I pointed to the team location on my map. "I'll be on standard V.H.F. The nearest guns hide here a few hundred meters north in a ring around the Falls. Can you guys have engines running at Dak To just in case?"

A senior warrant officer nodded. "We'll give him three minutes."

To Brillo I said, "You'll have to follow my headings exactly. The team will put a shiny on you in the final mile or so. Come in right on the deck. And egress due west."

"No problem," Brillo said.

"The instant you call outbound, the Falls will start exploding."

The jungle heat and humidity were oppressive. Cumulous clouds boiled up but never seemed to block the sun. By ten-thirty in the morning the red Dak To dust that coated my boots and flight suit began to stick to my neck and face.

Some of my sweat flowed for young Brillo. I figured his chances to be fifty-fifty--or less.

Shoebox walked up and heard me review the plan. "Plane's ready. Full of gas."

"We may need an hour to get the fastmovers out here," I concluded. "Let's try to execute around noontime. Any questions?"

I took off and requested four F-4s and four A-1s to meet at a rendezvous point well north of the scene of action to preserve surprise.

Shoebox passed the plan to the team on a secure radio. "Any delay getting aboard the chopper could be fatal."

"I can't shake the image of a twenty-three millimeter gun blazing away into a helicopter at point blank range," I said. "I'll stay well clear of the Falls.

Maybe we can catch the gunners while they're choking down their fish heads and rice."

"Brillo's a good one," Shoebox said. "He's cheated death before."

"Gunfighter four-one, check." The F-4s checked in just after noon.

"Two."

"Three."

"Four."

"Covey, Gunfighter Four-one's a flight of four, wall-to-wall hard bombs."

"Covey Five-nine-one, roger, loud and clear."

"Gunfighter's eighty miles out."

I gave them a target briefing on my U.H.F. radio. "Arm up, stay high, and be ready to hit my smoke. Target is near the Trail ten south of the rendezvous." I didn't mention troops on the ground. They'd figure that out when they saw the chopper. If everything worked, no troops would be on the ground when the attack began.

"Gunfighter, roger."

"Try to stay west of the Trail. We'll have A-Ones holding east."

"Roger."

"Jupiter, check." Three A-1 checked in.

"Two."

"Three."

"Covey, Jupiter, flight of three A-Ones." The pilots were Vietnamese.

I told Shoebox to launch Brillo, then briefed the VNAF pilots. At the end I said, "You'll strike after the F-Fours."

I knew Jupiters as excellent pilots. The leader usually spoke perfect English. Wingmen did not always understand. I watched them fly to the northeast, high, but well below the orbiting F-4s.

I moved east, looking for the Huey-driving lone ranger, my friend Brillo. A rotary-winged armada stirred up dust at Dak To. They would launch about three minutes behind Brillo, staying far enough away to avoid waking the gunners, but near enough to help in a disaster. To preserve tactical surprise, I stayed as far north as I could and still give perfect vectors.

Shoebox spotted Brillo for me.

"Come ten degrees right, six miles." I called directions out to Brillo.

The Huey responded.

"Five right, four miles. Lookin' good."

Brillo flew at nap-of-the-earth level. No sign of enemy activity sounded or flashed.

"Two right, two miles . . . one more ridge to cross." My stomach churned. "Shoebox, ask for a mirror flash on the chopper."

Shoebox complied. His role included directing the ground troops, and helping direct the choppers when my radio and my brain were saturated with controlling airstrikes.

"Get ready. Look for a shiny right of the bare trees and short of the road."

"Got it," Brillo declared.

"Gunfighter Four-one, move south. Standby for a mark in less than a minute."

"Rog."

The fragile craft stopped over the crater for one second . . . two seconds . . . three seconds . . . four seconds.

Stress pressed down like an anvil on my head. I could hear my heart pounding.

Descending northeast of the gunners, I hoped to distract them from the helicopter to their south. Within a ten-mile radius of the stationary Huey I knew trumpets sounded, people screamed, and all hell was breaking loose.

"We have everybody. Headed west."

I detected Brillo's forward motion and fired two smokes onto the nearest ridgeline to the escape route. Bam. Bam. "Gunfighters. Hit my smoke. Start on the north mark and work south. Call helicopter in sight."

"Lead's in. Helicopter in sight."

"Cleared hot." I watched Brillo move west.

Three five-hundred-pound bombs boiled red near my smoke.

"Gunfighter's cleared random attacks." I fired another smoke west of the Falls.

"Two's in, chopper in sight, taking heavy fire from the target area."

"Cleared hot. Don't call in, guys." I couldn't see tracers, but airbursts formed small clouds on the axes of the F-4 attacks.

Dropping three bombs per pass, the Gunfighters dove and twisted around again and again. When gray smoke obscured the area, I threw in a white one where I suspected gunpits hid under heavy camouflage. The military crest--two thirds up and one-third down the mountain--was my starting place. Over the past eight months, every wisp of smoke, flash of light, and all those tracers at night had gone into my memory.

After sixteen passes Gunfighter leader said, "We're winchester bombs."

"Copy," I said. "Please hold high with twenty-mike-mike to cover the A-Ones."

"We can stay six more minutes."

"Roger, break, Jupiter flight, hit my white smoke on the east side of the area. Please drop all your bombs in one pass."

"Brillo's climbing out to the south now," Shoebox said.

"Jupiter One, in."

"Cleared hot."

Jupiter leader rolled in from the east. Tracers rose and burst to meet his attack. He only dropped one bomb.

"Jupiter, please drop all bombs in one pass."

"Roger, Covey, Jupiter has a target in sight."

Brillo rejoined four Hueys and two Cobras who had crossed the fence.

The sight of airbursts excited the Jupiter pilots as they exchanged lively chatter in their native language. When I could squeeze a word in, I requested, "One-pass, haul-ass." I told Shoebox, "They've picked up something on the ground that I can't see. But I don't want to work a rescue operation that requires a passport check in this area."

The A-1s climbed to a higher base altitude. "Jupiter One is in." A thousand feet away and above me, the flight leader rolled and seemed to hang in midair. I counted thirty silvery airbursts in strings around the huge green-and-brown Skyraider, as it began a near vertical dive at the ground.

This time Jupiter leader released the remainder of his bombs.

A large square fire erupted south of his hits. Jupiter flight emptied their wing pylons of bombs in the vicinity of the huge secondary, and no more airbursts came.

"Thank-you for your help today, Gunfighter Four-one. You saved some lives. Break. Jupiters, nice work. One large secondary explosion. Cleared R.T.B."

I felt as if I had aged ten years physically and maybe a hundred psychologically.

Shoebox held his deadpan expression and offered an understatement. "I suggest we move ten miles north."

"I'm exhausted. What's up?" I flew north.

"A team that's humped the hills for three days is running from an N.V.A. patrol."

I switched my comm panel to listen to the team. "Do I hear whistles and dogs?"

Shoebox nodded, confirming the enemy troops were on the good guys' heels.

The normally whispered calls came through in a loud and breathless voice. I relayed the Prairie Fire Emergency to Hillsboro and made low passes to get a fix on the team. "At least this team has reasonable distance from the big guns."

Shoebox launched choppers and asked in a casual tone, "How good are you at close air support with smoke rockets?"

I tried to smile as I reached up to arm my second rocket pod. "What the hell else can go wrong?"

At five hundred feet during my third smoke rocket pass, a large red light labeled Rear Engine Fire illuminated on the top center of my instrument panel.

"Damn." I cursed, but the light stayed on.

I climbed, turned, and checked mirrors but detected no smoke trail. The rear engine instruments showed normal operation. "Shoebox, I think the team is in more trouble than we are. We'll hang around. Tell them to prepare for hard bombs."

Another Jupiter flight checked in, and I briefed them.

Two Cobras arrived and found an L.Z. for the team. The Cobra leader said, "I'm making my blades pop. Run to the sound." He flew a tight circle around a small clearing.

I switched my radio control panel and listened to the out-of-breath reply from the team leader.

The number two Cobra attacked the N.V.A. where my smokes were still drifting up from the green ocean of jungle canopy.

Jupiter number two made my day when he called a chip light. Animated Vietnamese chatter followed his announcement.

"A chip light is caused by metal in the oil supply," I told Shoebox. "Imminent engine failure. I have to send the A-Ones home."

With one eye on my red light, still bright on the center panel, I lobbed a rocket onto the Trail at the north end of those nasty Falls. "Jupiter flight, please dump all bombs in one pass and escort the wingman home."

"Roger, Covey. We can stay."

"No. Take your wingman home. Thank-you, Jupiter."

"Roger, we'll hit your smoke on the road. One pass."

"Thanks." Those Jupiter pilots were as tough as anyone who ever flew A-1s.

"We're a hundred meters out," the team leader called.

While the Cobras continued to fire on the N.V.A., two Hueys landed. When they lifted away with the team, the Cobras joined them.

Now the skies were clear, and the radios were silent. Only minutes earlier I heard tension, even desperation, in many voices here.

Pointed for home at two-thirty, I stared at the Rear Engine Fire Light. In a final angry gesture at the point of light that threatened our well-being, I thumped the damn thing.

It went out.

Chapter 10
Hippy Cowboy Two

February 1971

A Vietnamese N.C.O. in tiger-striped fatigues met me on the ramp at Kontum one morning. He wore a commando hat with one side pinned up and a light green silk scarf tucked under his collar. I smelled perfume.

I shook hands but looked over his shoulder at Sixpack. My eyes asked, "What the hell, over?" Sixpack answered, "Meet Hippy Cowboy Two. Have you read the paper, sir? Fifth Special Forces Group is leaving. You're flying with a seasoned trooper. He's done his time on the ground."

I nodded. "Hippy Cowboy Two?"

"Yes, sir. At your service."

"We have our callsigns. They have theirs." Sixpack smiled and shrugged.

We climbed aboard the Oscar Deuce and took off.

I missed flying with my American colleagues, but I soon learned a fearless soldier was behind Cowboy's permanent smile. He wanted to run everything and fly the airplane, too. We searched the sector for several hours. I assumed he was planning future infiltrations.

"Fly north." Cowboy looked at his watch. "We must insert a two-man team here." On his map he pointed to a deep valley at the northeast corner of Command and Control Central's area of operations.

"Helicopters should be safe enough in that area." I counted ridgelines and turned toward the target. "Very far from the Trail and the guns." A quiet L.Z. sounded like a great way to start the action. We could rehearse for operations later that required landing zones in range of the larger antiaircraft weapons.

Cowboy made some radio calls in his native language. Soon he pointed to a white single-engine airplane. "Cess-na one-eight-five."

I nodded. "VNAF?" I wanted to confirm the small Cessna belonged to the South Vietnamese Air Force.

He nodded and spoke more native words into his microphone.

The reconnaissance team's target area was a remote and rugged section of Laos. I spotted the only feasible landing zone--a grassy clearing at the bottom of a narrow rocky valley. The white Cessna flew down the valley then orbited north of the L.Z. and below our altitude.

Cowboy pointed south and resumed his Vietnamese conversation.

I recognized the large bulbous nose of the approaching Sikorsky H-34, an older helicopter in bright green paint. I remembered Marines at Danang calling this tall chopper the Shudderin' Shithouse.

The chopper descended to the treetops and landed in the valley. After a short pause, the H-34 lifted off and climbed out heading southeast. The white Cessna circled three times then flew away.

"Do you have an okay from the team?" I had to ask questions instead of making assumptions. Appearances could deceive.

"Yes," Cowboy said. "Team okay."

"We must refuel at Dak To. Then you can look for tomorrow's landing zones."

"Okay."

We flew briefly over Laos after the pit stop. Cowboy searched the jungle with his binoculars, but he didn't seem enthusiastic about the next day's plan. "Can we go to Kontum?"

"Sure." I pointed southeast. "What infantry unit do you come from?"

Cowboy turned and smiled. "Vietnamese Special Forces."

"I noticed your aftershave lotion smells very strong." In the span of a few hours I had gotten to know Cowboy well enough to broach that subject.

"Yes. Aftershave. Camp have no shower. Use aftershave."

"I see."

I pulled a tour as duty officer, glued to the Covey Alpha ops counter for twelve hours. I had to insure the paperwork was right for each sortie and handle incoming calls on the radio and phone. During mid-afternoon, I received a strange radio call.

"Covey Alpha, this is Covey five-three-three. I have an emergency."

"Roger. Go ahead." I looked at the schedule. The caller was a new guy on a solo visual reconnaissance of Cambodia. I had seen him hanging out with Major Major, but I didn't know him personally.

"My seat back is broken. It lays back flat."

"Well, climb into the right seat and finish the mission from there." I motioned Captain Skinny over and filled him in.

"I don't know if I can fly from the right seat." He seemed to moan his words.

"I know that guy," Captain Skinny said. "He's the kid with his nose up Major Major's ass all the time. I call him Lieutenant Major."

"Can you sit up straight and fly right from the left seat?"

"I'm not sure." More moaning.

"You be careful, y'hear?" I turned off the radio.

"Sir, you're not supposed to do that," my radio operator complained.

"No, he's not supposed to do that. I'll turn it on in a few minutes when my anger at this half-man subsides."

Lieutenant Major survived his ordeal and surprised me by not writing himself up for a Silver Star.

The next day at dawn I landed at Kontum and taxied to the parking ramp. I saw a jeep waiting, so I left the engines running. Hippy Cowboy Two climbed aboard. That fragrance hit me again.

"How are you?" I welcomed my smiling amigo.

"Fine." He shook my hand then strapped into the right seat.

We launched. "What would you like to do today, Cowboy?"

"We must pick up the team in the north."

"Sure." I called A-1s just in case.

Cowboy spoke Vietnamese on the radio as we approached the landing zone. He repeated his message several times. Finally, someone answered. After several lengthy conversations, he told me, "Helicopter will come in thirty minutes."

I checked my arming switches while we sailed around in circles. "Here comes the Cessna one-eight-five." I pointed to the small white airplane as it descended into the valley.

The tiny plane pulled up and circled below us. An H-34 arrived, landed for a moment, and took off.

I asked Hippy Cowboy Two, "Were both men okay?"

"No. Only one man come back."

"Only one? What happened to the other guy?"

Cowboy shrugged. "Maybe dead."

"Maybe dead . . . maybe dead? Can you be more precise?"

"No." Hippy Cowboy Two smiled.

"What happened to the other guy? Surely the survivor had some idea."

"We put in two. Get back one. Fifty-percent good, right?" He looked at me expectantly.

"You say the glass is half full. I say half empty." Maybe the guy defected, I told myself, or maybe he enjoys the jungle life.

"Survivor have bullet hole in hand." Cowboy smiled and touched his palm.

Maybe dead. "I have much to learn about your culture, Cowboy."

The following day, while flying over rolling hills in northern Cambodia, my right-seater, Hippy Cowboy Two, answered an excited Vietnamese caller on his radio. Then he told me, "Have three-man team. Ready to come out."

"Okay, but this area has lots of enemy soldiers. Let me call for air support." I passed coordinates in secure mode to the headquarters at Kontum.

"We'll launch some Cobras," the voice said. "Should reach you in thirty."

"Rog." I turned to Cowboy. "Can your helicopter be here in thirty minutes?"

"Yes. I tell him. Thirty minutes."

While we circled, I switched one F.M. radio to a frequency the Cobras commonly used. Through my binoculars I picked up a tiny human figure under the sparse jungle cover of the landing zone.

My radio came to life. I heard the Cobras planning their mission. "This is a Vietnamese operation. Things could get really screwed up. Let's not hang it out too far."

"Rog. We'll give them a good prep, then get the hell out."

I understood the Cobras saw nothing to die for in this Vietnamese operation. But I also sensed the Vietnamese weren't committed to these missions either. The culture gap loomed like an inscrutable encyclopedia I didn't have time to read.

I confirmed Cowboy's intercom was not set to listen to the Cobra's uncharacteristic conversation. In the past they had always hung it out. I advised my Vietnamese partner, "Tell your team to lie flat on the ground. Cobra gunships will attack on all sides."

He made a call, then passed a thumbs-up signal.

I briefed the Cobras when they checked in on the V.H.F. radio and cleared them hot when they reported the team in sight.

For five minutes they fired and turned and fired again. Rockets, grenades, and bullets slashed a wide fiery circle in the thin jungle around the team. Flames licked the outer edge of a thick black donut with the team in marshes in the middle. Then the Cobras departed.

"Cowboy, you may bring in your helicopter."

He nodded.

Soon the little white airplane showed up with the H-34 trailing. While the Cessna 185 circled, the green chopper recovered the team with no resistance.

On the Cobra's F.M. frequency, I said, "Thanks, guys. You did better work than I anticipated." I knew they'd get the job done.

They didn't acknowledge.

"We go home now?" Cowboy asked.

"Sure." Dare I ask? "Is the team okay?"

"Yes. Both soldiers okay."

"I thought you said the team had three men. Where's the other guy?"

"Maybe dead."

"Two out of three?"

"Not bad, huh?" Cowboy smiled.

After landing at Kontum, Cowboy and I waited for a jeep in the shade of my O-2. Watching a small white airplane turning onto final approach for landing, I wondered if the VNAF had more than one of these. Probably not.

After a nice landing, the Cessna taildragger swung around and taxied toward the ramp where we sat. The airplane turned off the runway onto a small taxiway three hundred feet away, then drove quite deliberately into a deep ditch.

Crunch. The engine stopped immediately. The right wing broke off at the root.

I joined a dozen helicopter crewmen who were sprinting to the scene. I counted six little guys, as we called the indigenous soldiers, climbing from the left door, which now opened skyward.

The first American to arrive asked the pilot, "Anyone else inside?"

"No. Everyone is safe."

"What happened?" I couldn't understand how he had hit the ditch. What the hell were six people doing in that small airplane? Probably cooking nucmam and rice, for all I understood of this culture.

The troops in the plane were participating in an accelerated training program. Too little and too late, I supposed, but the war had been going on forever. Like Alice in Wonderland, I was a stranger, reacting in awe to events the Vietnamese considered normal.

"After I land, I look inside at some papers," the pilot said. "Airplane go into ditch." With a sheepish grin he shook his head.

I walked to the Duck. *Holy shit. They can fly. They can accomplish the mission. But they can't taxi to parking.*

". . . a major test of Vietnamization."

I entered the vault as George, our intelligence officer, began his briefing to a crowd of Coveys crammed into the small room.

"The operation is called Lam Son Seven-One-Nine. Twenty thousand ARVN troops comprise the ground invasion force. They are attacking west, down French highway nine, into Laos. If they reach Tchepone, they'll cut the

Ho Chi Minh Trail."

"How do you rate their chances of success?" someone asked.

"They have all the American airpower they need. The White House says the mission is to eliminate sanctuaries and stockpiles in Laos that threaten remaining Americans during our pull-out."

"*Stars and Stripes* says protest marchers are out again in droves," O.K. Bryant said. "More non-support from the folks at home."

"Nixon probably calculated the political heat would be lower with no American ground troops involved." George showed his grasp of the politics involved.

"How will the operation affect us?" I asked.

"It already has. We were tasked to provide one O-Two airplane and two O.V.-Ten pilots. Art Moxon and Wayne St. John were volunteered by our commander. They're both great guys, but . . ." George scanned the room.

He's looking for field-graders. More political saavy.

"But the commander thought they were troublemakers."

"Art was accused of rearranging the bar furniture up onto the roof, but nothing was ever proved," I told O.K. over the chatter. "Later that night, his handwriting was found on the wall of the female latrine over at the Army infirmary."

O.K. shook his head. "The hospital has a ton of nurses, and they're both ugly."

"He's been here a long time." I tried to rationalize my friend's single crazy night.

"Too long, probably."

"Wayne asks a lot of crazy questions, but he's no troublemaker," I said.

"I think he drove the Covey van to the infirmary that night. Art was riding on top."

"I see."

When the buzz subsided, George continued. "FACs from all over Southeast Asia are using the Hammer callsign operating twenty-four hours a day from Quang Tri. Initial feedback is that the Hammer FACs are living in tents and using hot bunks. One guy gets up to go fly, and another crashes in his bunk after twelve hours in the air. Art reports a target-rich environment, and the invasion is going slowly but surely. The brass is still looking for volunteer ground FACs to move with the Vietnamese units."

"Driving a Jeep instead of an airplane? I don't think so," I said. "If I were stuck with visual recon of Cambodia, rather than Prairie Fire and night missions, I might go for a the thrill of riding a jeep into hell."

O.K. and I had to fly later that night, so we adjourned to quarters. We stopped for a soft drink in the hooch bar, where we encountered Captain

Skinny and Lieutenant Ecstatic, who were celebrating.

"What's up?" I asked.

"The wicked witch is dead." Captain Skinny had flown earlier and was finding his relaxed mode.

Lieutenant Ecstatic rarely drank alcohol, but he raised a beer can. "Major Major has left Pleiku. He got a job at N.K.P. with the Nail FACs."

"Yeehaa!" Captain Skinny sounded off.

"He made me write an Igloo White Mission Operating Instruction before he left."

I asked Ecstatic, "Why?"

"Because he fucked up one of those sorties and blamed me for his ignorance. I was the duty officer, and I placed the maps and photos with his mission equipment. You know, the picture where headquarters wants us to lay the truck-sensor string."

"I know," I said. "You're directed to fly as low as you have to go to find the objects in the photos . . . like individual trees that mark the beginning and end of the string. Then you have to hit them with smoke rockets."

O.K. joined in. "The fighters have to slow to three hundred knots, and they can't deliver in bumpy air. That's why they set Igloo White sorties for the still morning air. So, what did Major Major do?"

"Apparently he just found the rough coordinates and tossed in some rockets. Sensors were nowhere near where they were supposed to go. Rendered them useless."

I began to laugh. "Those things cost millions--state-of-the-art electronic sensors that look like jungle plants."

"Seventh Air Force was pissed," Ecstatic screamed. "And I took the blame."

"Even though the commander doesn't know half of the shit that idiot caused around here," I said, "he has to be happy to be rid of Major Major."

Captain Skinny raised his beer can. "He got a sedan out of the deal. Maybe he'll give his jeep to Major Boubek. Here's to the wicked witch."

"Which one?"

As the laughter subsided, a captain who was a former Strategic Air Command tanker pilot entered the bar and took the last empty seat on the far end of the couch. Tall and stocky with short auburn hair, Captain SAC had taken a strategic approach to the war by flying higher than any other FAC. We knew he was afraid, but he lived in denial. Anyone could become airsick by staring at the ground through binoculars for too long, but, with help from a sympathetic flight surgeon, Captain SAC had parlayed his airsickness into a long term grounding.

At the bar O.K. spoke in a low voice so he would not be heard at the couch across the noisy room. "In pilot training, they referred to airsickness as 'manifestation of apprehension.' A lot of guys washed out for M.O.A."

"Here." Captain Skinny said and handed me a green plastic helmet liner that normally would fit inside the steel helmet we wore during rocket attacks. He had drawn a goofy face on the front. On the back he also sent a message to our slacker captain. "Pass this to Captain SAC."

I tossed the helmet along. The Covey who caught the helmet looked at the drawing and passed it down the line. The amusement continued until the hat reached Captain SAC. He laughed at first then his face changed to terror. He tossed the hat down and left the room.

When the helmet stopped spinning on the floor, two words became visible. Captain Skinny had written "Jeep FAC."

Several days passed. I sat at a desk in the intel vault, studying reports of gun activity along the Trail, preparing for my next mission. "Today's been quiet. No gunfire in the past twenty-four hours."

"Probably because the weather's been awful for the last few days." George's assistant, a young airman, handed me another stack of reports.

O.K. Bryant walked into the vault. "Did you hear about Captain SAC?"

"No," I said. "What's he done now?"

"Flight surgeon found spots on his lungs. He's in the hospital at Cam Ranh."

"He probably stuck bubble-gum on his chest for the X-ray."

"He's gone," O.K. said. "He was no help here."

"You're back two hours early," I said. "Was the war getting too hot for you, too?"

"The thunderstorms were. Nasty green fire-breathin' monsters. You'll never see the ground. I'll call Seventh Air Force and give them a pilot weather report."

We walked to the duty desk. O.K. told the duty officer, "Hand me the Buffalo Chip hotline."

The lieutenant stood and handed O.K. a receiver from a phone marked Blue Chip.

"Good evening, Colonel . . . yes, sir . . . I just landed, and I suggest we weather-cancel the next sortie . . .yes, sir . . . yes, sir . . .." O.K. looked up with wide eyes.

"Am I canceled?"

"Nope. He hung up on me. Didn't want to know about the weather. Sorry."

"Thanks for trying," I said. "Sortie count for the Air Force is like body count to the Army. Makes us look like we're doin' something."

"FAC sorties are a lot cheaper than fighter sorties, too. Have fun." O.K. slapped me on the back and departed.

I took off at ten p.m. with Alfalfa aboard. We entered the clouds at a thousand feet and circled. "Let's stay over the field until we break out of the soup. If we turn northeast, we could cruise into a thunder cell and not know it until the aircraft starts bouncing aroound like a pinball."

"Rog. We're shakin' pretty good as is."

We broke out at ten thousand feet into a surreal world. Thunderstorms stood like a forest of huge green mushrooms. Lightning inside made the angry furnaces of energy flicker and flash. High purple death-clouds moved through the cumulus. White clouds below were sculpted in streaks and odd ripples by wind gusts and shears. A blinding finger of lightning blazed across the sky in front of us.

"This place reminds me of Carlsbad Caverns." Alfalfa had resigned himself to grinding out the mission, bad weather or not.

"We'd be a lot safer inside Carlsbad Caverns. Let's tell Moonbeam what's going on. They'll let us go home."

"Do it." Alfalfa leaned forward and confirmed the V.H.F. radio was set to the airborne command post frequency.

"Moonbeam, Covey Five-nine-one." No answer came, so I called again.

Alfalfa moved the squelch disable switch on the radio, deactivating a circuit that filtered out weak transmissions and background noises.

The radio began to hiss. "Sssssss. Covey Five-nine-one, this is Moonbeam. Sssssss."

"Those guys are probably orbiting over Thailand," Alfalfa said. "When a line-of-sight transmission is this poor, the source could be over Kansas."

"Moonbeam, Covey Five-nine-one. We're not going to win the war tonight. Haven't seen the ground since take-off."

"Roger. Anybody with common sense is indoors tonight. You're cleared home, Covey. Be careful."

On the first evening after my cycle of six night missions ended, we Prairie Fire pilots attended a party hosted by the Pleiku VNAF A-1 pilots, whose callsign was Jupiter. A hardy group with lots of combat time and high spirits, Jupiters welcomed us into their squadron building, where a long table set with white linen stretched the full length of a large room. The building had previously been the home of an American A-1 squadron. Pictures and trophies adorned the walls.

Shouldering cases of beer, we received a hearty welcome, not by name but by callsign. I felt immediately at home, and soon I sat down between Captain Skinny and Jupiter 21 with a traditional Vietnamese feast before us.

The squadron commander stood. "I am pleased to host our American brothers, who are so far from their loved ones at home. We appreciate your efforts against our common enemy--communism." He raised his glass. "To our friends, the Covey FACs."

"Hear, hear," everyone chimed. Some of our group stood and raised beer cans to their own tribute. From the far end of the table a voice shouted, "Fuck Communism."

The fun continued as delicious food arrived in waves. I enjoyed a sausage that floated in my tepid soup and melted in my mouth. I asked what kind of meat this delicacy was.

The A-1 driver seated next to me said, "Blood."

"That fact would account for the texture," I said.

One tough little guy called to me throughout the evening, raising his beer mug, "Covey Five-nine-one, you are cleared hot!"

I would rise and laugh and drink.

He carried on into the night, until I finally raised my empty glass and said, "Covey Five-nine-one is Winchester."

"Okay, you make dry pass."

The party wore on, and many accounts of the airstrikes shared in recent months were recounted with both FAC and fighter pilot versions. We adjourned from the table to the squadron lounge, a small room with a bar across one end. Pictures of A-1 Skyraider aircraft covered the walls. I learned that Jupiter 21 had been a flight leader on several strikes I had controlled.

"Five-nine-one," he asked, "do you remember the wingman who dropped the five-hundred-pound bombs one hundred meters from the friendlies?"

"He was supposed to be shooting rockets."

"Yes. He is sorry about his mistake." He motioned to a humble-looking Vietnamese lieutenant, who stepped up and offered his hand.

"We live and learn," I said, shaking the kid's hand. I walked with my Jupiter friend to a familiar face in the crowd. "Where have I seen you before?"

The young pilot had a receding hairline and a huge smile. "Jupiter two-six," he said, then moved his hands far apart. He brought them together like aircraft approaching head-on. Just before his fingertips touched, he moved his right hand down and away.

I remembered. "You're the guy who said hello to me a few weeks ago." I had first seen that smiling face up close from my O-2 cockpit. Focused on the helicopters below and right, I had looked to my left when I heard his engine. The huge A-1 had filled my windscreen then ducked under my flight path.

He extended his hand and laughed out loud, as though relieved when I shook his hand.

I joined his laughter. "You scared the shit out of me," I said. "Somehow the incident seems funny now."

"Tell me, Two-one, how do we bring the war to an end? When does peace return to your country?" Alcohol had lowered my inhibitions. Politics was not a proper bar subject, but that basic question burned in my mind.

My friend nodded. "The two Vietnams must become one."

"The obvious answer had escaped me. The gap between North and South Vietnam seems so huge. And neither country seems to have the military power and the political will to overwhelm the other."

"I do not know how or when, but the solution must be reunification."

I shook his hand and bade farewell. As I stumbled back to the Covey hooches, I remembered a *Stars and Stripes* article saying negotiators, after meeting in Paris a hundred times, had finally agreed on the shape of the table.

I arose the next afternoon, showered and went to see if coffee was brewing in the Hooch bar. I was scheduled for the ten p.m. mission over the Trail.

Captain Skinny nursed a glass of water at the bar. His flightsuit had sweat rings.

"Dawi Skinny." I used the Vietnamese word for captain. "You look groggy. Did you process all the beer from last night?"

"You left before they brought out the Skyraider cognac. They served it in little square bottles, like A-one sauce comes in. Smelled and tasted like the dregs from a fuel storage tank."

I shook my head and laughed. With baggy bloodshot eyes, my friend looked terrible.

"I had to hold my nose to get the stuff down. All I remember is climbing out of a ditch on the way back with Fat FAC." Captain Skinny referred to an O.V.-10 pilot who was large, not fat, but got the name anyway. "I think I'm going to give up drinking. Just go cold turkey."

"I do that every few months. How's Fat FAC doing?"

"He headed down to the flightline this morning, but I don't see how he could have flown. He's as embalmed as I am."

A familiar short figure entered the bar. With curly hair and a flightsuit bearing Army pilot wings, he strode to the refrigerator and took out a beer.

"Brillo," I said. "Where have you been?"

"Just returned from three weeks in Lam Son Seven-one-nine."

"Dawi Skinny, have you met the bravest or dumbest chopper pilot in

Vietnam?"

They shook hands.

"Sure feels good to be home." Brillo drained his beer.

"You'd better tell us about Lam Son before the beer starts talking," I said.

"I got shot down three times. Last time the fifty-cal round stopped in the webbing of my survival vest." He patted his left shoulder. "Lam Son was a shitty operation. During some of the last evacuations, we had to shoot ARVN troops off the skids to avoid crashing."

"Damn." I tried to imagine the hell my friend had survived.

"The Army brass who planned the initial invasion brought their Mekong Delta tactics up from Saigon. Waves of choppers flying at fifteen hundred feet were dog meat for the N.V.A. gunners in Laos. Over a hundred were blown away. On three different missions mine was the only chopper to come home. They finally let me do some of the planning. Things got better."

"Why did you volunteer?" Captain Skinny asked.

"Bad timing. I borrowed my commander's jeep. I brought it back just as he was ordered to provide volunteers."

"Welcome home, Brillo." I shook his hand again.

Chapter 11
Waiting for To Go

March 1971

Followed by a horde of Coveys, Ed entered the hooch bar after midnight.

I leaned on the bar and sipped coffee with friends before my two a.m. launch. "I know all of you didn't land in the last hour."

"Nope," O.K. Bryant said. "But Ed made a hell of a landing. Touched down minus most of his right wing."

The noise in the room subsided. Heads turned.

I expected Ed to speak, but he beamed a glad-to-be-alive smile and opened a beer.

"C'mon, Ed," someone said. "Let's hear the story."

Ed nodded. "One more time. I'm cleared to land, on final approach at about three hundred feet, you know, the point when the runway numbers become readable. I turn on my landing light, and all I see is helicopter."

Someone said, "Damn. Coming or going?"

"Head-on. Filled up my windscreen. We both broke left hard, but his blades caught my right wing."

"Damn." Murmured expletives broke the hush in the crowded room.

Ed continued. "I actually considered jumping out, but my chute never would've opened from that altitude. So I jammed in full rudder and aileron controls."

I pictured the huge former football player twisting the yoke and slamming his boot into the rudder pedal. I wondered if I could have responded as quickly.

Ed seemed unruffled--but quite happy to be alive. "The airplane rocked and buffeted, but stayed right-side up. The helicopter landed beside the runway."

O.K. added, "The tower guy said Ed wobbled to a landing. He's an old wobbler."

The crowd laughed nervously.

I remembered hearing tower call ground fire to me during my first solo night landing. I felt glad my warrior friend had survived. "You're lucky you didn't burn. The airport traffic pattern can be as dangerous as the Trail. Where did the chopper come from?"

Ed's demeanor showed a glad-to-be-alive euphoria. "He's with some Army unit out in the boondocks. Got completely lost. You know the old story, where the pilot asks for a practice direction-finding steer, and tower says, 'We don't do practice D.F. steers.' So the pilot says, 'Give me a real one.'"

Ed's joke carried the group back from the intense initial reaction.

"Approach Control brought him in directly opposite to Ed's landing direction," O.K. said. "Told him to contact tower and break left to Camp Holloway as he approached the runway."

"But he didn't break," Ed said. "He flew down the runway until I spotted him with my landing light."

After more laughter, O.K. asked, "Do you remember what they said at Theater Indoctrination School about helicopter pilot training? Before they graduate, some guy beats their fucking brains out."

Ed continued. "An Army colonel showed up. Blamed the whole thing on the helicopter pilot. Shook my hand and said he'd handle the problem."

"What can they do anyway, Ed?" I asked. "Make you a lieutenant and send you to Vietnam?"

Two hours later I crossed the fence with Covey AA, aiming to bash N.V.A. trucks. "Moonbeam, Covey Five-nine-one. On station with Alpha Alpha aboard."

"Roger. Contact Spectre Zero-seven on Tango frequency."

"Roger." I checked my code card and called Spectre, the A.C.-130 gunship, three times before he answered. I asked, "Where do you want to work tonight?"

"We'll stay south of Delta forty."

"Roger." I cruised to the north end of the sector and told my right-seater, "Keep your eyes open. Those gunships wander all over the place."

Alfalfa opened his window and stuck his night-vision scope into the wind. After an hour of searching, he called, "I have three trucks waiting to cross the river at the neck of the Dog's Head. The scope works great in the moonlight."

I called for air. "Hello, Moonbeam, Covey Five-nine-one has three trucks."

"Roger, Covey. Looks busy tonight." Moonbeam acknowledged, subtly indicating my target was small compared to the targets claimed by the Nails and Danang Coveys. I held the low hand in the TACAIR poker game.

Within five minutes I heard, "Jury, check. Two. Three. Covey Five-nine-one, this is Jury, three Alpha-Sevens."

I asked, "Are you here to work with me? I have three trucks." I had never heard such a prompt response to an air request. I thought he might be just passing through.

"We're coming out here as fragged."

"Sounds good enough to me. What's your lineup?"

"Three of the Navy's finest, two Rockeyes, and six Mark-eighty-twos apiece. Forty minutes of playtime." The fighters had launched from a carrier with two canisters of armor-piercing bomblets and six five-hundred-pound bombs on each airplane. Also, relative to the typical flight of F-4s, they had lots of gas.

I gave them a full briefing.

"We're over your Dog's Head in the river. Ready."

I carefully eased my gunsight down to where the southbound Trail intersected the dog's neck.

Bam.

My rocket worked as advertised.

"Hit my smoke. I'll hang south of the target at base minus one."

"One's in." Jury leader dropped his Rockeye bomblets on my smoke. Four square fires blossomed amid the sparkling shower of tiny bombs. Ten red tennis balls rose.

I turned so Alfalfa could scan the target.

"Four Alka-Seltzer tablets," Alfalfa said. "Rockeye is dissolving four trucks."

"Two's in."

"Same place," I said. "Cleared hot."

Two hit the same place. Ten more tracers arced up at us and burst with an audible rumble. "Nice job, two. Break. Three, move your Rockeye a hundred meters north, up along the road."

Number three hit exactly where I asked. Three more trucks flared. Fifteen tennis balls rose and burst over the target.

I told Alfalfa, "The angle of these tracers tells me the gun is sitting about one klick west of the target. What do you think?"

"I concur. He's the only shooter at the moment."

On the radio I said, "Jury leader, we see seven trucks burning. Would you like to try and silence this gun?"

"Affirmative. We have thirty minutes left."

"Can you drop singles until we get close?" I'd use one bomb per pass, then go for the kill with whatever the fighters had left when we zeroed in on trigger-happy Nguyen.

"No problem. Ready for your mark."

I turned to Alfalfa again. "The tracers start burning about a thousand feet out of the gun barrel, so I figure he's west of the first ridge."

Alfalfa nodded as I rolled in on my best guess of the gun location.

Bam. My rocket became an orange dot. More tracers knifed into the black sky. Five strings of five.

I passed a correction to Jury leader. "Five hundred meters west of my smoke. You're cleared random attacks. Stay above base altitude."

The fighters took spacing so they could aim in reference to the previous bomb, whose glow would last about ten seconds. The gunner, instead of quitting for the night, took the challenge and fired twenty, then thirty rounds at each attack. Red tennis balls filled the sky.

I told Alfalfa, "This guy's shooting everywhere. Keep your eyes open."

But the A-7s' bombs crept steadily closer.

"I think I saw muzzle flashes," I said. "I'll try to mark 'em." A drop of sweat rolled down my forehead and stung my right eye as I rolled up and over.

Bam.

Turning hard away, I watched a tracer stream streak to the spot from where I had fired the rocket. I rolled out. "That sonovabitch is aggressive."

Alfalfa leaned forward and looked out my window as the fiery balls drew silent red lines a hundred feet behind and to our left. "Fucking deadly game. Let's kill this guy."

"Jury's ready."

"Roger," I said. "Go fifty meters south of my smoke. Drop all your bombs."

"Leader's in."

"Cleared hot."

Tracers came up in strings of five. Five came, then five more, then two tracers at the same instant four five-hundred-pound bombs exploded.

"Did you see that?" Jury leader sounded excited.

"Nice bombs," I answered. "He only fired two rounds from his last clip. Two, drop yours on the south edge of leaders. Three, set up on the west edge."

A-7s numbers two and three cleaned their wings with no response from the ground.

"We're winchester, Covey." Jury leader called, indicating he was out of ammunition.

"Roger. Your bombs hit the target every time. I'm amazed."

"Thanks. The computer does most of the work. Good targets and good marks."

"Rog. I showed you on target at zero-one-ten and off at one-forty. One hundred percent of your ordnance was on target. We counted seven trucks destroyed, and one twenty-three-millimeter gun silenced. I believe you destroyed the gun, but we can't claim it without photographic proof."

"Fun working with you, Covey. Do you think you could get a hop out to the U.S.S. Hancock?"

"I'd love to, and I'll ask, but my boss is not of our cloth. Thanks again."

"Rog. Jury, go button five." The flight leader directed a radio frequency change.

"Two."

"Three."

Alfalfa took another look at the burning trucks. "This computerized bombing will up the ante on the Trail. The N.V.A.'ll have to drag missiles down here to stop the A-Sevens."

I turned north. "I've heard about Rockeye, but tonight's my first glimpse of the real thing. That shit really eats trucks."

Alfalfa peered into the darkness for well over an hour. "I've got six trucks at the Red Cliffs. They stopped as we flew by. Appears the drivers left their lights on and ran."

"Moonbeam, Covey Five-nine-one has six trucks."

In the early hint of dawn Alfalfa checked his watch. "We're almost outa time. Let's pass this one to the dawn patrol O.V.-Ten."

I rogered him as the radio began to chatter.

"Moonbeam, Spectre Zero-seven is firin' up six trucks north of Delta forty."

"He's right on top of us," Alfalfa said. "Let's get outa here."

"Spectre seven, Covey Five-nine-one is underneath you. Hold your fire."

Spectre did not acknowledge my call.

"That asshole was supposed to stay south tonight," Alfalfa said.

"Moonbeam, Nail Five-seven. Any word on my A-Sevens?"

I laughed and hooted on the intercom as we listened for the reply.

"Nail, Moonbeam, negative. They haven't checked in yet."

"You hijacked his airstrike," Alfalfa said, smiling. "Jury flight was on its way to work with the Nail. They called you for advisory purposes only."

"Roger that, partner. Eeeah! Those Nails have outbid me too many times not to enjoy this moment." I moved my thumb to the microphone switch.

"Moonbeam, Covey Five-nine-one has B.D.A. for Jury flight."

Alfalfa laughed.

"Go ahead, Covey," Moonbeam replied.

"On at ten past one. Off at four-zero." I passed encoded target coordinates with detailed B.D.A. "Also, please add a comment those A-sevens did excellent work. We're R.T.B."

"Roger, Covey Five-nine-one."

I set the nose ten degrees right of the pending sunrise, trimmed for level flight, and enjoyed a huge yawn. "I'm exhausted. How're you doing?"

Alfalfa shook his head. "My eyeballs ache from this unnatural schedule."

"I know. The fatigue never goes away."

"Yeah. When I get home, I'm going to sleep for a fucking year."

Alfalfa and I popped beer tops in the hooch bar at seven a.m.

A new captain brewed coffee. "You guys always start this early?"

"First of all, we earned these beers," Alfalfa said. "Secondly, if you're an O-Two driver, you'll learn the hour is late, not early. I'm Ron. Call me Alfalfa."

"Mark." He extended his hand. A handsome dude--tall and slim with blue eyes--his brown hair met military length restrictions but just barely.

I shook his hand and asked, "Where are you from?"

"I used to fly tankers."

"Oh shit, another SAC guy," Alfalfa said, sounding facetious. "Our first Strategic Air Command pilot grew spots on his lungs to avoid flying combat missions."

"Yeah. I've heard. Six months ago I was passin' gas on a Young Tiger rotation over here. I refueled a bunch of one-o-fives coming off targets in North Vietnam. We had turned for home when a lone fighter called. Said he had to refuel or jump out. So we gave him some gas."

"Sounds reasonable," I said.

"Our tanks in the fuselage were empty. I used fuel from a five-thousand-pound reserve tank up front. We're not supposed to touch that tank, because its weight keeps the tail from dragging on landing."

"So did you drag your tail on the runway?" I asked.

"Nope. I got a letter of commendation from the fighter wing commander and a letter of reprimand from the SAC wing commander."

"Really?" The new guy captured my full attention.

"I was holding one in each hand when I decided to put in my resignation papers. The Air Force doesn't pay me enough to deal with that kind of chickenshit."

"But you had a year left on your commitment, and they gave you an Oscar Duck."

Captain Mark nodded. "How'd you know?"

"A captain at Danang got the same deal when he resigned."

"The Crazy Man?" Mark had just come from the Danang checkout program.

"Yeah." I laughed when I remembered my first flight in Vietnam. Somehow that time seemed like years ago instead of months.

Alfalfa told Mark about our adventures with Jury flight and the mad gunner at the Dog's Head. "We must've killed him. The bombs interrupted his five-round clip."

"I'm not sure the Air Force pays enough to do that shit either."

"We don't do it for the pay," I said. "We do it for the fun." I couldn't believe I had said those words. I laughed at myself.

Mark laughed, too. "So, how often do you enjoy being shot at?"

"Actually, the gunners react to only three situations. When you offer an irresistible target, they'll take a shot. Unless you fly Prairie Fire, your tactics will keep you ninety-nine percent safe from those situations."

"What's number two?"

"When they don't want you to see something on the ground, they'll try to drive you off with gunfire. They stick a few tracers in your face, hoping you'll go away."

"And the third scenario?" Mark asked.

"You mean tonight's scenario," I said. "If they have the ammo, they'll always shoot when you attack them."

Alfalfa added, "The unwritten laws of triple-A discipline allow us to weave around inside their effective range to do our job of observing. When gunners give away their position, they get bombed. So they need a good reason to shoot. I agree with the distinguished asshole's three-situation rule."

"I'm not sure I want to become as hard-core as you two. The airlines would never hire me." Mark joined our laughter and raised his coffee cup.

"Another Crazy Man?" I said. "I think you'll fit in nicely."

"Holy shit. I need a drink." My old friend, Ken Blutt, entered the crowded bar the following evening with Major Reed. "I think we hit a U.F.O."

His words silenced the room.

"A what?" someone asked.

"A fucking hard object of some kind." Blutt sounded serious. "We were on TACAN final. We put the gear down, when boom. We hit something. I started a missed approach, but the engine instruments were all normal, so I landed."

With mussed hair and collar standing up Major Reed looked shaken. "We hit something. I'm dead certain. We couldn't find any damage to the airplane. I'm too short for this shit." The major banged a bottle of V.O. whiskey down on the bar. He pulled the tiny yellow ribbon with blue edges from the bottle and tied it to his watchband.

"What's that?" a voice in the crowd asked.

"My Short ribbon. Means I have less than a month to go. Maybe it'll change my luck." He held his arm out and admired his handiwork. Then he glugged his glass full.

Ken and Reed drank and re-told their story into the night, pondering an ominous list of solutions to their very real mystery.

I watched and listened, adding nothing. I knew danger lurked in the traffic pattern.

The next morning I began a duty officer tour at six.

A tall N.C.O. from our flightline maintenance unit walked up to the operations desk at seven. "I think I found the answer to the U.F.O. problem." He held out his hand.

"What's that?" I asked.

"Rice plants, I think. Found them on the wheels of the plane that hit the U.F.O. Looks like your buddies did a touch-and-go out in the boonies last night."

"Damn." I referred the gentleman to Ed's office.

Several hours later, a groggy Blutt arrived with pale Major Reed. He shook his head and smiled. "We misread our altimeter by a thousand feet. Touched down in a rice paddy about a mile out. Must have bounced real high to clear the dike."

"Are you sure?"

"We drove out and found our tire marks in the mud," Major Reed said. "The mystery's solved, but I don't feel any better. I now know we came within inches of dying. Fucking inches."

I felt a chill. "I'm glad you're alive."

Ken and the major walked away mumbling.

Near the end of my twelve-hour tour as duty officer, I noticed the unopened black briefcase stuffed with official paperwork from the day's Danang run lying on the edge of the radio operator's desk. The ops building had become quiet, so I opened the pouch. Placing letters in official mailboxes would pass the last boring hour of my duty day.

On top of the stack of paperwork was a new PIF. The Pilot Information File was required reading for pilots before each flight. I read the letter carefully. At first I thought I had found a fake document, but the signature matched the existing PIF letters. Marks from the copying machine matched marks from the old PIFs.

Since O.K. Bryant piloted the last mission of my desk tour, he could decide about the new PIF's authenticity. I posted it before he arrived at the counter to sign out.

"What the shit is this?" O.K. laughed as he read. "Jettison Procedures for the Piddle Pack. Are you serious?"

The PIF referred to a square polyurethane bag, six inches on a side, used for male urination during flight. The bag had expandable sides and a long neck.

O.K. shook his head and read key phrases from the directive. "A Daily Piddle Pack Jettison Report will be submitted to Seventh Air Force, giving eight-digit coordinates for the jettison location."

"Sounded strange to me, too," I said. "Two-thousand-pound bombs only require six-digit reporting."

"Prevailing winds will be logged," O.K. continued, "as well as clearance authority for jettison. You mean we'll have to ask permission from Moonbeam to pee?"

"I can only imagine the radio traffic on this subject." I laughed and shook my head. The PIF was surely a fake--but a brilliant one. The list of rules paralleled real bombing restrictions and rules of engagement issued by micromanaging politicians.

"Here's the best part," O.K. said. "Pilots will report the weight of jettisoned piddle-packs. Weight will be derived from the amount the neck of the bag stretches in a four-g pull."

"I had trouble visualizing that one."

"Look, they attached a chart with inches on one side and grams on the other."

"The letter's got to be fake. Should I leave it in the file?"

"Of course," O.K. said. "Let the colonel rip it out if he wants."

After dinner at the club, I adjourned to the bar and told Elf and a group of Coveys about the PIF.

"I heard about that letter this afternoon from a friend at Danang," Elf said. "Some guy they call Crazy Man did it."

I asked, "How did they find out?"

"They caught him red-handed faking another one. Something about Inspecting Toilets for Communist Snooping Devices."

The next afternoon I was burning my third load of avgas with Sixpack, the rider I had teamed with in my Prairie Fire initiation. American green berets had returned to flying duties after Vietnamization of the program had failed. We spent a sweaty morning inserting teams into dangerous lands. Now we babysat--waiting for the inevitable call for help. An O.V.-10 was at work over Laos. In our O-2 we covered Cambodia.

I asked, "Are you glad you'll get to finish your tour?"

"I dunno. I've done three years here. I was kinda lookin' forward to going home. Back in North Carolina I have a beautiful Mossberg shotgun--"

"Mayday, mayday, mayday. Yellowjacket Two-one just lost oil pressure. I'm fifty miles west of Pleiku at twenty grand."

"That call is from an F-One-hundred," I told Sixpack. "He's directly overhead with an engine that'll seize up any second now. I don't know if those jets can fly without hydraulics." I switched my U.H.F. transmitter to Guard frequency."Yellowjacket, Covey Five-nine-one is directly below you, if you have to jump out."

Sixpack and I searched the holes between scattered clouds overhead for signs of the distressed airplane.

"Thanks, Covey. I think I can make Pleiku. I'll set up a flame-out pattern."

"Good luck." I resumed listening watch over the teams, since the voice sounded like a typical fighter pilot--everything under control.

Sixpack educated me about his guns and knives back home while we completed our mission and the sun sank. "All teams report okay. I'm staying at Pleiku tonight."

Taking his hint, I flew east and began my descent. "Pleiku tower, Covey Five-nine-one, five miles west for landing."

"Roger, Covey. Pleiku is closed." The controller's voice sounded unsteady.

"What's up, tower? This Covey is outa gas as usual."

"The runway has pieces of aircraft debris everywhere."

I was curious about that remark, but my fuel tanks were empty. I had to land now. "Kontum has no lights. I'm out of options. Is any portion of the runway useable, or do I have a go at the taxiway?"

"Can you stop in the first two-thousand feet of runway two-seven?" The controller sounded stronger now.

"Affirmative. I'll clear at the first turn-off. Gear down. Thanks." I dropped full flaps, slowed to minimum run approach speed, and turned to final approach. As I touched down, I saw trucks and people in the lights at the far end of the runway. In the low jungle growth beyond the end of the runway, a slightly worse-for-wear F-100 rested next to a fire truck.

Elf greeted us at the door of the ops building. "You missed the big show."

"Maybe you did. We logged eleven hours of Prairie Fire."

Elf smirked. "An F-One-hundred came in with his engine out. He was haulin'--fast as hell on final. When he touched down, his nose gear collapsed, and that big air scoop scraped the full length of the runway."

"Damn."

"Took out the arresting cable. Snapped the thing like string. Sparks and airplane bits flew everywhere. His tires were smokin' when he went off the end of the runway."

"I saw the jet sitting in the boonies. Is the pilot okay?"

"He's dead. The airplane got airborne off that first little hill off the end of the runway, and the pilot ejected but was too low for his chute to deploy."

"I talked to him when he lost oil pressure--not ten minutes before he died, I guess." My parachute suddenly weighed a hundred pounds. "Fuck this place."

I grabbed a beer at the hooch bar and took a couch seat next to wild man Nick. "I don't think I congratulated you for shouting down Major Major a few weeks ago."

"Thank you," Nick replied. We klinked beer cans. "Say, I've heard your name mentioned as an instructor candidate."

"Don't butter me up, Nick. First of all, I have a Raven application pending. Secondly, everybody knows instructors give up flying Prairie Fire. No, thanks."

"I know. I miss those good missions. Most days I just drone around Cambodia."

"Ask the schedulers to fly you a two or three-day P.F. cycle. Ed and Elf both understand. What else is brewing?"

"The commander wants us to fly some contractor named Henckley to Ubon. He's that creepy old man who sits at the end of the bar. You know--he's always talking to himself."

I nodded. "He's a know-it-all asshole. He talks down to everyone."

"Right," Nick said. "He doesn't deserve an Ubon trip ahead of our maintenance guys, and the lieutenants question the legality of flying a civilian."

"If he's a contractor, why doesn't he buy a plane ticket?"

"This issue is really about the commander. Why is he so damn anxious to fly this civilian?"

After a short Prairie Fire day, I called the Group Headquarters in Cam Ranh, and spoke with Major Jerry Lippold, who had left Pleiku shortly after I arrived. Still a good guy, he said he'd try to slip my Raven application to the top of the pile.

I was ready to go to the bar on that bit of news, when the duty officer intercepted me. He handed me the van keys. "Go bring the troops down from the hooches. Ed's returning from his last mission in thirty minutes."

We unloaded the van in time to see an O-2 appear from the setting sun for a pass down the runway at a hundred feet. Oscar Deuce drivers cheered as Ed exaggerated his pull up to downwind, and turned to the runway for the last time.

A fire truck pulled up, and Coveys manned several hoses for the fini-flight tradition. I stood with my camera in the crowd next to O.K.

I asked, "Do I see Henckley getting out of Ed's O-Two?"

"Yeah," O.K. said. "Ed said the hell with the controversy and took him to Ubon."

"He killed an issue which was dividing the squadron, and he pulled the boss off our backs."

The lieutenants with the hoses attacked Henckley viciously. The old coot held his suitcase up as a shield, but a second hose crew flanked him. The water weapons knocked off his glasses and blew him to the ground. They kept the pressure on him until Ed climbed down from the right door--the O-2's only door.

Ed took his shower with a smile and waved a champagne bottle to the crowd. Then, the entourage boarded the van for the trip to the hooches.

As the driver, I initiated the next traditional event. "We're approaching the gate."

Like a true maestro, Ed led the chorus in a gradual crescendo. Starting with his hands near the floor, he raised them slowly. The troops intoned, "Ahhh," louder and louder as we approached the gate. The rising tones drew the attention of the Vietnamese guard. The American cop folded his arms. He'd seen this act before.

Twenty cynical college graduates screamed, "Ahhh," as loud as they could, until Ed slapped his hand down. The voices now screamed, "Fuck!"

The Vietnamese guard dropped his rifle like he'd been shot.

The American shook his head.

I laughed all the way to the hooches.

Henckley reveled in Ed's spotlight. "Why, I never expected you guys to hose me down. Made me feel like one of the boys. Heh, heh, heh." His ranting disgusted people who already carried anger for the nasty old coot.

I parked the van, and the crowd moved like a noisy herd to the bar.

Henckley carried his suitcase to a room in a nearby building.

An hour later I was drawn to that building by the flashing red lights of an ambulance and police vehicles. I spotted O.K. in the small crowd. "What's up?"

"Somebody rolled a tear gas grenade into Henckley's room."

I asked, "Is he all right?"

"Yeah. A green beret in the next room smelled the fumes and rescued the old bastard. Then he noticed an open suitcase on Henckley's bed--full of cash."

"Greenbacks?"

"Yep. Apparently he cashed a lot of checks in Ubon, and planned to triple his money on the black market, buying Vietnamese piasters, then converting to M.P.C., and his bank account. The Military Payment Certificate exchange rate is fixed, but dollars bring up to five times as much."

"The lieutenants were right. Henckley's a crook."

"Holding green is a strict no-no even for civilians in-country," O.K. said. "They're supposed to use M.P.C. like we do. Several months ago the green beret--the one who saved him--was on a team that ambushed a small N.V.A. convoy moving north. They were hauling dollars to Hanoi."

I shook my head. "Black market dollars go north to buy bullets."

We watched the police take Henckley away in handcuffs.

"Just between you and me," O.K. said, "seeing this little drama makes me wonder what kind of deal this jerk had with our commander."

At six the next evening I ran up my Oscar Deuce for take off. Alfalfa sat beside me as I made the standard call. "Covey Five-nine-one will be climbing over the field, blacked out to fifteen hundred feet."

"Roger, unable to approve blacked-out operations in our airdrome."

"Say again."

"Pleiku Tower is unable to approve blacked-out operations in our area of operations."

"Roger that, but be advised this aircraft has an intermittent electrical system tonight." I put my left hand on a switch that would extinguish all lights and turned to Alfalfa. "Sing out if you see tracers."

He nodded.

We rolled and my stomach churned with anger at one of the dumbest things I had heard and could not ignore. I circled tightly over the field without apparent incident, and called, "Tower, Covey Five-nine-one is departing your area and frequency."

"Roger."

My anger won a battle with my common sense. I added, "Have another cup of coffee."

Alfalfa laughed. "You're a little brutal tonight."

"No more brutal than their stupid rules. The first ground fire I saw was in the traffic pattern. Damn. I thought we had a mutual admiration thing with the comm guys."

"Why not say whatever they want to hear, but do what you have to do?"

"No wonder you're a captain, and I'm a lieutenant."

We had a routine night on the Trail, finding and harassing several trucks without great effect on the outcome of the war. I flew well clear, as Gunfighter One-one, a flight of F-4s, tried to strike triple-A positions at the Falls.

The aggressive leader took control. "I'm, turnin' my lights on, two. Get ready. I'm in."

"Roger." Number two sounded stressed--like a brand new lieutenant.

Thirty tracers rose in strings of five.

"Leader's off. Roll in on the gun, Two."

"I don't have you in sight any more . . .. I'm off dry."

Alfalfa and I laughed.

"Okay, Two, move in closer and keep me in sight."

"Roger." Heavy breathing followed his words.

"One is bright-flash with the lights, rolling in."

Forty tracers rose up at the flashing lights on the F-4.

"Get 'em, Two."

"I lost you, leader. Two's off dry."

After a long pause, Gunfighter leader said, "Two, turn on your lights."

Alfalfa said, "I give the leader an A for effort."

As we departed the area, we monitored another incident, unfolding on Moonbeam's frequency.

"Moon-beam, Stinguh requests ahR-Tee-Bee. We jest lost a jet engine." The A.C.-119K model gunship had a jet engine added to each wing. The pilot sounded like a Tennesseean.

"Roger, Stinger. We understood you only used the jets during take-off."

"Roguh that, Moonbeam. But we realluh lost this one. A twenty-three just cleaned it right off the wing. It's layin' on the ground up by Delta forty-one."

Moonbeam called, "You're cleared to R.T.B."

We laughed and joked during the cruise home.

Lieutenant Ecstatic was the duty officer and met me with the question, "What did you tell tower before you left the area?"

I had forgotten the blacked-out ops discussion by now. "What do you mean?"

"A tower controller called in tears saying they were only complying with some letter of agreement."

I doubted the tears part, but I called the tower to investigate. "This is Covey Five-nine-one. I understand you called my squadron."

"Yes, sir. Your remark about the coffee hurt some feelings up here."

"Your policy threatened my life. Your feelings are not my top priority."

"I understand, sir. I called earlier to tell you we were only implementing a letter of agreement your commander signed."

Now the real problem came into focus. "Can I come and read the letter?"

"Please do."

I drove out to the tower and climbed up to the cab. "You guys called out the first ground fire I saw over here. What's the deal?"

"Here's the letter, sir. Your commander signed it."

"Do you have a carbon copy I could take and show the other pilots?"

"Sure."

Chapter 12
Going . . .Going . . .

March 1971

More than a dozen lieutenants looked up when our tired-looking commander visited the lieutenants' sanctum sanctorium for the first time. Gray, stocky, and wrinkled, the boss stopped inside the door twenty feet from the refrigerator where I stood and spoke softly to a nearby lieutenant.

The hooch bar fell silent.

Someone had told me the boss' last job was as a scheduler at Military Airlift Command Headquarters. I pictured him standing in front of a large wall of plexiglas with a grease pencil in hand, trying to control a worldwide fleet of trash-haulers, flown by crews who didn't know he existed.

The buzz of conversation gradually returned.

I squelched it when I asked, "Did you come here to explain the letter of agreement you signed with the tower? The one where we have to leave our lights on at night?" I reached down for the piece of paper that had smoldered in my flightsuit pocket for the past twenty hours.

"We all know flying around without lights isn't safe. Heh-heh-heh."

Nobody joined his forced laughter.

"Colonel, I respectfully disagree. Having been shot at the only time I tried to land with lights on, I'd say the opposite is true."

"Heh-heh."

I felt my temperature rise as the old fart grinned. I took a short step onto my soapbox. "Do you mean if we have our lights on, and we get shot down, then our death is an acceptable combat loss? But a lights-off loss is a non-combat accident that threatens your career. Do we understand you correctly?" I felt angry enough to kill, but I took strength from using we--the collective pronoun.

Fifteen sets of angry eyeballs turned the room cold.

The commander stepped back to the door and departed, as if propelled. He had stayed near the door. Maybe he anticipated a quick exit.

I passed the letter around. "All bullets will be ignored, by order of the commander. I told the tower guys I planned to blow off this bullshit procedure. They agreed."

O.K. Bryant smiled and nodded. "I'd say you pissed him off pretty good."

"I spoke the truth. I was not rude. His staff may fear him, but I don't. I'd say the same words to a general officer if our commander wants to convene a court martial." I could understand how some officers got grenades rolled into their tents.

"Short of bringing charges, he could still fuck up your career."

"Career, hell. I'm a citizen-soldier. I joined the Air Force out of an immediate necessity to avoid the infantry. If all commanders are as full of horseshit as he is, I'll leave when my commitment ends."

"Why don't you say what you really mean?" O.K. joked, but I bit.

"We both know he's never flown a night mission. He doesn't fly combat, day or night. He makes rules that threaten our lives. Who's the fuckin' enemy here anyway?"

"You're preachin' to the choir," O.K. said. "We're worried about you."

Nick walked over with Sixpack. "I've got a bone to pick with you, asshole. You nearly got me killed. What do you think of that?" His dark wild eyes--slightly glazed by booze--stared down at me.

"I have no idea what you're talking about." I smiled and shook hands with Sixpack, who was radiating an alcohol glow.

"A few days ago," Nick said, "when I was bitchin' about not flying Prairie Fire missions any more, you said to ask the schedulers if I could fly a P.F. cycle. You said they'd understand." He smoothed his mustache, which stuck out in all directions from his upper lip.

I realized Nick was being funny. My anger subsided. "I remember now."

"I did. And they did."

"I gather you flew a good one today?"

"Good? I couldn't do shit for good, because of the fuckin' guns. They're everywhere."

I nodded. "We could use some B-Fifty-two strikes on a few choice interdiction points."

"They destroyed a Huey at the Falls. Two good guys got killed. I ran outa fuckin' rockets tryin' to shut down the damn guns." Nick made rocket passes with his hands.

Sixpack touched my arm. "Sir, today I accepted the fact I was going to die in an airplane. Lieutenant Nick was divin' and yankin' around the sky. He started marking gunners using his wing as a pointer. We were so low I made eye-contact with one of those N.V.A. bastards."

"Another Huey landed to pull the bodies from the downed bird." Nick shook his head. "Then, a Cobra took a twenty-three millimeter round in the rocket pod--peeled it open like a banana. Pilot made it home with four hundred holes in his chopper. His gunner took an A.K.-forty-seven slug in the knee."

"Lieutenant Nick did good." Sixpack raised his beer. "He got right in the middle of things--kinda like you just did with your commander."

A slim captain with brown hair and brown eyes greeted me at the squadron the next morning. He wore the patches of an evaluator from the 20th TASS headquarters at Danang. "Are you ready for your no-notice hundred-and-eighty-day checkride?"

"Sure. I've got nothing better to do." I had a lot of better things I could do.

He briefed me, then we launched. When I located the Ho Chi Minh Trail in the southern panhandle of Laos, the tactical portion of the check ended.

My evaluator said, "Let's go try some instrument approaches."

I rolled my eyes, but looked straight ahead.

An hour later we had climbed from completing another instrument low approach when the captain pulled the power on the front engine. "I'm simulating you lost your front engine. Recover."

"Okay," I said. "The front engine runs the hydraulic pump, so we can't lower the landing gear normally."

The captain nodded.

I removed the cover from a handle on the floor between our seats. "Pump."

The captain's jaw dropped.

"If I were solo," I said, "I'd unfeather the front prop so it would windmill the gear down. But I'm not. I think the technical order says three hundred good strokes will lock the gear down." I looked at him, then the handle, then back at his bewildered face.

The captain worked the handle. A trickle of sweat rolled down his nose.

"Tower, Covey Five-nine-one needs to extend the downwind pattern." I turned to the captain. "You have to pump harder."

"Roger, Covey. You're cleared."

The captain shook his head, groaned, and pumped. He grunted and toiled for five minutes, until green lights indicated the gear was down and locked.

I turned to the runway. "Covey Five-nine-one, gear down, low approach."

"Cleared low approach."

I descended until I could assure a safe touchdown and began a go-around.

Now drenched, the captain sighed. "I have the aircraft."

I hid my amusement as I passed him control of the plane.

We climbed out. The captain pushed both throttles to full power and turned north. He circled over a lake at the foot of low mountains. "All you had to do was unfeather the front engine. That hand pump is for emergencies only."

"I know. But I've heard of propellers that wouldn't unfeather, or wouldn't feather again after the gear was down."

"Those stories are bullshit." The captain pulled the front engine mixture lever all the way back.

The front engine died. When the captain pulled the propeller lever back, the prop stopped turning and aligned like a knife edge--feathered--into the relative wind.

"Now, watch." The captain slammed down the gear handle and pushed the prop lever to full increase. The propeller began to spin, and after ten seconds green lights flashed on the panel. He pulled the lever and the propeller stopped again. "Voila."

"Okay. I take your point. The stories are probably only rumors." I wanted to add I was only having fun at his expense, but I didn't. He had shut down an engine in a combat zone. He wasn't a warrior, but he knew the airplane.

The next day I flew the Danang run with Alfalfa. Cruising east approaching Chu Lai on the coast, we enjoyed good visibility with scattered clouds above and below us.

"Look," I said. "We have a bogey at ten o'clock low?" I pointed to a twin-engine transport, painted in brown and green camouflage passing left to right.

"Yeah. A C-Seven. Looks like he'll cross the TACAN station same time as we will."

I started a left turn and watched the C-7 in a right turn below us.

Suddenly the large airplane reversed to his left and brought his nose up.

"Do you believe that trash-hauler is trying to sneak up behind us?"

"Can't let that happen." Alfalfa leaned forward and looked left.

I rolled inverted and let the nose fall, aiming at the C-7 cockpit. "Don't fuck with the FAC, boy. If I fired a rocket now, you'd eat it."

The C-7 rolled to the west.

I pulled out of my steep dive and headed north. Just to be sure, I looked behind and below. "He's coming back for more."

The C-7 had continued a hard right turn, raising his nose to intercept our course.

I let the pesky trash-hauler close to half a mile, then I jammed in full left rudder and up elevator. The airplane pitched over to the left. Inverted, nose up, and pointed west, we watched the C-7 pass below. I pulled back on the controls and slid down behind him. "I'll hang behind him until he points west again."

"He's got spirit," Alfalfa said.

"True, and no cargo."

The C-7 turned hard right, but I pulled and rolled to stay on his tail. He reversed his turn hard, but I hung on. I flew lazy-eights behind him, placing my gun sight on the pilot, then rolling over to nail the copilot. "Wish I had my camera."

The C-7 rocked his wings and turned west.

I rocked mine and turned north.

"Weather looks shitty up toward Danang." Alfalfa opened the approach book.

"Yeah. We'll do the TACAN penetration to a radar-controlled final." I was reviewing the procedures when something flashed to our east.

Alfalfa said, "Did you see that?"

"I thought I saw a parachute with red and white panels. I'll call approach." I mashed the mike button and said, "Danang Approach Control, Covey Five-nine-one. We're twenty miles southeast. Did I just see a parachute? Has someone bailed out?"

"Disregard your sighting. Enter holding at one-two thousand. Altimeter two-niner-eight-zero. Expect approach clearance at four zero."

"Roger." I turned to Alfalfa. "A lot of spooky shit goes on over here."

"Probably an unmanned, surveillance drone. I can disregard with the best of 'em."

The airplane lurched and bounced when we entered the turbulent clouds. I remembered my bumpy rides in the recent past. We descended on headings given by the TACAN and Approach Control, breaking clear of clouds at five hundred feet. I held the nose ten degrees into the wind in order to fly a direct track to the runway, which approached through my left window. "Check out this nasty crosswind. Here I sit, workin' like a dog on my day off."

Alfalfa smiled. "We're livin' the FAC motto: One good deal after another."

"I use the kick-out method for crosswind landings. You do what you have to do with the controls to make the airplane take your ass where you want to go."

"No change from your normal flying techniques."

"Roger that." Just before touchdown, I banked right and kicked the left rudder to line up with the runway. At the same time, I chopped the power and raised the nose. The right wheel squeaked onto the pavement, then the left.

I slammed in full right aileron to keep the crosswind from lifting the right wing again.

After we parked and chocked the O-2, an airman approached.

I held up my hand. “Please don’t touch the airplane. Thanks.”

He smirked and left.

I filed my return flight plan and went to the club for hot chow.

Alfalfa walked to the Education Office to take a correspondence course test. We met at ops as the sun dropped behind green mountains.

I sensed something was wrong as I approached my Oscar Deuce. “The right seat is missing. What do ya think of that, Captain?”

Alfalfa smiled and shook his head.

I waved a senior N.C.O. over. “Excuse me, sergeant. Please replace my right seat.”

“Sir, that aircraft arrived without a right seat.”

“Are you saying the Captain here squatted like a mamasan all the way from Pleiku?” I wanted to call him a fucking idiot, but I held my high ground. I faked a twitch, and rested my hand on the wooden grip of my revolver, strapped to my survival vest.

“Sir, I didn’t steal your seat.”

“Did I say you did, sergeant?” My fingers wrapped around the pistol grip.

Alfalfa pretended to hold me back.

The sergeant stared at my right hand and stepped backward.

“I’m going inside to find a senior officer who gives a shit. Failing that, I know where I can find twenty right seats.” Speaking in a calm but emphatic tone, I surveyed the fleet of Danang-based O-2s.

The sergeant’s gaze stayed on my right hand.

“Let’s go.” Angry, but under control, I carried my irate lieutenant act inside.

I kicked the door open and stomped to the ops counter. “I want to confirm the configuration I signed in with included a right seat.”

A bald lieutenant colonel stuck his head out of an office down the hall.

When I glared in his direction, the head popped back inside. I whispered to Alfalfa, “I think we’ve just been cleared hot.”

“Yes.” A second lieutenant behind the counter moved his finger down the page of an open log book. “Right seat, back seat, and two empty rocket pods.”

Alfalfa held out open arms. “We need flight publications. Ours were in a pouch on the rear of the right seat that disappeared.”

The second lieutenant pointed to a nearby office.

I stepped to the door and said, “I need flight pubs.”

The airman inside rose and said, “Sir, you can have ‘em all.”

"Just enough to get to Pleiku." I took what I needed from his bookcase.

"We need a fire extinguisher," Alfalfa said.

I watched the airman's eyes widen as I palmed my pistol butt again. "I know where we can get one." I followed Alfalfa to the exit and slammed the door behind me.

"You're doing great," Alfalfa said, laughing. "The irate lieutenant, huh?"

"That's me." I started to smile, then I noticed the master sergeant installing a right seat in my airplane.

"Sir, I didn't steal your seat."

"Please. Stop lying. You're responsible, sergeant. The captain here would make a great witness at your trial. How'd you like to lose all those stripes?"

"I'm very sorry, sir."

I leaned down and looked into his face. "Yeah. Sorry for getting caught. You disgrace the uniform." I climbed in, cranked engines, and taxied away.

"Tower, Covey Five-nine-one is ready to copy clearance." I joined a long line of airplanes on the taxiway that paralleled the runway.

"Roger. You're number eighteen for departure."

"You were tough on that sergeant," Alfalfa said.

"That fuckin' thief? All the while I was thinking of Jerry. Remember? He was flying an aircraft that had been here for overhaul when an engine blew up."

Alfalfa nodded. "Do you think the maintenance troops at Danang were responsible?" He turned up the volume on the U.H.F. radio.

"For the blown engine? Yes."

An Australian sounded loud but calm on the emergency Guard radio channel. "Actually, I'm amongst wild flowers. Quite lovely."

"Roger the flowers. Save your battery. Come up again in fifteen minutes."

I remembered a report I had heard at the club. "An Aussie B-Fifty seven went down in the A Shau Valley this afternoon. Sounds like him on Guard channel. His transmission comes through like he's right next door."

"He sounds like a tour guide describing the flora," Alfalfa said. "They'd better get his ass outa there. The sky's turning dark."

We taxied forward with the slow line of airplanes and listened to the rescue.

Tower passed updates. "Covey Five-nine-one, you are number seven for departure. Break. Alpha Charlie Hotel, you are number ten."

"Neg-a-tive. Alpha Charlie Hotel not number ten." The accent this time was Vietnamese. I had seen a C-47 with local airline markings join the line.

Alfalfa laughed. "Tower insulted this guy. 'Number ten' translates to 'the worst' in Vietnamese. Everything's number one--good, or number ten--bad. They should have skipped ten."

"Sorry, Alpha Charlie Hotel."

Emergency channel voices chattered. "Okay, pop smoke now, and say color."

"Roger. Quite orange, actually. Almost vermillion. Say, I'm hearing rifle fire to the east." The Australian pilot sounded more serene than the tower controller who kept the line moving to the runway.

"Keep your head down. Jolly Green will be right behind the Skyraiders. Tally your smoke."

"That is one calm survivor," Alfalfa said.

"Covey Five-nine-one, switch to departure frequency, cleared for take-off."

I pushed the power forward; we rolled. Departure frequency was quiet. For an instant I relaxed in the comfort of being in charge of my own destiny.

"Jolly has the survivor. Taking fire from the east."

Alfalfa gave me a thumbs-up. The helicopter had saved the Aussie.

"Sandy one is in." A-1's covered the chopper's escape.

I smiled at the tiny slice of success.

"Covey Five-nine-one, you're cleared direct Pleiku. Climb and maintain eight thousand." Departure control then passed an altimeter setting.

I rogered, turned due south and trimmed for level flight. For forty-five minutes the blackness of Charlie's Vietnam passed below. I called the artillery unit stationed near home base. "Pleiku Arty, Covey Five-nine one is inbound on the three-six-zero radial."

"Sir, that radial is hot. Suggest you arc around to the zero-one-zero."

"What do you think? If we fly the arc, we'll probably miss dinner."

"Big sky theory." Alfalfa pointed straight ahead.

Boom. Boom. Boom. Three fireballs glowed in a straight line on the ground before us.

"Those fuckers are one-five-fives." Now Alfalfa pointed left.

"Covey Ops, Five-nine-one," I called on F.M. during a hard left turn. "Would you please call the club and reserve two hot meals?"

"I'd be happy to, Five-nine-one."

"The duty hog is cheerful tonight," Alfalfa said.

"The voice was Lieutenant Ecstatic. He'd be just as happy not to call for us, but I think we can anticipate a warm plate tonight."

At six the next morning I flew circles and called the Forward Operating Base at Kontum for the sixth time with no response. Frustrated, I unsynchronized my propellers and dove the airplane at the green beret compound.

ROWROWROWROW. The unsynched propellers made an unnerving droning that would wake the dead.

"Roger, Covey. Water buffalo is on the way."

After landing, I parked and waited fifteen minutes before a jeep arrived.

Shoebox staggered from the jeep to the aircraft. His eyes were red.

"What the hell is going on, my friend?" I asked, as I started and taxied.

"First of all, I'd like to inform you your unsynchronized engines made a noise that caused sphincter muscles to relax throughout the compound."

"Roger."

"Captain Howard took a call from the White House last night. They told him to come home and pick up his Medal of Honor."

"Howard's the quiet guy. He does everything by pointing and whispering. I've never heard him talk out loud. What did he do to earn The Medal?"

"Sir, the word 'fear' is not in his vocabulary."

"So you partied last night?"

"You could say that." Shoebox fumbled with his map. He pointed to a quiet area near the Vietnamese border. "We've got a good mission today, though."

"Out of range of the big guns. Can't be too lucrative."

"A big N.V.A. headquarters. We have a bunch of radio intercepts that all come from this peaceful little hillside. A fifteen-thousand-pound bomb will arrive in two hours to change that situation."

"Commando Vault. I've heard of those things. Never seen one." The huge conventional bombs were dropped singly--like a big black egg--from the back of a radar-directed C-130. Blockbusters left over from past wars could clear helicopter landing zones in triple-canopy jungle.

"Yep." Shoebox nodded. "We'll put a team in before the smoke clears."

"Immediate Bomb Damage Assessment? Sounds like a great idea. I doubt if they'll find much to assess after a fifteen-thousand-pounder goes off."

We climbed and orbited north and west of the target area.

Shoebox talked to other teams until the moment of truth arrived. He pointed up and east.

I spotted the C-130--a tiny black blob at eighteen thousand feet. "The book says we should stay three miles away. The concussion must be awesome."

"Bombs away." Shoebox used his uncanny vision to observe the falling speck with a tiny stabilizing parachute attached.

I finally saw the bomb, but caught a silver glint beside it. "Did you see the flash? Right beside the bomb. Must be the aluminum pallet the bomb sits on when they shove it out." I turned west to stay clear of the deadly frisbee.

"We have an oak tree over here." Shoebox gave the code word to launch the helicopters.

Nodding to acknowledge his call for chopper launch, I watched the huge black bomb pass our altitude. I turned right to view the last few seconds of the bomb's existence in solid form.

BOOM.

A monster fireball blossomed and a white concussion ring expanded across the jungle. Our O-2 banged into the shock wave as the fire faded into a tall gray mushroom cloud.

"Looks like a nuke," I said. "Choppers are in sight."

Two Hueys landed at the base of the wispy fungus, dropped off the B.D.A. team, then took off, joining three others they came in with. Two Cobras flew alongside like outriggers.

Shoebox collected an okay from the team.

I landed at Dak To. When I lowered the nose the aircraft rocked and shimmied. "I think we blew the nose tire. I'll ease off to the side here." I pulled clear and stopped.

Shoebox jumped out and confirmed the nose tire was flat.

"Moonbeam, Covey Five-nine-one has a flat nose tire at Dak To. Please relay to Covey Operations."

"Roger."

I climbed out and stretched. I could find no damage beyond the flat tire.

"It's only flat on the bottom." Shoebox grinned.

"Is that the official Army position?"

In two hours an O.V.-10 landed on the bumpy strip at Dak To. Elf shut down his right engine and waved.

A young airman with tire and toolbox climbed from the back seat. He stood by a large fire extinguisher while Elf restarted his engine, then ran to us while the O.V.-10 departed. "I love this action! The pilot said he'd come and get me in a few hours."

"He's probably good for that." I shook the young man's hand.

"He also said I should ask you something about hard landings."

"I'd expect no less from the Elf." I laughed.

Shoebox and I pulled the tailbooms down to raise the nosewheel off the ground.

The airman propped up the front strut and changed the wheel and tire.

We thanked him and departed.

I called Elf on F.M. "We're on station. What's up?"

"Choppers and A-Ones are inbound. Friendlies have colored signal panels out. You can see them in the clearing."

"Roger. Tally."

"The show is all yours. I'm outa gas. See you later."

I worked the A-1s for one pass so they understood the team's location. They held high while the choppers came in.

Shoebox chatted with the B.D.A. team until the choppers swooped them away.

"Well?" I said. "Tell me about B.D.A."

"Their intelligence was good. They found blood and bits of metal."

A message waited at Pleiku when I landed: "Please come to Cam Ranh as soon as possible for an interview. Signed Steve Canyon." I showed the note to Elf.

"I know. I did some checking. The boss won't let you use an O-Two for this," he said.

"What a surprise. Hell, I'd walk to the coast to get away from that asshole."

"A C-Seven will pass through here tomorrow morning. Destination Cam Ranh."

I was on it. After I arrived at Cam Ranh I reported to Lieutenant Colonel Shelton at the 504th Tac Air Support Group Headquarters. His office was small--almost cozy--with a small pad of brown carpet. A brass lamp sat on a table next to his desk. The colonel stood tall and distinguished with gray temples and wire-rimmed glasses.

I took the chair he offered beside his desk.

He asked a few questions about my family and why I had volunteered. Then he said, "We're looking for FACs who can work independently and make decisions without a lot of supervision."

"I take off most mornings at five-thirty, and come home twelve hours later. Do you know about Prairie Fire?"

He nodded.

"I checked out in November." I wanted to say no Pleiku senior officers came within fifty miles of Prairie Fire, and all my decisions were independent. But I knew they weren't looking for whiners. I tried to appear strong and silent.

He smiled as though he read my mind. He stood and shook my hand. "Congratulations and welcome to the Steve Canyon Program. The next scheduled opening will be in a couple of months. We'll send a message so your folks can cut orders."

Smiling, I walked to the huge Aerial Port hangar. Then I realized the good colonel had revealed nothing classified about the program. After joining, I still knew nothing. I felt snookered.

"C-Seven to Pleiku?" From behind the counter a sergeant directed me to a gate.

I climbed aboard and strapped in. Before my mind drifted too far into ignorant euphoria, I was brought back to earth by a horrible stench. I asked the loadmaster, "What's that foul odor?"

"Sir, I've tried gallons of disinfectant, scrub brushes and fire hoses. Does it still stink?"

I nodded.

"We've been hauling a lot of bodies lately."

The lieutenant colonel in charge of Covey reconnaissance missions over Cambodia pulled me aside as I entered the building one morning on a rare day off. "My morning pilot has a cold. Can you pick up the mission?"

"Sure, Colonel. Happy to fly instead of playing duty officer."

"I appreciate your helping us. Here." He handed me a 1:50,000-scale chart. "Please recce this real estate in detail. Put everything in your report."

"Everything?"

"I'm putting together a comprehensive picture for higher headquarters."

"Can do, sir." I grabbed my flying gear and flew the mission. I found no enemy troops. Mostly I saw remote villagers who waved when I flew over. I tracked one undocumented trail and wrestled with the idea of including elephant excrement sightings in my report. What the hell. The colonel said to include everything.

Five hours later, the colonel greeted me in the intelligence vault, where I was finishing my report. "How'd it go?"

"Just fine, sir. Here's what I found." I handed him a ten-page report.

"Great job." The colonel beamed. "The folks down in Saigon are saying our reports are twice as heavy as any others they're receiving."

"Is that what they do, Colonel? Weigh 'em?" I laughed hard at my little joke.

His smile faded.

For the next few days the winds at Pleiku blew across the runway at thirty knots. The O.V.-10s were grounded. O-2s operated five knots below design limits for crosswinds.

I began my takeoff roll with full control deflection into the wind. At liftoff, the airplane jerked twenty degrees left into the wind. I allowed the craft to weathervane and track ahead.

I repeated my near acrobatic flying at Kontum, and picked up Roundeye, also known as Steve Stevens, a new Covey Rider. I asked, "How long have you been in Vietnam?"

"About six years."

"Holy shit, Roundeye. Have you lost your mind?"

"I extend in six-month increments. The Army gives me thirty days leave and free travel with each hitch. I've been around the world five times. I go back to Denmark in a few months. Next year--South Africa."

"That's all fine," I said, "but what about the six years here?"

"I only have to deal with Vietnam in six-month chunks, and besides, you can stand on your head and gargle peanut butter for six months." He grinned.

I had to smile as I set up the assets to pull out a team.

In the middle of our ballgame, a fast reconnaissance jet shot past.

"What the hell was that?" a helicopter pilot asked. "I over-torqued my engine getting out of the way. I'm goin' to Dak To."

I decided to investigate. "Hillboro, Covey Five-nine-one. What's going on with all the traffic? It's a hazard."

"Sorry, Covey. No sector FAC due to the winds. You're the only FAC here, and we're sending everyone your way."

"That won't work. We're too busy to handle sector duties safely."

"You're the only FAC. You'll get all the calls." This voice sounded older than the previous one.

I called Paul Curs, the Cambodia FAC, on F.M. "Please switch to Tango frequency and come up here and play sector FAC. Keep all traffic north and west of the Falls."

"Roger." Like a hungry dog, Paul scarfed the mission.

I finished the day without further incident. At Kontum, the jeep driver relayed an invitation from his colonel for me to visit the bunker.

I explained the crosswind problem to an irate Army colonel. Halfway through my brief speech, I decided he would never understand.

"I've got one broken helicopter, and my soldiers' lives have been endangered by the intrusion of unwanted airplanes and radio traffic. Do you understand me, lieutenant?"

"Yes, sir."

"I can get help through SOG channels if I have to, and fucking heads will roll. Do you understand?"

"Yes, sir. We need to pull the Cambodia FAC up to Laos until the winds subside."

"I don't give a shit how. You just fix it. Dismissed."

Sixpack gave me a ride to the airplane. "Are you alright?"

"I'm not sure. I think about half my face has been ripped off."

"You'll be fine, as long as you are absolutely certain, speaking for the Air Force, the problem is solved."

"Thanks, pal."

I took my weary bod to the club and unloaded my troubles on O.K. at the bar.

"Look," he said. "Across the room I see the commander and his staff, chatting as if they had a fact to discuss. You owe the commander a heads-up on the angry colonel."

"With his entire staff, you'd think he could solve a little crosswind problem. Guess I should go over there." I walked to the table of the weakest humans I'd ever met.

The commander asked, "What can we do for you?"

I explained the situation. Finally I said, "Phrases like 'we're taking fire' were stepped on by airplanes passing through the sector. A helicopter was nearly hit by a recce bird. The Army colonel at Kontum is really pissed off."

The commander said nothing.

"We need to put up a sector FAC, even if he's an O-Two driver or an O.V.-Ten pilot in the right seat of an O-Two."

Nothing came back. The colonel looked at me as though he didn't have the slightest idea what I was talking about.

When I looked at the majors and lieutenant colonels on the staff, they averted their eyes.

"Thank you for your time, gentlemen." I walked to the bar in disgust.

"Did they help?" O.K. asked.

"He didn't know what I was talking about. The other assholes were afraid to speak."

"Guarding their little careers." O.K. smiled.

"They'd better guard more than that. If we have any trouble tomorrow, I'll give the boys at Kontum our commander's trailer number."

Chapter 13
. . . Gone!

March 1971

Boom.

At one a.m. the ground shook. Glasses and dishes rattled in the hooch bar.

Pow. Pop-pop-pop-pop.

Joining the crowd that flowed outside, I heard a Huey wop-wopping near the runway a mile to the south. Bright lights illuminated gray smoke boiling up from a point obscured from my view by buildings.

Several Coveys stood on the brick revetment beside the hooch. Drunker ones leaped from revetment to roof. From above they sent reports.

"They're firing on the perimeter, out beyond RAPCON."

"Can't see any bad guys, but fires are burning on this side of the runway."

"The cops have rolled up in an amphibious vehicle now, and they're shooting into the darkness."

"Hey, we could use a round of beer up here."

The shooting continued into the night. An A.C.-47 gunship arrived and poured red tracer streams into the darkness south of the base.

Coveys on the roof cheered.

The Warbler sounded, announcing an attack on the base.

Coveys cheered again.

I moved inside the bar.

A clearer picture of the attack came from crews who had escaped the squadron when the explosions began. "First we heard a dozen mortars hit near the middle of the runway. Next, an explosion took out the brand new control tower that opened last week."

One evacuee from the flightline was George, our stocky intelligence officer. "We've been expecting something for weeks. The Four-o-eighth Sapper Battalion sneaked in and hit the tower point-blank with an R.P.G.--rocket-propelled grenade. Seven guys were hurt. Sappers got away clean."

O.K. Bryant had been flying and arrived after the smoke had cleared. "They loaded the injured tower guys onto a MEDEVAC bird. Most should survive. The traffic pattern is being controlled now from a sandbag bunker beside the runway."

I pulled my pal aside. "I need to talk to you in private."

"Me, too," O.K. said.

We took beers out to a picnic table on the deserted patio.

"Before you came over here," O.K. asked, "did you go to Cannon Air Force Base for instant fighter pilot school? Only fighter-qualified FACs--designated A-FACS--can control airstrikes supporting American troops. I thought you were a B-FAC like me."

"Yes, I'm a B-FAC. That rinky-dink school is the Air Force's way of holding onto the FAC mission. The brass doesn't want Army helicopter pilots controlling airstrikes. Plus, more missions mean more budget dollars."

"I overheard the commander this afternoon, ranting and raving in his office. He wants to pull B-FACs--specifically you--from the Prairie Fire mission. I think ol' George saved you for the time being."

"What did George do?"

"I heard him ask, 'Sir, don't you believe the President? Our area of operations is Laos. We have no American combat troops in Laos. Then, the boss mumbled something I couldn't understand."

"That old bastard's going to get someone killed." I dismissed my thoughts of the chair-warriors.

"He's a piece of work, all right."

"Speaking of danger, O.K., what's the story with your Prairie Fire battle damage last week? I heard Sixpack laughing about an R.P.G. attack."

"Oh, that little incident. I have to swear you to absolute secrecy."

"You got it." Keeping a brother warrior's secret would be easy.

"Wednesday, I took off early, and nobody answered the radio at Kontum. So, I made a low pass. I had a lot of speed, so I added an aileron roll."

"Oh shit." I began to laugh.

"I never saw the antenna, but as I rolled out, it whacked my right wing. Pulling up, I saw a big hole in the leading edge. I had to use full left rudder to keep the wings level."

"What did you do?" Tears welled in my eyes. I couldn't stop laughing.

"I lowered the gear and flaps. Flying became a little easier after I slowed to approach speed. I landed and taxied to the ramp."

"Who was your rider?"

"A new guy. I'd never met him before. He climbed out of the jeep and pulled six feet of aluminum antenna out of the aileron control cables along the front of my wing."

"Damn." The picture he drew in words made tears of laughter pour down my face.

"I told him I couldn't go back to Pleiku. I'd be shot, then hung, then burned at the stake. I had to fly a mission and claim battle damage."

"And he got in the plane with you?"

"Yep. He said if I'd fly it, then he would. We used the entire runway to take off, and we took turns holding the left rudder--a real pain in the ass. We put a team in quick-like, then came home."

"Does anybody around here know?"

"Just you and Jim Lee. I asked the maintenance troops to fix it on the sly if they could. Told 'em I'd be in trouble for flying too low."

"And nobody's said anything to you?"

"Nope. I do know the commander finally found out. He called in a weapons expert--a civilian from Danang. The guy looked at the wing, shook his head, and said he'd never seen anything like it."

As we walked inside, I heard Elf say, "They missed the big show."

"Who's that?"

"Plumber and Plumber's Helper. They're in Ubon."

"Together? In the same airplane?" I couldn't believe what I heard.

I slept late the next day, played handball with Elf, and spotted four trucks on the Trail shortly after sundown. Alfalfa and I had given the north half of our sector to a Spectre gunship. We offered mixed reviews to a pair of F-4s who attacked our movers and woke a few gunners near the Falls.

"Covey, this is Leghorn. Come up New High on Fox Mike."

"Damn," I told Alfalfa. "Leghorn monitors teams. Something's wrong." I switched to F.M. radio and dialed the frequency listed for New High on my code card. "Leghorn, Covey Five-nine-one."

"Covey, can you go green?"

"Sure." I turned on the encryption device and waited for a green light. "Leghorn, Covey Five-nine-one's green."

"Roger, Covey, loud and clear. Please checkout the valley west of our position. We've counted a thousand campfires. You need a night scope to see them. Must be an N.V.A. division camped there."

"Roger." I flew north to the huge valley that extended from the steep ridge where Leghorn sat to the ten-mile Trail segment we called the Straightaway. I put the valley on the right side so Alfalfa could use the scope.

He peered down into the dark jungle. "Leghorn ain't lyin.' I see at least a thousand fires. Have a look." He handed me the scope.

Through a small window on my side, I peered through the starlight scope.

The scope was larger than the window, but I could see enough to appreciate the significant target. Black jungle became green, and campfires sparkled like a galaxy of stars. "Figuring at least five or six soldiers per fire, I'd estimate a division-size force is camped down there." On the radio I said, "Leghorn, Covey has the target."

Alfalfa said, "The target's huge but outside our rules of engagement."

"Not quite," I said. I called Moonbeam and used code words to identify a Prairie Fire priority for the target. I also had to pass my initials.

"Covey Five-nine-one, you'll have Gunfighter Five-one, a flight of three in fifteen minutes."

"Roger." I told Alfalfa, "We could use a squadron of BUFFs for this one."

"This target's so big, even Gunfighters could hit it."

Fifteen minutes later, we heard, "Gunfighter Five-one check, two, three. Covey Five-nine-one, Gunfighter's at the rendezvous, three F-Fours, wall-to-wall Mark eighty-twos."

"Roger. Orbit and look below for my beacon. I have a great target for you."

"Roger, Gunfighter, green 'em up." The fighters armed their ordnance.

I spit out a detailed briefing. "Your target's a mile square. Call tally on my red beacon, and I'll mark the corners."

"Roger. Tally . . . Say . . . are any other fastmovers out here tonight?"

"Negative. We have a Spectre gunship no closer than fifteen miles north."

"Gunfighter Five-two's breaking east. Head-on traffic."

"Covey, Gunfighter's got strangers up here. Break. Let's head for the tanker."

I offered an easy fix. "You can dump everything in one pass if you want."

"We're too spread out now, Covey. We'll go to the tanker and try again in about forty-five minutes."

"Roger."

Alfalfa said, "We're out of time here, ourselves."

"Moonbeam, Covey Five-nine-one. My fighters went back to the tanker. They had a near-miss incident with some other fastmovers. What's going on?"

"The only other fighters in your sector are Spectre's escorts."

"That explains everything. Thank you." I called Spectre ten times. No answer.

Alfalfa said, "What a damn waste! I wonder how many soldiers will die when this N.V.A. division spills into Kontum Province."

"If I could see that armed trash-hauler, I'd get his damn attention. For now, we may as well dump all our ordnance on these campfires." I climbed and took one more peek at the target through the starlight scope.

"Armament panel is set," Alfalfa said.

I rolled in and fired ten rockets into the enemy formation. As I pulled out, I changed switch settings and dropped burning markers into the fray.

Then we turned for home.

"We did what we could." Alfalfa rationalized the huge missed opportunity.

"We'll report what happened in a way that can't be misunderstood or interpreted. We're our own enemy in this fucked-up war."

Medicinal alcohol helped me sleep late and stay on the night schedule. The next afternoon I awoke and treated my frustration with a handball game with Elf.

"You were right," he said while we warmed up. "I should never have allowed the Plumber and the Plumber's Helper to go to Ubon together."

"Uh-oh."

"I guess everything went fine until they armed up at the end of the runway last night. While Plumber held the brakes, his Helper--I want to call him Baby Huey--leaned into the wind blast from the propeller and pulled the safing pins. He had trouble with some clips."

"Each incendiary brick has a clip at the end of the arming wire." I remembered learning this difficult procedure. "They're tight as hell. You have to really force them onto loops that hang from the rack."

"Apparently Plumber's Helper missed the loop and pulled the arming wire. The brick ignited on the rack."

My jaw dropped. "What?"

"Plumber hit the jettison button."

"That's a viable option, but the panic button drops everything off both wings."

"Right. Two pods of rockets, log markers, and a rack of bricks--one burning--slammed onto on the ramp at Ubon."

"What happened next?"

"Plumber waved his Helper aboard, and they took off."

"And left the ordnance burning?"

"Yep. Nick's the primary O-Two Instructor now. He said he'd hold a gun to the Plumber's Head and make him call and apologize to the fire department and anyone else he pissed off at Ubon."

"If Ubon refuses us our little escapes, Covey morale will hit a new low. Go ahead and serve, Elf."

I considered myself to be an average handball player. Ed had been the undisputed champ. Now Elf claimed the throne. After losing two games in a row, he turned and slugged the hardwood backwall. A large purple lump immediately rose near the last knuckle on his right hand.

"You broke it, Elf."

"Damn." He held up his injured paw. "It really hurts."

We walked over to the nearby clinic.

A large sergeant at the flight surgeon's desk looked at Elf's hand and said, "You're grounded." He offered Elf an official form. "Sign this."

"No, sergeant. I won't sign your paperwork. I'm not grounded."

I followed my friend out the door. "Better find some ice for that thing."

"Yeah. All that flight surgeon wants to do is ground people. Truth is, he can only recommend grounding. The commander's signature is required on the form. Any other commander would probably let me fly with some kind of splint. Not this guy."

I shook my head. "Don't let that asshole cause you to suffer permanent damage."

"Fuck 'em all, from that sergeant right on up the line. I'm not grounded."

When Alfalfa and I arrived at our airplane for the ten p.m. launch, we had a small surprise. I asked the crew chief, "What did you do to my seat?"

"The pilot's seats are being replaced with armored ones. My bird is our first one from Danang with the modification." The young man seemed proud.

"Guess I don't have a choice." I smiled and climbed in, but I couldn't squeeze my parachute pack past the seat's right edge, a six-inch strip of armor, welded at ninety degrees to the back. I put the parachute in first, then climbed in and strapped it on.

Once in the seat I couldn't reach around the side for access to items like the fire extinguisher and the instrument publications mounted behind the right seat. I squirmed through my ground operations but made my take-off time. The ground roll seemed measurably longer with the heavy seat added.

"You don't like armored protection?" Alfalfa asked.

"We don't need armor over the Trail."

"I'd think you'd take all the protection you can get."

"A triple-A round that hits us will explode and rip the airplane apart. This seat won't change that fact. This armor is for small arms protection, and we generally fly above the range of small arms. All we do is lose performance by adding extra weight to the Oscar Duck."

"Theoretically, you're right."

"The front edge of the seat has cut off circulation to my lower legs. They're both numb, and that ain't a theory. And what if I had to climb out of this thing to bail out?"

"You'd never make it."

"I'm sending in a hazard report when we land." I squirmed to find a comfortable position to complete the mission and keep blood circulating to my feet.

After landing I sent a long and specific list of seat hazards into safety channels, then crashed.

I had dinner the following evening with Alfalfa, then we adjourned to the hooch bar for coffee. We were scheduled for a two a.m. launch.

O.K. came through the door with a message in his hand. He shook his finger at me. "You stirred up some shit with your hazard report."

I shook my head. "I wasn't the only FAC unhappy about armored seats. And even if I was, everything I wrote was true."

"The engineers in the 'States agree." O.K. paraphrased the message. "They say armored seats will be removed."

"I'm impressed," I said. "Somebody finally did their homework."

O.K. continued. "They talk about all the testing they did, then they say, 'We did everything but sit in it.'"

"Sit in it, sit on it." That comment made me angry. "Are they trying to be funny? What kind of vacuum do they live in?"

"Further, our data indicates with a typical night ordnance load," O.K. read, "the single engine service ceiling of the O-Two is fifteen-hundred feet below sea level."

"No shit?"

"Because of the overgrossed condition," O.K. read on, "landing within one hour after take-off is prohibited unless all external stores are jettisoned."

"That rule will create a new generation of rack-FACs," Alfalfa said.

"The rear seat'll be removed."

"Great," I said. "I know a fat sergeant at Danang who collects O-Two seats. But how'll we do Prairie Fire checkouts?"

"I talked to the maintenance chief this afternoon," O.K. said. Until Danang gets the T.C.T.O.--the Time Compliance Tech Order--to remove them, they'll follow the current T.C.T.O. and continue to install them."

Now Alfalfa became angry. "Those shithead engineers should be expediting the new T.C.T.O. instead of making jokes."

"To appease hardcores like Captain Alfalfa," O.K. said, "we received local authority to remove the right side of the seat."

Alfalfa wasn't finished. "The Army has a saying--lead, follow, or get the hell out of the way. Does anyone not understand why this war drags on forever?"

We landed at dawn and taxied to parking. Cops seemed to be everywhere. I asked one, "What brings you guys to the flightline?"

"Mortar attack last night, sir. They put holes in thirteen aircraft. At the same time, sappers blew up a couple of storage buildings. No casualties."

"Did you get the sappers?"

"They got away clean."

I smirked at Alfalfa, and we walked to the ops building.

Lieutenant Ecstatic accosted us as we hung up our parachutes. "Did you hear the news? The colonel got orders. He'll command the Twentieth TASS at Danang. I mean, he's gone."

"Gone?" I laughed out loud, lifted by the good news. "Gee, I didn't receive my invitation to his going away party."

"That job is a promotion for him," Alfalfa said. "He probably sucked it up on one of his combat sorties to the headquarters at Cam Ranh Bay."

"The Peter Principle's at work," I said. "He reached his highest level of command incompetence here, so he moves to the next level."

"Oh, yeah? You're leaving, too." Ecstatic looked at me.

My mouth and eyes opened wide involuntarily.

"Report to some base in Thailand. Message says you will travel in civilian clothes. Congratulations. Peter Principle?" Ecstatic offered his hand.

I laughed, shook his hand, and nodded.

A few days later, O.K. flew me to Danang where the squadron would convert my message into orders that would turn the wheels for my move. As we descended along the coast near the base, my friend asked, "How long will your out-processing here take?"

"Three days. I'll catch a ride to Pleiku for the big party this weekend, then report to a special operations detachment in Thailand. Guess I'll disappear for awhile."

"Are you ready for the Steve Canyon Program?"

"I'm ready to leave. And I know as much as you do about what's ahead."

"Shit." He laughed. "You are clueless."

I gave my message to the 20th TASS administrative section, and they told me to stop by the next afternoon to pick up orders.

Several pilot training pals joined me at the dark, crowded bar of the Danang Officers Open Mess--the DOOM club. Short, blond Skip Franklin brought his guitar and sang cynical songs about the war. Everybody sang the choruses.

Dugan arrived and chugged his first beer. “Great to see you.”

“What’s the occasion? Good mission?”

“Standard. Just naped a bunch of bad guys. What brings you here overnight?”

“I’m short. Out-processing tomorrow. Going into the Raven FAC program.”

“I thought you had a month or so to go.”

“I did too, until I got the message the other day.”

“The Laos boys must have had unplanned attrition.” Dugan elbowed me.

“You have to expect a few losses in a large organization,” I rationalized.

“The organization you’re going to is small. I have spies on the inside. Speaking of losses, did you hear about the new TASS commander?”

“Hear what?”

“He’s gone--got fired today. They fired all field graders in the squadron.”

“Wow. He only left Pleiku last week to come here. What happened?”

“Do you remember our buddy Ferret, who couldn’t fly a box kite?”

“Yeah?”

“He’s stationed up at Hue-Phu Bai, a ten-minute flight north of here. He took off this morning for a Danang run. Left his ordnance pins in the pylons. He figured to pull them and fly a mission when he departed later from Danang.”

I shook my head, fearing fate had caught up with the poor skills of my friend.

“When Ferret put the gear handle down, the nose gear showed unsafe. No green light. Tower said it looked down, but the safe-and-locked indicator didn’t come on.”

“Oh, shit. Certain disaster in the making.”

“Ferret called the squadron and the chief of standardization read him the procedure right from the Dash One tech order. You know, keep a thousand r.p.m. on the front engine to power the hydraulics, then hold the gear handle down while you land and stop. When the maintenance troops pull down on the booms to raise the nose gear off the pavement, shut down the front engine.”

“Roger. Then they put the lock pin in the nose gear, and you can taxi to parking.”

“Apparently the new commander--your guy from Pleiku--had other ideas. He figured the nose gear would collapse anyway, so he told Ferret to shut down the front engine, feather it, and use the starter switch to kick the prop horizontal. He figured only sheet metal damage wouldn’t constitute a reportable accident on his watch.”

“Did he know who he was talking to?” I shook my head.

Dugan laughed and rolled his eyes. "So Ferret shuts down the front engine, but the prop won't feather."

"Shit. I've heard about those problems." I looked around the crowded bar for the evaluator who had convinced me the story was only rumor.

"Now, Ferret's going down, from the drag of the windmilling prop and the rocket pods he can't jettison because he left the pins installed. He grabs a double-handful of those mixmaster levers." Dugan moved his right fist back and forth, moving imaginary versions of the throttle, prop, and mixture controls that blossomed up for each engine from the center console.

"All he had to do was start the front engine again."

"Let's not forget who we're dealing with." Dugan laughed and swigged his beer. "Now, catch this. Ferret pulls off the mixture lever for the rear engine."

"He shut down his only engine?"

"Yep. Then he silently pancakes into a rice paddy short of runway three-five."

"Shit. Did he survive?"

"Crawls out of the rubble without a scratch."

"Here's to little Ferret. I'm glad the dumbshit's alive." I raised my beer.

"Long live dumbshits." Dugan joined the toast. "I heard he had to walk to operations. The rescue helicopter was flying nurses around."

"Helicopter guys need loving, too." I thought of the Keystone Cops as I ordered another round.

"You know what they say," Dugan said. "Danang sucks."

"I'm leavin', pal. And that old fart of a commander finally got what he deserved. In my rear-view mirror, Danang is all right."

I flew to Pleiku on a Friday with a stack of orders that would launch my new adventure. I looked forward to Saturday's dining-in, a formal military affair in more civilized regions. Here, we'd follow the traditional rules, but wear party suits. Then, we'd eat and drink too much.

On Saturday morning I rode down to the ops building and turned over my extra duties and extra weapons to F.N.G.s.

My close friend, O.K., was the duty officer. "Show me those orders. I want to see what a ticket out of here looks like."

A captain, followed by four spirited lieutenants in flight suits came through the front door. "My name's Peacock. We're ferrying five O-Ones to northern Thailand. How's lunch at your club?"

"Below average, probably." O.K. paged a new guy who was studying in the intel vault. When a face appeared, O.K. threw him a set of keys. "Take these guys to the club for lunch."

"Thanks," Peacock said.

"Mind if we look at your airplanes?"

"Help yourself," Peacock said as he led his troops to the door. "We love the Oscar Ace. It does everything at seventy knots--take-off, climb, cruise, land and taxi."

Five gray Cessna Birddogs sat in a line facing our squadron building.

O.K. and I joined a couple of other curious Coveys inspecting the perky little planes. They sat back on tailwheels at a jaunty, ready-to-fly attitude.

"I forgot how tiny they are," I said. "I flew in one at Hurlburt."

"You'll probably fly one of these same airplanes," O.K. said, "as soon as they paint over the U.S.A.F. markings. Northern Thailand is another way of saying Laos."

"I'm ready."

After an hour or so, the O-1 pilots returned from lunch and departed.

I took a vehicle full of Coveys to the club. I spotted Captain Skinny at a table near the door and joined him. "Where have you been lately?"

"I quit drinking after that party with the Vietnamese A-one pilots. Then, I quit complaining after Major Major left."

"Sounds like a low profile to me." I laughed and munched a mystery-meat burger.

"I fly everyday and write letters home. I feel a lot better, too. Say, you must be short. When are you leaving us?"

"Tomorrow. I'm hopping to Ubon in an O.V.-ten backseat. Maybe you--"

"One of those O-Ones is down," a lieutenant ran up and announced, breathless.

"Damn. I just met those guys."

"A Dustoff Huey took off from the Army clinic here."

"If anyone can save the day," Captain Skinny said, "Dustoff can. They're known from the Delta to the D.M.Z. for having balls of steel. Let's head down to ops."

Less than an hour later, we watched a Huey with red crosses on the front and sides approach and land in front of our squadron. Captain Peacock climbed out, soaked to the skin. He shook hands with the Dustoff pilot, then walked to our building.

"Welcome back," O.K. said. "We'll get you a dry flightsuit. You can enjoy our party tonight." He led Peacock to the intelligence vault.

After the captain changed and called home base, he told his story to George, the intel officer, and a room full of Coveys. "Not thirty minutes west of here, the engine quit. I was only a couple thousand feet up, so I didn't have a lot of time to think."

"What was the terrain like?"

"I was over heavy jungle. The only clear area was a small river. So I decided to ditch. Everything went well until I touched down. The airplane sank. I had to swim for my life."

"Any enemy activity?" George read from a pad on his clipboard.

"Not at first. I lost everything getting clear of the aircraft, then fought the unbelievable current to some large rocks on a sandy shore."

"Then did you call for help?"

"Lost my radio. My troops spotted me, and Dustoff answered their Mayday."

"What did you see on the ground?"

"Boot prints all over the sand. I wasn't afraid until that point. Then I became terrified. Fresh tracks. Everywhere."

I listened to the chilling story in quiet awe. This dose of reality took some glitter off my picture of the O-1 in my future.

I used fifteen minutes to pack my worldly goods and don the party suit. Then I joined O.K. and my pals on the officers club patio at five o'clock.

I raised a beer. "Short."

Everyone raised beer cans. Most held their beer with the middle finger.

"I'll miss you guys. I won't miss Vietnam." I felt sad when I thought about leaving my warrior brothers but took comfort knowing more warriors waited in Laos.

I stepped inside the door near the long bar for a refill. Blue party suits lined the bar, covered with patches offering information like billboards: Participant--Southeast Asia Wargames, Laos Highway Patrol--Dogshead Division, Yankee Air Pirate, Kill a Cong for Christ, One Hundred Missions Over the Suzy Wong--Shot Down Twice. The patches were limited only by the imagination of the wearer.

Someone handed me a full can of beer.

"Keep the noise down." The REMFs were up to their standard tricks.

In a flash of rage, I shouted, "I'm leavin' here tomorrow, and I intend to make all the fucking noise I can tonight."

The REMFs grumbled and cursed.

Still angry, I took my can of beer to the rear of a large cooling fan blowing humid air across the REMF tables. "This beer's for you." I dumped the golden liquid into the whizzing blades.

A white spray blew across the room like a blast of insecticide.

The crowd stood. Some departed. Some laughed and applauded. A few came over and congratulated me on surviving my tour.

Eventually, the aroma of steak drew me outside to the grill. I joined a crowd watching the large fist-sized hunks of beef sizzle and crack.

O.K. inhaled and shook his head. "That smell takes me back home. I close my eyes, and I'm on my porch in Alabama."

"Where'd the meat come from?" I tried closing my eyes, too.

"The Army," O.K. said. "We scrounged enough plywood to get a helicopter but opted for steaks."

"We couldn't have picked a more perfect afternoon for a party." I looked out from one of the highest points on the base at hazy meadows and rice paddies that faded into distant mountains. "The weather, the people, the ambiance. Everything's perfect."

Boom. Boom. Boom.

Three dark smoke columns boiled up in the infield, next to the runway, a mile to the southeast. The Warbler sprang into action. Loudspeakers announced, "Condition Red. Take Cover!"

O.K. shook his head. "Damn useless Warbler. The rockets have already announced themselves."

I agreed. "Only a direct hit on the grill will keep me from a steak dinner."

The chef abandoned his post at the grill, and Captain Skinny picked up the tongs.

The club manager attempted to lock us out on the patio.

A more sober Covey stopped him by asking, "Do you believe that wooden door is going to stop us from doing what we are going to do?"

"Sir, the club closes on yellow alert. This one is red."

"I know that. I repeat my question. Do you believe you or the Viet Cong or anything else is going to stop this group? Is it worth inviting damage the rockets were not capable of doing, just to prove a bureaucratic point?"

"But, sir, the club closes on yellow alert."

"Give me the keys, sergeant. You're off the hook. Go and seek shelter."

The REMF officers tried to make a stand and close the club. I joined Covey lieutenants who poured through their ranks to the bar.

"We're calling the Air Police," one REMF shouted.

"Call the goddam Marines, you prissy fuck," one Covey yelled back. The voice sounded like mine.

When the base commander arrived, his REMFs flocked around him like flies on a cow pie. The old lieutenant colonel looked to be about eighty and near death. He gave a sermon, but no one listened.

Our guys continued to cook steaks, pour drinks, and arrange tables. Larger

Coveys formed a perimeter. Someone shouted from inside the building, "Just go away. Go kill puppies. They won't fight back."

The old colonel gave me a hard look. I wanted to hit him. He was the enemy. I wondered if my facial expression showed my sincere feelings inside.

Probably minutes and possibly seconds before the lid blew off at Pleiku, our guest speaker arrived--Colonel Andy. His smile took away our anger. His upbeat manner removed the tension. He took the base commander aside.

Within five minutes, the old dead lieutenant colonel departed with his cronies.

Colonel Andy returned and announced, "I have good news and bad news. The good news is you can have your party. The bad news is you have to wear flak vests and helmets. Sorry guys. The regulations aren't mine to waive."

Mixed reviews turned to laughter. Alcohol made most of us feel bullet-proof. We dispersed to our quarters and returned, our party colors only slightly subdued by battle dress.

I sat with O.K. in the middle of three rows of tables that extended from a head table to fill the club dining room.

Elf passed me a plastic six-pack holder, stretched to form ridiculous protective goggles. "You'll be much safer with these."

"Excellent idea." I added the plastic glasses to my costume.

Field-graders shared the head table with Colonel Andy. Captain Peacock and the Dustoff crew drank wine at one end.

"Everyone has a toast to offer," O.K. said. "No time to enjoy the steak."

I nodded, feeling content in my own little world.

Finally, Colonel Andy stood to speak. "I counted 'em. One hundred and nine wine toasts. A new Air Force record."

The crowd roared, like Bear fans at Soldier Field.

"When the history of this war is written, the valor of the FAC force will occupy key chapters, alongside Dustoff." He raised his glass to the Army pilots.

Again the crowd exploded with cheers and toasts.

The handsome colonel responded with FAC adventures he'd seen in his tenure as commander. He owned the audience--in more ways than one. "Last week," he said, "the new commander at Quang Tri arrived and climbed in the back seat of an O.V.-ten with the old commander. Ten minutes later they were both dead. During an aileron roll at the end of the runway, they caught a wingtip in concertina wire. Concertina wire."

The crowd became temporarily sober. The coils of barbed wire he described only extended a few feet above the ground.

"The investigators brought me a cassette tape they found in the rubble. I hoped it would offer a clue as to what was going on inside the head of the pilot as he took this senseless risk."

The room became silent.

"The tape was from the family of the commander due to go home the next day. I had to listen to 'Daddy, we can't wait to see you.' I had every detachment commander in Vietnam listen to it. This war isn't worth losing our good people that way."

"Hard to argue with that concept," O.K. whispered. "But for the grace of God, he could be talking about me."

Colonel Andy finished on an upbeat note, and the lieutenants hauled him into the lounge and threw him over the bar. They grabbed me next and tossed me over. A fighter pilot tradition held that folk who were tossed over the bar had to buy a round of drinks.

As the colonel and I poured booze, he asked, "What's your crime?"

"My last night at Pleiku, sir. I go to the Ravens tomorrow."

"Congratulations. That's a tough cut to make." He shook my hand.

I felt proud at that moment. Dizzyingly drunk, but proud.

"Don't hang it out for nothin'," he said. "I went up there a few weeks ago. I was supposed to fly in a Raven's backseat, but at the last minute I had to meet a Laotian general. The Raven returned with a bullet hole through the backseat."

"I don't intend to die for no reason."

"Keep that thought," he said, and we toasted.

The evening faded into laughter and song.

At six a.m. I felt barely alive. A gallon of water later, I opened my locker in the life support section and found six mini-grenades remaining from my personal survival arsenal. I handed them to Lieutenant Ecstatic. "Be careful," I warned. "These little buggers are experimental. They just go off sometimes."

Ecstatic's eyes widened. His hands trembled.

I laughed and rose above my depleted condition. Following Elf to his O.V.-10, I climbed into the backseat. "I hope you don't feel as bad as I do."

Elf smiled. He gave me a smooth ride, although the heat and vibration of the O.V.-10 backseat made my stomach churn.

My hungover brain had locked onto a song I had heard and sung several dozen times the night before. I faded into sleep, mumbling, "Mary Ann Burns is the queen of all the acrobats . . .."

Chapter 14
Gone! My Turn

April 1971

Elf taxied the O.V.-10 to base operations at Ubon Rachithani and shut down the right engine.

From his back seat I watched the blades strobe hypnotically in alternate directions--like my feelings--before they finally stopped. Leaving behind stupid rules and inept leaders also meant saying goodbye to warrior brothers.

Elf said, "Good luck, my friend."

"See you back in the world."

I unstrapped, tapped Elf's helmet, and climbed out into the bright Thai sunshine. Sweat flowed down my neck and back as I retrieved my green B-4 luggage bag from the cargo compartment in the back of the airplane.

Elf had the engine started again when I walked back around the wing and saluted. His boom mike touched his bushy moustache when he waved his cast at me. A new flight surgeon had arrived, repaired his damaged hand, and let him fly with a plaster cast on his hand. Elf had insisted.

I smiled and watched his props make two whizzing circles that pulled him away. The heavy burnt kerosene aroma took me back to my first day on a flight line. A million memories fought for my attention. One thought dominated. I'll miss all you crazy sons-of-bitches.

Inside base operations I found a latrine and changed to civilian clothes, stashing my Nomex flightsuit in my bag--maybe forever. I stepped out in mufti.

A sharp-looking sergeant smiled from behind the base operations counter. A plexiglas board behind him listed aircraft by callsign. "Can I help you, sir?"

I waited while a howling F-4 passed overhead. "I need transportation to Udorn."

"The MAC Passenger Terminal is across the runway. The base shuttle bus'll stop out front in ten minutes."

"Okay." Another F-4 flew over and drowned out my words. "These airplanes make a helluva noise."

"We're the Wolfpack, sir. The Eighth Tac Fighter Wing."

"This sound is different." The F-4 cacaphony roared louder than the occasional droning reciprocating engines and wop-wopping Hueys at Pleiku. But howling was a new sound.

"I used to work on Phantoms. The boundary layer control system howls when it blows high pressure air through tiny holes in the wings."

"That explains it." I walked to the door.

"Good luck. Military Airlift Command runs Klong ops now."

"Klong?"

"The Thai word for sewage ditch. Also, the Klong is a C-one-thirty that flies a circuit from Bangkok to all the bases everyday. You have a couple of hours before the plane leaves, and you'll need all of that time." He shook his head, as though he wanted to say more.

Outside, the jet engine noise--whining on the ground and screaming in the air--seemed amplified by the hot concrete ramp. A blistering sun poured heat. White cumulous clouds boiled.

A blue bus took me on a tour of the base. Most buildings were made of a dark wood--probably teak--and landscaped in tropical flora. Tin roofs dominated the horizons. I felt odd riding on the wrong side of the road. Phantoms continued to roar overhead.

We finally stopped at a low building. I joined a line that stretched from a door along a sidewalk and around the side.

I asked the sergeant ahead of me, "Are you in line for the Klong?"

"Yep. But it sure ain't like the good ol' days."

"What do you mean?"

"Used to be, you could flash an I.D. card at the TAC pilot and jump on board. Now MAC's brought in a small empire of bureaucrats who screw the G.I. at every turn."

I inched forward in line and peeked around the corner of the building.

Near the door two young Air Policemen sat at a table opening luggage and rummaging the contents. A distraught N.C.O. watched with his hands on his hips.

The sergeant continued. "MAC prefers hauling cargo rather than people."

"Really?" I didn't mind playing straight man.

"Cargo doesn't complain about being hot, cold, late, or landing hard."

The last half of the line laughed loudly.

"A shelter of some kind would be decent." I wiped my forehead with my palm. “The sun’s like a torch. And what do they do when it rains?”

People around me grumbled.

After forty-five minutes passed, I reached the counter inside and presented orders to an airman wearing thick glasses.

“Sir, you need an M.T.A. to board a MAC aircraft.”

“A what?”

“A Military Airlift Command Travel Authorization. You can get one at the Transportation Squadron building on the other side of the base. Next.”

My temperature continued to rise, but I checked my anger. The wormy little clerk was only a cog in a big wrong-minded machine.

I lugged my bag out to the bus stop and waited. Finally reaching the transportation squadron thirty minutes later, I was surprised to find the reception area empty. “Excuse me,” I said, tapping the counter.

“What do you need?” The voice came from a back room.

I moved to the end of the counter so I could see the chubby clerk doodling at a desk. “I need an M.T.A., please.”

“You need funded travel orders for that.” He didn’t even look my way.

“I have funded travel orders.” I checked my watch. One hour to go.

The rude individual wore green fatigue pants and an olive-drab tee shirt that didn’t quite cover his hairy belly. He ambled slowly to the counter. “You must be in uniform to travel on MAC aircraft.”

“My orders direct travel in civilian clothes.” I wanted to kick this guy in the nuts.

He studied my orders for several minutes then slowly pecked a few words on an old typewriter. He handed me the form.

I confirmed I had what I needed then said loudly, “Put your uniform on.”

“My supervisor said--“

”Put your shirt on, mister, or I’ll call the cops now and file charges.”

He had to suck in his belly to button his shirt.

“Airman Johnson, you disgrace the uniform--a proud uniform better men than you wear to die in everyday. You’re overweight, lazy, and insubordinate. If I miss this flight, I’ll be back to file those charges and put your sorry ass in jail.”

He stood with his mouth hanging open. “But, sir--“

”Try harder.” I slammed the door, hoping to wake a supervisor, and jogged to the bus stop.

As I bounced in the firm vinyl seat during my third bus tour around Ubon, I recalled a Covey hooch bar seminar about Project 100,000--one of McNamara’s good deals for the military. The federal government forced the armed services to take as a welfare project one hundred thousand individuals who fell below recruiting standards. The military would convert them from sociopaths and semi-morons into useful citizens for the Great Society. The impact on N.C.O. morale and the Air Force mission was horrific. I decided I had just met Mr. Ninety-nine thousand, nine hundred and ninety-nine.

Three clerks later I sat on a bench of red nylon webbing in rear of the C-130 with five minutes to spare.

While the engines started, a loadmaster droned his mandatory briefing.

An Air Policeman led a panting German shepherd around the cargo bay on a last-minute drug inspection. The nice doggie left a gob of saliva on the crotch of my trousers.

Otherwise, the flight to Udorn was uneventful.

The thin officer wore green fatigues, glasses and a black baseball cap that told his story--Det.1, 56th SOW in white letters below silver captain's bars. Calling my name, he met me at the sweltering terminal at Udorn. We shook hands.

"I'm Mike."

"How'd you know my name?"

"We called the Klong. Checked the manifest. I came over and picked out the only passenger arriving in civilian clothes."

He took my suitcase to his jeep, parked outside near a sign that said Welcome to the 432nd Tac Recon Wing. "Hop in. I'll give you the tour."

He drove onto a road that paralleled the runway on our left.

"The club and all the support facilities are across the runway." He pointed left and stopped at a taxiway that extended perpendicular from the end of the runway across the flightline road and a quarter mile beyond. He turned right on the taxiway and flashed his ID card at a Thai guard who saluted. "We're entering the Air America ramp."

I nodded and took in the sights. Small hangars and buildings on both sides had parking aprons where various civilian airplanes sat. Large silver C-123s and green H-34s lined one side of the wide ramp. On the other side, near a row of blue and silver Hueys, several Thai workers in white coveralls stood beside a C-47. The left propeller began to turn, and the exhaust pipes belched white smoke as the engine started.

"On the left, behind these buildings is the Air America club. Over on the right is their passenger terminal. We own the big hangars at the end on the left." Mike nodded ahead where the taxiway widened to accommodate two dozen T-28s and several O-1s.

"You're well hidden."

"We don't need any visibility. The Det is made up of American volunteers who teach indigenous personnel every skill necessary to fly and fix aircraft of sundry types. In this way we're probably a typical special ops low-cost force multiplier." He smiled. "Oh yeah, we do Ravens, too."

He parked in front of a large hangar and handed me a key. "Give me your paperwork and put all your military uniforms in that conex container." He pointed to a dark green metal cube about ten feet on a side.

"Okay."

"Then come upstairs and meet the commander."

Five minutes later I knocked on the commander's door.

"Hi. Welcome to Det One. We want you to feel at home here throughout your tour of duty." Colonel Gleoggler stood six feet two. Wavy black hair with distinguished touches of gray was set above angular facial features that made him look like a dark-haired Steve Canyon.

"I feel great so far, sir. Your people are sharp."

"We'll help you in any way to prepare for what's ahead. You're in from Pleiku?"

"Yes, sir."

"Been there. Nice little base."

"The climate was perfect up in the highlands."

He nodded. "I guess you've figured out by now you'll be living in Laos."

"More or less." Rumors confirmed. I waited for more information.

"We'll check you out, then send you to Ventiane in a few weeks. The embassy makes the final decision on where you'll go next. You're wearing civilian clothes because Laos is neutral. We have no military combatants there. For the next six months, don't even think about wearing a uniform."

"Sounds reasonable."

"If you go down, you can carry a flight cap in your pocket and claim you were launched at no-notice on a rescue mission."

I chuckled. "I think I'd prefer to crawl out of the wreckage shooting."

"I understand." The colonel smiled. "The embassy will offer you cover stories, but they're bullshit. The N.V.A. knows the score. No Raven has ever been captured."

His last words stuck like an arrow in my cerebral cortex.

"We'll be here for you when you take your breaks from the program. But, be advised. I have one pet peeve--flamboyance. We don't need publicity. Up-country you can do what you have to do. But around here, I don't want to answer for any childish Raven antics."

"Don't worry about me, sir." I wondered what the hell he was talking about.

"Great." He shook my hand again. "Your trainer is Wally. He's a former A-One driver and an old Raven FAC. I'll show you to his office."

I followed the colonel down the narrow hallway.

"Got a new Raven for ya, Wally. See you later." The colonel departed.

Major Wally Krueger also was tall. With a square jaw and thin brown hair combed straight back, he looked like a fullback who'd stayed in shape over the years. His handshake confirmed that image. "O-Two driver?"

"Right."

"Another new guy, Denny Morgan, is due in from Vietnam later today. With a fleet of two O-Ones, I'll check you guys out quick as I can."

"I'm ready." I had no clue what would happen next.

Wally pinched the fabric of his dark brown shirt with a pencil pocket on the left sleeve. He wore matching pants and jungle boots. "Most guys pick up a few of these walking suits outside the gate at Brother Armajit's place. If you believe in cover stories, Forest Ranger colors are green and brown."

I nodded.

"Don't tell Armajit anything. He's probably a spy, but he makes good walking suits. Some guys wear jeans and t-shirts. Be comfortable." Wally smiled.

I liked how Wally hit his main points and moved on.

"You can stay at the Sri Som Chin Bungalow. On your way out, ask Mike for directions and a key. I'll see you and Denny here at eight a.m. tomorrow."

"Great." I turned for the door.

"One more thing. Keep a low profile at the club."

I nodded and departed. The Det's offices occupied the second floor of a long row of offices in the middle of a large double-hangar. I watched a busy crew of technicians riveting and sanding the wing of a T-28 in the huge hangar bay as I descended the open stairs. The gray, single-engine propeller-driven trainer had been converted for attack duties. Similar in appearance to the A-1, the T-28 was smaller with tricycle landing gear.

A small fleck of gray paint fluttered into my left eye and stuck directly over the cornea. I became suddenly blind in that eye. I bumped into the colonel at the bottom of the stairs. "Excuse me, sir. Something blew into my eye."

"Let's see." He looked at my eye.

"It's stuck over the center."

"Yep. I see it." He handed me the keys to his jeep. "Follow the main road around the base. Turn right just before the club. Hospital's a few blocks down. Hurry."

I climbed in and fired up the engine. The jeep had a left-side steering wheel. Away I went. My confusion with the road and sense of urgency caused me to swerve wildly a few times. I had no depth perception, was sitting on the wrong side of the vehicle, driving on the wrong side of the road.

Slow down, I told myself. You're going to get killed before you ever fly an O-1.

The colonel's directions worked, in spite of my disorientation. I parked and entered the emergency room. "I have something in my left eye."

"Come in here." A technician led me to a table under bright lights. Several others--all wearing white--joined him.

"I think a piece of paint stuck on the surface." I hoped they wouldn't amputate.

"I see it." Someone held my eye open. A doctor stepped in and used long tweezers to pull the object away. My depth perception returned. Next, someone squirted liquid into the wound.

"Thank you." I felt relieved from the feeling of helplessness. And I knew I'd fly tomorrow.

"Close your eyes." A nurse piled gauze pads in my eye socket.

I heard a wide strip of tape rip. Then it stuck to my cheek and forehead. Then another. I sat up.

"You have tiny lacerations on the surface. Wear the patch for twenty-four hours. Come back if you have problems." The doctor shook my hand and left.

"Okay." I nodded to a half dozen technicians who surrounded me. "Thank you very much, ladies and gentlemen. I'm impressed."

Someone led me to a desk near the door. "Sign here, please."

"Maximum help and minimum paper. You're my kind of professionals." I signed the log and departed.

At the club two beers later I lost the patch.

When I lived at Pleiku, I never went off-base at night. Thailand was different. Dirty streets full of smiling people welcomed me to Udornthani. Outdoor food stands and bar after bar lined my passage around several traffic circles.

Sri Som Chin was a small two-story apartment building a half mile down the street from the Two Friends Bar. I found my room and unpacked, then scanned an O-1 training manual at a table in the sparse common area at the top of the stairs.

A blond, wiry kid about five-foot-six entered and trudged up the steps. "Is this the See Some Chins?"

"Something like that. Today's my first day here." I introduced myself.

"Denny Morgan." He shook the hand I extended. "Where are you from?"

"Chicago--by way of Covey-Pleiku. I flew O-Twos on the Trail. You?"

"Cam Ranh Bay. I served with the ROKs--the Republic of Korea forces."

"I've heard they're a tough bunch."

"Yeah. Hard as nails. They don't take shit from anybody."

"Was Cam Ranh your first assignment?"

"No. I started in the backseat of an F-Four. They didn't have training slots to upgrade me to the driver's seat. I ended up in the Oscar Duck."

"Do you have any family?"

"I have a wife in Florida, but I couldn't resist the lure of the Steve Canyon Program. I think she understands. How about you?"

"First assignment. No family." I opened the refrigerator in the corner of the room. "Somebody left beer in here."

The door downstairs slammed with a bang. An excited-looking young man clomped up the wooded steps. His walking suit and gold I.D. bracelet told me he was a Raven. He adjusted a large bandage on the left side of his head. "Is that beer for me?"

"Sure. I don't know who bought this, but I'll replace it tomorrow." I handed him a cold one and pulled out two more.

"Jim Hix. Raven Two-two."

We shook hands and traded introductions.

Denny said, "Should I ask what happened to your head?"

"Nearly lost my ear going through a T-Twenty-eight canopy this afternoon." Hix had a strong physique, with thin curly brown hair, and intense blue eyes. He joined us and rested his boots on the small table.

"You ejected?" I noticed his left biceps was bandaged, too.

"My engine oil was all over the windscreen. I couldn't see anything. And I plan to kill that asshole, Tom King, who was in an O-One nearby. He said I was over a friendly site. 'If you have to jump, do it now.' Shit. He was only twenty miles off."

"How were you injured?"

"The Yankee ejection system is supposed to blow a hole in the canopy and pull you through it. The hole was too small for my head. If you check out in the Tango, wear a helmet. And don't put pens in the sleeve pocket." He patted his bandaged arm.

Denny and I glanced at each other. His facial expression matched my thoughts. Holy shit.

I said nothing, hoping to hear more of Hix's story.

"I remember the ejection like slow motion. I saw my thirty-eight pistol float out and bounce off the wing of the doomed airplane. Probably a good thing, because I'd have used it on Tom King when he started making low passes." Hix grinned.

"Who picked you up?" Denny went for more beers.

"Air America was on the scene in no time--fortunately for King--because

I was in the middle of bad guy country." Hix accepted a fresh beer with a smile and a nod.

I asked, "Are things pretty hot these days up-country?"

"We've lost three guys in the last month over the J."

I had no idea what the J was. "The what?"

"P-D-J. Plain de Jars. A large piece of real estate the North Vietnamese try to capture each dry season. They take about half of it, then we bomb 'em back to the border."

"Three guys, huh?" Denny shook his head.

"Good friends--Chuck Engle, Grant Uhls, and Park Bunker."

The night faded into beer and stories. I tried to learn about Hix and understand how he found his troubles. I wondered if I'd be as matter-of-fact if I had just bailed out over Laos.

Hix would be back in the air before the bandages came off.

Larry Ratts had nestled into the Lao culture deeply enough to earn the title Lawrence of Laos. With a sea captain's hat in his hand, he introduced himself the next morning at the Det. We found an empty office and chatted. He had a round face, innocent blue eyes and a quick smile.

"I was a Covey at Pleiku, too." He described his hooch room.

"You'll be honored to know they knocked down the wall and added your room to the bar area." I told him the latest Pleiku news.

Larry whipped his cap behind him as the colonel passed the doorway.

I laughed. "What's the hat thing about?"

"A few weeks ago, the colonel got a nasty call from the wing commander. Someone had reported an unmarked O-One taxiing across the road into the Air America ramp. The pilot was allegedly wearing a bright yellow scarf, Smokey-the-Bear hat, and an eye patch. He was singing and making music while he taxied."

"You seem to have detailed information."

"The squeeze-box gave me away. I'm the only Raven concertina player."

I nodded. Obviously, Larry enjoyed driving people crazy. I liked him.

"The colonel was hot. Lectured me about flamboyance. He even threatened to send me home."

"He's the boss around here," I said. "But who keeps track of hats, scarves, and eye patches?" Larry's stunt seemed so harmless--weird, maybe--but harmless.

Larry smiled. "Are you busy now?"

"Denny's flying this morning. I'll go this afternoon."

"Follow me." Larry strode down the hall and grabbed a set of jeep keys from Mike's office. Then he gave me the real tour. "Air America is the airline that supports the war in Laos. They fly all types of fixed-wing craft and helicopters supporting of the logistics needs of Laotian and other friendly government forces."

"Who pays the bills?"

"Money comes through C.I.A. channels. We call 'em the Company. They lurk behind the scenes here, and they have field agents everywhere, running pieces of the war. Be discreet and protect their identities at all costs."

"How much do you deal with them every day?"

"A ton. They advise large units and lead smaller ones. They have great intel. I'm living at Pakse now, but I've been all over Laos. The Company relationship with Ravens is informal, unofficial, and close."

"So, how do you meet these guys?"

"I'll introduce you to a few today. They seem to prefer working one-on-one. Up-country, just stay cool. The field agents approach you when they need help. After the door is open, use them to get the intel you need." Larry drove to the Air America passenger terminal and introduced me around. He then drove to Club Rendezvous--the Air America club--for an early lunch.

But for the heat and heavy tropical flora, the scene could have been a stateside pilot's lounge. Men wearing gray trousers--some wore khaki--and open-collared white shirts sat at most of the tables in the bright room with large windows along one side. Most wore stripes of rank on their epaulets. Several greeted Larry as they passed.

As I finished my pork fried rice--Larry had ordered kow-pot-muu for me--I said, "Judging by what I've seen so far, Air America has to be huge."

"Biggest hazard when you bail out over Laos is having an Air America chopper collapse your chute." Larry grinned. He reached into his pocket and handed me a well-worn bony rabbit's foot.

"What's this?"

"You need a good luck charm. A good buddha. The locals call it good Phi." He pronounced it pee. "That rabbit's foot has been passed along by Ravens who came from Pleiku."

"But won't you still need it?"

"Nah. I've never been shot down, and I'll be leaving in a few months. Time to pass it along."

"Thanks." I rubbed the charm and put it in my pocket.

A few hours later, I sat in an O-1 with Wally in the backseat.

"Cleared for take-off."

When I pushed the throttle, propeller, and mixture levers to maximum, the loud noise surprised me. We rolled forward, and I had to feed in right rudder to counter the engine torque and keep the nose on the centerline. At thirty knots the tailwheel came off the runway. At about fifty we lifted off. I raised the flaps and adjusted the power back to climb settings. "This airplane goes up like an elevator, compared to the Oscar Duck."

"Never flew the O-Two." Wally was a man of few words.

"This airplane is a hoot!" I felt at home in the cockpit by the time we reached the working area. The engine noise had fallen off to a steady drone. I began a list of flight maneuvers with slow flight, lowering flaps to sixty degrees and slowing the indicated airspeed to zero.

"Turn into the wind." Wally pointed to the right.

I turned, and we tracked slowly backward.

"Okay," Wally said. "Keep an eye on your cylinder head temperature. Engine heats up fast with no cooling air."

I checked the sparse instrument panel which had a vacuum-driven attitude indicator and fewer than a dozen flight and engine gauges. Beside the seat I found three radios and an Automatic Direction Finder receiver for navigation between radio beacons. "Visibility is super. All the references you need to do the mission and fly this thing are outside the cockpit. You gotta love it."

Wally directed me through the standard stalls and falls, then we turned for the traffic pattern. "The O-One has one big tactical advantage over other FAC planes. With the windows open, you can hear and pinpoint the source of ground fire."

"You fly with the windows open?"

"All the time. And when you hear the first bullet pop, change altitude, airspeed, and heading. Jerk the plane around. Go ahead and practice a few jinks."

I yanked and banked the airplane.

"You can yank harder. And don't forget the rudders."

I thought of a roller-coaster as I jammed and stomped the controls.

"At the same time you should be calling for airstrikes. From the report of the weapon you'll know exactly where the gunner's hiding."

I asked, "You routinely strike small arms gunners?"

"Every time. You owe your fellow FACs that much. By pounding the gunners, you discourage the bastards from taking casual shots. You push Darwin's Law on 'em."

"Then you can work even lower without being hassled."

"You learn fast," Wally said.

We flew ten traffic patterns for practice and met Denny in the debriefing room.

Wally went straight to the point. "I'll solo you guys tomorrow. Next day, we'll pair up--one solo and one dual--and go down to Nam Phong for landing practice. Meanwhile, we'll work a few airstrikes, controlling the Tango-twenty-eight training sorties here."

"Nam Phong?" Denny asked.

Wally pointed to a map in the wall. "The U.S. built a ten-thousand-foot runway about forty miles south of here. F-One-elevens were going to launch from there for night bombing, but four of the first six they brought over--Operation Harvest Reaper--disappeared without a trace."

"Sounds like Grim Reaper to me." Denny raised his eyebrows.

"I just realized something. You guys aren't going to benefit from landing on a concrete runway. We'll take a bag of chalk and mark lines in the infield grass."

Denny and I glanced at each other.

"We'll make a three-hundred-foot strip. When you can stop comfortably in one hundred feet, I'll certify you combat-ready."

The fun of flying made the next few warm, sunny days fly by.

One day with Wally in my backseat, I watched Denny land in the grassy infield at Nam Phong. He stopped in two hundred feet.

Then I had a go myself. The engine backfired when I chopped the power to idle and rolled into the final turn. With sixty degrees of flaps, the approach looked steep--like a forty-knot rocket pass. Just before impact I pulled back the stick to flare and touch down. I started to flare smoothly, but I ran out of time. The ground rushing up at me caused me to make abrupt adjustments. "Yikes!"

After several bumps and bounces, Wally said, "The idea is to run out of airspeed and altitude at the same time."

I nodded and added power. From the downwind leg, we watched Denny touch down, then lose control as his aircraft whipped around in a circle.

After a pause, Denny took off again.

Before I could comment, Wally said, "I'll pass you an old proverb about tail-dragger pilots and ground loops . . ."

I turned around to look at him.

". . . those who have and those who will." He grinned.

On the bombing range I learned to aim using the third rivet on the center beam of the windscreen. The O-1 had no gunsight. After expending the four rockets on each wing, I practiced dropping smoke grenades out the window.

Wally said, "I guess accuracy is the fighters' problem."

Denny and I became fast friends. I enjoyed his sense of humor. He found fun everywhere. Our last evening in town began at the club, where I showed off my skill at flipping stacks of beer coasters from the edge of the bar and catching them in mid-air.

Denny flipped a beer coaster into a major's bowl of chili. The major didn't see the humor I did, and I laughed even harder as Denny went through the motions of a humble apology.

We departed.

Following Denny around the bars downtown became an exercise in human hilarity. My jaw ached from laughter by the time we stopped at the Two Friends Bar for a few nightcaps.

The midnight hour approached, and the owners of the tiny watering hole wanted us to leave. An older Thai woman came to our table. "You drunk G.I.s. You go home now. We close."

Denny kissed her hand. "Maybe we drink all night."

"One more round. Then you go."

"Work hard, play hard." I raised my beer bottle.

"I'll drink to that," Denny said and clinked his beer against mine. "You know, I admire the décor in this establishment."

The interior walls of the Two Friends Bar were covered with styrofoam shipping containers, probably the work of an American G.I. On one wall an original oil painting featured two colorful butterflies whose antennae curved around and eventually connected. A small counter faced the door with a jukebox and a few tables taking all the remaining space.

"The art or the architecture?" I asked.

"Cluster bombs over here." Denny pointed to the front wall. "And over there we have the basic M-nine-oh-four fuze container. The ammo crate ambiance, I'd say--a class by itself. What do ya think?"

"I think we should we make these people truly happy and leave." I had exceeded my alcohol limit.

"Samlar race. From here to the bungalow. Okay?"

"Might as well. I'm too drunk to walk."

We staggered out the door where several of the common Samlar pedal cabs waited. The front half of the vehicle looked like a bicycle. A large red seat in a hard plastic shell sat on the rear axle between two large bicycle wheels.

I bartered, offering two baht--about ten cents--for the ride home. "*Bi Sri Som chin, song baht, mai krop*?" Larry Ratts had taught me a few useful words.

"*Song baht*. Okay, G.I." The young Thai driver smiled and bowed.

"No, G.I.," Denny said. "You pedal. He rides. We race."

The Samlar drivers laughed. They had seen this act before.

My driver said, "*Ha baht, krop*."

"He wants a quarter just to let me drive."

"Pay him, you cheapskate." Laughing, Denny climbed onto a nearby Samlar and bartered with the owner-operator.

Before my driver climbed into the passenger seat, he put his foot on a small pedal above the sprocket. "Brake here. No brake here." He moved a small handle under the right handlebar grip, and a small bell rang. Ding.

"On three, ready? One, two, three." Denny took off.

I chased him down the dark, narrow street.

When I pulled within half a Samlar length, Denny edged me toward a side ditch. I paused then swerved behind and passed on the other side. I sailed to the front door of our small apartment building and mashed the small pedal with my heel. The brakes squealed like a pig, and the Samlar shuddered. But we stopped.

Denny flew past.

Ding-ding-ding-ding-ding.

"Oh, shit." Denny hit the klong, a drainage ditch, where it emerged from a culvert beside the street well past the finish line.

I laughed at the crashing and cursing noises. I was still laughing when Denny staggered up the stairs. Black mud covered his shoes. Small gobs dotted his face.

"My Samlar didn't have any brakes." He began to laugh. "The guy wanted twenty bucks for a new front wheel."

"So did you pay him, you cheapskate?"

The next day, Air America hauled us to Vientiane in a Porter--a large single-engine taildragger that could land in only a few feet by using great pilot skill and the reversing power of the turboprop. From the copilot seat I surveyed the flat expanse of rice paddies and the occasional village moving slowly below. Trees sprouted in villages and in distant hills. I soon spotted the muddy Mekong River and the sprawling Laotian capital on the north bank.

After we landed, a quiet staffer--probably an airman or sergeant--pulled up in a jeep and took us to the U.S. embassy for briefings. Near the end of the day we visited the office of Raven Zero-one, the Air Attache's action officer for Raven FAC issues.

Tall and thin, Zero-one looked nervous to me. He welcomed us and bantered about the training program at Udorn. Then he got down to business. "I guess you want to know where you'll be living for the next six months."

I glanced at Denny and smiled when he rolled his eyes.

"We have an opening at Vientiane--"

"Vientiane?" I interrupted angrily. From my sparse knowledge, I knew the only combat action I'd see at Vientiane would be with the headquarters types. I wanted to go to a place called Twenty Alternate--Long Tchien--near the P.D.J. "I've been in the thick of Prairie Fire for six months. I came here to fight a real war, and I know the action is further north. If you don't need me, please send me back to Pleiku."

"I'll take Vientiane." Denny volunteered and took me off the hook.

"Okay," Zero-one said. He turned to me and folded his arms. "You get to go to Lima Five-four, Luang Prabang, the royal capital."

My eyes opened wide. I had never heard of the place.

"And don't worry. They have a nice little war going on up there."

Chapter 15
Bienvenue a' Luang Prabang

April 1971

The next afternoon, Denny gave me a jeep ride to a silver Air America twin-engine tail-dragger for my flight to Luang Prabang. "I heard an embassy guy call this run the Courrier," he said. "The Fifty Kip flies the same mission to the southern sites."

Since two-thousand kip equaled a dollar, I felt some comfort to be riding the Courrier. "See you at Udorn in a month."

"You're on. Samlar races." Denny wanted a rematch. He grinned and pulled away.

I climbed aboard and sat by a window. My green luggage bag was smaller without uniforms, so I slid it under my seat. The bag was malleable except for survival gear. The cold steel of my CAR-15 rifle's flash suppressor protruded from the zippered opening.

A large American woman sat beside me. "Hi. Are you going to Luang Prabang?

That's where the airplane's going. I smiled and nodded.

"I teach English there. I've been in Laos a year now."

Nodding again, I wanted to shake my head. *I know you don't teach logic.*

Her lip movement persisted.

Tired and hungover, I didn't care to talk to anyone about anything.

Finally she asked, "So what do you do?"

I thought about trying a cover story. She sounded air-headed enough to believe one. Then I thought of what Denny might say in this situation. "I'm the world's greatest fighter pilot." I watched her eyelids rise before I turned away and dozed off.

Screech.

I awoke and looked out my window as the aircraft pulled off the runway and rolled to a stop. I had traveled one hour forward and thirty years backward in time. Refugees packed the parking ramp. A huge, ragged-looking audience wrapped around the perimeter, barely held in check by soldiers. Several groups of people were running and yelling. The chaotic scene reminded me of black-and-white World War II newsreels. People carried everything they owned. Dogs, pigs, chickens, and children ran loose among the tattered villagers.

Outside, I looked around. Peaceful green mountains filled every horizon. Closer to the chaos a control tower stood near an Esso fuel pump. A few hundred yards behind me the wide brown Mekong River flowed below the peaks.

An older gentleman--probably a lieutenant colonel--wearing a walking suit motioned to me. He leaned against a jeep parked on the ramp.

I moved to him through the crowd.

"Ed Bender. Welcome to Lima-Five-Four."

We shook hands.

I introduced myself. "Thank you. Great to be here, I think."

"You'll love this place. Toss your bag in back."

I climbed in, and we drove slowly through the crowd to the main road. On both sides dirt trails wound down from the road to the ramp through five feet of jungle.

Bender spoke about the refugees. Larger Air America planes were moving them to areas safe from N.V.A. attacks. I heard USAID, meaning Uncle Sam's money, was helping, but most of his words competed poorly with the noise of the masses and the jeep's whining engine.

After he turned right onto a gravel road, he pointed to a cluster of twisted steel girders. "One-two-two-millimeter rockets hit the C.I.A.'s ammo dump a few weeks ago."

I was happy to be riding on the right side of the road again. "Do you get a lot of rockets here?"

"Not in town where we live. We had more attacks at Pleiku, where I flew A-ones a few years ago." Bender pressed the accelerator as the jeep labored up the slight incline.

I nodded.

Bender pointed left again. "A couple of miles out you can see the sleeping elephant mountain. Over on the right is the Buddhist shrine called the Wat Phousi."

A huge green pachyderm dominated the southern horizon. To the north a golden spire pointed skyward from the top of a five-hundred-foot hill.

"If you can't see the Phousi, don't take-off. Clouds that cover the wat also fill the mountain passes. The airfield has a radio beacon, but it's not reliable enough to make an instrument approach."

I nodded.

"Luang Prabang has about twenty-thousand inhabitants and over a hundred temples. The Lao pilots are typically very superstitious, and their Buddhist ways include animism. They make operational decisions based on the spirits."

"I've heard about good Phi." I rubbed my right pocket and felt the rabbit's foot.

We passed the Bienvenue a' Luang Prabang sign as we neared a wooden bridge with a green steel trestle.

"This small river is the Nam Kahn. It feeds the Mekong and marks the eastern border of the city." Bender held his speed as the jeep bounced up onto wooden planks over a hundred-foot ravine with a dark brown stream at the bottom.

Half a mile later we reached a T-intersection.

Trying to stay oriented, I counted one right turn followed by a left. Primitive thatched houses grew among newer buildings that showed French influence.

Finally, Bender swung left down a long driveway and waved at an armed civilian standing beside a huge palm tree. "Welcome to the AIRA compound. That's Air Attaché to new guys."

"Nice digs." I was still using Denny's phrases.

He jerked the jeep to a halt in front of a two-story ivory-colored house with sturdy concrete and terrazzo finishing. "The dining and living rooms are here. The enlisted quarters are upstairs."

I climbed out of the jeep and retrieved my baggage.

Bender led me across a graveled courtyard to a long low building in front of the main house. "My quarters are on the end near the big house. The medic has a dispensary in the middle. FACs have the two rooms at the end. You'll bunk in the last room with Bill, the chief FAC."

I walked to the door he pointed out.

"Go ahead and unpack. You can meet the guys as they drift in from the flightline."

Half an hour later in the high-ceiling living room of the main house, Bender filled in blank spaces in my picture. "Laos has five Military Regions. Lima-Five-four here at Luang Prabang is headquarters for M.R. One. FAC callsigns start with the Military Region designation. Bill is the senior FAC, Raven One-zero. You'll start auspiciously as Raven One-three, until Frank Birk leaves next week. Then you'll be One-two for the next six months. Dirty Ernie is Raven One-one."

"What's the mission up here in the far north--away from the Trail?"

"Kill North Vietnamese soldiers. We can't let them take over the government in Vientiane or displace the king, because we need their permission to bomb the Trail in southern Laos."

"And we bomb the Trail to stop the flow of supplies to South Vietnam."

"Yeah. Something like that."

"What is your role here?" I asked.

"Air Operations Commander. I try to make this whole thing work."

Bill arrived around five o'clock. Short with thinning hair, he resembled a compact Johnny Bench and seemed businesslike in demeanor. "I see you've already moved in to my room." Bill laughed as we shook hands.

I knew immediately humor would be a mainstay of this relationship.

With Bill came Dirty Ernie, a Rodney Dangerfield type, who showed an outer layer of humor with his mispronunciation. "Welcome to Lang Prabang."

Frank Birk arrived last. Tall and slim with brown hair and piercing hazel eyes, Frank seemed more serious on first impression. "Welcome. Raven thirteen, huh?"

I drank beer and listened to the day's war stories while the Laotian cook brought out pork ribs, vegetables, and homemade bread. Bill introduced me to the enlisted troops when they arrived as a group: Henry, Charlie, Fred, and the Chief. "You'll get to know these characters soon enough. Also, Dit and Swick work in the intel vault out back."

After a delicious meal, Bill pulled me aside while the others set up the evening movie. He lit a Marlboro. "What do you think about Luang Prabang?"

"So far, so good. I think I could fit into the family here."

"These guys are super. I flew O-Ones with Dirty Ernie at Tay Ninh. He was the fiercest Sundog FAC in Vietnam. Now he's having some kind of internal struggle with the mayhem and risk of it all. But he gets the job done."

"Does his nickname come from his interest in Playboy centerfolds or his sense of humor." I had observed both tendencies in the few hours I'd known him.

"Both." Bill laughed. "You'll replace Frank Birk, and I've asked him to give you a local area checkout."

"He seems like a great guy."

"Absolutely. But be careful. He's fearless, and he's brought home bullet holes every day for the past week or so--up from once a week. Several months ago an interpreter was killed in his backseat."

"Does he hang his ass out for nothing?"

"He's doing the job the way he sees it. Raven Zero-one was going to send him home, but Frank talked him into another chance. He'll go to Pakse in M.R. Four where the situation's relatively quiet at the moment."

"I'm ready to kick the tires and light the fires."

"Get some rest. You'll go with Frank in the morning."

I showered and climbed into bed feeling on top of the world. I liked everyone, and the leadership showed not one ounce of political encumbrance or careerism. Nothing stood between me and the mission but my humanity.

At seven in the morning I took a cup of coffee and joined Frank and the radio operator in the intel vault. A console with stacks of radios covered one side of the room. Maps and a bulletin board covered the opposite wall. The only furnishings were a filing cabinet, a safe and several chairs.

Frank perused messages on a row of clipboards.

Steve Swick manned the radio console. A muscular lad with carefully combed brown hair and glasses, he raised his coffee cup and smiled. "Good morning, Mr. Raven One-three."

"Good morning, Mister Swick. You're Army, right?"

"Special Forces. My specialty is crypto."

"Where are you from?" I detected a familiar accent.

"Crawfordsville, Indiana."

"Small world. I went to Wabash College."

"Ten thousand miles, and I can't seem to get away from you college boys."

"Who'd have thought I'd run into a Townie in northern Laos?"

Swick grinned.

Frank interrupted our joking. "We'll take the U-Seventeen up the Nam Ou this morning." He moved his hand on the map along a river that meandered northeast from Luang Prabang. Then he pointed to the Lao-Burma border. "This afternoon we'll go out west. Any questions?"

"Only a million or so. What's a U-Seventeen?"

"Cessna One-eighty-five Skywagon. It cruises twice as fast as the O-One and carries six hours of fuel versus the O-One's four-hour load. The U-Bird's seats are side-by-side, and it has a yoke instead of a stick."

"We have an O-One and a U-Seventeen?"

"Yep. And a T-Twenty-eight. We use the O-One for close air support in the local area because things are easier to see and hear from that platform."

"I like the Oscar Ace."

"The U-Bird is best for interdiction work farther away. When you're solo in the seventeen, remember you have a blind side above and below on the right. Also, the windows seal out ground fire noise. Ready to go?"

"Yep." I went to my room and retrieved a web belt with a pistol, knife and two survival radios. I also brought my CAR-15 with a bandoleer of ammo.

Frank sat in the jeep. "I'll drive. You fly."

As we bounced down to the airport, I memorized the route again. We sped across the ramp where I had arrived the day before. Refugees camped in the grass, but the once-paved surface was clear. We continued along a dirt road beside the runway to the west end then crossed the runway. The taxiway on the other side curved into a cluster of tall steel revetments.

Ahead, I counted ten T-28s, parked two per stall. Bombs nestled like eggs under the wings of most birds. On the fuselage behind the wing, some planes had a round symbol, the erawan--a white three-headed elephant--painted on a red background. I noticed the erawans were painted on removeable plates. Every one of these gray, oil-stained beasts had a spot of color on each side of its large radial engine. The cowl flaps--small engine-cooling doors--had a rearing horse stenciled in black on a yellow background.

"Their callsign is Mustang," Frank said.

We parked in a corner behind a gray U-17 whose only markings were small black tail numbers, 5-2-2. Four rockets on each wing hung in pods of two each, exactly like the launchers on the smaller O-1 parked alongside.

"You need to remember two particular items when you fly the U-Seventeen."

"My mind's a blank page." I could see the U-17 had a larger cockpit.

"Lock the tailwheel and keep the fuel selector in the Both position. Otherwise, she flies like the O-One." Frank's academic lesson sounded simple enough.

"I can do that." I fired up the large taildragger, launched, and leveled off at about a thousand feet.

Frank pointed to the Mekong.

I banked hard and moved to the middle of the muddy river. "She's a piece of cake to fly."

Frank nodded.

The drone of the engine sounded smooth and strong. At cruise power the airspeed needle pointed to one hundred and forty knots. The large cockpit reminded me of the O-2, with side-by-side seating and a bench seat behind. The U-17 had a few more gauges than the O-1.

"I see the knob on the bottom center is labeled Cigar Lighter," I said. "I'll have to get some cigars."

Frank smiled, but he didn't say much. "Seven or eight hundred feet above the ground works for me. If the engine quits, zoom as high as possible and make a distress call. Then land."

I laughed internally at Frank's understatement. Cruising northeast along the brown Mekong, I saw a picturesque village at the base of the first ridgeline west of the airfield. A ring of magnificent palm trees surrounded fifty thatched houses.

"Bad guys own most of the area beyond this village." Frank checked in with Cricket, the northern Laos airborne command post and counterpart of Hillsboro. "Raven One-two, airborne out of Lima-five-four with Raven One-three aboard. Working frequency three-fifteen-point-five. We could use F-Fours in about twenty minutes."

"Raven One-two, Cricket, Roger." The voice sounded businesslike.

Frank reported airborne to the AIRA house. "One-two's airborne with one-three."

"Roger." I recognized Swick's voice.

Frank pointed out friendly positions on a ridgeline near the Mekong. "They have no lines here, only small enclaves. The plantation on the south bank is the King's farm."

Where the Mekong began a wide turn to the north, the Nam Ou joined it from the northeast.

"Go that way." Frank pointed to the Nam Ou. "The N.V.A. hauls a lot of shit down this river. Then they shoot it at us. Count the boats you see. They're all bad."

"Okay. What do you call that karst ridge with the huge cone?" One steep ridge formed a C-shape around an inverted ice cream cone reaching up over two thousand feet.

"Pa Theung. The caves at the base are free game, too."

Jinking and searching for the next eight miles, I tallied thirty boats hidden under vegetation along the bank. We came to a set of bends.

"We call this place the W. North of here you'll need to keep the nose moving a little more." Frank searched the banks and looked behind us, too.

I began to zig-zag across the river.

After five more miles Frank pointed to a small tributary flowing from a wide valley to our north. "The small river is the Nam Bak. The Lao pilots won't fly north of here. They think this valley has bad spirits."

"What do you think?" I genuinely wondered.

"I'm not superstitious." Frank took control of the airplane to show me something. He banked hard to the right and climbed.

On my map I saw the Nam Ou jogged east-west between two sheer three-thousand-foot karst ridges. Looking outside I could see Frank was flying up the southern ridge.

Frank flew a few feet above the peak. "Arm one rocket and get set to fire."

"Okay." I reached up and raised one of eight red-guarded switches on my left.

Frank moved the controls wildly. We lurched left to inverted and nosed over the cliff. Falling toward the river, he rolled out in a steep dive. "Look at 'em run. Fire."

I pushed the pickle button.

Bam.

Several khaki-clad soldiers scurried the hundred-meter distance from the river's edge to a large cave opening. A fireball blossomed near the river, then became white smoke as the soldiers disappeared into the dark opening.

Frank rolled right and pulled away. "I surprise those guys every day. You have the airplane."

Following a wide bend to the north, I resumed my river recon mission. "Do you ever hit anybody?"

"Sometimes. But I take most of my hits there at Pak Bak--all in the tailfeathers so far. The gunners don't know how to pull lead when they aim at airplanes."

I nodded. "My boat count is over a hundred." I had spotted all kinds of water craft, from dugouts, larger sampans, and motorized bamboo rafts. Most were pulled up on the bank or parked under vegetation. Some had been camouflaged. Taken together, they presented a significant logistics target.

Five miles ahead, the Nam Ou flowed from due north between four-thousand-foot cliffs. On the east bank, the vertical wall was slightly lower and broke for the confluence of a perpendicular valley.

"This place is called Muong Ngoi. Lots of bad guys here. You'll always find targets in this valley or west of here in the Nam Bak valley. Dien Bien Phu is about ten miles northeast."

I climbed to a thousand feet.

"Speaking of targets . . .." Frank pointed to a suspicious shape under trees on the river's east edge. "I've got the airplane." When rolled ninety degrees, the nose sliced down in a neat wingover. He dove toward the water at maximum speed.

I looked up at the eroded faces of the gray limestone cliff faces. "I see gunners in caves on both banks of the river."

"Yeah. They're awake now. We'll wait for the F-Fours." Frank pulled the U-17 straight up, and leveled off with another wingover at three thousand feet. "What did you make of the target?"

"About the size of a semi-trailer. Covered in a blue tarp. Supplies?"

Frank nodded. "Check your map. You do the briefing and control the strike."

"This airplane zooms up nicely. Better than the Oscar Deuce."

"Yeah. I flew the O-Two at Danang."

I copied coordinates and elevations for the briefing. Frank was testing me, but I knew the answers.

"Raven One-two, Cricket. You'll get Falcon Two-one in about five minutes."

Frank said, "Send them to the three-five-five radial for ninety miles off channel one-oh-eight."

I briefed Falcon flight.

Frank watched in silence as I prepared to mark the target.

Rolling in, I noticed the U-Bird had an iron sight welded to the cowling on the left side. I lowered the nose, lined up, and fired.

Bam.

My smoke hit near the tarp.

"Falcon has the target. We'll drop pairs. One is in."

I turned below and behind the Phantom. "Cleared hot."

Two bombs arced down and hit the tarp. Orange fireballs flashed, then gray smoke boiled into the sky.

"Nice bombs."

"Two's in."

"Cleared hot." I was back in the saddle. After directing all their bombs onto the same target, I searched with Frank's binoculars.

"See anything?"

"Just smokin' holes." I passed good bomb damage assessment and said goodbye to Falcon flight.

"What are these white flakes? The valley's full of 'em."

I dove lower to examine the particles that floated like heavy snowflakes. "We must've cooked a several-years' supply of rice."

"Amazing. Let's check the Nam Bak valley and follow it south to the river."

I flew west. "Lots of trails under the trees here."

"The N.V.A. has logistics base camps and training areas all over the place, but the Lao pilots won't fly past the W. Use F-Fours for the larger targets."

"What's the T-Twenty-eight drivers' problem?"

"A few months ago, a four-ship flight came up here in terrible weather. They never came home. Now anything north of the W has bad Phi. I get tired of that bullshit."

Except for answering a few questions, Frank remained silent while I flew home. Approaching the airfield, he said, "Cricket, Raven One-two's over the friendlies."

"See you later, One-two."

The U-Bird landed as easily as it flew. I greased a three-pointer and taxied a mile to our revetments.

"I usually fly a standard approach like yours, but I add power and fly along a few inches off the runway. Chop the throttle a couple hundred feet before the end."

I nodded.

Homemade bread made my large lunchtime ham sandwich taste delicious.

An hour later--in the U-17 with Frank--I followed the Mekong River west toward Burma.

About sixty miles into the trip Frank pointed out a military outpost on a hill on the north bank. "You can see small structures, trenches, and antennas. But the embassy won't clear you to strike it. I don't know why. Maybe the President doesn't want us to kill Chinese at this time."

"My map says the small village at the base of the hill is called Pak Beng."

"One of our backseaters, Mr. Seo, has family in that village, so be careful if you strike the area. You'll have to convince the embassy the outpost should be destroyed."

I nodded. "What are the Chinese doing here?"

"Building a highway to Thailand. The approaching China Road ends a few miles north. No need to go there. I visited the area once to help pull a Company roadwatch team out. I saw thirty-sevens in rings of six each. They don't bother to camouflage the gunpits."

Forty miles past Pak Beng the Mekong turned ninety degrees right and ran north. Thirty miles further, on the Burma border near Ban Houei Sai, Frank showed me Lima Site 25, a runway with three levels and steep grades connecting them.

"Without strong winds," he said, "the best landing approach is uphill, and the best take-off is downhill. Let's see if anybody's home."

Frank gave me a history lesson as I lined up to land. "The U.S. government paved the runway because the semi-precious stones in the ground lacerated airplane tires."

"We're near opium poppy territory, aren't we?"

"The Golden Triangle." Frank nodded.

We landed and stayed long enough to say hello to a surprised Company man, who lived in the back of the operations shack there. He showed us stored ordnance for the T-28 and a supply of aviation fuel.

During our takeoff roll we bounced once off the first plateau, then leaped off like Superman from the second. I flew forty miles south to L-69, a one-thousand-foot strip of red dirt built atop a steep hill.

"Be careful," Frank advised. "If you land short, we'll hit the hill. If you land long, we go off the cliff on the other side."

Landing on the short runway was easier than thinking about landing there.

In a screened hooch at L-69 Frank and I drank cold lemonade and listened to an intelligence update from two civilians. "We have a small supply of fuel and ammo. N.V.A. activity is sporadic. Just remember, we don't cry wolf. When we call for airstrikes, we really need help."

I surveyed the wide valley below Lima-69 and came to the naive conclusion that enough land existed out here for everyone. Why were they fighting?

On the way home we made pit stops at L-69A, another dirt strip in the valley below L-69, and L-118A near the China border.

During the hop back to Luang Prabang, Frank emphasized the importance of staying in contact with the company people out west. "We have a huge area of responsibility. You never know when or where the next crisis will pop up."

After landing at Luang Prabang, Frank drove me to a small building on the other end of the runway. Inside, he knocked on the open door to a small office. "Sir, I would like you to meet a new Raven FAC." He turned to me. "Meet Major Oum Pang, the commander of the army unit that fights harder and better than any outfit in Laos."

"We like to find good targets for the Ravens to destroy." Oum Pang rose from his desk to his five-foot nine-inch height. His intense eyes and sincere smile added power to his words. Quickly, his personality overflowed the room.

I shook hands with this warrior. "We like good targets."

"Let me show you where my commandos usually operate." Smiling, Oum Pang led me to a large map of the local area and pointed out several firebases.

"We give Major Oum Pang's commandos top priority," Frank said. "He has the radio frequency for the AIRA house, and I stop by here every day to see my good friend."

The next morning I flew the O-1 with Bill in back. He showed me the exact locations of all the friendly units in a sparse ring around the city. After landing he drove me to a large wooden building where our backseat interpreters had their office.

The senior backseater, Seo, introduced himself. "When I worked airstrikes from the ground, they called me Black Widow." Short, and handsome, Seo spoke excellent English. He introduced me to Sai and Piang, two small, quiet characters.

I said I'd be back after lunch to pick up one of them.

I used three of the O-1's four hours of fuel touring the local area.

Seo set up shop in my backseat, chatting and sometimes yelling in his native language. He gave me detailed knowledge of each ground commander as we worked T-28 strikes on targets passed from ground units. "I have called one more commander," he said. "He requests the Raven to fly over while he is moving his troops."

"Show me," I said. Airpower escort normally discouraged enemy attacks.

Seo pointed to the second ridgeline from the Mekong, less than fifteen miles from the city. "He is marching his men on the top of this long mountain."

I found the string of soldiers clad in green uniforms moving near the crest of a ridge that pointed to the airfield. "We can look around the area, but the fighters have landed for the day. And we, too, must land soon." I leaned my fuel mixture, just in case.

"I understand." Seo spoke more Lao on his radio.

I weaved along the ridge and scouted the terrain ahead, finding no sign of enemy troops. The point man had half a mile to go to reach his destination.

Boom.

A mortar round exploded fifty feet in front of the column. The point man fell.

The N.V.A. attack had fooled me. I had searched out to rifle range but not mortar range. I felt my anger rise. *You've challenged me professionally, but I take it personally. You assholes will pay.*

The din of small arms firing brought me to reality. I called Swick at the AIRA house. "We've got a battalion-sized fight going. Tell one of the FACs to get a set of T-Twenty-eights out here."

"They're eating dinner, and I think the Royal Lao Air Force is done for the day."

"And I'm nearly out of gas. But the N.V.A. is on a different schedule. They have a nasty little attack underway. Send help, please." I scoured the flat area at the southern base of the mountain.

Twenty N.V.A. soldiers, crouching in light colored uniforms, stood and crossed a dirt trail. A kilometer farther south two mortar positions blinked as they launched their small bombs at the hilltop.

Below me, the friendlies were organizing a perimeter. Their disarray matched the frantic radio calls in their native language.

"Hang on," I told Seo, and yanked the airplane to the right, slicing down in a two hundred and seventy degree turn, passing over the friendlies. I armed a rocket and aimed at the closest concentration of enemy troops.

Bam.

I pulled off hard right, just above the smoke, then reversed left toward the mortar flashes and armed another rocket.

Bam.

I could hear the distinct pop of rifle fire below me as I whipped the airplane toward the friendly lines. One rocket left. I could use a small nuke.

I heard Frank's calm voice. "What's all the commotion about?"

"Looks like a company or more of N.V.A. with mortar support are attacking one of our battalions. I'm outa gas and about to fire my last rocket at the next N.V.A. face that comes out of the jungle."

"Where are you?"

"Rolling in on a platoon that just ran across a clearing on the right flank of the attack." I armed a rocket as I passed about ten feet over the friendlies. From point blank range, I fired at a large clump of trees.

Bam.

This time I passed though the bitter smoke cloud.

Pop-pop-pop-pop-pop.

I flinched as rifles blinked fire at my airplane. I jerked the nose around to the friendly position. "I'm ten miles west of the field. No gas. Come out here if you can."

"Usually the N.V.A. attacks at night," Seo said.

"They picked the perfect time for this one--after the T-Twenty-eights landed and before the A.C.-Forty seven takes off." I could understand the reluctance of the other FACs to respond. Here was the new guy, describing a large fight on his first solo in their war zone.

"The friendlies say you slow down the attack," Seo said.

I slashed down the side of the mountain again, but I had no more rockets to fire.

"We're sending someone to you, One-three." Swick's voice came through.

"Roger. Thanks." I hadn't seen a fight this big since one night on the Bolovens Plateau when P.S.-22 came under attack. Never had I witnessed this many N.V.A. troops in one place along the Trail. Now I watched individual soldiers advancing on a one-mile front. Hundreds of muzzles flashed. I saw movement everywhere.

"Friendlies have machine gun now." Seo pointed to flashes at the end of the column. "Have mortars soon."

"The enemy seems to be ignoring us." I pressed down to where I could see faces in the fading light. After several passes, I heard Frank's voice.

"I'm airborne in the seventeen. I have you in sight."

"The valley floor below me is crawling with N.V.A. You can see movement everywhere. Friendlies are up on the ridge. I'm outa gas."

"Show me the mortars, then go home."

Using the wing of the Oscar Ace as a giant pointer, I pylon-turned the last firing positions of the mortars.

"Wow," Frank said. "You've stirred up a real target here."

"Have fun. I'm leaving." I watched two T-28s set up an orbit overhead.

With one eye on the runway, and the other on the fuel gauge, I landed, taxied to the revetments, and shut down the engine. I crawled out, drenched.

Seo climbed out, walked to the edge of the revetment and threw up.

One of our two O-1 mechanics, a Philippine national named Ramon, handed me the binder full of aircraft forms.

I scribbled 4.5 in the flight duration block, initialed the pilot block, and handed the paperwork to Ramon.

He shook his head. "I think you leaned the engine too much."

I smiled and thought about what he said. "You mean if I had properly adjusted the mixture--"

Boom.

We both looked east when the first bomb cracked from the T-28 attack under Frank's control.

"The enemy is nearby?" queried Ramon.

"Temporarily."

Chapter 16
All in the Family

April 1971

Skreek.

Bill halted the jeep beside the O-1. He motioned for me to climb in.

I shook the hand of my crewchief, Ramon. "Good airplane. Thanks."

"No problem." He smiled as I turned to board the jeep.

I ducked under the jeep's brown canvas top, laying my rifle and map bag on the floor in back. "I appreciate the lift."

My backseater from the roller coaster-like mission, Seo, finished vomiting. He climbed on his motorbike, waved and buzzed away.

Bill smiled. "You earn a free ride home when you find an N.V.A. regiment."

"Sounds like a good deal."

"Nice work. Frank called in. He's herding what's left of 'em back to Hanoi." Bill lit a Marlboro and aimed the jeep home.

"In truth, they found me. I was escorting a Lao infantry unit along the ridgeline, and the N.V.A. came outa nowhere, like boom." I felt physically exhausted, as though I had just run a long race.

"Frank taught you well. Finding lucrative targets starts with the Company intel reports, radio cuts, and a close look at where the strikes have been going. Then check the actual terrain for flaws in their camouflage, straight lines, colors, or a wisp of smoke from a campfire. Throw in a few classic items like water sources and military crests--you know, one-third down and two-thirds up the mountainside. The friendly ground commanders will fill in the rest of the picture."

"Those guys on the ground gave me dozens of coordinates--like an artillery target list. I asked Seo to make them justify every one. And they did. Lights, noises, patrol contacts--I hit all the legitimate targets they gave me."

"How do you feel after your first solo day?"

"Tired." I flipped up the cover of my small green notebook. "Did I really put in sixty-two airstrikes today?"

"Find your second wind. The guys want to give you the tour tonight."

"The tour?"

"We have three semi-decent bars in town." Bill turned onto the rutted main road.

"I'd feel more comfortable socializing with them if we could review the cast of characters. The Chief is the New York City guy--hair combed straight back?"

"Right. Tough as nails on the outside. His troops are his first priority."

"The chunky guy with glasses--sounds like he's from Tennessee--who is he?"

"Henry. Tunes engines like a maestro. Works his ass off in the sun all day. But he has a subscription to Screw Magazine, just to keep up with trends in the civilized world."

"I see." I hadn't read publications like that in Indiana.

"He really does." Bill laughed out loud.

"Tall ordnance guy, curly black hair, pock-marked face. I forgot his name."

"That's Charlie. He's quiet most of the time, but he loves to talk about silver bullets--B-Sixty-ones. He spent years maintaining nuclear weapons."

"Okay. And Fred's the medic--the mature one of the bunch?"

"Yeah. Fred's a super doc. He spends a lot of time with the kids in town. Makes sure they have vitamins and stuff."

"I feel as though I know Swick, the radio operator, since he's from Crawfordsville. He lives in the Army house, right?"

"ARMA--for Army Attaché. You'll like the officers, too."

"Finally, Dit is the little white-haired guy who works in the intel vault."

"Yeah. He's a crusty ol' master sergeant. Really loves his job."

"Have I met everyone?"

"Yep. We're short an A.P.G. guy--that's Airplane, General mechanic. Should have one in a few months."

"Okay. End of interrogation."

"No problem. I'll let you buy a round later."

I splashed water on my face and thought about a shower. I washed a sandwich down with a beer, then slid into the jeep behind Bill and Ernie. Several enlisted guys clambered into the Chief's black Scout.

Bender watched from the small porch with his small can of Beaujolais. He stayed above the restlessness of the troops.

"We'll try the Bungalow Bar first," Bill said. "Ernie and I go there almost every night." He turned onto the hard-packed dirt of the main road.

We passed a theater with an over-sized marquee and nearby movie posters that resembled billboards. In brilliant hues they captured the passion of the current fare and previewed adventures involving a vicious tiger.

"With no television, the locals love their cinema," Bill said. "I think most of their movies come from India."

"Have you been to the theater here?"

"Hell, no. You could get V.D. from the toilet seats." He laughed and turned toward the city center. Eventually he pulled into the gravel courtyard and parking lot of a small hotel.

When the Scout stopped beside us, troops tumbled from the doors.

"Follow them," Ernie motioned.

A small path wound around tropical bushes and palms. I saw a round thatched roof covering an open-air bar. "I like the looks of this place. Nice ambiance."

As the first customers of the evening, we filled half the circular bar.

Bill sat beside me. "Meet Chris, the owner, and his lovely wife, Deng."

I shook hands with the handsome couple. "How do you do?"

"Nice to meet the new guy." Chris wore a white shirt and tie.

Deng tossed her long, thick tresses. On the floor opposite us a small girl played with a black cocker spaniel.

"Were you born in Luang Prabang?"

"No. When I was a young man, I emigrated from Hanoi. They gave us a few months to leave the country in nineteen-fifty-four."

"When the politicians divided Vietnam?" I knew vaguely about the evacuation.

"Yes. About one million people left at that time."

"We don't worry about Vietnam anymore." Deng showed her striking smile. "Many merchants in Luang Prabang came from Hanoi."

"The Bungalow is my favorite night spot," Bill said. "The crowd is small and friendly, music is mellow, and the food is excellent."

"We hope you have a good experience in Luang Prabang." Chris said goodbye. He and Deng walked to the hotel. Their daughter followed with the dog.

A bartender served up cold cans of Tiger Beer.

I took a swig of the bitter liquid. "Where is this stuff brewed?"

"Singapore," Henry said.

"Yeah," the Chief added. "You can taste the delicate bamboo aging."

The crowd laughed, but I agreed with the Chief.

"Another round, please." I acclimated quickly.

An hour later Bill parked along a dirt road near a two-story wooden building. "This stop on the tour represents a major slide down the social ladder."

Ernie nodded. "The huge gate across the street opens to the local jail--the monkey house. We call this mine shaft the Prison Bar."

"One of these nights," Bill said, "the authorities are going to open both gates and herd the bar crowd across the street and straight into hell."

I felt safety in numbers as our troops joined us on the wooden porch. The swinging doors were missing, but in every other respect we seemed to step into a dark, shadowy bar in Dodge City in 1875. I wished I had brought my six-shooter.

"Let's grab one of these large round tables," Bill said.

When my eyes adjusted to the nearly complete darkness, I saw a stage at one end of the bar. A teenager stood center-stage, making horrible sounds with a guitar. Another kid sat in a chair beside him, doing nothing. I wanted to leave. I lifted a shot of cheap scotch. "Here's to the road. May we be on it soon."

Henry laughed. "After you've been here a while, sir, you'll love this place."

Sinuane, a Lao T-28 pilot stopped briefly but with a flourish at our table. He greeted each enlisted man as an old friend. "Raven-One-three, you must change your callsign. One-three is a very bad number. Maybe you die."

I laughed. "I'm probably in more danger in this bar than over the Nam Ou."

"You fly too low."

"I fly low enough to find good targets for you to strike."

"You must wear this when you fly." He handed me an amulet.

"I can't take your protection away."

"No sweat. I have many buddhas." He pulled up his gold neck chain with eleven small buddhas attached.

"Thank you, my friend. I'll carry this on every flight." I downed a shot of White Horse Scotch and felt immediately safer.

Our final stop seemed hidden in the jungle on the west end of town.

After Bill pulled up before a small building on the dark narrow road, he took care to turn around and park facing civilization. "We call this place the P.L. Bar."

Ernie said, "That stands for Pathet Lao. This place has bar girls, and it's so remote that the other side stops here, too."

"No weapons, and nowhere to run. What the hell have I gotten myself into now?" I stumbled to the door.

We found seats around the last empty table in the corner. Perfumed ladies floated by, but my thoughts stayed closer to survival. "Would anyone be surprised if a sword-wielding Commie bastard burst in here and started hacking at us?"

"I would," Henry said.

"You're not uneasy here?" I asked.

A large-breasted girl sat down on his knee, making my question moot.

"Have a beer," Ernie said. "Relax. Man cannot live by war alone."

Airborne in the U-17 then next day, I cruised up the Mekong and chatted with my rightseater, Piang. "I plan to go up the Nam Ou. Ask if the local commanders have any targets near the river."

"Okay." Small and shy, Piang wore green fatigues with a red beret. He sounded ten feet tall on the radio.

After a few minutes he reported. "About ten boats bring soldiers down Mekong last night. Stop near Nam Ou."

I flew up the Mekong and saw a cluster of wooden boats on the sandy west bank. Nearby, a footpath meandered up the steep incline and disappeared into a grove of trees. I searched the bank and the trees. I asked Piang, "Do you see any soldiers?"

"No."

"I don't either. But we can make them walk home."

I called Bill, who was working the local area mission in the O-1. "Send me a set of Tangos when you can."

"Roger."

Five minutes later I briefed Mustang Green, a flight of two. "The boats must go."

"Roger, Raven One-three." The T-28 leader's voice belonged to T.Vant, a handsome and affable fighter pilot, rumored to be related to the king of Laos. "Mustang Green is in on the boats."

The gray T-28 overhead rolled slowly beyond ninety degrees, and its nose found the target.

"Cleared hot."

A five-hundred-pound bomb fell and whumped in the center of the boats.

"Hold high and dry, please." I dove into the angry gray smoke of the bomb. None of the boats remained intact. "I see some caves on the hillside. Near the path."

"Mustang Green, roger."

"Get ready to hit my smoke." I zoomed up and away, then brought the nose around to the hill. I fired one rocket.

"Mustang Green is in."

"Cleared hot on the caves." I watched the T-28s pillage the dark openings. Bombs and rockets smashed into and around the target for about two minutes. Smoke rolled up from several dark openings.

"Mustang Green is winchester."

"Thank you. See you later."

I turned back to the Nam Ou and counted boats.

After lunch I went to the airfield early and hung out with the T-28 pilots for awhile. I met Chin, also known as Mustang Red, the squadron commander. A tough-looking dude, he had a mole on his chin that sprouted a two-inch hair. I didn't ask.

"I've spotted a lot of boats on the Nam Ou," I told him. "Forty or fifty are south of the W. Many more to the north."

"We can hit the boats, but our first priority must be here, near the city."

"I understand. If we close the Nam Ou, we cut off the tail of the local N.V.A. forces."

Chin smiled. "One day. Maybe soon."

I nodded and shook his hand. I vowed to keep the pressure on these guys to hit enemy targets wherever we found them.

When Piang arrived on his moped, we launched in the U-17. I reported airborne to Cricket and the AIRA house.

"Look at your left wing, near the strut." Bill's voice replaced Swick's.

"It's still attached."

"Look at the surface. See anything shiny?"

I spotted a bright one-inch square. "I think I see what you're talking about."

"Aluminum tape. Ramon put it over the A.K.-forty-seven hole after you landed this morning."

Damn. "I don't get no respect." The only place I flew low was near those boats.

"Thought I'd let you know. Keep your eyes open."

"Thanks." Why did I say thanks? I wish he'd have told me over a beer after dinner. I felt violated. In all my crazy O-2 days I had never been hit by ground fire. I had lost my cherry without even knowing it had happened.

Piang took an interest in the bright thing on the underside of the wing. "Bullets?"

"Only one. We didn't deserve that hit."

"N.V.A. shoot from trees." He pointed ahead, where a dozen sampans now resembled a pile of burnt toothpicks on the river's edge below barren hills.

I nodded. "Cricket, Raven One-three. I have targets if you have air."

"Roger, One-three. Twenty-minutes."

I flew north on the Mekong for ten minutes. No other targets offered themselves. I put my briefing together then turned around.

"Raven One-three, Falcon One-one."

"Falcon, Raven, go ahead."

"Two fox-fours. Wall-to-wall Mark eighty-twos."

I briefed them. "I'll mark a stand of trees, about a klick square. Please put all your bombs in those trees."

"Rog. Whatcha got?"

"A platoon of N.V.A. Watch for small arms fire. They put a round through my wing this morning from those trees." I looked over at Piang, who nodded. From a mile away I took aim.

Bam.

A column of white smoke rose from the middle of my tiny forest, isolated above a sparsely vegetated section of the river.

I pulled up and located the leader, a black speck on a clear blue sky.

"Hit my smoke."

"One's in."

"Cleared hot."

Dropping three bombs at a time, the Phantoms gouged fiery divots from the green patch.

"We're winchester bombs. Would you like some twenty mike-mike?" The flight leader offered to strafe. Due to the increased risk of this tactic, the brass had placed restrictions on gun passes. Normally, I had to beg for this ordnance.

"Cleared hot. Spread it around."

Falcon made the woods sparkle then departed like the wind.

I gave them credit for accurate attacks, although I couldn't see specific damage. I shrugged at Piang, who shrugged back.

The cold beer felt perfect as it cooled my mouth and throat. I sat in the vault giving Dit the details from my day, while Swick manned the radios and ran paper tapes through an encryption device.

Swick smiled as he listened to my story. "So the Wabash man is going to carry on the Frank Birk tradition? One hit per day?"

"No way, Townie. Today was a fluke."

Bill entered and bolted the heavy door behind him. "I have some news. Frank leaves tomorrow for Pakse. You're now officially Raven One-two."

"Maybe my luck'll improve."

"Mine already has," Bill said. "I'm going to the States in a week. Gotta put my marriage back together."

"Good for you. I wish you the best."

"Plan on going to the daily four o'clock A.O.C. meeting while I'm gone."

"Sure. But before you leave, would you talk to the Lao colonel at the ops center? See if he'll give us all or most of the Tango sorties for one day just to kill boats."

"I'll try, but the local Army commanders depend on airpower."

"Sell him on the efficacy of air interdiction. You're eminently qualified to advocate airpower. Meanwhile, we'll clean up the Nam Ou like a Roto-Rooter."

While Bill enjoyed the States, I flew twice each day. One typical evening with Ernie at the Bungalow, I hoisted my third beer. "I've been talking to the Tango pilots about the Nam Ou."

"They're no help north of the W. They believe the river has bad ju-ju."

"The N.V.A. owns that river. It feeds, clothes and arms them. We can take it back with airstrikes."

"Let's do it."

"First we need good numbers on the boats. Are you ready for a high-low mission?" I wasn't sure if Ernie would go for my plan.

"As long as I'm the high man." Frank had once called Ernie Astro-FAC.

"Don't fly so high you don't deter the gunners. I'll call out what I see, and you write it on your map."

"I'll fly the O-One and do the writing."

"No. You take the U-Seventeen and do the writing. I need the maneuverability and quick response of the O-One."

"Okay. You're making this difficult for me."

"How, asshole? All you have to do is write."

"Fine. Just don't get blown away."

We launched early so we could return in case of a crisis in the local area. I leveled off at five hundred feet in the cool morning air. I watched Ernie climb to about three thousand. "How's the weather up in the stratosphere."

"I'm ready to copy when you're ready to send." He descended to fifteen hundred feet and circled at Pa Theung.

Turning to follow the Nam Ou, I rolled over and let the nose fall. Like a carnival ride, the Oscar Ace took me down steeply. I jerked the nose right, then started a smooth left pull across the river, my wingtip a few feet above the dark brown ripples. The dry season had made the river narrow, and I could dash across the two or three hundred feet in only a few seconds--exposure time I considered reasonable. "The view down here is fantastic. Eight boats, left wing."

"Copy."

Crossing the bank, I pulled up and rolled back toward the other side. Under the bushes I saw more boats and piles of supplies. "A dozen boats and wooden boxes on my nose."

"Copy, One-two."

"Wow, what a view." I pulled up into another crop-duster turn, and brought my wheels within a few feet of the water.

"Five boats at my one o'clock." I looked behind my rudder where a shooter might likely hide, then pulled the nose up and over for the next run. My initial nervousness about flying this low got lost in the sweaty maneuvering moment. I reached up and flicked a red-covered switch. "I'm arming a rocket in case I have to put somebody's head down."

"Roger."

Yanking and banking like a madman, I inventoried the N.V.A.'s brown water navy. At the W the river valley widened. I climbed out of the cover of the trees along the banks. I powered up to seven hundred feet over the wide flat section. "I'm taking a break."

"Roger."

"How many so far?" I searched for Ernie, spotting him up at five thousand feet.

"About a hundred and forty."

Passing over the W, I stretched my arms and torso. I cupped my hands in the slipstream to divert cool air onto my face. Then I rolled over and began again. "I'm sweating like a pig here."

"Should I write that down?"

"No."

Occasionally I heard popping noises behind me. By now I was comfortable with the low altitude. I added jinks and false starts where I could. Finding boats in groups of ten or more, I also called out large stashes of supplies along small tributaries. At Pak Bak, I climbed and searched the sky but didn't find Ernie. Then I dove again, heading north to Muang Ngoi.

"What's the count?"

"I quit writing at three hundred."

When I heard that remark, I climbed up to seven hundred feet, angry as hell. I turned for home.

"Are you done?" Ernie was a speck, at ten thousand.

"Why should I search if you aren't going to write?"

"Good point, One-two."

I cornered dirty Ernie in the revetment after landing. "What the hell were you doing at ten fucking thousand feet?"

"I can write at ten just as well as at five thousand."

"But you don't deter any shooters when you're above two." I shook my head.

"When I saw how low you were, I wrote you off. I hung around just in case you needed a rescue effort." Ernie laughed.

I didn't know if he was joking or nervous, so I didn't know how angry to act. "I'm living proof that proper tactics give you the advantage you need sometimes. But part of those tactics is keeping the high man in view of the enemy. You, my friend, were in fucking orbit."

"Look, if you want to die beside the Nam Ou, go ahead. I'll try to scoop up what's left and get it to a proper burial in the States."

"If you had flown the proper altitude, I'd have never heard a single gunshot."

"I added fifteen hundred feet to the highest point in my map sector."

"Don't go there." I began to laugh. I decided Ernie really might be afraid. Maybe he had done this FAC-thing too long.

"I would have done a good job with your SAR. Maybe bagged a Silver Star."

"Do me a favor, asshole. Take a clean map and write down what I called out. I'll take it to the operations meeting this afternoon. Next time you'll be the low man."

A few days later Bill returned on the courier flight, and Ernie boarded the same plane for a few days off in Udorn.

After dinner Chin and Neuheng stopped by the AIRA house. Chin was the T-28 leader, Mustang Red. Neuheng was a young pilot who wore mirrored sunglasses and never stopped laughing. His common trick was to mash the mike button in his airplane and only laugh.

"We came for the beer," Chin said.

Bill asked, "The mission beer?" Then he turned to me. "We give four cases of beer to the flight leader and two cases to the wingman with the most combat missions each month. These characters usually win."

Chin smiled.

Neuheng laughed.

"Have a cold one while I go get your cases." Bill went to a storeroom behind the kitchen.

I handed my Lao friends cold beers. "How many missions did you fly?"

"Two-hundred and eighty-six," Chin said. "And Neuheng fly two-eighty-three."

"Wow. That's ten a day. Every day."

"The targets are close to the airfield. We fly many sorties."

Bill rolled out the beer on a handcart. "Is Budweiser okay, guys?"

Chin lifted the top four cases. "Thank you very much."

Neuheng laughed and hauled the remaining two cases out the door.

Bill and I followed them out and drove to the Bungalow.

I asked, "Do you believe two-hundred and eighty-six bombing missions a month? That number is a combat tour for American fighter pilots."

"You've probably noticed they hit what they aim at," Bill said as he pulled into the courtyard parking lot. "Practice makes perfect."

We walked over and greeted Chris, who tended bar.

After my second beer I told Bill, "You look invigorated. How was your trip?"

"Wonderful. We worked everything out. We'll be all right now."

"Long way to go just to get laid." I laughed and elbowed Bill.

He laughed, too. "Twenty-thousand miles. A damn long way."

"Did Ernie tell you about our recon of the Nam Ou?"

"Yeah," Bill said. "You found three hundred boats, and he flew too high."

"I'd say he stayed within gliding distance of Lima-five-four all the way to Moung Ngoi. I mean, he reached ten thousand feet."

"When we were Sundog FACs together at Tay Ninh, Vietnam, Ernie was a real killer. He blew up everything in sight. If he couldn't get fighters, he'd call in artillery. If he couldn't get artillery, he'd throw out green smoke grenades. Bad guys thought it was poison gas."

"Awesome," I said. "What happened?"

"I think he's wrestling with the meaning of it all. Bullshit like that. He still does good close air support. Otherwise, he seems to be moving into a survival mode."

"Maybe he needs a break from the daily intensity."

"A trainer slot opens in Vientiane in about a month," Bill said. "I've put his name in the hat to train new guys for awhile. He's agreed to go. Maybe he can relax and get his head screwed on right."

"Good idea. I like Ernie a lot. But mentally, he's no longer in the fight."

"Yeeeha." Bill sounded elated as he climbed down from the O-1 cockpit around noon a couple of days later.

"Good mission?" I had been waiting in the jeep for fifteen minutes after landing from a Nam Ou boat-buster ride.

"Just like the one you had three weeks ago. Last night an N.V.A. regiment overran the last friendly outpost this side of Pa Theung. Dumb bastards were trying to hold it this morning." Bill climbed in and lit up.

I headed home. "Did you put any airstrikes on their little commie heads?"

"Oh, yeah. I got F-Fours first. Showed 'em the position. They saw troops moving around the network of trenches on the hilltop. Told 'em they were all bad."

"Troops in the open--a target that makes a fighter pilot's heart pound."

"These guys dropped singles. Twelve passes apiece. Afterward, a few N.V.A. were still moving, so the F-Fours gunned 'em. Total havoc. Damn. Sure feels good to kick Commie ass."

I remembered a Covey song. "An arm over here and a leg over there, doo-dah."

"You don't find targets like that one every day."

"Nope."

"I put thirty sets of Tangos on a group that ran to the north," Bill continued. "That regiment ain't gonna bother anybody for a while, if ever."

"Nice work."

"Thanks. Try to land in time to go to the four o'clock meeting with me today."

"Sure."

Bill and I sat on the left end of the front row, among twenty interested parties at the Air Operations Center's daily briefing. The center occupied a small building near the flightline. A small army of RLAF clerks sat at desks and tables in open rooms whose walls were covered in maps, charts, schedules, and lists. The place looked authentic enough. I wondered how many beers they got for being tidy.

A husky RLAF colonel stood before the group and summarized air activity for the past twenty-four hours. "During the night a North Vietnamese company took the friendly position near Tango Hotel two-three-two-one. This morning, T-Twenty-eights attack this position and kill many enemy. Now the Lao Army re-takes the position."

A tall American, about thirty years old, wearing jungle fatigues with no name or insignia raised his hand. "Colonel, I just returned from that location."

"Go ahead, Mr. Sword."

"We counted a hundred and nine N.V.A. bodies on that position after the F-Four and T-Twenty-eight attacks. We believe an entire infantry company was killed by air."

Bill smiled proudly and nodded. "A hundred and nine K.B.A. Not bad."

"That's a good job by Mr. Bill and the air forces," the colonel added graciously.

Sword nodded. "One more thing. Don't put that number in the U.S.A.F. DISUM." He referred to the daily intelligence summary--our primary daily report.

"Why?" Bill asked. "The F-Four pilots deserve to hear details when they do well. Most of the time we ask them to make toothpicks out of trees around here."

"I understand," Sword said. "But sources could be compromised if that number found its way to Hanoi."

The DISUM is classified secret," Bill said.

"I understand," Sword insisted.

"I think we should let the Americans solve their problems. Thank you all for coming." The colonel adjourned the meeting.

Bill stayed angry as we drove home. "Screw the C.I.A. and their fucking sources."

"Why don't you stop by the Triple-Nickel Squadron on your next trip to Udorn? All he said was to keep it out of the DISUM."

Bill smiled. "Good idea. Say, you've flown everyday for a month, and the U-Bird is due a hundred-hour inspection in Udorn." He laughed and moved his hands from side to side. "We may have a match here. Go ahead and fly to Udorn tomorrow. Take a few days off. I saw Denny when I passed though Vientiane. He said you guys have a Samlar grudge match coming up."

"Yeah. Denny enjoys life to the max. He's a bad influence." I smiled.

I flew a morning mission, then launched for Udorn after lunch. Alone with my thoughts, I watched steep green mountains pass slowly below. My left brain monitored my compass and clock details, while part of me drifted back to my old pals at Pleiku. *Damn, I've been busy. No* Stars and Stripes, *no radio, no television. All I've done is fly--twice a day, every day. I've flown more in a month than I did in three months in Vietnam. I could probably do that for the rest of my tour, but an escape in Thailand can't be bad. Time to relax and tune in to the real world.*

After forty-five minutes, I felt relieved to see the wide brown Mekong with the flat urban sprawl of Vientiane on the near bank. I tuned the Udorn radio beacon.

I slipped into the traffic pattern using the U-17 tail number as a callsign--as a real civilian would do. I parked the airplane in front of a large hangar where Air America would take it apart and put it back together in three days. Walking across the hot concrete ramp toward the Raven conex container, I spotted Frank Birk.

"How're you doing?" he asked.

"Not bad. Just delivered that U-Bird for a phase inspection. See the silver tape by the left strut? Your pals on the river put a hole in the wing."

"Only one?" Frank asked. He motioned to the large hangar.

We walked inside. Technicians had removed the right wing of an O-1 parked in the corner near the huge door.

"Looks more like a hulk than an airplane, now," Frank said. "The right wing was hanging on by a thread."

"What did you do, Frank?"

"I only flew across an open field--a bit low. A fifty-cal gunner did the rest. Battery's burned up, and all the Plexiglas is gone. He hit me twenty-six times."

"You're lucky to be alive." You're too good to die stupidly.

Frank showed me a small scratch on his right thumb. "Cut by Plexiglas--finally got myself a Purple Heart," he said with a big grin. "The guy really trashed the airplane, though."

"See you at the bar, Frank."

I completed a few errands that required sobriety, then went to the barbershop in one end of the dark teak frame building that housed the officers club.

A heavy-set lieutenant colonel with red hair entered wearing a Triple Nickel patch on his flightsuit. He sat to wait his turn. He seemed to watch me suspiciously.

Every time I shifted my eyes to the colonel, he was staring at me. Part of me wanted to tell him to screw off. A different part wanted to tell him the only barbers in Luang Prabang worked with mechanical clippers under a tree in the town square. He was probably concerned about my mutton-chop sideburns, but soon they were on the floor.

As I left, I checked his name tag and smiled at Colonel Joe Kittinger. "How do you like the cut, colonel?"

He nodded.

I walked down the hall to the main lounge. Drawn to the middle of the bar where a large round table had the Det.1, 56 SOW patch painted on top, I plopped down in an empty chair.

A T-28 instructor recognized me as one of the two most recent arrivals. "Did you hear what happened at Paksong this afternoon? Denny got killed."

Chapter 17
The Tea Party

May 1971

"What? Denny?" I couldn't believe what I heard. The noisy Udorn officers club became silent inside my head.

"Mid-air collision with an Air America Porter." Rich Fleisig, the T-28 instructor pilot continued his grim tale. "Not many details have come out. Apparently he made a clearing pass and pulled up to downwind. The Porter was belly-up, too. Sounds like they blind-sided each other."

Visions tumbled through my brain--a laughing, blond kid flipping a stack of beer coasters at the bar, running me off the road in a samlar race, breaking into loud laughter during debriefings with Wally. Words failed me. When I realized I could do nothing to change this news, a chunk of my soul shriveled away.

Frank joined us. "What's up?"

"A new Raven, Denny Morgan, was killed this afternoon." Rich repeated his story.

Frank raised his beer. "Here's to Denny."

"To Denny." We all clinked glasses.

I remembered our last evening on the town. "You guys should have seen Denny during our Newby Night. The Long Tchien Ravens were spending nights in Vientiane, so they showed us a rowdy time. And Denny led the pack."

"You mean visits to the steamier joints in the city--the cigarette show at the White Rose and Madam Lulu's Rendezvous de J'Amour?" Frank shook his head. "They couldn't invent a better shock treatment to prepare new guys for the Raven program."

"Denny was funny. At two a.m. we were in this huge nightclub crowded with locals. Denny took the microphone and sang a goofy song about the Hamburg Zoo--complete with sound effects. The orchestra backed him up.

I don't think I've ever laughed so hard." As I spoke, a tear leaked out.

"I'm takin' an O-One to Ubon tomorrow," Frank offered. "Backseat's empty."

"Most of my Udorn memories were shared with Denny." Thoughts of Ubon Rachithani drifted into my mind like the fragrance of sandalwood. I had escaped there from Pleiku a few times. "I'll go, but I have one huge question."

"What's that?" Frank asked.

"Can you keep bullets out of your backseat, even in Thailand?"

Frank laughed. "Another round, please."

After several drinks the Det.One T-28 drivers departed, and we joined a small but loud group at the nearby table which had a large green and white Triple-Nickel patch painted on top. Crews from the 555th Tac Fighter Squadron were relaxing vigorously.

"Whiskey for my friends," I enjoined the waitress. "Water for the horses."

"Looks like a couple o' FACs to me." A handsome black-haired fighter pilot flashed a huge smile. "I'm Leo Thomas."

After introductions and more whiskey, Frank baited the F-4 pilots for poor bombing accuracy.

"The only targets we get are these damn tree busters," Leo said.

"If you can't hit it," Frank asked, "what difference does the type of target make?"

"You fellas spend too much time in th' jungle," Leo drawled. "Ya'll got rough edges."

"Right," I said. "A lecture in decorum direct from the hills of Tennessee."

"Kentuckeh, actually." Leo smiled.

"Sorry." I pretended to apologize. "Show him your war wound, Frank."

Frank held out his thumb with the tiny scratch on it. "Worth a Purple Heart."

The F-4 drivers oohed and aahed.

When I stopped laughing, I said, "I saw his O-One this afternoon. Twenty-six fifty-cal hits. I can honestly say he destroyed the airplane before flying it home safely."

"Hot damn," Leo said. "You guys are all right. Let's go to the Golden Palm for breakfast." He referred to a Thai restaurant about a block away on base.

The room spun when I stood. I staggered along with the crowd.

Approaching the lights near the door of the restaurant, Leo said, "The base commander owns this joint. Food tastes pretty good."

"Base commanders are a pain in the butt." I felt a surge of nausea. "Holding interest in this business proves corruption at the highest levels."

"That's the Thai base commander," Leo said. "We don't work for him."

I emptied my stomach on the trunk of a large palm tree in front of the place.

Late the next morning I awoke to Frank's pounding on the door of my hotel room.

We found medicinal coffee on the way to the base and departed for the two-hour flight to Ubon, buzzing along at five hundred feet above rice paddies, jungle, and the occasional village.

"Did I have a good time last night?" I opened both rear windows for maximum wind blast effect. I took deep breaths and fought off thoughts about Denny's death.

"I think so. You tried to buy a round of drinks with Laotian kip. The Thais prefer baht, of course." Frank glanced over his right shoulder, then shook his head.

"Did I cause an international incident?"

"No. Leo bailed you out. You owe him a couple o' bucks."

"When I lose a friend, I drink too much. Doesn't change anything."

"Yeah," Frank said. "One of my pals at Pakse got shot up a few weeks ago. Frank Kricker--the senior FAC. Opened his leg to the bone. We weren't sure he'd make it, but I heard he's doing better now."

"That's great news."

"Krick was closing in on three thousand combat hours."

I had about seven hundred.

"He got hit over the same location where Lloyd Duncan got his toe shot off not long ago. We changed Duncan's callsign from Raven Four-two to Raven Four-toe."

"Pakse must be a laugh a minute."

After a significant pause, Frank said, "I got engaged on my last trip home."

"Wow!" I said. "Congratulations. More good news."

"She lives in Selma, Alabama, where I went to pilot training."

"So far, so good."

"She's super, but I worry about her brothers. They live for one thing--hunting turkeys. I hope that isn't a genetic trait."

Three days later I felt revitalized after relaxing in Ubon. I had grabbed a hop to Udorn and was flying a renewed U-17 into Laos. I called the Vientiane operations center as I approached the Mekong. "I'm overhead. Any word?"

"Yep. We have a passenger for you. Come on down."

"Okay. Tell him I don't intend to shut down."

"Rog."

Five minutes later I taxied to the front of the trailer housing the American Air Operations Center in Vientaine.

A sturdy gentleman wearing a gray walking suit loaded his bag in the back and climbed in. "Ed Troxel. I'm the new A.O.C. up at L.P." The new air operations commander looked like a brown-haired Elvis.

I introduced myself. "Ed Bender departed?"

"Yesterday. How about giving me a checkout in this thing on the way up?"

"Sure." I climbed over to the right seat while he walked around to the left.

Mr. Ed strapped in and scanned the instrument panel.

"Two simple rules will keep you out of trouble in the U-Bird."

"Okay. Let's keep everything simple."

"Lock the tailwheel for take-off and keep the fuel selector on Both."

"I can handle those items." Ed located the levers I mentioned.

"I'm not a real instructor in this airplane." I smiled at the new boss.

"That's okay. I don't think I'll need much instruction." Mr. Ed taxied to the runway, locked the tailwheel, and took off smoothly. "So how do you like Luang Prabang?"

"I love it. Any bad news has to be above my pay grade. How's Hurlburt Field?" I confirmed he was here on a six-month Project 404 rotation from the First Special Operations Wing in Florida. Had a year passed since my days on the beach?

"Florida's great. I hear L.P. is nice this time of year."

"I love it. I usually cruise this route around six thousand feet."

He nodded and leveled off.

I supplied power setting information as we droned along. Finally, I asked, "What's your background?"

"I flew N-model Hueys--gunship support for SOG--out of Ban Me Tuot."

"CCS--Command and Control South?"

"Yep. And once upon a time, I was a pilot training instructor in T-Thirty-threes."

"I flew thirty-eights. I heard the thirty-three was fun," I said.

"Do you remember that safety film--it became a classic--where the crew chief gets angry and steals a T-Thirty-three?"

"I do. The film featured several shockers to make us safety-minded, I guess."

"I was flying that night, when Fort Worth Air Traffic Control Center called and asked me to join up and help the guy."

"Really?" I felt connected to a major historical event.

"Yeah. He was a mess. He had no parachute or helmet. He wore earphones. Never raised the landing gear, and the poor guy had the power cobbed to maximum."

"Why did he steal the jet?"

"He was angry at his supervisor and depressed as the Christmas holidays approached. Apparently he had a civilian pilot's license, but by the time I joined on him, he realized he'd made the mistake of his life."

I noticed the radio beacon had locked on to the station at L.P.

"I talked him into a power reduction," Mr. Ed went on, "and pointed him in a descent to the Dallas airport. During a left turn to final, he probably became disoriented. The stars blended with the city lights that night. He rolled until he was pointed straight down." Mr. Ed illustrated with this left hand.

"Holy shit," I said. "The safety film didn't reveal the ending."

"I screamed at him and barely pulled my jet out in time. When I looked back, he was a fireball in a Sears parking lot south of Interstate Twenty."

"Incredible." I felt chilled by the horrific ending.

Mr. Ed looked at his watch. "Are we there yet?"

"See the large mountain down at eleven o'clock? That's the sleeping elephant. The runway's just beyond."

He nodded and reduced power.

I called the AIRA house as we descended.

Mr. Ed flew over the runway and turned downwind short of the Mekong. He leaned forward, looked out my window, and turned to land. "Two-one-nine, base, touch-and-go."

"Touch-and-go?" The radio crackled. Laughter followed.

Mr. Ed raised his eyebrows and looked at me.

"Lieutenant Neuheng. Tango driver. Always laughs on the radio."

"Do they all have a flight discipline problem?"

"They're not used to training flights around here." I tried to hide my amusement.

Mr. Ed flew three perfect patterns and landed, turning off at the end of the runway. He parked with a few directions from me. Then he smiled and said, "Thanks," as he pulled out his luggage.

A small committee greeted the new boss and swept him away.

I waited in the FAC jeep for Bill to land.

When he climbed in, twenty minutes later, he shook my hand and slapped my shoulder. "How're you doing?"

"Fine, I guess."

"I'm leaving tomorrow to escort Denny's coffin home." Bill seemed shaken. "He and I flew F-Fours together in Florida. His wife is like family."

"Pass my feelings to his folks. Denny was a free soul who lived a joyous life."

Bill nodded. "I know. I will. Ernie'll come up here while I'm gone."

"The new boss seems like a good guy. I checked him out in the U-Bird."

Bill laughed. "Bender's predecessor was killed in a T-Twenty-eight. Bender and I bumped heads from time to time. I'll withhold judgment on Mr. Ed. And you be careful."

I flew early the following morning.

Henry had insisted. "We have to beat the crowds for Pi Mai Lao--the Lao New year. Some call it the water festival because people douse each other. You'll love it."

After an unusually quiet mission, I stashed my gear at the house, except for my camera, and joined Ernie and Henry in a jeep convoy to the Mekong. Kids along the roadside threw scented water on us as we passed.

Henry laughed from the backseat. "The holiday is about cleansing. The locals pray for Buddha to bring rain, so they can grow rice."

"Ah, the rainy season," Ernie said. "Great flying weather."

"Most Lao festivals have some kind of fertility angle." Henry raised his eyebrows.

At the river's edge, we parked and climbed into one of many small wooden boats.

I asked, "Where the hell are we going, Henry?"

"We have to cross the Mekong and visit the cave of a thousand Buddhas. Five hundred years ago, the locals hid valuables there when an invasion came. Now they look on it as a shrine."

"Henry's a real expert," Ernie said. "Thanks to his long-haired encyclopedia."

"Yes, sir." Henry beamed. "I got the whole set."

Two rowers held course against the lazy current. We made the journey more quickly than I had guessed and climbed onto the sandy shore of no man's land.

"Here I go again," I said. "Wandering around in the damn boonies with a couple of guys who don't give a shit about their own survival."

"The bad guys take this day off, too." Henry laughed at everything.

"Yeah, relax," Ernie said. "Blend into the culture."

"At six-foot-two, you blend in all right." I felt like a target.

We mingled among the families having picnics and crowds of kids drinking sodas from straws stuck in plastic bags. I munched what I hoped was chicken meat a vendor had barbecued on a bamboo stick. We walked east along the beach about a mile to the shrine. Peering into the dark cave opening, I saw hundreds of golden images of the Buddha. Over my right shoulder I saw the mouth of the Nam Ou. "Are you guys ready to go?"

"See the guy over there in the purple shirt?" Henry nodded toward the river. "He's the crown prince. Don't you feel safer knowing the royals are out here?"

I clicked his picture. "No."

"Let me offer you a small history lesson," I said. "During the siege of Dien Bien Phu in nineteen fifty-four, the Viet Minh threatened to overrun Luang Prabang. The king refused to leave, giving the place a political significance it might not have otherwise deserved."

"What encyclopedia have you been reading?" Henry smiled.

"Bernard Fall," I answered. "Hell In a Very Small Place."

"Oh."

"History is repeating itself. Before he left this morning, Bill told me the king had been asked to evacuate to Vientiane. He refused."

Ernie spoke up. "Maybe we should stay with the crowds and head back to town."

"Great idea." I felt relieved.

I flew at least twice a day for the next few weeks, immersing myself in a personal N.V.A. eradication program, and drawing the T-28s farther up the river every day. I buried the pain of Denny's death under layers of cheap thrills along the Nam Ou. Exhaustion waited like a straight-jacket at the end of each day.

Mr. Ed became a fixture in the revetments, driving his radio jeep. He stayed late most evenings and missed supper. Occasionally we'd chat over a beer.

I attended the A.O.C. meeting each day. I had asked the Lao colonel to allow the T-28s to strike boats, and the day finally came.

"The local situation is quiet--perhaps too quiet," the colonel said in measured tones. "Tomorrow most attack sorties will work with the Ravens on the Nam Ou."

I launched early the next morning. Within an hour I called the AIRA house. "Please tell One-one to launch. I'm out of rockets."

"Roger," Swick answered. "He's on his way."

By the time Ernie arrived, I had thrown my last smoke out the window. I felt sweaty from twisting and turning, but I had found more than eighty boats for the T-28s, callsign Mustang, to attack. "I hope you brought smoke cans."

"Six or eight."

"I'll be back in an hour with a case of 'em. Maybe we can fly two-hour shifts this way." I didn't want to waste this golden opportunity.

"Roger, One-two."

"Smoke from those cans takes forever to rise above the trees. When they hit water, the smoke won't rise at all. I suggest you pitch one when the Tangos call passing Pa Teung." I felt as though I was preaching.

"Roger, One-two." Ernie sounded as if he was hearing a sermon.

An hour later I returned with eight rockets on my wings and twenty-four cans in my back seat. I spotted Ernie about a mile above the river. "How's it going up there, One-one?"

"You're right about the smokes. See you in a couple of hours."

"Roger." From about seven hundred feet, I marked another sixty boats in groups of six to ten and watched them vaporize. The Mustangs were coming all the way to Muang Ngoi in a steady stream.

"Mustang Blue, Pa Teung. Hahahaha." Somnuck and Neuheng called inbound.

"Roger. Fly to Pak Bak."

Trees along a crooked tributary east of the Nam Ou offered decent cover for a dozen boats. The stream joined the Nam Ou where a sheer rock cliff formed the opposite bank.

Pulling the pin, I rolled in, dropped a red smoke grenade out the window and pulled up. The can hit the water, leaving a pink mist. With a lazy wingover, I reversed and dropped another. Another water shot produced only mist. I pulled the pin on a third grenade while holding the spoon against the olive drab can with my right hand. Flying left-handed, I yanked the airplane roughly to the hidden fleet of sampans, and threw the can vigorously from point blank range.

Plunk. The grenade hit the water and disappeared. I pulled up and turned. Reaching back for another grenade, I caught a shadow in my periphery. I instinctively jammed full left rudder, pulled hard and rolled.

The jagged texture of the cliff face passed a few feet beyond my left tire. *Shit. They're only boats.*

Bill came back to L.P. after a few weks. Ernie returned to Vientiane aboard a courier flight that passed through while I was flying.

I walked into the living room around five.

Behind the bar, Bill grinned. He was sending Henry to nirvana with stories about mini-skirts and hot pants.

"Once again," I said, "the new guy gets to visit Thailand, while the boss gets America."

"Somebody has to reconnoiter the war back home. Protesters are everywhere."

I shook his hand. "Life's a bitch. Good to have you back."

"You're wearing a hard look I don't remember."

"Fatigue. I've been the only one bringing in B.D.A. lately. We sank the N.V.A.'s entire brown-water navy the other day. Three hundred warships."

"I heard. Nice work. I'll take the O-One in the morning. Sleep in if you wish."

"You're on. Hand me a beer. Shit. Hand me two."

"The Ambassador is visiting L.P. tomorrow. We have a luncheon buffet at the USAID house." Bill made his announcement with a small flair.

"Why don't you cover for me? Tea parties are my weak suit."

"We work for the Air Attaché, and he works for the Ambassador. Figure it out."

"I've never been big on bureaucrats, especially high-placed ones. I'll go kill Commies while you curl your pinkie around a tea cup." I laughed at the disgruntled look on Bill's face.

"Ambassador Godley's a warrior. You will enjoy meeting him."

I nodded, then chugged my beer. "Groovy."

Bill shook his head. "Godley's the guy who keeps the generals out of Laos. He and the military attachés are where the State and Defense Departments meet and decisions are made. He has the power of a four-star, and he's our best friend. Hell, he doesn't ask Washington what to do. He tells 'em what we did."

I said, sincerely this time, "I'll go to your little tea party."

At ten p.m. I fell like a tree and slept for twelve hours. Then I took a hot shower. It felt so good, I took another one. A cup of coffee made me feel nearly human again as I stepped out into the warm but fresh morning air.

The Chief motioned for me to join him in his black Scout with all the troops. "How're you doing? Ready to meet the big boss?"

I climbed aboard. "I feel great this morning--really alive. How about you?"

"I'm doing fine," he said, grinning. He pulled away.

"Me, too," Henry said. "Must be the good life I lead here."

"I plan to keep my mouth shut and survive this little doily party," I said.

"I haven't worried about what words come out of my mouth in a long time."

The Chief smiled.

I looked around to the back seat occupants. "What are you laughing at, Henry?"

"I'm going to do what you do, sir." He burst into giggles as we pulled away.

Turning down a narrow street, the Chief parked behind the FAC jeep. "I didn't figure Mr. Bill would be late."

"No," I said. "He knows the game."

We walked up wooden steps, through a screened porch, then into a large crowded room. A long table in the center held piles of succulent meat and oceans of colorful tropical dishes.

"I have died and gone to heaven," Henry said.

I confirmed he was staring at the food, and not a waitress.

Bill waved from the other side of the room.

I joined him in an informal line that inched its way toward a tall figure in a loose orange shirt with an African motif.

G. McMurtrie Godley dominated the room. Smiling graciously, he bowed and spoke to each person who stepped up to shake his hand.

I made a sandwich, then walked back to Bill. "I like his shirt."

Bill nodded. "He's not your average bureaucrat."

I finished eating as Bill introduced us to the Almighty Godley as the local Forward Air Controllers.

The Ambassador greeted us, then placed his huge hands on our shoulders. "The Ravens are my boys. I'm so proud of what you guys do."

"We enjoy helping the little people fight for their country," Bill said.

"I know that," Godley said, as the crowd seemed to push us. But Godley took his time. "If there's ever anything I can do for you guys, well, I want to know about it."

I thanked the Ambassador, and walked away with a sense of pride. I felt as though Godley had passed down a share of the power he vested.

I took a glass of iced tea and followed Bill to the edge of the crowd.

He handed me the keys to the FAC jeep. "You know that first ridge off the end of the runway?" Bill spoke quietly.

"Yep." I nodded.

"Huge slabs of rock stick out of the ground on the near end, right?"

"I see it everyday."

"The place is crawling with N.V.A. Go do something about it."

I touched my rabbit's foot and nodded.

I picked up Seo and took the Oscar Ace for this mission close to home. "Cricket, Raven One-two's airborne outa' Lima five-four. Two souls. Working freq three-fifteen-five. I've got targets if you've got air."

"Roger, Raven One-two. Weather's bad over the P.D.J. We jest might ship ya some F-Fours this afternoon." The voice sounded familiar, but I couldn't place it.

"Thanks." I approached the ridge where Bill had found the bad guys. At its base, a beautiful village lay in ashes. The wide circle of royal palms had wilted in the heat from the burnt thatched homes.

Seo confirmed what I had surmised. No bomb craters here. N.V.A. had torched the place as they passed. "My ground commanders say the enemy hides nearby."

I nodded to Seo and climbed five hundred feet above the ridge that stretched for five miles ahead and rose a thousand feet above the Mekong. At the near end gray slabs of rock protruded at forty-five-degree angles from the crest of the green hill. I looked at the rocks and caught movement. "Get your personal affairs in order, boys. Seo, please tell the friendlies nearby to get down flat. We're gonna move a mountain."

Seo smiled. "Sounds like I need to make my seatbelt tight."

"You could say that, my friend."

Soon my fighters arrived. "Raven One-two, Falcon One-one."

"Falcon, Raven, go."

"Two fox-fours. Wall-to-wall C.B.U.-Forty-nine. Lot's o' playtime." The flight leader sounded crisp and ready.

"You're gonna like this one, Falcon-One-one." I gave a careful briefing, then saw the fighters approaching as two dots ahead of two black smoke trails. "The target's on the first ridge east of the runway. Keep your pattern south and east. I'm in to mark."

"Roger, Raven One-two."

I rolled and fired.

BAM. A rocket streaked ahead into the huge boulders.

I pulled straight up and over my left shoulder. "Hit my smoke."

"Raven One-two, this is Jody flight."

"Go ahead, Jody." That callsign came from F-4s based at Korat Air Base, Thailand.

"Jody copied your briefing. We're outa gas, and we'd like to clean our wings in one pass."

I asked, "Okay by you, Falcon?"

"Falcon's moving south. Go ahead, Jody."

"Target is N.V.A. troops among the rock formation at the top of this ridgeline. My smoke is on 'em. What are you haulin?"

"Eighteen mark-eighty-two's apiece. One's in."

I watched the F-4 diving steeply perpendicular to the ridge. "Cleared hot."

"Roger."

I thought of a B-17 as bomb after bomb trickled off the belly of the F-4. The cluster of black eggs looked on line but long. They missed the top of the ridge and sailed a half a mile down the other side, erupting in fire and boiling smoke.

"We went long, didn't we?"

"Yep."

"Two's in. FAC in sight."

"Cleared hot." Number two was lined up with the ridge, pressing through his release altitude. As if they had eyes, eighteen five-hundred-pound bombs rained down on the enemy troops. The F-4 snapped straight up.

The rock formation disappeared in bright fiery flashes that turned into reddish black smoke.

"Nice work, two."

"Thanks, Raven. Falcon, too. Jody's bingo fuel. We'll check messages for results."

"Roger." I'd report this one in the DISUM. "Falcon One-one. Get ready while I have a look."

"Jody, go button five." The leader changed frequency.

"Two." His wingman followed.

"Rog. Falcon's one minute out."

I rolled in on the hill that now resembled a volcano. "Falcon, this is Raven One-two. N.V.A. troops are spillin' down the south face of this hill like ants. Put your cluster bombs on the hillside."

"We're on the way."

I had pulled off in a lazy climb to the south while I watched the scene behind me in fascination. A hundred khaki-clad soldiers stumbled and scrambled for their lives. Looking up, I saw an inverted F-4. My airplane was directly between a hungry Falcon and his prey. I pulled and rolled right as hard as I could. I glanced at Seo, who was smiling and hanging on.

"One's in. Bend it around, sport."

"Cleared hot." Pointed west, I cranked my head around and watched five-hundred knots of brown-and-green aluminum smoke down past my tail feathers.

"Two's in."

I spotted number two, cleared him, and watched one pull up. The hill began to sparkle as thousands of baseball-sized bomblets exploded. Ground movement ceased.

"They're down there, two," Falcon leader said. "Make every pass count."

"Two's off right."

"What's going on, Raven?" Falcon leader asked.

I looked at the target. Two T-28s rolled in and dumped four bombs apiece into the rocks atop the ridge. "Falcon, go through high and dry. The Mustangs want a piece of this one. Sorry 'bout that." I told Seo to tell the T-28s to stay clear for five minutes, and they could have their way with the target for the rest of the afternoon.

Delayed-effects bomblets sparkled steadily on the crushed enemy.

Falcon came around again and again. "We're winchester C.B.U. I see a few movers. Mind if we strafe?"

"Cleared hot."

I watched the gray smoke trail, then heard the twenty-millimeter cannon growl. RRRRRROW.

The Falcons gunned everything that moved. Then they lifted up and away. "We're bingo. R.T.B."

"Sierra Hotel, Falcon One-one. Take a hundred K.B.A." My estimate of the killed-by-air total was probably low.

"We haven't seen troops like this before. Thank for the target, Raven One-two."

"These guys could have hurt us tonight," I said. "You saved our bacon."

"Triple-nickel. Come see us. Button five."

"Two."

After dinner, Mr. Ed brought out a box of Manila Coronas. "Cigars for everyone."

Bill and I joined him at the small bar built in front of the stairwell at the back of the living room. We fired up the stogies. I poured a shot of bourbon over ice cubes.

"Don't ruin the ambiance with that rot gut sour mash." Ed raised a bottle of Chivas Regal. "Fighter pilots drink scotch."

I looked at Bill who shook his head.

"Humor me, boys." Ed grinned and poured us generous portions.

"Tastes smooth enough," I said. "Are we celebrating something?"

"Don't you know?" Ed raised his glass to me. "The Ambassador held up his departure to watch your airstrikes. Stood beside his C-Forty-seven in awe for an hour."

"Killing N.V.A. is my cup of tea," I said.

Bill looked as though he wanted to say something.

"Before he departed," Ed said, "he said fine things about the L.P. country team."

Bill nodded. “I was beside the Air Attaché. He reminded me U.S. fighters are prohibited within ten miles of Luang Prabang.”

“I did what I had to do. That N.V.A. company, or regiment, would be cutting our throats by now.” I took a large swig of Chivas.

“The Attaché knows.”

I still felt defensive. “Those F-Fours blew away over a hundred N.V.A. today.”

“We’re not attacking you. I told the Air Attaché we had no choice when this large formation showed up so close to the airfield.”

“What did he say?” I wasn’t ready to go home yet.

“He understood. He’s an old F-Four jock.” Bill lowered his voice. “I think he got a hard-on when they started strafing.”

Chapter 18
The King Wants BUFFs

June 1971

When someone knocked on the door to the AIRA house around five-thirty, Bill, Ernie, and I turned from our comfortable stances at the bar.

A smiling lieutenant colonel in green Army fatigues entered.

"Colonel Smith," Bill called. "Welcome."

"Just checkin' up on the Air Corps." The older gentleman walked over to the bar. "I knew you guys would have the beer flowin' by now."

White salt rings below his armpits were evidence of the otherwise dignified officer's long day. Removal of his cap revealed receding gray hair.

"Here, Colonel." I handed him a beer.

"Colonel Smith officially exists," Bill said. "He gets to wear a uniform as the assistant Army attaché for this region."

"I have to wear the uniform," Smith said. "I spent the afternoon on that ridge you guys blew up for the Ambassador the other day. I should've joined the Air Corps."

I pointed to Bill. "He found the target. I just marked it."

"Most of the damage on top was done by that first strike. All those bombs came right down the throats of the N.V.A. They were protected by twenty feet of granite on all sides except that overhead angle." The colonel explained the fortification in detail.

"Eighteen five-hundred pounders," I said. "How many N.V.A. bodies did you find on top?"

"Over a hundred, judging from the body parts--real grisly scene. Another hundred on the hillside."

"Here's to a day's work," Bill said, raising his beer can and grinning.

I swigged my beer, hoping those souls would come back as non-communists in the next life. "They could've hurt us if they had come down the hill."

"I'll drink to that." Smith took a long sip. "They'd have owned the airfield and burned down half of Luang Prabang by now."

Ernie finished his beer and pulled up another one. He shook his head.

The increased scale of the fighting around Luang Prabang made me wonder if I would tire of the killing as Ernie had. So far, so good. I could still find 'em and kill 'em. And I hadn't turned to jelly. I probably drank too much--small price to pay.

"I'd better go. I only wanted to check in on the Air Corps." Smith walked to the door. "How's Swick doing?"

"Great," Bill said. "We're going to make him our morale officer."

"The Crawfordsville flash," I added.

Smith opened the door, then turned back. "Keep your eyes open for a follow-on force. Their doctrine says another fighting unit would roll in behind the initial attackers to exploit any successes."

"We'll find 'em," Bill said.

And kill 'em.

After dinner, Bill and I turned the living room chairs to face the movie screen on the wall near the door. We crashed in two recliners that comprised the front row.

Steve Swick loaded a reel onto the projector while the rest of our troops and a couple of Air America pilots drifted in for the show.

Another knock and Chris and Deng from the Bungalow entered. Deng held her daughter's hand, and their black cocker spaniel followed.

We stood and greeted our friends.

"You have Clint Eastwood tonight?" Chris asked.

"As a matter of fact, yes," Bill said. "Welcome to the movies." He ushered them to a couch that was quickly emptied for them. On his way back, he grabbed us a couple of beers.

Comfortably seated, Bill said, "Roll 'em."

I enjoyed the first part of the film, an escape into really top-notch make-believe killing.

When the reel ended, Bill headed for the bathroom.

Rather than re-winding as he usually did, Swick snapped the next reel in place, turned the lights down, and rolled part two.

The black cocker spaniel walked around, sniffed my boots, and jumped into Bill's empty chair.

Bill stumbled into the dark living room and found the arm of his recliner. He walked around to the front and reached behind him for the seat as he bent to sit.

"Yeowww!" Bill screamed and leaped up. The unexpected feel of a furry thing in his chair caught his full attention.

Swick flipped on the lights.

With a possible grin on his face, the black pup trotted to the couch.

I laughed uncontrollably. Raven One-zero had been spooked by a puppy.

"What the--"

"Big bad dog scare ya?" As was my custom, I gave Bill no mercy.

While the laughter subsided, Mr. Ed entered and motioned for me to join him at the bar. "You know that small tributary south of Moung Ngoi?"

"Flows in from the east?"

"That's the one." Ed had to whisper, as Swick had started the movie again. "Ten or fifteen boats are stashed along that stream, and they ain't going anywhere tonight."

"What did you do?"

"I was over Moung Ngoi at sunset when I spotted the convoy. A motorized raft was in the lead--loaded with fifty-five gallon drums."

"So you pounced."

"Not at first. Most of the boats peeled into that tributary when they heard my engine. The raft turned around and tried to go north. But his little motor only held him stationary against the current."

"Then, you pounced?"

"Yeah." Ed smiled broadly. "Two Mark-eighty-twos. You should have seen the fireball. Sent his ass off to meet Buddha."

Over strong coffee the next morning, I continued to tease Bill. I met him in the commo room with Swick. "You didn't have bad dreams about cocker spaniels, did you?"

"I didn't expect to feel anything but cushion." He shook his head and laughed. "I'll leave all the denizens to you for a few days. I have a big meeting in Vientiane. Apparently the king is jealous of General Vang Pao's power on the P.D.J. He's asked the embassy for B-Fifty-two strikes up here."

"We rarely have targets big enough to justify BUFFs," I said. "Even if they could hit a pinpoint target."

"I doubt we have the required radar support, since Lima Site Eighty-five went away in sixty-eight."

"Stay out of trouble in Vientiane. I'm going boat-hunting."

Bill exaggerated a salute.

I picked up a new right-seater named Somnuck. An hour later I maneuvered the U-17 around nasty boiling cumulus formations, along the way to Moung Ngoi.

Somnuck looked ill but gave me a thumbs up.

I noticed when I banked right, he leaned into me. I centered the ball in the turn and slip indicator. More rudder, I figured, and he'd be fine.

I counted twelve loaded boats exactly where Mr. Ed had described.

"Cricket, Raven One-two. I have twelve boats. Any F-Fours today?"

"Roger, Raven One-two. We can send ya some Falcons in 'bout half an hour." Again, the voice sounded familiar, but I couldn't place the name.

"Roger. Rendezvous three-five-four for ninety miles off channel one-oh-eight."

I prepared a briefing and located several back-up targets, since the weather seemed to be changing. The surrounding thunderstorms moved quickly for their size. At the moment I had blue sky overhead, and Somnuck looked green.

Falcon 61 checked in, and we went to work.

I marked the target, which looked like solid jungle from farther away than fifty feet. "Hit my smoke."

"One's in." The dark F-4 rolled over and lined up in a steep dive.

"Cleared hot."

Three bombs fell away. The Phantom pulled up and rolled.

"Two's in."

I watched the leader's bombs explode beyond the target. "Cleared hot on my smoke--three-hundred meters short of lead's bombs."

Two's bombs hit the target.

"One's in." The angry-looking Phantom pounced again.

"Cleared hot. Hit left of two's smoke. The boats are strung out to the east."

Again, the leader hit long.

"Two's in."

"Left of your last ones. Lookin' good. Cleared hot."

"One's in." The pilot sounded pissed. "You're going to tell me my wingie hit the target again, aren't you?"

I refused to cut him any slack. "A-ffirmative. Cleared hot."

Leader hit closer but still long.

"Two's in."

"Cleared hot. Work east."

Two hit the target a third time.

"Sierra Hotel, Two. One's cleared hot."

They repeated their attacks with the same results.

"Falcon Six-one, you were on target at one-five, off at two-five. All ordnance hit within three hundred meters. You destroyed ten boats loaded with supplies. Five boats damaged."

"Roger. Thanks, Raven."

"Raven One-two, this is Falcon Six-one Bravo."

"Go ahead." To Somnuck, I said, "The leader feels so pissed off about his bombing that he lets his backseater talk on the radio."

Somnuck smiled.

"Can you take pictures of this target for us?"

"I'd be happy to, Bravo. I'll deliver them personally." I had the clear feeling this guy didn't trust me. I wondered what he'd say eyeball-to-eyeball.

"Thanks. You be careful. You have weather rolling in."

"Falcon Six-one, go button five."

"Two."

I pulled out my Pentax camera with a 200-millimeter lens and 400 A.S.A. Tri-X film. I set the camera for 800 A.S.A., lens wide open, shutter on 1/1000th of a second, and focus on infinity, creating a sophisticated point-and-shoot camera. These settings produced clear prints from shots taken under conditions that would blur normal photography.

I spent the roll in three passes, then turned for home.

An ominous black wall covered the Nam Ou at the W, stretching to both horizons and reaching higher than the service ceiling of the U-17.

I turned to Somnuck. "We must fly under the storm."

He nodded. "I understand."

I set the vacuum–driven attitude indicator for level flight and opened my window so I could track the water below. I descended to just above the surface of the Nam Ou, now swollen and red from recent storms.

When we entered the deluge, my visibility decreased to about a hundred feet. I concentrated on staying over the red water below.

Somnuck began to throw up, then pulled out his airsick bag. The open window brought in a small hurricane that whipped vomit particles around the airplane. Pieces hit the back of my head. Grains of rice stuck to the glass face of the attitude indicator. A putrid stench filled the cockpit.

I concentrated on the river. When I detected blurred greenery on my left, I banked right, then left to stay centered on the river.

Somnuck had trashed the right window--I only looked that way when I had to.

Lightning cracked and flashed. The smooth purr of the engine faded into barks of Somnuck's loud retching. When the outside visibility allowed any time at all, I used a map to scrape stuff off the altitude indicator.

At times the rain gushed into the cockpit like a fire hose.

After ten minutes that seemed like a year, we emerged into the relative calm and steady rain near Pa Theung and the Mekong. Another black curtain approached Luang Prabang from the north.

I pushed the throttle up.

Using fifteen degrees of bank to hold course on final approach, I squeaked the right wheel down gently, then eased down the left. When the tailwheel touched, I turned full controls into the crosswind that tried to bully me off the runway.

I taxied into the revetment and shut down the engine. Waving to Ramon, I opened the door and stepped into the cleansing rain. "We have a small mess in here."

"No problem."

"Somnuck, the rules of military aviation say you must help."

Nodding. He staggered out and clung to the wing strut.

I headed for the showers.

At dinner I kidded Mr. Ed, who made a rare appearance. "I put Falcon Six-one flight on a bunch of boats this morning. Blew them away."

"Up near Muong Ngoi?" he asked.

"As a matter of fact, yes." I joined in on his laughter.

He shared his story of raft-bombing with the rest of the group, because, I surmised, Bill wasn't around to argue that air ops commanders weren't supposed to fly combat missions.

"The Mustang pilots are meeting at the prison bar tonight," I said. "They invited us to tip a few in celebration of recent successes."

"I could probably do that," Ernie said.

"I'll join you guys, if that's okay." Mr. Ed smiled.

The three of us piled into the FAC jeep and bounced through the mud to the Dodge City saloon replica across the street from the monkey house. I spotted several pilots hanging around the door, and they weren't smiling.

"Lieutenant Neuheng, what's up?"

His smiled returned, and he motioned us inside. "Do you know the French Army officers? They live here in Luang Prabang?"

"I've seen them. A tall, thin lieutenant and a short, fat major." Following Neuheng inside to a large round table, I remembered these men from a USAID party.

"Yes." Neuheng motioned for us to take seats. "They start to make trouble, but now they go home."

I bowed to the assembled pilots and took a seat between Neuheng and Sinuane, who was the wingman and close friend of Chin, Mustang Red.

Two chairs down, Chin seemed agitated, but he shook my hand. "Raven One-two, you are a good friend of the Mustangs."

Neuheng handed me a white bottle cap full of whiskey.

"I always enjoy the company of my fighter-pilot friends." I downed the booze as Neuheng slid the fifth of White Horse Scotch along the table top.

Following tradition, I filled the cap and offered it to Sinuane.

He tossed back the scotch, then spoke in a low voice. "French officers say Lao people are lazy. We must make them leave."

"The French are always pissing somebody off. Don't worry about it."

"Okay, but I do worry you fly too low." Sinuane laughed.

"I use every tactical advantage when I go down to look at a target."

The White Horse bottle made two more passes.

Suddenly, all hell broke loose. The T-28 pilots sprang up, shouting and knocking chairs in all directions.

I saw a tall French lieutenant in a khaki uniform swaggering in through the door, followed closely by a stocky major. They wore round caps with small leather bills.

Chin, who was more than a foot shorter than the lieutenant, walked to the door with Sinuane and the others in trail.

Neuheng said, "Wait here. Lao business." Then he joined the formation.

We Americans stood at the table in a subtle state of cringe.

Chin nailed the French lieutenant with a quick roundhouse right to the jaw. The lieutenant fell unconscious into the major's arms.

Sinuane pulled out his forty-five and fired once into the ceiling.

Bang.

The deafening report reverberated in the large, closed room.

In the instant of silence following the shot, a woman screamed.

"He hit someone upstairs. Holy shit." Ernie bolted for the door.

"This dive has an upstairs?" I asked, following him.

"Yeah. A whorehouse. Henry told me about it."

Mr. Ed joined us. "Discretion being the better part of valor, I say we get the hell out of here before they open the gates to the monkey house."

We joined the wild herd, pushing, shoving, and stumbling through the door. Drunker ones fell and were trampled.

Chin held his boxing pose. He wanted a piece of the major who had his arms full of the lieutenant.

I told Chin, "Let's go. We'll live to fight tomorrow. Come on."

He reluctantly followed, grumbling in his native language.

Ernie had the jeep running when Mr. Ed and I sprinted up.

I swung into the backseat as the hunched-back owner of the bar trotted past with a mini-skirted young woman draped over his shoulder. Recoiling at a trickle of blood on her thigh, I thought I detected a slight smile on her face. At least she was conscious.

Now jeeps were doing what individuals had done inside. Chaos ruled.

While Ernie swerved and spun the wheels, I watched for activity at the prison. Finally our tires found traction. We raced home.

I flew early and long the next morning, pretending the night before had been a bad dream. I immersed my mind in business as usual on the Nam Ou.

After lunch, Mr. Ed pulled Ernie and me aside. "I try to have a little fun with you guys, and you drag me into a shoot-out."

I shrugged and smiled.

Ernie shook his head. "Life's a bitch."

Mr. Ed spoke in a low tone. "The girl is okay. The bullet only grazed her."

I sighed. "Thank you for that bit of good news."

"The Lao wing commander took corrective action." Mr. Ed folded his arms across his chest. "For the next thirty days, the Mustang pilots have to wear their pistols at all times--even while sleeping."

Ernie asked, "What does that prove?"

"Rather clever," Ed continued. "By punishing the entire group--including the troops who don't go to bars--he assures peer pressure will come to bear on the guilty party without the embarrassment to the Royal Lao Air Force of a formal investigation."

I felt a wave of relief. "I'm glad the girl isn't seriously hurt."

Ernie shook his head. "I'll never go to that bar again."

I met Bill in the commo room where I went to debrief a long day.

"I can't turn my back on you guys for two days." He laughed loudly.

"Somebody told you about last night?"

"Yeah."

"What's up with the Big Ugly Fat Fuckers?" I changed the subject.

"B-Fifty-twos aren't feasible. We're offering the king L.G.B.s."

"Laser-guided-bombs?"

"Affirmative. I think the N.V.A. are using that huge cave at Pa Theung--and other caves in the area--to stage supplies for their operations around Luang Prabang."

"So we plunk a few two-thousand-pound precision bombs in there?"

"Exactly. At the very least we make them afraid to set up in a cave. They'll spend the rainy season in the rain."

"When do we start?"

"Two o'clock tomorrow afternoon. This operation will combat test the L.G.B.s. F-Fours will drop a smart bomb and a dumb bomb together. The dumb bomb should always hit long, since it doesn't use up energy chasing the laser beam."

"We should've nailed the Pa Theung cave a long time ago."

"You can take the first one. I'll scout around for more caves."

In the same room twenty-four hours later, Bill waited with Dit for my debriefing. "So tell us how it went."

"The first L.G.B. tumbled. I could tell because it was painted brown on top and white on the bottom, just like fuel tanks. The pilot got pissed when I asked if he had pickled off a tank by mistake."

Bill laughed. "You have no tact at all, do you?"

"What the fuck do I need tact for? Sometimes you have to intimidate these guys--challenge them to come on down and get the job done."

Dit looked up from his note-taking. "Rules say the fighter-bombers are supposed to release their bombs at forty-five hundred feet."

"Which is fine if they can hit the target from two-miles of slant-range." I felt angry. "If not, they need to press lower. Fuck stupid rules. Otherwise we're all wasting our time here."

"Get off your soap box," Bill said. "What happened with the L.G.B.s?"

"I guess the bomb malfunctioned and stalled out. May not have been the crew's fault. "The next laser bomb flew into the cave mouth like a cough drop. Plunk."

"And . . .."

"And nothing . . . for about twenty seconds. Then a stream of fire and smoke blasted out of the cave mouth like a dragon's breath. Saw a few secondary explosions and fires, too. Must have arrived as a real surprise to the folks inside. Like two thousand pounds of HELLO!"

Bill flew cave busters for the next few days. Then Ernie flew the O-1 to Udorn for a hundred-hour inspection. On the fifth day of laser bombs, the U-17 had an engine problem. Ramon needed parts before the craft would be available to FAC the next afternoon's laser mission.

Bill called the embassy to try and cancel the F-4s. When he hung up, he said, "Raven Zero-one will bring a U-Seventeen up here for the strike. He'll arrive at one thirty. You can take this one. You need to build rapport with the guy."

I laughed. He was Bill's boss, not mine. I really didn't know much about Raven Zero-one.

I parked the jeep at 1:15 in the FAC revetment next to the broken U-17. On Bill's advice to play by the rules, I carried a helmet along with my survival gear and Larry's rabbit's foot. I had always worn earphones during my O-1 tour. I walked over to a crowd gathered near the T-28 wing of T. Vant, also known as Mustang Green.

T. Vant smiled and shook my hand. "Fifty-cal." He pointed to his left flap.

I leaned down to view the clean half-inch hole. "Did you see the gun?"

"Yes. About halfway to Pa Theung. Second ridgeline from the Mekong. I saw the flashes." He pulled out his map and pointed to the spot.

"This means a dedicated anti-aircraft unit is close by," I said. "Pass the word."

T. Vant nodded.

Behind him a U-17 flew a descending base turn and landed.

I walked to the end of the runway and climbed aboard with Raven 01.

His white helmet squeezed his face red. "Nobody's answering my calls to the tower," he said.

"That's common. Winds are light. We can take off from here." I strapped in.

Zero-one turned the aircraft around and pushed in the throttle. Eight-hundred feet later we were airborne. "Head for the peak over there." I pointed to Pa Theung.

Zero-one nodded and leveled off at fifteen hundred feet above the ground.

I asked, "Do you want to run the strike?"

"Naw. We're in your backyard. You can do the strike."

"We have about twenty minutes before the Time-On-Target.

Mind if we look around on this ridgeline? Start a circle to the right."

"What are we looking for?"

"Fifty-cal. A Tango just brought home a bullet hole." I searched carefully. In my peripheral vision I saw Zero-one's hand nudge the throttle forward subtly. The nose came up slightly. We circled and climbed. I pulled out binoculars and scanned for movement or the glint from a long gun barrel.

"See anything?"

"Nothing at all." I put the binoculars away. We were beyond their useful range.

"Raven One-two, Falcon Five-one." The fighters called me.

"The cave's over there." I pointed at Pa Theung. "Can I fly for a second?"

"Sure. You have the aircraft."

"I've got it." I mashed the mike button and descended using high-banked turns. "Falcon Five-one, are you ready for a briefing?"

Go ahead, Raven."

I delivered the words the fighters needed and leveled off around a thousand feet. "Nothing left but to clear 'em hot. You have the airplane."

Zero-one took control and said "cleared hot" twice.

The bombs behaved like cough drops, and the fighters went home.

Zero-one turned for the runway. "The L.G.B. issue is important to the Ambassador. We have to show our support for the King."

"Care to do a little recce?"

"Nah. I have enough gas to reach Vientiane. I'll drop you off and head on back."

Bill was waiting when I returned to the house. "How'd it go?"

"Okay, I suppose." After he climbed into the jeep, I pulled away for the four o'clock meeting. "He had no interest at all in looking for bad guys."

"We knew that. But something is going on around Pa Theung."

I told Bill about T. Vant's hit.

He nodded. "I know they're out there. We should be back to full strength soon. Ramon will have the U-Bird parts today, and Ernie should return with the O-One."

I nodded and yawned.

"You've flown thirty days straight. Why don't you take a few days off? I'll pop caves and have the enemy situation figured out when you return."

"If you insist. I'll hitch a ride with the first C-One-twenty-three in the morning." I referred to the steady stream of Air America transports that delivered pallets of bombs.

I parked, and we joined the meeting. The Lao colonel expressed his pleasure with the laser-guided bombing program and described enemy activity near Pa Theung.

When he asked if anyone had questions, a Company intelligence officer waved a scrap of paper. "I have information that may be of interest to pilots. We received this information in a radio intercept." He read from the paper. "The four-oh-seventh anti-aircraft company has moved into the vicinity of Pa Theung with the mission of shooting down airplanes."

"May I see that?" Bill asked.

"Sure." The C.I.A. man passed the paper down the row to Bill.

Bill read the message, then rose to his full five-foot-four-inch height. "This message is dated a week ago. You sat on this vital information for a week?"

"I didn't realize--"

"We've located a fifty-cal. Or it located us. After all we do for you guys, don't tell me this is the best you can do."

"I'm sorry--"

"Unbelievable. Road watch teams, rice drops, medevac missions--all the fucking times we hang it out for you guys, and now you stab us in the heart." Bill shook his head.

"Tell him how you really feel, Bill." I tried to lighten the moment. I was angry, but I couldn't change the past.

"So, I think the Americans have to discuss some things. Now this meeting is over." The colonel adjourned diplomatically.

Bill stormed out to the jeep.

The Company man held up both hands. "I'm sorry. Please come over and look at everything I have."

I nodded. The offer came too late in this case, but I vowed to visit him later.

Udorn offered a big-city-Saturday-night feeling, and I needed the escape. After running errands, I made the inevitable trip to the officers club. I noticed an older guy wearing blue jeans dominated the agenda among T-28 instructors at the Det One table. I introduced myself.

"Dick Defer," he replied, shaking my hand. "How are you doing?"

"Good. Are you a new guy?"

"Second Raven tour. Been at Pakse a few weeks now." Defer's speech was high-pitched rapid-fire with a Dixie accent.

"I've been at Luang Prabang a couple of months. Life is good."

He smiled and continued his animated tale. "So if I have any rockets left at the end of the day, I go over where the river makes two right-angle bends. I fire from max range." He made a tall arc straight ahead with his index finger. "Really pisses off the gunners."

"South southeast of Pakse?' I asked. "Where the trail crosses the river?"

"Yep."

"At Pleiku, we called that place the Western Ford. Those gunners are good."

"I believe you."

"I realize you've been around, but you need to know those twenty-threes were the most accurate guns in the Covey area of operations. Don't do anything stupid."

Defer shrugged.

In the background I heard the Cricket airborne controller voice--a slow drawl--that had intrigued me for weeks. I looked around to the ABCCC table and spotted my O.T.S. pal, Neil Upmeyer, sitting with a couple of friends. I walked over and sat beside him. "So, how's the pride of Beaumont, Texas? Or is it Houston?"

Upmeyer leapt to his feet and slapped my back. "Colonel, let me introduce Raven One-two. We survived Offisuh Trainin' School togethuh."

I shook hands with a large bald lieutenant colonel.

"Bill Alexander. Pleasure to meet you."

"I think I met you once before at Vance."

He nodded and offered me a cigar. "I was a FAC for a short time. I'd been at Danang for a few weeks when the commander did something that got us both fired."

I lit my cigar and remembered. "What did you do, Neil, to get sent here?"

"Washed out o' pilot trainin'. Volunteered a few times. I'm havin' a blast."

"His earthy humor keeps everyone in stitches." Alexander finally smiled.

I nodded and shook Neil's hand again. "Some things never change."

I awoke at noon, and my throat was aflame. Coffee was no remedy. Eventually I made my way to the Det to see Doc Smith, a reputed friend of the Ravens.

The young energetic flight surgeon took a look, then went to his bookcase and pulled down several volumes. "Hmmm . . .."

"Does it look as bad as it feels, Doc? I had a few drinks last night."

"Ugh . . .." The doctor only grunted and referred to another manual.

"What's going on, Doc? A little post-nasal drip? Must've been the cigar."

More grunts.

"Doctor Smith. Two minutes ago I thought I was doing the right thing by coming here. Now I'm not so sure."

The former football player looked up sadly. He closed his books, removed his reading glasses, and sighed. "Your throat . . . well . . . is showing signs of . . . withdrawal. You need a drink, boy!"

I laughed and laughed some more. "Happy hour approaches. Let's get out of here! Do you have a jeep?"

"Hell, boy. I've got an ambulance."

"Don't call me boy! Can we stop at Triple-Nickel? I have to drop off some photographs."

"Dirty pictures? That's all those fighter guys understand."

"Nope. Just boats. I have to resolve a credibility issue with one of their navs."

The 555th Tac Fighter Squadron building was almost empty, but we ran squarely into Captain Leo Thomas. "Leo, meet Doc Smith, world's greatest flight surgeon. And say, I owe you a few dollars from that wasted night at the Golden Palm restaurant."

Leo laughed and refused my money. He pulled out a clear plastic bag. "I take this with me on every mission. Here's the flag of the great state of Alabama. My pals in Selma sent it over. I wore these dogtags on my Thud tour."

"You aren't superstitious, are you?"

Leo showed us a few more small keepsakes. "And I recently added this five hundred kip note I got from a drunken Raven FAC. Don't spoil it by telling me how little it's really worth."

"I hope it brings you more success than it brought me that night."

He tucked his bag away. "Why's a civilian hangin' around a fighter squadron?"

"Exactly ten days ago Falcon Six-one Bravo asked for these pictures." I handed him a large envelope I had picked up from the wing photo lab.

Leo opened the envelope. "Looks like firewood to me."

"That debris was ten loaded boats before Falcon Six-two dropped his load. These five are intact but filled with water. I reported them as damaged in the B.D.A. report."

"Why did he want these pictures?"

"Target was under the trees. I guess he didn't believe me. You can tell him that's no excuse for missing the target. My smoke was good."

Leo checked a clipboard with old flight orders. "That guy's a known extrovert. I'll pass these to him later. Let's go to the bar."

My throat burned. I turned to the flight surgeon. "Does your siren work, Doc?"

Leo led us to the Triple-Nickel table in the center of the noisy bar.

My throat felt better when I sipped my first glass of whiskey.

"This place will be packed tonight." Leo looked around the room. "Brigadier General Robin Olds is passin' through. He's touring all the fighter bases one last time before he retires."

"Robin Olds?" Doc Smith asked.

I ordered a round of drinks from a pretty waitress, then answered the good doctor. "He commanded the Eighth Tac Fighter Wing at Ubon--the Wolfpack. Killed four MiGs. Added to twelve kills from World War Two, that makes him my hero. Speakin' of my heroes--"

"Hi, guys." Frank Birk pulled up a chair and joined the mirth. He, too, ordered a round of drinks, although everyone at the table had glasses lined up.

"Did you have a bad month?" I asked.

"No. Just nervous about gettin' married in a few months."

"Scotch is good for nerves, too. Deaden's 'em." I felt woozy. "Doc's helpin' me cure a sore throat."

"I hear Robin Olds is coming tonight," Frank said. "I knew him at the Academy."

Several rounds later the guest of honor arrived. Tall and fit, with the trademark moustache, Robin Olds entered and dominated the room. He took the seat of honor in front of a small stage where several flight-suited guitar players sat drinking.

A lieutenant colonel led the crowd in an hour-long songfest. Finally, the crowd sang about Robin and the Wolfpack, and the colonel presented General Olds with a chrome cartridge belt.

The general gave a short speech, then sat at our table.

Shortly after the amenities, Frank fired his first salvo. "You know, Colonel Olds, the F-Four might work okay in the air-to-air mode, but it's a lousy bomber."

"Frank, do you see this star on my shoulder? I'm not a colonel."

I began to laugh.

"I'm sorry, General. But, damn it, Colonel Olds, the F-Four can't hit shit on the ground." Frank was drunk.

"That's General Olds, Frank. And the F-Four is a fine warplane."

Several Nickel troops tried to change the subject, but Frank persisted.

I laughed and laughed.

"Sorry, General . . .."

In Luang Prabang by lunchtime, I had a sandwich with Ernie.

"You can take the O-One this afternoon." Ernie looked tired.

"Anything going on I should know about?"

"Bill's been cave-busting. This morning I got reports of an enemy company near Pa Theung." Ernie pulled out his small green memo book and gave me coordinates. "You can see a patch of dark green trees next to the river. Check it out."

An hour later I droned around Pa Theung, making easy turns with a small, quiet backseater named Piang. He collected target coordinates from ground units.

I requested F-Fours from Cricket and searched.

Using binoculars from about seven hundred feet, I studied Ernie's dark green forest and found tiny peep holes though the leafy coverage. "I see something strange here, Piang. The ground under the trees is bare. No jungle, no grass."

"Friendly commander across river say many enemy go to this place."

I flew a wider circle and continued to scan.

A sentry with a rifle on his shoulder looked up at me. He seemed to be guarding a pile of boxes near one edge of the clearing.

I only caught glimpses through the treetops, but I could see the soldier tracking me with his eyes. He didn't shoot, so he probably thought his cover was secure. But a force large enough to clear the ground and set up sentries had to be a company or larger.

"I got 'em, Piang. Tell the friendlies to take cover."

Two flights of Falcons called, and I briefed them. "Falcon One-one, drop all twelve bombs in one pass. You must hit the patch of trees. Press if you have to."

"Roger. We can do that. I see a cone formation near a river intersection."

"Tally, I'm at your two o'clock low over the smaller river. I don't plan to use a smoke. Let's surprise these guys."

"Tally ho."

"Target's on my left wing--the dark green trees. Attack parallel to the river. Friendlies are on the other bank."

"Green 'em up, Falcon." The flight leader armed his bombs. "One's in."

"Cleared hot."

Like its namesake, Falcon screamed down on the target. Irrepressibly, the powerful beast spit loose twelve bombs.

Half the small forest bloomed red.

"Shit hot, Falcon. Two, hit the other half. You're in sight, cleared hot."

"Two."

Number two smashed the other half.

As if in slow motion, small trees tumbled end-over-end above a fiery hell.

By the time the smoke cleared, I had briefed the second flight and ordered more. Trails, bunkers, trenches, and piles of supplies lay open for attack. I put L.G.B.s on large bunkers. Two hours later, the green trees were gouged to bits, like a tough beard swiped by a dull razor.

After dinner I thanked Ernie for the target.

"Did you find something?"

"A company of N.V.A. Hit 'em with four sets of F-Fours and ten sets of Tangos. Friendlies on the other bank said arms and legs were flying outa there."

Ernie looked disgusted. He didn't seem to know if I was kidding or not.

I seemed to have detected a soft spot, so I continued. "Yep. They said body parts were splashin' in the river.

Chapter 19
R AND R and a SAR

July 1971

As June ended sheets of monsoon rain became a standard background for my landings. The engine still purred, then backfired normally when I chopped power to touch down. Gusty winds shook the airplane and fought me through the flight controls. The tires squeaked on, then flung up roostertails.

One day soon after I shut down, Bill halted the jeep near my wingtip. "Climb in."

I ignored the warm rain and walked to the jeep. "Thanks for the lift."

"Did you earn it?" Bill gunned the jeep for home.

"I found clear air and wiped out a platoon." I described a long day of dodging thunderstorms the seasonal winds pushed across Laos.

"What about the laser-guided bombs?"

"I put them on E.C.-Forty-seven radio cuts--coordinates from Dit's daily reports. Found a small cave about four miles up the Nam Ou and a mile east of the river. When I went down and looked into the opening, I saw tables and chairs."

"Those electric-gooney-bird reports give a good display of the enemy order of battle. Sounds like a regimental headquarters." Bill parked in front of the house.

"You know how I hate those headquarters types. I put both two-thousand-pound bombs in the cave."

Bill laughed. "Wasn't the second bomb a bit of overkill?"

"What's overkill?" I grabbed for the last laugh.

"Overkill is flying and fighting for ten months without an R and R." Bill led me into the living room where Mr. Ed leaned on the bar.

We stopped for beer.

"I spent a week in Bangkok about a hundred years ago," I said.

"You can travel to Australia at taxpayers' expense, if you leave tomorrow."

"I dunno. Can I trust the defense of northern Laos to you rascals?"

"Don't worry about the war," Bill said. "It'll be here when you get back."

Mr. Ed jumped in. "When you stop at the Manila airport, you'll see a guy who sells fine cigars. Check him out. He'll tailor a stogie to your own persona."

"In that case, how could I possibly refuse?"

The next morning I rode a C-123 to Udorn, then boarded a C-47 headed for Saigon. Finally, I climbed on a bus marked R and R Processing Center.

I sat beside an in-country FAC named Rob, whose callsign was embroidered on his luggage bag. He seemed quiet but friendly.

I only told him I was an out-country FAC.

He probably guessed the rest from my civilian attire.

The bus pulled into a compound called Camp Alpha. Stepping off the bus and into a long line, we became the temporary property of the Army.

"The Army's getting even with the Air Force," Rob said, "They're making us suffer the standard humiliation and indignity they impose on their conscripts."

I began to believe him after I signed a receipt for bed linen and a towel, then reported to an open bay barracks with fifty bunks. The Army didn't charge us for lodging, and I figured the price was about right.

Back in line, we slowly snaked around buildings and into a screened latrine. Everything except the porcelain was painted olive drab.

A private handed us a toothbrush and toothpaste. "Brush 'em."

I felt like a prisoner of war. "Someday I'm going to write a story about all this shit, and people won't believe me."

The soldier shrugged.

Another station featured a cretin inspecting haircuts. At the bank I wrote a check, and the teller recorded the transaction on my immunization record. Until proven innocent everyone was treated as a black-marketing criminal.

Finally Rob said, "I've got a belly full of this horseshit. Let's go talk to that Army captain over there. He looks like he's in charge."

We walked over to our brother officer in green fatigues.

"Excuse me, sir," Rob said. "We're officers, not draftees right out of the boonies. Does everyone have to endure the same degrading conditions here?"

He said, "Yes," and walked away.

Rob's jaw dropped.

"I would've phrased the question more subtly," I said, "but now I understand why the Army has a problem with fragging."

After four more hours in line, we reached a station that issued tickets to Sydney.

I shook my head and looked at the slip of paper. "These tickets aren't free."

Rob shared my frustration. "Tan Son Nhut Air Base has an officers club. Why don't we grab a cab and get the fuck outa this sewer for awhile?"

"I'll drink to that," I answered. "We'll find out if the gate guard's job is to keep bad guys out or good guys in."

Less than an hour later in the air-conditioned club, I lifted a cold draft. "Here's to a separate Air Force."

Rob clinked his glass against mine. "Do you know why the Army resents the Air Force? We go off to foreign shores and build the mandatory runway, then, with the leftover concrete, a nice club. So what's wrong with that? We have to eat."

"And drink." I raised my glass again. "We're caught in a culture clash. The Army goes somewhere, digs a hole to live in, and dreams about edible food."

"Sometimes," Rob said, "the only thing the Army and the Air Force agree on is hot steel on the enemy."

"Sometimes?" I asked.

Twenty-four hours later, our Boeing 707 pilot reduced power and began a gentle right turn near the east coast of Australia.

The pretty flight attendant made standard seatbelt announcements, then added, "Below us is Botany Bay, where Captain Cook came in seventeen-sixty-nine. In a boat, of course."

I told Rob, "She's made the R and R run before."

We continued our descent, and our tour guide did also. "On your left, near the new Opera House, is Sydney Bridge, which used to be the longest of its type in the world. Then the Americans built one six inches longer. Six bloody inches."

"Definitely," Rob said. "But six inches can be important."

After landing, we were bussed to an R & R Center, where we lined up to book accommodations and tours. Most of our group took the bus to Kings Cross.

When I reached the counter, I asked, "What's the nicest hotel in Sydney?"

She smiled. "King's Cross is where you'll find the ladies of the evening."

"I'm not in the Army."

Rob began to laugh. "The Army's corrupted this culture, too."

"I'll ply the lovely ladies of Australia with my obvious charm rather than my dollars." I told Rob, "I didn't travel four thousand miles to mingle with drunken grunts and whores."

The girl at the counter consulted her files. "The Wellington is nice."

"I'll take it." The image of Camp Alpha lingered in my brain.

Rob opted for less expensive digs, also away from Kings Cross.

"Would you like to book a tour? The outback bobbie is very popular."

"Bobbie?" I had no idea what she meant.

"Bobbie-que. You Americans claim to have invented it."

"Sign me up."

Before departing, Rob also signed for some tours. "What do you plan to do first?"

"I'll sleep in a huge soft bed for about twenty-four hours. Then, I'll need a few winter clothes. I packed for Bondi Beach, thinking July was summertime here."

Concrete and city cuisine helped me regain hope for civilization. On one hand, I felt reassured the entire world wasn't bent on death and destruction. On the other hand, I was certain the folks at home could not possibly understand the war in Laos.

I read a paper for the first time in months while waiting for a tailor to alter a houndstooth jacket of burgundy wool--pure Australian. The headline indicated three Soviet cosmonauts had died upon re-entry to the earth's atmosphere.

"Too bad about them spice blokes!" the tailor said.

I nodded. Probably a quicker death than the gulags.

Although I tried to go slow and savor the culture of koalas and kangaroos, the outback, and Foster's Lager, the week flew by. Too soon, I sat on an R and R bus answering a roll call. A throng of tearful women crowded next to the line of buses.

My Camp Alpha combat buddy, Rob, took a seat beside me. I hadn't seen him since the bobbie.

Rob smiled. "I've heard weddings often result from these Sydney R and Rs."

"You might be right." I looked outside at the ladies. "But I'm sure most of these tears will dry before the next bus convoy pulls in."

A few troops failed to show. One character arrived so doped up the police hauled him away. The airliner took off on time.

When we landed in Manila for fuel, I deplaned and immediately spotted Mr. Ed's cigar stand--a rolling humidor offering tobacco in every shape and size for the avid aficionado. I selected a long narrow cigar, and it immediately caught fire, lighted by a small man who seemed to appear from nowhere.

"Too long." The Philippine gentleman frowned. "Try this one."

More fire and smoke billowed.

After two more attempts, I found my cigar and bought a box of them. I picked up a box of coronas for Mr. Ed. A short nap later I walked down the ladder in the rain at Tan Son Nhut.

"Midnight in Vietnam," I said to Rob. "Four months ago I left this place forever."

Rob suggested we avoid the Army R and R boot camp. "Let's take a cab and try the local economy."

The only taxi we could find was a modified gas-powered golf cart. It looked like Santa's sleigh with our bags piled in the back. With a grizzled old papsan of an elf at the wheel, we putted off into the dark drizzle.

We stopped at five hotels. All were filthy and full.

At one a.m. we stood, drenched, in the linen line back at Fort Benning East.

The private issuing towels showed us a flight schedule for the camp. The next Udorn flight would arrive in five days.

Rob looked at me. "Tomorrow we're outa here."

"At any cost."

At five a.m. the lights flashed on in the barracks. A loud Army N.C.O. stormed down the middle aisle like a small tornado, banging the metal bunks with a steel garbage can lid. He shouted, "Rise and shine, gentlemen. You must clear this barracks within thirty minutes."

I joined Rob and a dozen other angry and sleep-deprived Air Force troops at the chow hall. "We're planning an escape to Udorn. How many are with us?"

A dozen hands waved at me.

"We have to keep our plan a secret," I said. "Remember survival school."

The chief master sergeant next to me nodded.

"Rob," I said. "Let's pursue all our options. Why don't you go to the Aerial Port at Tan Son Nhut? Take a list of names and numbers. Book us on the next available flight to Thailand. I'll take an N.C.O. to base operations, since I'm too angry for lengthy negotiations. Let's meet here at ten. Chief, would you organize the troops in groups of two or three so we don't attract attention when we leave?"

"Sure," he replied. "We'll see you guys at ten, right here."

A hike and two taxi rides later, a master sergeant and I arrived at base operations. "I'm encouraged," I said. "They have a C-Forty-seven parked out front."

The sergeant at the counter inside offered us coffee.

We accepted. My master sergeant accomplice explained our plight.

"I'll have to call the colonel," the duty sergeant said.

"He's in his office."

"Which colonel?" I didn't want to deal with a base commander.

"My boss," the sergeant said. "He's the gooney-bird pilot."

"By all means," I said. "Please call him."

A tall gray-haired lieutenant colonel entered from a hallway. "How many Air Force troops do you have over at Camp Alpha?"

"At least fourteen, sir."

"Okay. We've done this before. Be discrete, but be here at thirteen-hundred hours. We'll haul you to Udorn. No human should have to go through the crap the Army dishes out over there."

I shivered when I remembered how close I had come to Army conscription.

My trip to Luang Prabang was uneventful.

When I handed Mr. Ed his box of Manila Coronas, he reached under the bar and lifted up a bottle of Chivas Regal.

Bill joined us. "I'm glad you're back on time. I sent Ernie down to Vientiane for a month or so. Are you ready to fly and fight again?"

"Sydney's a great escape. In one respect, I feel brand new. But had you told me about Camp Toilet, I'd have never left." I filled them in on my recent adventures.

During the next week, I acclimatized to rainy season flying again, popping caves and sinking boats until solid ceilings pushed low enough to ground me.

I rode with Bill to the airfield on a nasty gray morning. Dark clouds seemed a stone's throw overhead and steady rain had saturated everything, including the jeep seat. I noticed the Mekong had grown high, wide, and swift.

Bill halted briefly on the runway. "What would you call this ceiling?"

"Dog shit. Maybe three hundred feet." I scanned the horizon. All the surrounding hills appeared chopped in half by the cloud layer.

"We'll spin by the A.O.C. and make sure the local area is quiet. I'll remind them today's ideal for using field artillery. Then we'll make sure Major Oum Peng has the radio frequency for the AIRA house."

"Sounds like a plan." I yawned. "No way could we get out of the local area except over the river. And if we found anything, we couldn't strike it."

"Nothing I know about justifies operating in the small arms envelope all day."

Later that morning we threw darts over our shoulders using a survival mirror to aim.

Suddenly Swick burst into the living room. "Cricket wants two Ravens airborne out of Lima-Five-four!"

"Tell Cricket the weather here is delta sierra, as in dog shit." Bill looked at me and shrugged.

"Roger that." Swick disappeared for one minute, then returned, laughing. "Cricket doesn't want a weather report. Cricket wants two Ravens airborne out of Lima-Five-four. Fly twenty-five miles south."

"Holy shit," we said in unison.

I felt dread and urgency as Bill bounced the jeep down to the airfield. I kept my hands busy checking the batteries in both survival radios on my web belt. Raindrops beaded on the blue steel of my revolver. Earlier, I had wiped my Smith and Wesson Combat Masterpiece with oil and loaded five rounds. I normally kept the twelve o'clock chamber empty. I had two hundred and twenty rounds ready for my rifle.

Bill parked in the corner of the revetment. "I'll take the O-One. First one to the runway is the leader."

I nodded and untied the ropes anchoring the wings of the U-17. After pulling the rocket-safing pins, I kicked the chocks away and climbed in. "Seat belt tight, rocket switches safe, mixture, mags, and battery on." I verbalized what my hands were doing, then yelled, "Clear prop."

Bill strapped into the O-1 parked beside me.

I hit the start button.

The prop turned in sync with the coughing engine then disappeared in a blur as the engine roared to life. Two-hundred and forty horses--enough to get this kite off the ground and into deep shit. I had joined up for the action, but I couldn't avoid trepidation for what lay ahead. I felt something between anger and fear while I resigned myself to my best effort.

When the oil pressure steadied, I taxied.

Bill waved as I pulled out and turned in front of him.

"The tower's empty today," I said, pulling onto the runway.

"Rog. Cleared for take-off." Bill turned the corner onto the runway.

I pushed the throttle to the wall. After lifting off, I raised the flaps and turned south a hundred feet above the jungle. I saw Bill following in the O-1. On V.H.F. I said, "Cricket, Raven One-two is airborne. Raven One-zero's right behind me."

"Roger, Raven One-two and One-zero. Search an area twenty-five miles south."

I rogered and called Bill on F.M. "I'm going around the sleeping elephant."

"Tally." Bill stayed back about a mile.

The ridge behind the elephant stretched horizon to horizon.

"No way but over the top of this one." I added power and climbed into the mist, watching the trees below with occasional peeks at my attitude indicator.

"How's the weather in there?" Bill kept the banter going.

"Visibility is about thirty feet. Stay close to the trees. I peaked at twelve hundred." I retarded power in a dive down the backside and broke clear in another east-west valley.

"I don't have enough power," Bill said. "Turning around."

"Use flaps." I could only imagine the desperate turmoil he faced on the other side of the mountain. I flew lazy-eights and waited for five minutes.

As he popped out of the cloud layer, Bill said what I was thinking. "Damn. This ain't fun."

"About three more of these ridges should be twenty-five miles."

"You're trying to kill me, aren't you--scraping me off on the trees."

"You can have the lead if you want. Ain't no other way to skin this cat."

"Go ahead. I need to catch my breath."

I cleared three more ridges with Bill in trail. We broke out in a wide valley. The next ridge was about five miles long--an oval with a peak in the clouds.

"Okay, Cricket," Bill said. "Ravens One-zero and One-two are on scene. What are we searching for?"

"Look for a package."

"A package?" Bill paused. "Is it Christmas-wrapped?"

"It has a parachute. That's all I can say."

"One-two, this is One-zero. Did you copy?"

"Roger on the package." I laughed at Bill's righteous indignation after the severe adventure of getting here. I turned back over no-man's land with only lush green jungle below me.

Bill took control. "Search this next mountain up and down. Fly a spoke pattern to the left. I'll go right."

"Roger." I flew just below the clouds toward the mountain. At the last second, I turned left and searched an outbound leg. At best I had three hundred feet of altitude.

Bill turned away to the right and flew a similar pattern.

BAM.

A white object flashed by my right wing.

Was that a rocket? It's moving too slowly for a rocket. I called Bill. "Watch out. I think I just fired a rocket."

"You what?"

"It launched itself. All my switches are safe." I noted an empty launcher.

"Tally ho. You missed me." Bill sounded angry.

"I'll need a new seat cushion, too. Must have been static electricity."

Bill grumbled and continued the search.

After half an hour my pattern brought me to the southwest end of the ridge. I felt claustrophobic operating under the low gray ceiling. Even in the slow U-17, I had to bank and turn constantly to stay in clear air.

"Cricket, Raven One-zero," Bill said. "Your toy is lying on the north slope of this ridgeline under a fifty-foot ceiling. I'll pass coordinates shortly."

Dashing through tunnels formed by cloud and mountain, I joined a half-mile behind Bill. Orange and white nylon panels draped the jungle scrub below him. A small black airplane was tethered to the chute. *A drone. I wonder where that baby's been.* "Nice goin', pardner."

"Thanks. I'll relieve you in about three and half hours." On V.H.F. he said, "Cricket, Raven One-two'll hang around while One-zero R.T.B.s for gas. We'll give this thing constant coverage." He turned north and disappeared.

"Cricket concurs. What's your fuel status, One-two?"

"Four hours."

"Roger. You can work with Jack now. He's overhead your position organizing the next move. Cricket will monitor."

"Raven One-two, roger." I remembered the Jack callsign as a specialized Seventh Air Force command and control bird--a C-130 that controlled rescue assets.

Bill took a final jab. "Do you think you can keep that thing in sight, One-two?"

"You just worry about those ridges you have to cross twice!" My smartass remark got the last laugh.

For the next few hours I circled around the wide valley and memorized the lay of the land. The nearest man-made feature was a red dirt airstrip on an adjacent ridge about five miles from the package. I carefully confirmed the range and bearing so I could use it to relocate the target area if required. I dodged ragged cloud bottoms and noticed a few thin spots above.

At one point the cloud cover broke momentarily. I spotted a C-130 flying at four thousand feet.

"Jack, Raven One-two. Bend that big airplane around to the left and take a look at your package."

"Roger." The Hercules rolled steeply. "Tally ho."

"Come on down here and scoop it up."

"Raven One-two, about all we can add to the fight is eight side-firing thirty-eight pistols and forty-eight rounds of ammo."

I laughed. "You might call Lima Five-four on V.H.F. I'm too low for line-of-sight contact. Tell Raven One-zero to come out here above the clouds and find a hole . . ."

The hole above me closed.

". . . or a thin spot to penetrate. Might save him a few heart attacks. He's old, you know."

"Raven One-two, this is Bobo." The U.H.F. radio came alive.

"Go ahead."

"Roger. We're here to take pictures. Got under the clouds with our radar."

I knew the RF-4 had terrain-avoidance radar capability, but the tiny space below the clouds would challenge any fast-mover to stay there. "Tally." I spotted the recce bird a mile north, moving around peaks like an angry shark in a green ocean.

"How's our heading?"

"Come fifteen left. Half a mile to go."

"Rog." The jet jerked left. "Tally."

I dropped to the treetops to stay clear.

The RF-4 blew across my windscreen and pulled up into the clouds. "We saw the target, but too late to get pictures. We'll let down again on a north-south run."

"Roger. I'll stay low and look for you."

After a few minutes, the recce pilot said, "Bobo's underneath. Southbound."

"Ten degrees right. One mile."

Bobo jerked, rolled out and pulled up over the target. "I don't know if we got anything that time. We'll give it one more pass."

"Roger. Looks like a southwest run-in gives the best ground clearance."

"Roger." Then after a pause, he said, "We're underneath."

"Tally. In five seconds go fifteen right. Target's around the next hill."

"Rog." The RF-4 stood on its right wing, causing a cloud of heavy white condensation to streak from the top half of the airplane. Bobo rushed at the target then rotated upward and disappeared.

"Another run?"

"Don't think so, Raven. We've seen enough. Thanks for your help."

"So long." I noted the time in my green memo book. I had been airborne for five hours, and I was hungry.

"One-two, this is One-zero on Fox Mike."

"Did you bring me a sandwich?"

"No, but they saved you one. The ceiling at the airfield has holes."

I saw Bill's O-1 arc around a hill north of my wide valley. I pulled straight up. "Nothing going on at the moment. An RF-Four passed through. See ya in three hours."

"Rog."

My recovery and landing at L-54 proved simple compared to the earlier ordeal of departing. I pulled into the revetment, spun around, and shut down.

Ramon waved and chocked the wheels. "Everything is okay?"

"I had a problem with a rocket tube on the right wing." I climbed out. "Don't put any more rockets in that empty launcher. Check for short circuits if you have time."

"No problem."

I signed the aircraft forms and turned for the jeep.

Ramon began to laugh and pointed to my right wing.

Walking around the tail, I checked the empty tube. I reached up and put the tip of my little finger in the bullet hole six inches behind the front end. "A.K.-Forty-seven."

Ramon giggled and nodded. "I'll change the launcher."

"Save it to show Mr. Bill. He thinks I shot the rocket at him."

"You are lucky the rocket does not explode."

I raised my eyebrows. Until that moment, I hadn't thought about a catastrophic explosion. *Holy shit.*

I took a sandwich to the commo room. First, I told Swick, "Call Cricket. Tell them I can confirm the presence of small arms in the target area." Then I gave a full report to Dit.

He took all the details, then asked, "How are you feeling?"

"Tired. I'll get a shower and go down to the airfield. This afternoon's mission has to be easier. I used up all my adrenaline this morning."

The rain had stopped as I climbed through the overcast on a southerly heading. I reported airborne, then spotted two A-1s circling in the distance.

"Raven One-zero, One-two. I see A-Ones. You've been busy."

"Sandy One and Two are circling a hole two miles southeast. We're waiting for Jolly Green Five-four to finish refueling. Come on down."

Over the hole and under the Skyraiders I rolled and descended. I pulled through to a heading of north. "Nice place to let down. A thousand feet of space below the clouds."

Bill circled ahead where the ceiling dropped much lower. "We're almost ready. I'd like to stay for the pick-up."

"Check your fuel gage."

"Okay. I'll head home. Sandy flight's on U.H.F. See you later."

"Rog." I turned left into the valley where the drone lay undisturbed. Then,

I returned to the A-1 orbit and switched my mike switch to U.H.F. "Sandy One, Raven One-two. Tell me when you're ready."

"Roger. One-zero briefed us. Any groundfire down there?"

"I took an A.K. hit this morning. Suggest you arm your cannons before you drop down. Low ceiling requires eyeballs outside." I saw a large HH-53 helicopter approaching from the south.

"Roger."

"Negative friendlies in the area. You're cleared in advance to return groundfire."

"Rog. Thanks. As soon as Jolly Five-four sets up, you can take us down."

I followed the A-1s until Jolly 54 checked in. This operation will be easy, I figured. The bullet hole from the last sortie did not enter my calculations.

"Jolly Five-four, Sandy One. Stay over this hole in the clouds while we troll."

Roger."

"Raven, Sandy's ready to descend."

"Roger." I rolled to ninety degrees of bank and let the nose slice down through the wispy hole that was trying to close. Passing two hundred knots, I looked, but didn't see Skyraiders.

"Raven, we missed the hole. Can you come back?"

"Sure." I turned hard and climbed into the thin ceiling. I popped through and saw the Skyraiders turning about three miles away. "I'm at your twelve low. You have a thousand feet clearance below the clouds at this point. Say when."

In trail formation the A-1s approached to about a mile. "Okay. We're ready."

I rolled inverted and pulled the nose straight down. "I need airspeed to stay in front of you guys. Head north when you get below the ceiling."

"Roger."

Under the clouds, I sped to the darker overcast up north. I saw the A-1s behind when I turned left. "I'll overfly the objective, then move out of your way."

"Roger."

I opened my window and flew across the drone. "I don't hear anything."

"Roger. Tally." Sandy flight split and made a dozen passes over the objective. White contrails followed their wingtips like string as the camouflaged beasts of war turned and dared the enemy to show himself.

I held low and clear to the north. "If you want to circle in the valley, I'll hold directly over the helicopter."

"Sounds like a plan, Raven. Break. Jolly Five-four, the Raven will bring you in. All seems quiet down here."

I went back for the Jolly Green Giant.

"Jolly has tally, Raven. We can follow you down."

"Roger." This time I pulled the power and dropped through the clouds at a hundred knots with Jolly in tow. I turned left and overflew the drone. "I'll try to stay overhead. Sandy owns the valley."

"Roger." Jolly Five-four moved across the treetops a hundred feet below me. The huge chopper slowed to a low hover above the drone. Someone had once told me the pararescue jumpers, or P.J.s, were the bravest of the brave. One of them showed me this quality when he jumped out, cut away the parachute, and hooked a cable to the drone.

"Jolly, Sandy. How's it going?"

"Just picking up the P.J. We'll be climbing out shortly."

I was turning left to stay over Jolly 54 when the huge spinning rotor vanished. The Jolly Green disappeared. At first I thought he might have lifted into the clouds. "Jolly Five-four, Raven One-two."

Jolly didn't answer.

I slammed bottom rudder to slice the nose down and buzz across the drone. "Sandy, Jolly Five-four is upside down on the ground."

The A-1s moved in.

I moved out. "Jack, Raven One-two. Jolly Five-four is on the ground inverted. We need help."

"Roger. Any survivors?"

"Affirmative. I see movement near the wreckage. No smoke or fire. He went straight down and rolled over." I had to clear my dry throat. "Sandy is giving close cover now."

"Roger. Help's on the way."

I looked up at my U.H.F. radio. From ten pre-set frequencies on the old control panel, I selected Guard channel. A Jolly crewman said he had two serious casualties and negative groundfire at the moment.

Swallowing hard, I reacted automatically and fought my shock symptoms. The situation seemed unreal. I struggled to believe the disaster outside, and my training took over. I watched my thumb press the transmit button. "Jolly, this is Raven One-two. Help's on the way. If you can, move your injured to a suitable pick-up point. If you hear anything, call me or Sandy.

"Roger."

"Raven One-two, this is Jack. We have an Air America Huey and an H-Thirty-four inbound. They'll check in on SAR Delta frequency."

"Roger." I did not have that frequency among the ten pre-sets. I turned on a small survival radio, moved my headset, and held the radio to my ear.

The calm voice of Sandy leader boosted my confidence as he reassured the survivors. "Tell us what you need. You'll be home in no time."

"Raven One-two, this is Alpha Charlie Hotel. I'm outa fuckin' gas."

"What is your position?" I assumed I was speaking to an Air America pilot.

"Somewhere over fuckin' Laos." His radio signal was strong. He was close.

"Can you see a long green valley?"

"I see a million fuckin' long green valleys, and I'm still outa fuckin' gas."

Annoyed by the bad attitude I heard, I fired a rocket up at a thirty-degree angle on a heading of due south. "Call me when you see a white smoke."

"Roger, I see a fuckin' smoke."

"Go three miles north from the smoke."

"Roger."

I spotted the blue and sliver chopper and guided the pilot's eyes to the crash site. Bill checked in on V.H.F.

The Air America Huey hovered between the drone and the Jolly where downwash from rotor blades flattened the tall elephant grass. "I'll take the two injured troops to Luang Prabang."

"Raven One-two, Jack."

"Go ahead, Jack."

"Roger. Can you discretely escort the Huey to Lima Five-Four?" The V.H.F. voice whispered, as if avoiding pissing off the foul-mouthed Huey pilot, who spoke on U.H.F. "He sounds like he has a low fuel condition."

"I'll follow the Huey." I wanted to say, "fuckin' Huey."

"Raven One-zero, Jack. Plan to stay until the H-Thirty-four picks up the other survivors."

"Raven One-zero, wilco." Then, Bill called me on F.M. "What a fine mess you've made out here. I had everything set up for you."

I laughed. "Watch out for the A-Ones. They're everywhere. The Huey's moving north now, and I'm following."

"Roger. I'll escort the Thirty-four, then come back and work up some kind of plan for tomorrow."

I dove down behind the Huey. "You may need to fire a smoke to guide the next chopper. Scenery's bland down south. Good luck."

"See ya later."

I chased the Huey over the green jungle canopy under thinner clouds than I had seen earlier. We cruised around the small hills and over the big ones. Until now, I had never thought of helicopter flying as an art form. That caveman could fly the shit out of a helicopter.

The Huey flew to the parking ramp near the control tower at L-54.

Breaking right to set up a landing toward the revetments, I noticed a fuel truck and an ambulance beside the runway. By the time I had taxied to parking, filled out the paperwork, and drove the jeep to the ramp, the vehicles and the Huey were gone.

Two Air Force flightsuits on a grassy knoll beside the ramp caught my attention. The H-34 must have dropped off the Jolly pilots. I was surprised at the speed of the chain of events. A silver-haired major and a sturdy captain chatted nervously.

I strolled over. "How are you guys doing?"

The major eyed me suspiciously. "Fine, thanks."

"Are you going to stay overnight? We have at least one good bar in town."

"No, no way," they said. "We're waiting for a C-One-thirty ride to Udorn. Say, uh, who are you?"

"I'm sorry." I introduced myself and shook their hands. "I was your FAC, Raven One-two. You disappeared right before my eyes. How are your troops?"

"The flight engineer has a broken back, and one P.J. has a smashed jaw," the major said. "They're tough. They'll make it." He seemed friendlier, but the captain stared at the six-shooter I wore over pinstriped, bell-bottom trousers and a blue polo shirt.

I recognized they were in shock after the crash and bewildered by their present surroundings. "I know you guys have been through a lot. Can I do anything for you?"

"Yes," the major said. "I'd like to retrieve our helmets and survival vests from the ambulance that took the injured troops to town."

"You can probably write that stuff off."

"We really would like to get them." The major insisted.

"Sure. Jump in the jeep. I'll give you a quick tour on the way to the hospital."

They followed me to my jeep.

As we lurched along the muddy road to town, I started a conversation. "The Huey was low on fuel, and I had to fire a smoke rocket three miles south to help him find you."

"Your rocket scared us." The captain cleared his throat. "We reported the noise as incoming."

"The radios in the U-Seventeen are old. I missed a few calls until I pulled out my survival radio. What brought you down?"

"Small arms, we think." The major shrugged his shoulders. "We were taking slack out of the line when something went wrong. Next thing I knew the heavy load began to slide down the hill and yanked us into the trees. I had no power to recover."

"I took a small arms round this morning. Hit a launcher tube and fired the rocket. Surprised me pretty good."

They didn't laugh.

What the hell. They just crashed.

I pulled in beside the Swiss Infirmary, the local version of a hospital.

The helicopter pilots secured their survival gear as orderlies brought out their crewmen on stretchers for transport to the airport. The pilot and copilot said encouraging words to both injured men.

I pointed to an Air Force C-130 approaching from the south. "I think I see your ride coming."

We hustled to the airport, shook hands again, and the Jolly 54 crew departed--somewhat the worse for wear.

Bill landed as the sunlight faded, and the longest day in several lives was over.

"I'll launch first tomorrow morning." Bill leaned on the bar with Mr. Ed and me. "Jack scheduled an early pick-up attempt with two A-Ones and three choppers."

"That force ought to handle the job." I puffed on my stogie and sipped scotch. Fatigue from ten busy hours in the air would soon own me. I looked forward to sleeping late. "I hope you have a boring sortie."

We raised our glasses.

Bill had a boring sortie.

Around eleven a.m. I joined two A-1s circling a thin spot in the cloud deck below. I moved my transmit selector to F.M. "One-zero, this is One-two. What's up?"

"All quiet here. Hobo Two-zero's overhead. We're waiting for a flight of three CH-Fifty-threes, callsign Knife Two-five."

"Roger. Go get gas. See ya in four hours."

"Okay. Don't try to win the war by yourself."

"Ha ha." I dove below the clouds and checked the objective area. The drone and the helicopter appeared unmolested. Several low passes didn't draw fire. I took out my FAC camera and shot a roll from fifty feet.

"Knife Two-five, check-in."

"Two."

"Three."

Back at the rendezvous point, I finished a detailed briefing to the Hobos and Knives with the words, "Arm up now. Cleared to return groundfire."

"Raven, Hobo Two-zero will go down first. Come back and bring in the Knives after we check for groundfire."

"Knife Two-five."

"Raven One-two copies." I rolled inverted and let the nose fall into the clouds. "You have a thousand feet to work with at this point. More like a hundred at the target."

"We're right behind you."

With power at cruise settings I zoomed to a northerly heading.

Two A-1s pulled abeam my left wing. "Which way, Raven?"

"Hang a left at the valley ahead. Objective will be off your left wing near the top."

"Roger." Hobo flight took wide combat spacing. When they rolled left, contrails streamed from both wingtips. The flight leader flew over the drone at ten feet. *These guys are really trolling.*

His wingman came across from the opposite direction, same altitude.

Hobo flight searched every inch of the valley. "Raven, go get the Knives."

"Roger." I flew back and climbed above the clouds.

"Knife Two-five has a tally, Raven. We're ready."

"Follow me." I pulled power and eased through the hole.

After the third chopper appeared underneath, Knife Two-five gave instructions. "Two-six, you have the lead. Hold outside the valley ahead while we go for the pick-up."

"Knife Two-six."

Knife Two-five followed me to the target.

Climbing slightly, I flew a tight circle over the chopper. My eyes never left him. Hobo flight rolled constantly, pulling tight lazy-eights in the valley.

A rope ladder fell from the side door. A P.J. started down.

"Knife Two-five's hit. We're movin' out."

The big helicopter tilted forward and eased away. The ladder with the P.J. retracted into the side door. "Fire came from the trees to the north. We're headed to Alternate. One casualty. Not serious."

"Hobo flight, hit the trees to the north." I followed the Knife to the intersecting valley where his wingmen joined him. "Good luck, Two-five."

"Roger. I'll take Two-six home. Two-seven will hang around for awhile."

"Sounds good." I turned and watched twenty-millimeter shells cut the jungle like a sparkling chain saw. As one A-1 turned off, the other rolled in.

I looked hard at the hillside below the target. "Hobo, I see steady muzzle flashes a bit south of your hits. I can mark it if you wish."

"Rog. Come on in."

I rolled and aimed.

BAM. BAM.

"Put your C.B.U. between those marks and work it north."

"Hobo's in."

"Cleared random attacks." I moved to the large valley.

Pass after pass, the Hobos came around, plowing rows of smoke and fire. Unseen shards of steel slashed the jungle like an angry reaper.

Finally, I heard, "Hobo's winchester, R.T.B."

"Raven One-two, Knife Two-seven. Can we refuel at Lima Five four?"

"Standby. I'll ask. How much gas do you need?"

"Four thousand pounds of jet fuel, J.P.-Four."

"Rog." I climbed up and called the AIRA House. "I need a favor. Can you call the Company and ask if we can have four thousand pounds of J.P.-four."

Swick's voice sounded slightly garbled, but I understood a "Roger." "Raven One-two, this is Jack. Hobo Four-two is inbound to you."

"Roger. We hit the groundfire, but I think it's time to ask the big question. Do we destroy everything on the ground, or does somebody think this objective is worth more blood?"

"Good question, One-two. We'll ask."

I cleared the next Hobo flight to strike the same area.

For twenty minutes hell rained from the sky. Hobo's furious attacks extended to possible escape routes. The price paid under the barrage had to be high.

I climbed up and called Swick. "Any response from the Company?"

"Roger, One-two. No problem at all. But they would like to know what the hell you're going to do with four thousand pounds of C-Four."

I laughed. C-4 was a plastic explosive. "No. You misunderstood. I said J.P.-Four. Juliet Papa Four."

"Rog."

"Raven One-two, this is Jack. More Hobos are inbound. Cleared to strike both objectives--the helicopter and the package."

"Thanks, Jack. We'll get right on it."

"One-two, this is One-zero, on fox mike. What have you done now?"

"Knife Two-five took hits. I've been blasting all around the objectives."

"Roger. I'm just coming into the area."

"Working this little target is like flying around in a living room full of bad guys. We have clearance to hit both objectives."

"I can handle that little chore."

"Hobos are inbound. Bad guys are north of the drone. You can see where the earlier strikes went."

"Roger."

"Be careful. I saw steady muzzle flashes halfway down the hill. I'm R.T.B."

"Roger, One-two. One more question."

"Shoot."

"What were you going to do with two tons of C-Four?"

The replacement A-1s had arrived and dropped down through a hole in the cloud cover. I spotted them near the objective, but they were heading away toward the old dirt strip I had used as a southwest reference.

"Hobo, this is Raven One-two. You're flying away from the target. Turn hard left, roll out heading zero-four-five. Target's behind the first ridge."

"Roger, thanks." The A-1s turned.

"Raven One-zero is on scene and in charge."

As I climbed out and turned north I heard Bill shouting expletives. I called on F.M. "What's the deal?"

"I nearly got run over by two A-1s. That's the deal."

"Oops. My fault. They were headed the wrong way. I turned 'em around. I thought you were listening on U.H.F." I went home and returned two hours later.

Bill left the Jolly smoking, and the drone would never fly again. But headquarters wanted complete destruction. Cricket sent F-4s with snake and nape. Their valor under the clouds proved superb, but their bombs missed.

I landed at sunset.

Tink.

On the opposite end of the long bedroom we shared, Bill opened his lighter.

I awoke every morning to that tink.

Bill drew in his first Marlboro. "Fuck that drone. Why don't you go out for a weather check? Unless you call, I'll send you some T-Twenty-eights in two hours. Pop that S.O.B."

"I can do that." After pre-flight rituals, I took off and found broken skies over the drone. I delayed the T-28s for one hour.

Finally, Mustang Blue checked in under clear skies.

I briefed him and fired a smoke rocket.

"You want to hit the little airplane?"

"Affirmative. Can you shoot rockets first?"

"One's in." Mustang blue's first rocket hit the drone.

Gray smoke rose, then the nose cone flared into white metallic fire.

What incredible marksmanship. Tango pilots were the best. I took close-up pictures and marked the chopper for the rest of Blue's ordnance.

I landed early and found Bill in a jeep with Mr. Ed. I held out two white film cartridges. "This one's before. And this one's after."

"I give up. Before and after what?"

"Mustang Blue. Lieutenant Somnuck incinerated it with a rocket."

"Take the film to Udorn. Be back in time to fly a morning mission tomorrow."

The wing intelligence officer at Udorn seemed almost as happy to have proof of the drone's destruction as I was to have an afternoon off. I gave him a verbal report to accompany the photos and went to the club.

After cashing a check, I walked into the dining room for a late lunch. The long room had tablecloths in squadron colors, staking territory as painted patches did on the lounge tables. I recognized a familiar face alone at the maroon recce table.

"Mind if I join you?"

Major John Fragos, my former T-37 instructor in pilot training, welcomed me like an old friend.

"You got a FAC job after Vance," my Greek friend said, "and I'll bet you have a Raven callsign now, judging from your attire and excessive hair."

The dark-featured major was bald, but I resisted the urge to tease. "Local barbershops are unsanitary. My callsign is One-two. So, recce's your cup of tea now?"

"Yep. I love it."

"I remember a dawn patrol mission in Oklahoma. You buzzed a railroad and turned on your taxi light in the face of an oncoming train. Made him think you were another train."

"I was only showing you the plane worked just as well at ten feet as it did at ten-thousand." The major tried to hide a smile.

"Have I seen you at work lately?" I wondered if he was the pilot who punched through the clouds over the drone two days before.

"No. I've been working over North Vietnam. Weather's been horrible."

"Heard about Jolly Five-four? One of your friends took pictures of that."

"Roger that. Were you the FAC?"

"I was one of 'em. I logged twenty-four flying hours in the last three days." I told him about the mission.

When other recce troops joined us, Fragos said, "Meet Raven One-two. He's been doing the Jolly Green SAR."

"There goes my low profile." I shook hands with everyone.

A lieutenant asked, "How long have you been in the war?"

I confirmed the date on my watch. "In two weeks, I'll have been here a year." *Holy shit. A whole year.* My mind drifted momentarily. *Maybe I should think about going home.*

Chapter 20
Are You Right-Side Up?

July 1971

I took off from Udorn at seven a.m. As I approached the Mekong I called the A.O.C. at Vientiane. "Anything for Lima-Five-four?"

"Affirmative. One passenger."

"Roger. I'll land in five minutes." I touched down gently in the still air and taxied to the trailer that served as the operations center.

A stocky Hispanic troop wearing civvies put a suitcase in the backseat of the U-17, climbed aboard, and shook my hand. "Staff Sergeant Sanchez. Call me Pancho."

I taxied out and launched to the north. "What's your specialty?"

"I'm an engine man."

"You're Henry's replacement. Welcome to the family."

Pancho smiled and looked wide-eyed at the jungle terrain.

I leveled off at six thousand feet, above scattered clouds.

Pancho asked, "Do you have a map?"

"Sure. It's in the pocket behind your seat."

He reached around and pulled out an aeronautical chart. "Why don't you use it?"

"I'm only required to carry it, not use it."

"What?"

"I'm kidding. I'd look at it if I had to. Every day I use the one-to-fifty-thousand scale charts. I don't have a good feel for the rate I move across that one-to-two-fifty."

Pancho nodded. He continued to ask intelligent questions. The clouds below us became a solid white carpet, so he stowed the chart. "How do you plan to locate Luang Prabang now?"

"Dead reckoning. Magnetic course to Luang Prabang is three-five-four.

Crosswind is moderate from the northeast, so I'm using a three-five-eight heading to hold course. Are you a private pilot?"

"No. I've never flown in a small airplane. I just like to know what's goin' on. What'll you do if we get to Luang Prabang and the clouds are still solid below us?"

"The trip takes fifty minutes. If I can't see the ground after forty-five, I'll go down and look for a hole. We have enough gas to go to Udorn if the weather's really bad."

Entering clouds, I climbed to eight thousand feet to stay on top. "You can fly if you wish, Pancho."

"Sure." His eyes opened wide.

Pointing to the compass, I took my hands off the controls. "Fly north."

"Okay." Pancho giggled like a child. He flew well for a novice.

I answered more questions and gave him an idea of what lay ahead. We approached Luang Prabang over a puffy cloud deck.

"I'll take control now." I turned left and descended to the top of the clouds.

"Do you see a hole?"

"Not yet." I skied along and dropped into a crevice between young thunderstorms.

Passing left and below us, a tiny hole gave me a glimpse of the jungle several thousand feet below.

I rolled inverted and reduced power. "Are you okay, my friend?"

"Doin' great, sir."

"Hang on." I pulled until I felt the tickle of a stall, and we shot straight down through the hole. Continuing to haul back on the controls, I leveled off below the deck. Next I had to avoid a gray rock face--a huge vertical feature of a lush green mountain. Stomping right rudder, I rolled hard past ninety degrees. With enough pressure on the controls to keep us seated, I let the nose follow the slope down to the treetops of a narrow valley and pushed the throttle to cruise power. Holding two hundred knots, I swooped left again to follow a small stream at the valley bottom.

Our compass showed us heading west.

Pancho smiled. "Nice flying. What do you call that maneuver?"

"A modified split-s and a couple o' whifferdills."

"I didn't realize they had names like that."

I nodded. When the reddish brown Mekong came into view, I thanked God quietly for giving me an easy path home. I stood the craft on the right wing and rolled out, heading north a few feet above the water. "Your new home waits around the corner."

"Wow. What a ride."

"I'm impressed you're not airsick." Following the surging river around a huge bend to the right, I popped up and checked in with the AIRA house, adding, "Tell Henry his replacement is on board. He owes me."

"Rog." Swick sounded indifferent as usual.

"Here's the city of Luang Prabang. Temples, palm trees and dirt roads."

"I love it already--a beautiful sight." Pancho stared out his window.

"Do you see the runway?" I pointed ahead and called tower for landing.

Pancho nodded.

The heavy U-17 settled nicely through my flare to a three-point touchdown.

A joyous reception committee escorted Pancho away while I helped Ramon slide eight rockets into the wing launchers and top off the fuel tanks. For the next few hours I scouted the Nam Ou but couldn't strike anything because of the overcast.

After lunch the overcast broke.

Bill and I drove to the office where our Laotian backseaters hung out. I one-upped my friend with a few Lao phrases I had been practicing. "*Sambadee. Chao bi bin nam coi, bo?*" I asked Piang if he wanted to fly with me.

"*Bi.*" The tiny soldier nodded, climbed up on his desk and retrieved a gold chain with several Buddhas from the wooden frame around a picture of the king.

"Me lot, bo?" I asked if he had transportation and elbowed Bill.

Piang nodded, and adjusted his red beret. He usually rode his moped to the field.

Bill recovered from his daze. My use of the Lao language had apparently befuddled him. "I don't know what to say. Does anybody care to fly with me?"

Somnuck jumped up. "I'll fly with Mister Bill."

In the U-17 two hours later we waited for another set of T-28s to arrive. We were supporting a friendly army unit that ran into N.V.A. near the king's farm along the Mekong south of Pa Theung. We had bashed the resilient enemy with ten two-ships of Tangos.

I saw Bill's O-1 over another ground unit about ten miles south.

I pointed to the fuel gauges. "Do you see only the left wing tank is feeding. It's near empty. The right wing tank is still full." I verbalized my thoughts, not expecting Piang to understand.

Piang nodded and shrugged.

"I don't like empty fuel tanks. When I flew the O-Two, we always left enough gas to get us home in each tank before we switched to another. This airplane switches automatically, but only after the left side is empty."

Piang nodded.

"I'm leaving a little gas in the left wing." I moved the fuel selector from Both to Right. "Seems like the right thing to do."

Piang smiled. He had no choice but to trust my judgment.

"Raven One-two, Mustang Green."

"Mustang Green--"

My purring engine stopped. The silence was deafening. The nose fell. "Hey, Bill. My engine just quit."

"Well, you better get it started."

Moving the fuel selector to Both and the mixture handle to Rich, I could hear Bill's laughter, too. The windmilling propeller made a whooshing sound. On my left I spotted a smooth-looking sandbar on the edge of the Mekong. Landing on that spot would take us into the water, and we could try to swim away from the angry North Vietnamese soldiers nearby.

"Engine is not turning?" Piang's eyes looked like saucers.

"Not at the moment." I switched on the fuel boost pump and descended in a left turn. My landing pattern would take me over people I had been bombing for an hour. "Tighten your seat belt. Can you swim?"

"Yes."

Pop-pop-pop-pop-pop.

The dreaded pop of small arms fire distracted me as we glided over the bad guys. I rolled out heading west over the edge of the river. Throttle open, battery and mags on, prop full increase. Shit, this scene is for real.

"Raven One-two, Mustang Green. You fly very low."

I could see the texture of the sandbar as I lowered flaps to full and began my flare.

ROWWWWW.

At the last possible moment, the engine roared to life.

Damn. I climbed steadily, raised flaps and looked at Piang. "We're okay now."

"Thank you very much." Piang smiled.

"Don't thank me." I felt my heart start beating again.

"We go home now?"

"We should. But I want a piece of those N.V.A. who were shooting at us. I know exactly where they're hiding now." I turned back and fired a rocket.

Bam.

"Mustang Green, hit my smoke. Friendlies are in the king's farm."

"Roger."

I turned for home and called Bill. "I'm goin' home. I suspect vapor lock.

Tell your backseater to check on the action at the king's farm."

"Roger. See you later."

I set up a long straight-in final approach and received landing clearance from the control tower. As we crossed the approach end of the runway, I pushed the throttle forward to level off and fly to the other end. Nothing happened. The engine was dead. I glided to a smooth touchdown.

"Engine stop again?" Piang asked.

"Yeah. We'll clear the runway here in the middle." I let the aircraft roll onto a muddy road that paralleled the landing strip. I turned my switches off.

As we climbed out, Ramon pulled up on his motorcycle.

"I think the fuel lines have vapor locked."

"No problem."

Mr. Ed picked us up in his jeep. "Most airplanes work better when that big blade in front goes round and round."

"I appreciate that advice. I know it comes from many, many years of experience."

After dinner Bill said he wanted to show me a message from Seventh Air Force. As we walked to the radio room, he teased me about my bad day. "Poor throttle technique. Gets you every time."

I changed the subject. "Is Mr. Ed flying?"

"Yeah. The weather broke. He's out killin' Commies."

"Ed's done a lot to improve the Twenty-eight pilots' flight discipline. Now you see tight formations and crisp radio talk instead of gaggles and giggles. But have you noticed his discipline is slipping?"

"Yeah," Bill said. "Henry showed him how to unwire the high blower--adds power, but shortens engine life. He's started buzzing the revetments. Says low passes are good for morale."

"I've seen that act. Takes your breath away when he roars over like a bat outa hell."

Bill pushed the metal vault door open. "Speaking of things from hell, read this." He handed me a message that filled several sheets of printer paper.

When I held page one, four feet of paper unfolded to the floor. "What's this about?"

"The Attaché forwarded this to us. Headquarters isn't going to send us anymore laser-guided bombs. They said we expended them on unauthorized targets."

I read the terse language of the opening paragraphs, asserting we never reported the cave closed at Pa Theung. So the computer automatically fragged daily L.G.B. sorties. Then the message listed targets we struck in the succeeding months--a four-foot list. My anger matched any that headquarters types could generate. "So we were supposed to ask some asshole colonel at Seventh Air Force for permission to hit the other caves?"

"That's the gist of the message."

"Tell them to send that colonel up the Nam Ou in a boat. That way he could be in a position to approve targets. Of course the N.V.A. would probably skin him. But I wouldn't let him in the house. He'd probably guard the toilet and tell us when to shit."

Bill laughed. "I spoke to the Air Attaché. He forwarded this message for us to enjoy. He has more than enough power to turn off whiny headquarters types. He said if we need more L.G.B.s, let him know."

The next morning I waited in the FAC revetment while Bill boarded the U-17 with the Lao colonel who ran the A.O.C. A week earlier the colonel had scheduled an orientation flight with me, but a huge black thunderstorm had blanketed the sky that afternoon.

The overcast ceiling had hung around all week like a dark premonition.

Standing with several T-28 pilots, I saluted as the U-17 taxied out. I planned to take the O-1 later.

The U-17 roared down the runway and climbed straight ahead to about three hundred feet. Then the engine stopped. The aircraft turned like a bat, then reversed to line up--silently--with the runway. Bill dead-sticked the U-Bird safely.

Mr. Ed drove out, retrieved the crew, and returned them to the FAC revetment.

Bill pointed to the O-1. "I'll try this one now."

I couldn't resist. "Watch your throttle technique."

We paraded through the local bars to hail Pancho and farewell Henry. Another new guy, Andy, arrived in time to join the fracas. He was our long overdue A.P.G. man--an airplane general mechanic.

Mr. Ed issued instructions at the Bungalow Bar. "Only one drink at the Prison Bar--enough for Henry to say good bye to his closest friends. And would someone please check Andy's I.D. card? He looks about sixteen to me."

Baby-faced Andy had fair skin and dark hair. "I'm twenty-three . . . really."

"Welcome to the family." I shook his hand.

"I know I'm lucky to be here. I hope I can make a contribution."

"Great to have a fresh perspective on board. Sometimes the guys can act a bit world-weary, myself included." I shook my head, wondering how much this innocent kid would change in the next six months. "Where are you from?"

"Fayetteville, North Carolina."

"Southern boys know how to work hard in the hot sun. You'll do fine."

He smiled and nodded.

After a couple of beers, Charlie, our munitions man, pulled me aside. He worked hard but rarely spoke. "You know I think you FACs are overpaid. All officers are."

"Your assessment sounds reasonable to me." I laughed hard.

"I thought I should tell you something. Ol' Pancho over there thinks you walk on water. I don't know what happened on the trip up here, but he thinks the world of you. I thought I'd let you know."

Thank you, Charlie. He did most of the flying. He's got good hands."

Bill joined in. "Speaking of flying, I'm taking the U-Seventeen to Udorn tomorrow. Ramon thinks he solved that fuel problem, but we'll do a major overhaul."

"When are you coming back?" Until he returned, Ernie and I would fly the O-1.

"I'll bring a new plane back tomorrow. I'll take Henry to meet the freedom bird. Then I'll scoot back here after lunch. Also, if you want to extend your tour, let me know. The embassy discourages extensions, but you have the option."

Those words got my full attention. "When do you have to know?"

"Sooner is always better, I suppose."

As the evening faded into song and story, I watched Henry laugh and cry. He'd miss us and be missed. But he was going home.

Everybody looked forward to going home, right?

Bill launched in the U-Bird at nine the next day with Henry aboard.

I followed in the O-1.

When Cricket answered Bill's check-in, I recognized Neil Upmeyer's drawl.

I checked in as rapidly as possible to test Upmeyer's controller skills. "Crick, Raven One-two's airborne in the Ugly Seventeen, one soul, working freq three-fifteen-five. I'll be ten miles east. I've got targets if you've got air."

"Roguh, Raven One-two."

I had to laugh. Neil took a pass on the fast-talking game.

I realized Bill was probably laughing, too, because I had said erroneously

I was in the U-17. Any search and rescue effort would start two hours late unless I corrected the mistake. I had to 'fess up.

"Cricket, this is Raven One-two with a correction to my last transmission. I am in the Oscar Ace, not the U-Seventeen." My face felt warm from embarrassment.

"Are ya shore?" Upmeyer joined the game.

I imagined Bill laughing so hard he had to give Henry control of the aircraft, but I didn't give up. "Stand-by, Cricket."

Bill's laughing voice sounded. "Cricket, this is Raven One-zero. One-two is in the smaller aircraft. I can confirm it is an O-One."

"Roguh that!" Game, set, and match to Upmeyer.

Several days later, I returned from a Nam Ou boat-buster mission. As I approached Pa Theung, I saw an O-1 a mile left, approaching perpendicular to my flight path. Ernie, upon his return from several weeks in Vientiane, was scheduled to fly the O-1. *Surely he's not trying to slide in behind me.*

Ernie had never before tried this silly stunt.

I'd teach him a lesson. I pushed the throttle to full power, planning to use the U-17's speed and climbing advantage to go vertical if he turned.

He snapped hard left.

I pulled the nose up and bat-turned to his high six o'clock position. When I saw him looking up at me, I pushed the nose over to point directly at him.

Ernie whipped the airplane around while I danced up and down like a yo-yo behind him.

Go on down, Ernie--close to the terrible ground. Get your adrenaline pumping. I stayed close enough to scare Ernie because he had started the fight. And I owed him from the high-low mission he had screwed up.

He had hinted in the past he thought I was crazy--too aggressive.

I played hard on that thought. Say uncle, Ernie. I wanted him to picture my propeller chewing his rudder.

He dove to escape.

I followed and forced him into a valley pointing west from the river.

As Ernie approached the valley bottom, I pulled up and away, noticing the valley stopped a few miles ahead with a steep cliff face.

Ernie must not have seen me leave, because he continued down the dead end path.

Climb, you dumbshit. I watched the O-1 slow and begin a maximum rate climb.

Ernie lowered his flaps, and the O-1 seemed to stop moving forward. He cleared the cliff by a few feet.

I smiled and raced to the runway. *You're the crazy one, Ernie.*

After parking, I hung out with Neuheng and several other T-28 pilots near the entrance to the revetments. I should have just taken the FAC jeep after Ernie's attack, but I waited around to gloat over my air-to-air victory.

ROWWWWW.

We ducked as a T-28 buzzed over the top of us doing full speed at twenty feet.

"Mr. Ed." I shook my head. My brain etched a close-up picture of the oily gray T-28 belly with no bombs and only rocket pods on the wings.

The T-28 continued over the town and pulled up into a graceful Immelmann, a half-loop, then a half-roll.

Neuheng pointed to the temple on a nearby hill. "He flies over the Wat Phousi. Very bad phi. Very bad."

The next morning a passing storm sent strong gusts that required me to taxi the O-1 down the runway, turn around, and takeoff toward the revetments.

I noticed Mr. Ed sitting in his jeep on the taxiway, so I aimed the O-1 at him, rather than climbing out. Time for revenge had come.

He fumbled with his keys, then started his engine. The jeep's black smoke trailed him into the revetments.

I followed him also, letting my right wing slice the air above his canvas jeep top. Then I climbed out and called Swick at the AIRA house. "Raven One-two's airborne."

Mr. Ed called me using the radio in his jeep. "Are you right-side up?"

Chapter 21
A Deadly Impulse

August 1971

The first couple of days in August brought clear blue skies--a hint of the dry season waiting impatiently around the corner.

With three FACs in town we flew dawn to dusk.

Bill pushed away from the dinner table. "A few more days like this, and we might have to declare victory."

In those same few days I had destroyed nearly a hundred small boats on the north end of the Nam Ou. "River traffic is way down. Between the bombs and the rain, the average enemy soldier must see this time of year as the worst. Something's always fallin' on him."

"I'll drink to that." Bill headed for the bar. "Beer?"

"I'll take one to the vault. I need to catch up on my reading."

"See you in a bit." Bill handed me a beer and joined the others who were setting up the room for a movie.

I walked to the communications room where Swick sat at his radio console. Picking up a clipboard, I perused enemy activity reports. "What do you plan to do after the war?"

"I may just stay over here forever." Swick gave unusual answers.

As I was polishing a suitable response, the chief interrupted with a radio call from the airfield. "Sparegroup just went in."

"Roger," Swick answered routinely.

My mind went into afterburner. The chief had misused the term, but Sparegroup was a callsign the administrative system used for personnel issues. Each of us had a sparegroup number--a tag from the embassy so they didn't have to broadcast our names on the radio. The only person flying at this hour would be the boss, Mr. Ed. But "went in" didn't sound like "landed."

"Sparegroup just went in . . . with passenger," the chief said. "Looks like total destruction."

"Oh shit." I bolted through the door and into the house, blurting to the group, "I just heard a cryptic message from the chief. Sounds like Mr. Ed crashed at the airfield."

I grabbed my pistol belt and followed Bill to the FAC jeep. *I don't want to believe this nightmare is happening.*

Bill spun the jeep's wheels as he backed out and headed for the main road. "Exactly what did the chief say?"

I repeated the words I had heard. "God, I hope I'm wrong. Who was his passenger?"

"The new guy--Andy. I hope you're wrong, too." He raced around the curves to the straight dirt road that crossed the bridge over the Nam Khan.

As we emerged from the trees, I saw a column of black smoke curling skyward. I felt my heart pounding. The wind left my sails in a huge sigh.

Bill shook his head. "Shit. I knew this was going to happen. A.O.C. Commanders aren't supposed to fly combat. Ed Bender honored the rule, but his predecessor died in a T-Twenty-eight."

Pieces of wreckage covered a ten-acre field off the near end of the runway.

Bill turned off the road and parked beside the chief, who had pulled up earlier. "What the hell happened, Chief?"

The chief was pale with shock. "You know how he always does the buzz job after he drops his bombs?"

"Yeah," we answered together.

"He usually pulls straight up and rolls right-side-up. This time he tried to pull her through for a loop-the-loop."

Two more vehicles arrived from the house and parked beside ours.

I surveyed the debris. "He must've been haulin' ass when he hit."

"I thought he was going to make it." The chief's voice was breaking. "He was pulling the nose up just before the explosion. And that wonderful new kid was in his backseat."

"Okay," Bill said. "Spread out and look for survivors. Yell if you find anyone."

I walked to the middle of the field. Two large fires crackled near the end of the runway, where the wings with fuel inside had probably been ripped away from the fuselage. Smaller fires burned across the field in a line with the runway.

Several local civilians waved to me.

I ran to them.

Whoosh.

Something passed overhead.

I looked up but didn't see the rocket I expected. As I approached, the crowd parted, and I saw the inverted front cockpit of the T-28.

Mr. Ed, wearing white pants and a purple shirt, lay unconscious, still strapped in the ejection seat. All the plexiglas from the canopy was gone.

Whoosh. Whoosh.

"Over here," I yelled and ducked the flying objects. What are those things?

I checked Ed's wrist. I felt an erratic pulse.

His eyes moved slightly. His only visible injury was a twisted back.

"He's alive," I shouted over my shoulder. "Hang on. We're going to get you out of here." I hoped for a miracle.

Bill and Ernie arrived.

Other troops hustled up behind them with a stretcher.

Bill took charge. "Slide the stretcher down there, then hold him while I undo the straps. Let's go real easy now."

We eased the boss onto the stretcher. The enlisted troops carried him to a large green ambulance Ernie had driven to the airfield, since we were between rotations of our medics. We strapped him in firmly.

"Ernie," Bill directed, "drive to the Swiss Infirmary. Stay there with Ed. The rest of you come and help us find Andy."

We fanned out again.

Whoosh.

I ducked the objects again and followed Bill to the runway, expecting to find the rear cockpit behind the front. "What do you make of that whooshing?"

"Probably fifty-cal rounds firing from the wings. Those large fuel fires are masking the noise of the shells cooking off in the internal guns. They're firing right out of the belt and tumbling through the air."

Bullets? Damn. I crouched lower and continued searching in the fading light.

As we walked down a gentle slope toward the fires and the runway, Bill said, "Here he is."

Whoosh.

Andy, too, remained strapped in his seat. He had facial abrasions, but, like Ed, his body had survived the crash intact.

Checking for a pulse and respiration, I found neither. "I think he's dead."

"Yeah," Bill said. "But let's still haul him in as quickly as possible."

I helped carry the stretcher.

Bill ran to the jeep and drove toward us until he bogged down in deep mud. He spun all four wheels in both directions.

I watched the jeep sink into the muck. "Charlie, grab another jeep. Offer ours as collateral if you have to."

Ten minutes later Charlie returned driving a Lao military jeep, stopping short of the bog. Rear seats had been removed, leaving open space, but the stretcher still wouldn't fit.

I climbed in back, and the troops eased Andy into my lap.

Bill jumped in beside me.

Charlie hit the gas pedal, and the jeep slithered steadily to the road.

"Be smooth, Charlie," I said. "Quick but smooth."

We raced along as darkness fell like a shroud.

I looked at the pale face in my arms. "I'm afraid he's gone. If his heart were beating, this gash on his cheek would be bleeding."

Bill nodded. "What a senseless tragedy for so many people."

"I can feel his body cooling off. He's drawing heat from me."

Charlie slid around a corner as we raced through town.

Andy's body grew cooler.

We pulled in beside the ambulance.

Orderlies took Andy inside on a stretcher.

Bill followed.

Ernie stood ghostlike beside the door. "The doctor just arrived. After I got here, I gave Ed mouth-to-mouth resuscitation for forty-five minutes."

The rest of our troops arrived and looked at us expectantly.

Pancho asked, "Any word?"

I shook my head.

Bill walked out. "They're both pronounced dead. Nothing more we can do here."

Charlie asked, "Do you want perimeter security at the crash site?"

"No," Bill said. "Someone needs to recover our jeep. Tell the RLAF the ammo is cooking off--a fact that should keep everyone out. I have calls to make."

"I can do that." Pancho waved and left quickly, as though he needed a distraction from the intensity of the moment.

Bill and I rode home in the ambulance with Ernie.

Bill broke the silence. "Are you alright, Ernie?"

"For forty-five minutes . . . I gave him mouth-to-mouth resuscitation . . ." Ernie seemed to want to say more, but no words came.

"Don't blame yourself. No one could have saved them. They hit the ground too hard. Internal injuries killed them. I'm sure they felt no pain."

When I sighed, Bill looked at me. "The pulse you felt was only fibrillation--the heart's last desperate spasms reaching out to us like a cruel trick."

"I know." I could still feel the warmth from my body being drawn to Andy.

When we parked at the AIRA house, I took my pistol belt to my sleeping quarters. I noticed lights and laughter in Ed's room. After depositing the gear, I knocked and stuck my head inside.

Several of Ed's friends from the American school sat on his bed. One said, "Hi. Is Ed flying late as usual?"

"Wait right here. I'll be back."

I walked to the main house where several troops sat in a gloom.

"I need help. Ed's friends are in his room. Could someone without Ed's blood on his clothing please go break the news?"

Charlie stood. "I'll go."

"Thanks." I followed him out the door, passing near enough to Ed's room to hear gasps and a muffled scream.

I pitched my filthy clothes into a hamper and stepped into the shower, letting the water splash my face for longer than usual, as if warm water would clean away the pain and horror. No denial phase this time. I was too close to deny anything. What's next? Anger? Damn. What a terrible waste.

An hour later I sipped Chivas in a quiet living room full of shell-shocked troops.

Bill emerged from the radio room. "Is everyone okay?"

No one answered.

"The embassy's sending a C-130 in the morning for the remains. The Air Attaché will fly up and survey the crash scene. I don't know when a replacement will come, but I'll do my best to wear both hats."

Most of the group sat in silence. Some nodded.

"Ernie," Bill continued, "a life support technician--a sergeant in real life--will arrive on the courier to inspect all the ejection systems. When he's done, you can take him to Alternate."

"Okay." Ernie spoke absently. He had idolized Ed.

I could sense immense pain and sadness burning through his shock.

Then Bill turned to me. "You'll fly at least twice a day. Watch like a hawk for N.V.A. shenanigans. First thing in the morning, go to the crash site. Take pictures of the major aircraft components and plot a chart of where you took each one. Then go fly. You should expect to fly your ass off until a new A.O.C. commander comes along."

"Can do." I sipped the straight scotch and felt it burn my throat. Would I think of Ed every time I lifted a glass of this smooth liquid?

Bill finished his speech. "Any questions?"

Pancho asked, "How did the crash happen?"

"Chief," Bill said, "let's get this over with. Tell us exactly what you saw."

The chief pushed away from the wall he was leaning on. "He came across the revetments, just like always. Scared the shit out of me. Then he pulled straight up. Instead of rolling right-side up, he pulled 'er back down. I thought he'd made it, then boom. He hit the ground."

Pancho persisted. He squinted at Bill. "What went wrong?"

Bill shrugged. "We may never know exactly what happened. I do know a loop is an altitude-gainer. You pull an easy four g's on the front half, then a tight five g's on the back. From the side a loop looks like a nine." He waved his finger to demonstrate.

Pancho still held a question mark in his facial expression.

"If you pull too hard on the front of the loop," I added, "then you start the backside too low without enough energy or altitude to pull through. Pulling g's takes energy, and Mr. Ed ran out. And he didn't have any altitude to trade."

"But Mr. Ed was such a good pilot. Why would he do such a thing?"

"Another excellent question, my friend." I remembered an afternoon spent answering Pancho's queries in my cockpit. "My guess is he planned the Immelmann and changed his mind at the top. He decided to pull through on an impulse."

"A deadly impulse," Bill added.

Broken gray clouds heralded a dismal dawn. Standing near the runway's end, I wrote, "One--Initial impact point," on a page of my clipboard. I snapped a picture of a shallow groove in the earth that grew gradually deeper. Ed had hit tail first. I saw tiny grains and shards of metal spread around the spot like powder. He was pulling as hard as he could. The metal had begun to shred on impact.

I documented where the wings had broken off and burned. Half a mile ahead I found the engine. It had rolled into small bushes like a lost soccer ball.

The propeller had walked off a quarter mile to the right.

I trudged to the end of the runway.

Bill stood with a colonel in a flight suit.

I recognized Colonel Curry, the Air Attaché, and handed him the roll of film and sheet of paper. "In case anyone ever wants to know."

"Thanks. Do you know who owns that bulldozer?" He pointed to a large yellow Caterpillar tractor on the far edge of the field.

Bill answered, "It belongs to the contractor who's constructing a new Air Ops building on the other side."

"Why don't you slip him a few bucks and ask him to dig a hole in the middle of the field? Then have him push everything in." The colonel made a sweeping motion.

"Just bury it?" Bill asked.

"The sooner, the better." Curry turned to his C-47. "And you be careful. A.O.C. Commanders at L.P. don't have much of a track record lately."

I flew a morning mission, returned, and found the O-1 still parked in the revetment. I hailed Bill in the A.O.C. Commander's jeep. "Busy day?"

"Yeah," he said. "I don't expect to fly for a while."

"The perimeter seems secure. Flooding along the Nam Ou makes N.V.A. logistics difficult. I smashed what I found. What's Ernie up to?"

"He's got bad diarrhea." Bill shrugged. "He took our tragedy harder than the rest of us. He felt close to Ed--really admired the guy. I think the resuscitation attempt traumatized him."

"I can empathize," I said. "But my intestines are fine." I had placed the incident in a compartment in the back of my brain where I would forever carry the chill of that evening. If I had to, I'd deal with it later.

"Good. After lunch you can deliver the life support guy to Alternate. Then fly a combat mission."

During lunch I calculated a heading that would take me to within visual range of Alternate fifty miles southeast. I took off soon after eating. My passenger seemed mature and well informed as we chatted, flying along at two thousand feet in the U-17.

"You finished your business quickly. How'd the inspection go?"

"I was ordered to finish quickly, sir. I found a few minor items that can be fixed without my help--"

Pop-pop-pop-pop-pop.

"Hang on." I slammed right rudder and pulled straight back on the controls. We rolled up and over. I saw a dozen soldiers in dark uniforms scurrying into old bunkers along a trail we were crossing. I hadn't climbed to compensate for the rising terrain, and my steady barometric altitude had brought me to about three hundred feet above the ridge.

"What's going on?" My sergeant passenger remained calm.

"N.V.A. We caught a platoon in the open. They hosed a few rounds at us. Normally, I'd take the time to kill the little commie bastards."

"Maybe you can get 'em on the way back."

"Right." I had changed my mental status from admin run to combat mission. "Hang on while I turn and clear the ground below." I pointed out the enemy soldiers hiding like a row of dark peas in a pod.

The sergeant asked, "Those black lines beside the trail are soldiers?"

"North Vietnamese," I said. "Tell your friends you've actually seen N.V.A."

"No, sir. I can't tell anybody anything."

I flew on to Alternate and squeezed into the landing traffic flow of one of the world's busiest airports. What I saw and heard was precisely what the dictionary called chaos. A tall karst stalagmite at the end of the runway forced pilots to take-off opposite to the landing direction, regardless of winds. "Keep your eyes open for other airplanes. This place is a mess."

Cleared to land, I ducked below a silver C-123 that took off in my face. Another cargo plane cleared the runway when I touched down. I zipped to a row of FAC planes and parked.

The sergeant followed me to the nearest building.

Inside, I met the A.O.C. Commander, Harry Light. "Here's your life support expert. He's a good man."

The sergeant shook hands and departed.

Light shook my hand. "Coffee?"

"Sure." I accepted a steaming mug.

"What the hell was Ed thinking?"

"I don't believe he was thinking at all. Pure impulse led him to try the loop."

"He was a good man."

I told him a few stories about Ed while I finished my coffee. "I found a platoon of N.V.A. on the trail that divides M.R.-one and M.R.-two. Any problem if I kill 'em?"

"Go ahead. Use Luang Prabang's T-Twenty-eights, though. We've got high priority ops on the P.D.J. today."

"Okay. Any clues on getting out of here safely?"

He laughed. "Traffic pattern's a free-for-all. Keep your head moving."

"Thanks."

Ten minutes later I lifted off. I raised flaps and turned hard right, climbing up over the karst and a steep mountain called Skyline Ridge. I soon found the trail where the N.V.A. had taken their cheap shots. Now the place was quiet--void of any trace of enemy.

I buzzed and searched but found nothing.

I landed at Luang Prabang, flew an afternoon boat-smasher, and landed again.

Neither the O-1 nor the FAC jeep had been touched.

I drove to the side of Bill's A.O.C. jeep where he sat with the chief. "Is Ernie alive?"

Bill smiled. "He can't stray more than ten feet from porcelain at the moment."

"Does he have those tiny tablets--cement pills, as we used to say?" I remembered a medicine called Lomotil that had once worked a miracle for me.

"Yeah. They go right on through."

"A fate worse than death." I laughed and drove home for a shower and a beer.

Two hours later Bill entered the radio room where I sat alone, writing up my intelligence debriefing. "I inherited a little problem." He looked serious.

"Want my advice? Do what you have to do and drive on."

"Right," Bill said. "Ed told me last week he had found an unmarked brown package in the hell hole--the cargo compartment in the belly of a T-Twenty-eight. The door was hanging down, and Ed was alone in the revetments at lunchtime. He's been holding the package to see who would come along and claim it."

"Uh-oh." I thought about the infamous golden triangle near Ban Houie Sai, one of the world's major sources of opium.

"I was packing up his things, and I found the package."

"No one claimed it?"

"No. Ed told me he would pull all the Americans out of here before he would allow anyone to use tactical aircraft to smuggle contraband."

"Where had the airplane been?"

"Ban Houei Sai."

"Damn. Who was the pilot?"

"A new guy, and he denied any knowledge of the package."

"Did Ed open the package?"

"No, but I did. It contains money--lots of Lao money."

"Oh shit," I said. "The plot thickens."

"The chief says if no one claims it after a reasonable time, we should throw a party down on the flight line."

I laughed. "Leave it to those cunning enlisted troops to come up with creative solutions to tough problems."

Bill asked, "You agree?"

"Sure. Have the pilots and mechanics bring their families. Roast a few pigs and chickens. We'll have a great time."

"I'm tired of looking at the package. Let's have a party."

Ernie's acute bowel distress continued for a week. Mostly he stayed in bed.

I flew two or three times a day. I felt fatigue consuming my energy reserves, but day-to-day combat had my full attention. I slept well, but at some internal level, I felt tired all the time.

During a local area mission in the O-1, I supported Major Oum Peng's commandos near the king's farm. They reported enemy fire, and I struck the area they described. I stopped to visit Major Oum Peng at the end of the day.

"My commandos thank you for the airstrike." He was gracious.

"Did they report B.D.A?"

"No. The enemy runs away." Oum Peng moved to a map. "You put airstrikes here." He pointed to a spot between the road and the Mekong.

"Yes," I said. "I saw freshly-dug fighting positions."

"I am sure. But most of the enemy are here." He slid his finger to a streambed further east. "Tomorrow morning, eight o'clock. You can go with me?"

"In a jeep?"

"Sure. We'll have my bodyguards." He smiled.

For good and bad reasons, I couldn't refuse. "I must come back and fly a mission tomorrow afternoon."

"Okay. See you at eight."

We bounced along a dirt road that paralleled the wide Mekong fifty meters to our north. An immaculate green jeep held Oum Peng in front with his driver and me in back with two bodyguards. We had traveled about eight miles from the airfield along the base of a high ridge to our south. I thought about my strikes on the rock pile atop the ridge.

Oum Peng seemed to enjoy speaking English. "Mr. Bill cannot come today?"

"No," I said. "He even suggested I might be crazy for riding a jeep instead of an airplane. But I told him Ernie needed to fly again. And I needed to see your target."

Oum Peng spoke Lao to his driver, and we slowed, passing the burned-out hulk of an armored personnel carrier. "Last week we have ambush here."

Beside the fire-scarred APC lay three small piles of ashes with a steel helmet on top of each.

"Three people die." He shook his head and spoke to his driver.

After another mile passed, we pulled off into a field on the Mekong side.

I saw bomb craters among a semicircle of fighting positions. "This position is where I put the airstrikes."

"Yes. And some enemy are here." Oum Peng reached down and picked up an oval steel hand grenade with a wooden pin. He handed it to me and said, "Chinese."

I passed it to a bodyguard.

"You must see over here." Oum Peng pointed several hundred meters east to where tall trees followed a stream from the road to the river.

As we walked to the jeep, I noticed small yellow bomblets--unexploded remains of C.B.U.-14--scattered in the field and beside the road. The primitive cluster ordnance had a high dud rate. I pointed to the bomblets. "What do you do about the pineapples?"

"The Army has people who pick them up."

"Another way to clear the field is to take cover and shoot the bomblets, if they are in your way."

Oum Peng nodded and spoke to his guards.

One of them aimed his M-16 and fired.

POOF.

Fifty yards away a yellow bomblet exploded in a puff of gray smoke.

I wasn't sure Oum Peng would understand my next point. I wanted to pass him a few things I had learned from an Explosive Ordnance Disposal trooper I had met in Vietnam. "If you hit the side--the yellow part--the ordnance will usually explode low order. If you hit the silver primer, the weapon will function high order--as designed."

Oum Peng translated again, and his guards poofed more pineapples.

One of his guards pointed to the CAR-15 rifle I carried.

Oum Peng nodded.

I extended the stock, chambered a round, aimed, and fired.

The bomblet spun around. A large yellow chunk was missing.

I moved a bit closer and fired again.

Another hit spun the bomblet around.

Oum Peng raised his eyebrows, as though I had missed.

I stepped forward and fired again.

BANG.

The concussion from the high-order explosion lifted me up and backward. I landed flat on my back to a howling audience.

"If you are okay, we can go now." Oum Peng climbed into his jeep with his men.

I followed, slightly embarrassed. I was certain I had hit the yellow part.

We drove down to the line of trees and stopped.

Oum Peng led the way to the dry streambed.

Sophisticated L-shaped caves had been dug into the bank. Several weapons, including green B-40 rocket-propelled grenades lay strewn about the cave floor. The enemy had left in a hurry. In the middle of the streambed a large rock swung gently, attached to a forty-foot vine suspended from a platform in a treetop.

"Sentry hide here," Oum Peng pointed upward. "When airplanes come, he can swing the rock. Everybody go in caves."

"Not everyone." I pointed to bloodstains on the ground and picked up an N.V.A. belt buckle.

"My commandos want you to put airstrike here and over there."

"You're right, Major Oum Peng. I should have put the airstrike over here, too. The trees make a good hiding place with protection and escape routes to the sides." I took pictures of the simple but effective N.V.A. bivouac location.

"We go back now." Oum Peng smiled at me. "Or maybe you want to shoot another pineapple?"

I skipped lunch to fly the afternoon mission. When I landed I could smell the roast pork from the runway. Turning into the revetments, I taxied past a drum barbecue pit with a huge pig rotating over hot coals. Another metal barrel had been halved to hold ice and yellow cans of Tiger Beer.

I signed the aircraft forms and handed them to Ramon. "Will I meet your family today?"

"Yes. My wife and five-year-old son will come to the party."

I felt drawn to the barbecue aroma. Along the way, Chin handed me a capful of White Horse Scotch. When I arrived, the Chief handed me a beer.

Families filled the dark revetments with colorful outfits and joyous little children. When Bill arrived, I pulled two cold brews from the barrel and walked over to his jeep. "I could close my eyes and float all the way to Texas on the scent of that barbecue."

"Me too, partner. Feels like Saturday afternoon in San Antonio." Bill seemed mellowed by fatigue.

We clinked beer cans.

"How's Ernie?"

"Still spending his days in the can. He wanted to fly today but didn't make it. I'm sending him on an R and R. He needs to move away from here and get well."

"Sometimes I can't believe this week happened. I feel empty. One day they're among us, smiling. Then, in an instant they're gone. Forever."

"This party is something I think Ed and Andy would have wanted. I think it's a suitable memorial." Bill gestured to the crowd of happy people.

"You're right. Ed's probably watching us from some place with a stogie in one hand and Chivas in the other, or the spiritual equivalent."

"Amen, brother."

Chapter 22
Northern Excursions

August 1971

He deserved a royal salute, but the new A.O.C. Commander arrived in Luang Prabang without fanfare.

Steering the FAC jeep into the AIRA compound at the end of a sweaty day, I spotted him slouched comfortably against a large column outside the front door.

He wore jeans, a polo shirt, and custom Wellington boots--probably kangaroo skin. He stood about five-foot ten, with intense dark eyes, black hair and a thick mustache.

I walked up to the door and introduced myself.

He smiled and extended a firm hand. "Hi. I'm Jerry Rhein."

I'd heard of Jerry. A long-time special operator, he had flown combat tours in the A-1 and run the A.O.C. at Alternate. The previous November he had led the A-1s on the Son Tay Prison Raid near Hanoi.

We shook hands and went inside.

"Great to have you here," I said. "My beer-low-level light is on. Has anyone shown you where we hide the booze?"

"Not yet. I'm happy to be at Luang Prabang. I've heard things are stable--almost laid-back here, compared to other places I've been. Bill's done a great job of holding everything together."

"He's been working his ass off for the past few weeks." I handed Jerry a beer.

"I hope to complete a six-month tour here."

"Yeah. Two of our past three A.O.C.s died on the job."

"No." He laughed. "I'm not worried about dying. If General Vang Pao finds out I'm back in country, he'll drag me down to Alternate. That place is always in crisis, and sometimes the general can be difficult. Of course, I'd go if he called."

"As you know, we work for the king--more or less. We've been killing N.V.A. in good numbers for the five months I've been here."

The AIRA contingent began to drift in and surround the new boss. After dinner we gave him the saloon tour.

Although I could tell he enjoyed playing the boss role, Bill welcomed Jerry. With the A.O.C. responsibility lifted from his shoulders, Bill could relax a little, and humor raised its ugly head again in the AIRA house.

A few days later I drifted into the communications room after flying.

With his feet propped on the console and a huge grin on his face, Bill sat in Swick's chair. He was alone in the small enclosure.

As I wrote my reports for Dit to type and Swick to encrypt, I sensed in our way of visual communications Bill wanted me to ask him about the radios. Stubbornly, I remained silent.

Finally, Bill dropped his feet to the floor and turned to me. "Swick checked me out on all these radios. I can cover this job for extended periods."

"That's nice." I continued to write.

"Seriously. I can operate all these H.F. radios." He swept his hand, indicating the wall of fifteen or twenty black boxes.

"Right." I stifled a laugh and continued writing.

"I can tell you don't believe me. Watch this." He flipped a few switches and turned some knobs. Then he called Vientiane. When a voice answered, he said, "I'm doing some tuning. Give me a short count, please."

"Roger, one, two, three, four, five, four, three, two, one, out."

I shook my head. "For cryin' out loud, Bill. Anybody can call Vientaine."

Bill took the bait and began to push buttons and turn knobs on every panel. "Ah, but I can contact all the other sites. And here's the Det at Udorn . . .."

I put down my pencil and crossed my arms on my chest.

Bill worked his way across the wall, lecturing and turning knobs. He tapped a radio in the corner. "This baby's a spare. Swick has it set up on a Ham frequency."

A one-hundred-decibel blast came through the speakers. "ALPHA CHARLIE HOTEL, THIS IS BRAVO KILO VICTOR, OVER . . ."

When two more channels opened at the same volume, I began to laugh.

Bill's jaw dropped. He turned knobs again, frantically, but he couldn't abate the noise, now approaching the pain threshold.

I slid from my chair to the floor and laughed until my sides hurt.

Bill looked down and also began to laugh. His mouth moved. "Shit."

I rolled and crawled to the door, opened it, and crawled outside. After latching the heavy steel door, I could still hear the speakers blasting.

Bill had decided Ernie's best recovery option was a lengthy escape, so when he finally emerged from his sickbed, I gave him a ride to the airport.

His pale white skin contrasted with the huge black sunglasses he wore.

An Air America hop would kick off two weeks of R and R. Ernie had selected Hong Kong, and the Det offered an open Sydney slot for the following week.

"Two R and Rs?" I refused to play amateur shrink, but I didn't plan to let him off easy. The only psychology I understood was reality therapy. As we pulled onto the muddy street, I wondered if he could handle our normal exchange of subtle insults.

"I've lost over ten pounds in two weeks," Ernie said. "R and R cures terminal diarrhea."

"But you'll need bed rest when you get back from two R and Rs." We crossed the Nam Khan bridge under a high overcast sky.

"I plan to spend lots of time in bed in Hong Kong. Do you have any good phone numbers in Sydney?" Ernie smiled mischievously.

"Go to Kings Cross. And beware of Camp Alpha." I looked across the smooth field that had been strewn with torn aluminum a few weeks ago.

"I have friends I can stay with in Saigon."

"The bulldozer erased any sign of the crash site. It's gone forever," I suggested. I followed a narrow road to the Air America ramp and halted the jeep.

"Yeah, forever. Kinda like the shits." Ernie eased out with his small suitcase.

"Don't forget to wear your rubbers." I waved. I envied his imminent vacation. He'd dumped his workload on me, but I knew he wasn't malingering. I scooted to the revetment where my backseater, Lieutenant Sai, waited.

Ten minutes later we flew over the wide red Nam Ou in the U-17.

"Not many boats down here," I said. "I think we can find the enemy up north."

Sai nodded. A large man, he was brave but excitable under fire.

Dark limestone karst on both sides of the river at Muang Ngoi rose several thousand feet above us as we cruised into the valley at seven hundred feet. Overhead, solid gray clouds gave an eerie cast to the available light.

"I see a trail." Sai pointed out his window.

I pulled the nose straight up, and whifferdilled to reverse directions. Looking through a single jungle canopy, I spotted the trail, white and wide from heavy use. It followed the base of the karst along the east side of the river. "Let's see where it takes us."

Sai nodded. "I think many enemy around this mountain."

We turned away from the river through a gap in the gray karst, entering a huge valley carpeted with green rice fields. A small stream snaked between an erratic pattern of dikes.

I stayed focused on the trail that zigged and zagged along the base of the mountain. On the backside of the mountain, the trail disappeared under trees, then emerged, bending into a cave opening. From five hundred feet, I could see the trees hid the camouflaged roofs of five structures.

"Cricket, Raven One-two. Send air. Rendezvous three-five-five for ninety-five."

"Roger, Raven One-two."

I flew to the Nam Ou. "We won't go back until the fighters come."

Sai smiled. "Yes. Maybe we surprise N.V.A."

North of Muang Ngoi about five miles, the Nam Ou turned due west.

I followed a small stream meandering northeast from the sweeping bend. I soon spotted empty boats lined up along the stream. "Look. They don't even hide their boats."

Sai nodded. "You'll shoot boats?"

"I might wait until they're full." On the northeast horizon I saw a runway. Buildings in the area had been reclaimed by nature. I checked my map as we crossed into North Vietnam. "Do you know the name of that airfield?"

"No." Sai shook his head.

"Dien Bien Phu. Lots of history at that place." I searched for Fire Base Eliane, where incoming artillery shells exploding every ten seconds in three feet of mud and blood inspired Bernard Fall to name his account of the battle, Hell in a Very Small Place.

"Raven One-two, Falcon Seven-five." My fighters checked in.

Turning south, I gave them a detailed briefing as they descended into the area.

"What kind of weather do you have?"

"The rendezvous point has a hole at about eight thousand feet. You should be able to do fifteen-degree dive passes below the clouds."

"Rog."

"The target's at the base of a karst wall. Attack east to west. Negative friendlies. And keep your pattern tight. We're on the edge of serious bad-guy radar coverage."

I figured that'd be the case, comin' up here." The leader sounded ready to fight.

"As soon as I see you, I'll fire a smoke, so you can make your first pass hot." I climbed and eased into the huge valley.

"Falcon Seven-five, green 'em up." Leader called for weapons arming.

I spotted the dart silhouette pulling through the only opening in the clouds in northern Laos. I rolled and fired a smoke at the cave.

BAM.

"Hit my smoke. Target is the cave and the trees to the left."

"One's in."

"Cleared hot."

In a shallow dive, the F-4 bored straight at the karst.

Three dark green bombs leaped away from its belly. Their mesmerizing arc carried my focus to the cave opening.

WH-WHUMP.

Billowing fire and smoke obliterated the cave and surrounding karst.

"Two's in."

"Left of lead's hit. In the group of trees. Cleared hot."

"Roger."

For five minutes the F-4s attacked, methodically bashing the target area down to crumpled rock. After his last pass, the leader said, "Falcon Seven-six, lead will extend straight ahead for the rejoin."

"Two." His wingman acknowledged and attacked.

I rolled in and told Sai, "Let's take a look up close, right behind two's bombs." I dove into the smoke and flew across the target. A major supply cache lay open and scattered. I estimated the supplies had been stacked in a ten-foot cube.

"Falcon Seven-five has SAM firing warnings, six o'clock." My fighters' radar warning equipment had detected a surface-to-air missile.

"That's affirm." His wingman confirmed a radar lock-on.

Suddenly Sai shouted, "I see enemy shoot. Over here." He pointed emphatically out his window.

Pop-pop-pop-pop-pop.

Pushing the power up, I dropped as low as I could. Well past the target, I pulled and rolled left, climbing over the karst. The radio stayed silent while I put together a bomb damage assessment.

I took a deep breath and lowered my voice--a macho thing. I had heard fighter pilots do this when they wanted to sound calm in the most chaotic situations. "Falcon Seven-five, Raven One-two has your B.D.A."

"Ready to copy." The F-4 pilot had also lowered his voice.

"All ordnance on target. Five military structures destroyed. A thousand cubic feet of supplies destroyed." I added times and coordinates. "A beautiful show."

"Thanks. That makes a lot of the shit we put up with worthwhile."

"Great work. Beautiful. Thank you."

"Triple Nickel. Come see us. Falcon Seven-five, go button five."

"Two."

Since climbing out, I had noticed level flight required forward pressure on the controls. Nose down trim didn't fix the problem. Suspecting a broken trim cable, I slowed and climbed to a couple thousand feet over the river.

The higher altitude allowed me to hear an urgent call from Cricket. "Roger, understand Raven Two-three is down. Say location."

Flying at a higher altitude allowed me to hear one side of Cricket's conversation with a Raven out of Alternate who was on the ground. I turned the V.H.F. volume down and switched my U.H.F. radio to the rescue channel.

"Roger. I'm fine. The engine quit. I had no place to go but this sandbar."

I recognized the voice of John Swanson.

"Chopper's on the way. Any activity down there?"

I didn't recognize the voice of the FAC he was speaking to.

"No. Nice and quiet at the moment. But don't delay the chopper or anything."

Swanny's funny. On the ground and cracking jokes. For the rest of my life, I'll tease that guy about his fuel management--assuming we both survive our tours.

"Air America is two minutes out. Standby."

"Roger. Tally. See you at the hooch."

Half an hour later I approached home base toward the revetments, adding power to level off a few inches above the runway surface.

A T-28 took the runway, facing me.

"He'll wait for us to get by," I told Sai.

Two more Tangos pulled onto the runway, and the leader ran his engine up.

"He released brakes," I said. "Shit." I jerked the throttle back, landed, and taxied into the soft turf on the left side of the runway. My left wheel began to bury itself in the mud, so I hit the right brake and gunned the engine, hoping to free the left tire and swing my right wingtip clear of the runway.

But this action only drove the left wheel deeper into the mud, and the left wing almost touched the ground.

The first T-28 roared by. The pilot waved.

I shut the engine down. "These guys are screwin' around again." I felt embarrassed but glad to be alive.

Sai looked bewildered.

The T-28 wingmen passed, smiling and waving.

Piang, Bouathong, and Neuheng. I recognize you clowns. I told Sai, "Everything's okay. They're only having fun at our expense. Let's climb out on your side of the airplane."

Ramon raced to us on his moped.

"You may have to jack the wheel out of the mud and clean the brake," I told him. "Also, the elevator trim doesn't work. Sorry about this mess."

He parked his bike. "No problem."

The next afternoon I returned to the northern Nam Ou. I found the boats near Dien Bien Phu partially loaded. According to the map at home, this target was too close to North Vietnam to permit U.S. Air Force strikes under current rules. I was on my own.

At this point in my combat tour, stupid political rules frustrated me no end. My primary directive was to kill N.V.A., and I could do that as well as anyone.

I circled to about three thousand feet, armed a rocket, and dove straight down.

BAM.

My first rocket blew the bottom out of a boat.

I fired six more times in vertical dives. Four more boats burned.

I was circling up for my next attack when I heard Cricket call.

"Raven One-two, do you read? Bandits in the barrel. Slow movers R.T.B. All slow movers R.T.B. at this time." Cricket's MiG warning sounded broken. He was probably orbiting over Korat.

"Roger, Raven One-two copies." I turned for home, because Cricket had insisted the MiG hazard was a threat to me.

Faintly, Cricket said, "Bandits out of Bullseye. Two-seven-zero for seven-zero miles. Headed two-seven-zero."

Shit. If Bullseye is Hanoi, those MiGs are close. I armed a rocket on each wing and dropped to treetop level. *I've seen fast movers try and fail to hit stationary objects on the ground. I'll be safe down here. MiGs need a clear air background for a heater shot, and I can outturn a strafing attack.*

I flew straight home without seeing MiGs. Lucky for them.

The next day I took the O-1 up the Nam Ou with Seo. I refused to be bullied away by North Vietnamese MiGs, although dark storms threatened to push me around.

As we entered the canyon north of Muang Ngoi at seven hundred feet, I noticed something looked different. "Look down at that cave." I pointed left. "Do you see anything?"

"The trail from the river to the cave shows heavy use by enemy troops."

"Yep. But something else is wrong with that picture." Half a mile past the cave, I rolled left and sliced back the way I came, my wheels barely above the surface of the river. Ahead, the trail meandered fifty meters from the cave to a cluster of trees at the river's edge. As we came abeam at seventy knots, I saw the trees were a sham. A blue corner protruded from one edge.

Seo also noticed. "The enemy hides supplies under the blue cloth."

"You're right." I called for an airstrike, then moved into the Nam Bak valley to find a back-up target in case the weather worsened. I followed a trail and found a few possible base camps.

After an hour, my fighters arrived. "Raven One-two. Falcon Five-one's inbound. Two fox-fours with Mark-Eighty-twos and C.B.U.-Forty-nine."

I told Seo, "Hard bombs and cluster bombs--a nice mix."

I briefed the fighters and turned to the Nam Ou. Approaching five miles south of the target, I pulled out my binoculars.

I reported what I saw to the fighters. "Two uniformed soldiers with rifles are walking from the cave entrance down the path. Now they're running to the trees. They are in the trees now. They must think they're safe. Call when you're ready for a smoke."

"Negative, Raven One-two. Don't scare 'em off with a smoke. I see a white path from a cave to a dot next to the river. Is the dot our target?"

I looked back to see an F-4 bending around in a steep screaming descent into the area. "I think you're on it. I'll fly straight past 'em. Cleared hot on the dot."

"Roger." The F-4 Phantom seemed to move faster than usual, pouncing on this juicy offering.

"Three away." I helped him count his bombs.

The first bomb hit fifty meters short, and the second hit exactly on the target, shattering the blue tarp to bits. The third hit slightly long.

"Wow. Nice hit. Two, same place."

Debris now covered the area. Two more bomb passes further fragmented the target, then a layer of delay-fused C.B.U. let me go down for a close look. While random explosions every second or two kept potential shooters' heads down, I snapped pictures from fifty feet of the junkyard the fighters had created.

"I estimate two thousand cubic feet of supplies destroyed. And two K.B.A. Nice work."

"Pleasure working with you, Raven. Falcon, button five."

"Two."

I parked in the revetment. Seo and I climbed out after four long hours.

Bill drove up in the A.O.C. Commander's jeep. "Another good day up north?"

"Damn right. Big supply dump. Two K.B.A." I smiled.

"You didn't see any MiGs?"

"Not today. But keep your star-stencil handy. Why are you driving Jerry's jeep?"

Bill grinned. "It's my jeep again. General Vang Pao found out Jerry was in-country. Jerry left for Alternate an hour ago."

After supper Bill and I sipped Chivas Regal at the bar while the troops set up the movie projector.

A couple of Air America pilots walked in wearing dark gray trousers and white shirts. They waved and sat at the couch.

"Those guys always want something when they show up for a movie." I laughed, offered them a beer and whispered to Bill, "I'll bet they have a helicopter operation south of Ban Houei Sai tomorrow."

"Nah, they're here for John Wayne," Bill answered under his breath.

The AA pilots walked over. "Sure. We've been known to sip beer from time to time."

We shook hands. I handed them cold brews.

Bill asked, "What's up?"

"Just stoppin' by for the flick," one said. "John Wayne tonight?"

"And to see what you guys are up to tomorrow," the other added.

Bill nodded. "Yeah . . . okay."

"We're moving troops around out west," the first pilot said. "Ban Houei Sai is nasty with N.V.A. these days. We'd sure feel better with air cover."

"I'll look into it," Bill said. "What time will you start?"

"Around ten? We're flexible."

Bill laughed when I subtly elbowed him. "I'll call the Company at Lima-six-nine-alpha if we have a problem."

"Thanks, guys." They returned to the couch.

"I'll talk to the A.O.C. folks," Bill said, "but you plan to cover the mission."

"I'll take the U-17 out there around eight."

I called Lima-69 at 8:30 a.m. Near the Burma border, this short dirt strip sat on a hilltop with a small Company shack beside it.

"Roger," a voice answered. "Land at Six-nine. You'll find all the players there."

I spotted several helicopters and a Twin-Otter parked beside the three-thousand-foot clay strip in the wide valley below Alpha. I joined them.

I met the helicopter pilots from the night before. They introduced me to John, a field agent wearing infantry gear but no rank.

Barrel-chested and rugged looking, John chatted with us. I learned he was part Cherokee. He was clearly in charge. "What time will the Twenty-eights be here?"

"Ten o'clock." I said. I hoped.

"Here's the plan." He pulled out a map and explained details of an operation that would put a company of mercenaries onto a ridgeline near the Mekong at ten fifteen.

I asked, "What would you like us to do?"

"Bomb the ridgeline before we go in there. Look around for bad guys. Currently no friendly troops are within five miles of the objective. We know the N.V.A. have a sizeable force up here. Find 'em and kill 'em." He laughed as though he knew how grossly he had oversimplified the problem.

"I'll take off at nine-thirty and return here after the force is secure."

"Great. I have a ground FAC named Mo."

"Mo?" I hung around and talked with the helicopter pilots, then launched. I found the ridge quickly and looked hard but found no signs of N.V.A.

Mustang Green, flight of four, checked in at ten.

I bracketed a three-mile segment of ridge with two smokes. "Please drop one bomb at a time, and go from the west smoke to the east."

"Roger, Mustang Green is in."

"You're cleared hot. I'll orbit south."

With laser-like precision, Green blasted the area as I requested. "Mustang Green is winchester bombs."

"Roger, here's a smoke for your rockets." I rolled in on the nearest steep green mountain peak which overlooked the operational terrain.

With fire and steel, Mustang Green flight made the entire hill untenable.

"Super job, Mustang Green. Please hold your strafe until the helicopters arrive."

"Roger." The T-28s spread out and circled the ridge.

A line of six helicopters snaked up from the north. Their spacing was perfect. As one unloaded troops and departed, the next one landed. "Raven, this is Hotel Six-six. Can you hang around for a couple more lifts?"

"Affirmative." I relayed the request to the T-28s, who obliged.

After forty-five minutes, the last helicopter departed, and I released Mustang Green. Then, I flew to L-69.

Big John seemed pleased when he approached and shook my hand. "I'd sure appreciate if you could hang around. My people are asking for four more twenty-eights this afternoon. We have indications of trouble to the west of the L.Z."

I had planned to spend the afternoon on the north Nam Ou.

"We'll buy you lunch at Sixty-nine-alpha."

"Sure. For lunch, I'll stay here all day." I climbed into the Twin-Otter.

We flew to the hilltop for chicken salad and lemonade.

Several hours later I directed another four-ship on targets requested by Mo, then landed again at Lima Sixty-nine.

John thanked me profusely. "I'm sure we'll need your help again soon." He shook my hand, climbed on the last remaining helicopter, and departed.

I was alone on the dirt strip in the middle of absolute nowhere. I climbed into the U-17 and hit the starter.

The engine chugged but didn't start.

Damn. I tried three more times.

The engine still wouldn't catch.

I advised John via radio of my trouble. "I think a fuel line has vapor-locked. I'll have to let it cool off for an hour or so."

I waited under a wing for an hour while the sun slid low in the west. I tried again, unsuccessfully. The engine still felt warm, so I waited a bit longer. I didn't want to run the battery down on futile starting attempts. At least the ground is clear for miles in all directions. If the bad guys come, I'll have ample warning.

The wind vanished with the light. Total darkness fell.

Under billions of stars, I listened to the insects. *I haven't felt this alone in a long time. Good thing I'm not afraid of the dark. Shit.*

After a lonely hour passed, the Twin-Otter landed, and John jumped out. "I brought a drum of avgas and a trusty mechanic."

"I appreciate your stopping by." Not being alone in the dark made a huge difference in my vital signs. Friendly conversation covered my pounding heartbeat.

We rolled out a drum of fuel. I had enough gas to reach Luang Prabang, but I figured the act of refueling would take my mind off unpleasant alternative scenarios. I climbed up on the wing and held the nozzle while the mechanic cycled the hand pump.

After replacing the drum, the mechanic fiddled underneath the cowling.

I held his flashlight.

"I think you're right about the vapor lock," he said. "I can't find anything wrong."

"Let's give 'er one last shot," I said. I hit the starter again.

Chug-chug-chug-chug-chug-chug.

The engine coughed and coughed and finally caught.

I shook the mechanic's hand and gave John a thumb's up. "Thanks, guys."

After the mechanic buttoned the cowling, I swung the airplane around and cobbed the throttle to the wall.

The U-17 rolled downhill and lifted easily into the dark sky.

Slipping into the psychological comfort of a familiar cockpit and the reassuring hum of a purring engine, I climbed and climbed, hoping to reach gliding distance of Luang Prabang as soon as possible. I decided my present good fortunes would reverse if I screwed up the navigation, so I eased north to the Mekong and followed it eastward.

"Alleycat, Raven One-two's airborne Lima Six-nine, enroute to Lima Five-four."

"Roger. You're out past curfew, aren't you?" The controller on Alleycat, Cricket's nighttime counterpart, referred to the prohibition of single-engine night flying.

"Had a little engine trouble. Doing fine now. Can you relay to my home base?"

"Rog."

I perceived a glow I assumed was the city of Luang Prabang, when I saw a strange bright light at my two o'clock high. Much bigger and brighter than a star, it hung motionless in the black sky.

"Alleycat, do you show any air traffic near Lima Five-four?"

"Negative."

"I have visual contact with a large flare at about ten thousand feet."

"Negative information for you, Raven One-two."

"Roger." *I think I'll put this crate on the ground and give it to Ramon.*

I did. I suspected the flare must have been a signal dropped from a Chinese transport. I could never confirm it as any indentified flying object.

A few days later, in order to keep abreast of the tactical situation out west, I stopped by the Company's office near the airfield.

The agent I had met at A.O.C. meetings welcomed me in. "What can we do for you today?"

"I'd like an update on your operations south of Ban Houei Sai. If we can keep an airpower eye on the situation, maybe we can avoid a crisis."

"Sure. He handed me an inch of reports on a clipboard. Let me know if you have any questions. Say, we have an interrogation underway. Would you care to watch?"

"Sure."

"Drag your chair over here." He led me to a door, which had a small two-way mirror.

"This N.V.A. private walked in with a psyops leaflet in his hand. He wants to start over in South Vietnam. He signed up for a one-year tour in Laos three years ago."

I peeked inside. In the middle of the small room sat a gaunt, khaki-clad soldier. He appeared to be cooperating with several agents conducting the interview.

"His unit," my agent friend translated, "the Three-thirty-fifth Independent Regiment, has taken serious losses from airstrikes. They're hiding during the rainy season."

"Let me know if he gives you coordinates." I smiled at the prospect of erasing an entire Communist infantry regiment from the face of the earth.

"The unit'll need heavy reinforcements before it can conduct offensive operations."

I wondered which airstrikes had done the number on the 335th.

"He spent the last month husking rice and listening to stories of Uncle Ho told by his unit's political officer. All the caves were bombed, and his shelter stays wet and uncomfortable."

I laughed and shook my head. "I wish I could send that information to a certain colonel at Seventh Air Force."

The soldier began to sob.

"They asked him about his family back home."

"I feel strange. Seeing this interview brings the war down to a personal level. I smash soldiers like this everyday. What's going to become of this guy?"

"Oh, don't worry. We're not going to push him out of a helicopter or anything."

Remembering the N.V.A. had never taken a downed Raven FAC alive, I asked, only half-jokingly, "Why not?"

Chapter 23
For a Good Cause

September 1971

"Oh, I've seen fire and I've seen rain," James Taylor intoned from stereo speakers as Bill and I sat at the Bungalow Bar one drizzly evening.

I had modernized the bar's musical inventory with J.T. and Carole King albums.

"Do you want the good news or the bad news first?" Bill asked. "I had a long talk with your pal, Raven Zero-one." Bill had delivered the U-17 to Udorn for a phase inspection. On the way home he'd attended a Senior FAC Meeting at the embassy.

I snickered. "I'll try the good news."

"I'll be leaving soon, and my replacement is Doc Russell. He's at Alternate now. Used to be an Air Force dentist."

"Shit hot. You get to go home. I get flossing sermons. What's the bad news?"

"Ernie is effectively gone. He'll return next week to say goodbye and pick up his stuff. You'll have to do local area checkouts for all our replacements."

"Bring 'em on. Deep down, I'm tired. But I can fly and fly some more."

"As the sole keeper of corporate FAC knowledge," Bill warned, "you'll have to watch the enemy situation closely. Don't let training issues distract you."

"Get Doc here first. I'll make him the local area expert. Then I'll spend time on the Nam Ou and out west with the other new guys. Ban Houei Sai is heatin' up." I lit a cigar, and wiggled my brows like Groucho Marx.

"Raven Zero-one says you can't go home until Doc is satisfied with the checkouts."

"Screw Raven Zero-one. I can check 'em out as fast as he can serve 'em up."

"You've got an attitude."

"No, he does. I'm more than pleased to train everyone. I'll stay an extra month, if I have to. But edicts from chair-warriors make my sphincter muscles relax."

Bill laughed at my crude humor. "Then you're really going to hate what I have to say next."

"Fire away. I'm sure you're gonna say something about downtowners." I viewed them as administrative speedbumps, who rarely strayed from Vientiane. They seemed to exist to offset high morale in the field.

"I realize you missed the layaway payment on your stereo at the Udorn exchange last month. And I know they're threatening to sell it. I saw the message."

"I'm buying top of the line equipment. Amps, speakers, tape decks--shit we never even saw at Pleiku. Layaway is my little piece of the real world. I'm two payments behind."

"At our meeting this morning, the bald downtowner, Bruce, said you can't take the O-1 to Udorn as planned because we only have two FACs here at the moment."

"Bruce," I said. "The guy with the hair implants? I've flown twice a day for over sixty days in a row. Where does he get off--"

"He tracks aircraft utilization." Bill looked serious. "It's his job."

"I'll stop at Vientiane and rip out his goofy lookin' hair implants. He'll change his mind." Now I probably looked serious.

"No," Bill said. "I already corrected him. I'm the senior FAC and acting A.O.C. Commander at Luang Prabang. He's not. Take the O-One Friday afternoon. Come back Saturday. If he says one word to me, I'll let you pull his hair."

"Deal. Tell him to get his personal affairs in order. Quote me." I waved at the bartender. "Another Tiger, please."

"Our assignments should be out soon--unless you decide to extend."

"I'm thinkin' about it. My worst nightmare is returning to training command and working for some jerk who's been hiding from the war."

"I've seen fire, and I've seen rain." The stereo blared.

"Or worse, a downtowner?"

We laughed loudly.

On Friday, after flying two combat missions, I landed at Vientiane and parked near the A.O.C. trailer beside another O-1.

Leo Metz, the tall blond A.O.C. Commander at Vientiane, walked out and waved.

"This airplane has ten hours left before phase inspection," I said. "I assume the other one is due a trip to Udorn."

Leo nodded. "Tell Bill we appreciate the ten hours."

"I will. He's only trying to do the right thing, in spite of the downtowners."

Leo laughed.

I climbed in and took off in an ancient O-1A. The log showed over 15,000 flying hours. Level flight required me to hold the stick aft and right. *What a piece of shit.* I pressed southward.

"Udorn Tower, six-two-five's an Oscar Ace, ten north for landing."

"Roger, six-two-five. Three-sixties on downwind, please. F-Four minimum fuel recoveries in progress."

"Wilco." I flew circles over the city while a long line of nose-high Phantoms painted final approach with a fog of black exhaust. One-by-one, they touched down.

After half an hour, F-4 activity ceased, but the tower didn't call.

"Udorn Tower, six-two-five is base, gear down and welded, full stop."

"Roger, Six-two-five, down and welded."

I heard laughter in the background of the call from the tower. They had expected to hear, "Down and locked."

"Cleared to land."

I paid my bills. The base exchange would hold my stereo gear until I showed up with a final check and orders to my next duty station. I stopped at the barbershop, then found the crowded bar at the officers club.

Lieutenant Colonel Joe Kittinger, commander of the 555th Tac Fighter Squadron, leaned on the bar with navigator Captain Roger Locher, an F-4 GIB, or Guy-In-Back.

I ordered a scotch. "How are you?" I introduced myself to Roger and the red-haired colonel, since I didn't wear a nametag.

"What's your callsign?" Colonel Kittinger obviously recognized my Raven attire.

"One-two." I raised my glass. "Here's to Triple-Nickel."

He smiled and raised a beer. "I worked with you a few days ago. Up on the river."

"Really? We've wiped out a bunch of N.V.A. lately."

"You gave me credit for two kills," Kittinger said.

"I remember." I began to laugh. "You hit a target without the benefit of a mark."

"You'd have scared 'em off with a smoke rocket." He laughed, too. "Roger was my GIB on that mission."

"I took pictures of the debris left after your strike," I said. "I'll bring you copies."

"Great. Let me set you up for an F-Four ride. How long will you be here?"

"Not long, sir. According to Vientiane, I'm not supposed to be here at all. I've flown sixty-two days in a row, but who's counting? And I have to fly back tomorrow morning."

"Then let me buy you a drink. Bartender, a double." He pointed to my glass.

With hardly any effort, I became inebriated. The evening passed in a swirl of laughter and tall tales.

The hotel clerk pounded on my door. "You say wake up eight o'clock."

"Kop kuhn, krop." I thanked him and took a long shower. Later, when I stepped out into the sunshine, I reached into my pocket and found a receipt for a pair of shoes. I vaguely remembered a shoe shop the night before. The name on the receipt matched a nearby store. I walked inside.

The smiling gentleman took my receipt away and returned with a pair of ankle-high shoes with the leather on the inside. The outside surface was the reddish-brown-and-white hairy hide of the cow.

"I ordered these?"

"And pay for, too." The smiling cobbler bowed.

The shoes reminded me of the coloration of my grandfather's prize-winning bull, Storm. How many times had I crossed the Louisiana pasture for my chores in the barn with one eye on the path and one on old Storm? I wondered if my unconscious choice of these shoes represented a rite of passage.

An hour later I tossed the gross shoes into the storage conex at the Det.

The O-1 would not be released from phase until the.afternoon, so I hung around the ops desk at Det One.

Bill had sent a message for me to pick up paperwork at Vientiane.

I acknowledged and told him of the delay.

By the time I left, cumulous towers covered northern Thailand. I maneuvered around a few stone-like columns and landed at Vientiane.

Inside the A.O.C. trailer, Leo handed me an envelope for Bill.

I took a large drink of water, thanked Leo, and climbed back in the O-1.

A black thunderstorm encroached upon the north end of the field.

As I taxied, wind gusts whipped my flight controls to the limits.

Using both hands I couldn't hold the control stick steady. I taxied back to the trailer and tied down the O-1. I told Leo, "I think I'll wait this one out."

"You're the first smart Raven I've ever met."

"Funny man." I almost revealed I'd learned about thunderstorms the hard way.

The storm raged for two hours, dumping over an inch of rain, mostly sideways. When blue sky appeared, Leo asked, "Do you plan to stay overnight?"

"In the same city with the downtowners? No, thanks. I'm outa here."

I took off and climbed northward. The sun set behind my left wing, and I checked in with airborne control.

Alleycat had no traffic at the moment. The controller was in a jovial mood.

I spoke to each position on the staff, trying to isolate a stuck microphone button. The banter helped pass the time as the mountains grew darker.

My A.D.F. set found the radio beacon at L-54. Then, a glow on the horizon became the town of Luang Prabang.

Easing the nose down, I called, but no one answered at the AIRA house. I picked out where it should be and flew over as low as I dared in the darkness.

"Roger, One-two," Swick said on the radio. "One-zero's at the airfield."

I pulled up and aligned with the runway. Lowering flaps, I eased down to the dark strip.

At touchdown, the nose jerked left.

Instantly, I shoved the throttle forward and pulled the O-1 into the air.

A bulldozer and a grader loomed off the left side of the runway.

The left brake had apparently stuck, so I slipped the aircraft down on the left tire and banged it on the runway surface several times. My anger made the procedure easy.

Then I tried landing.

The airplane rolled out normally.

I stopped and taxied back. Nosing into the FAC revetment, I shut down and wrote "Left brake sticks" on the aircraft forms.

Bill pulled up in the jeep. "What the hell kind of landing was that? Let me smell your breath."

"Stuck brake. I bounced a few times to loosen it up."

"I was sitting here waiting. Couldn't see the runway. Then screech, roar, squeak, squeak. squeak." Bill jerked his head back and forth. "You should have heard the racket you made. I thought you'd rolled up in a ball." He handed me a cold beer.

"Murphy's Law."

I told the cockpit side of the story, and we laughed as he pulled away for the house.

"Meet Bill Conley and John, his assistant," the chief said one evening. "They're E.O.D. guys--Explosive Ordnance Disposal. They'll stay with us for a few days."

Bill and I shook hands with two large gentlemen in civilian clothes.

"We've been here a while," Conley said, "rounding up unexploded bombs and staying with USAID. But since we're Air Force on the inside, the chief invited us to stay with you guys. He says you show better movies."

"Welcome," Bill said. "Let us know if we can help."

"We'll need your help," Conley said. With freckles and flat-topped red hair, Conley had huge forearms and a barrel of a chest. I pictured him carrying a five-hundred-pounder under each arm. "We've collected most of the unexploded bombs from the boonies and the broken ordnance from bomb dumps and stacked it a mile off the end of the runway. We need somebody to warn aircraft when we blow it."

Bill pointed to me. "He can help you with that little chore. I'm too short."

Everyone laughed.

I spoke with Conley while the others set up the movie. "How much stuff will you destroy?"

"About fourteen thousand pounds of ordnance. We'll use nine hundred pounds of C-Four plastique explosive."

"Damn. Where do the bombs come from?"

"All over the area. USAID has a program where they rebuild homes that were destroyed by U.S. bombing. So every villager with any damage at all makes a claim."

"We don't target civilians. We don't bomb villages. How many claims to the contrary do you get?"

"We've pulled bombs--mostly nose-fused two-fifties--from half a dozen places. I think they were all dropped by T-Twenty-eights, not American airplanes."

"Why do you say that?"

"The U.S. doesn't load two hundred and fifty pound bombs anymore. And all U.S. bombs have nose and tail fuses--instantaneous and point-zero-one-second delays."

"Right. They can select a functional delay from the cockpit."

"Can't blame the little people for wanting new houses."

"Yeah," I said, "but the program encourages fabricated stories that make bullshit headlines back home."

On a foggy morning two days later I rode with Conley in his ton-and-a-half weapons carrier, the official name for his large green truck. He slid and spun down a muddy road that took us into the jungle off the east end of the runway.

I wore my pistol belt and carried a portable U.H.F. radio. "I'm short, too," I said. "Don't get me in any big trouble today."

"No, sir." Conley smiled and pulled the truck off the road. "We'll walk from here. The site is about four minutes ahead over the hill."

We hiked to a clearing where bombs, shells, and weapons were stacked like cordwood--six feet high, six wide, and twelve long. Gray blocks of C-4 dotted the pile, each block connected to another with detonation cord like a dark brown spider web.

Conley moved some shells to the pile, placed C-4, and attached a blasting cap and det cord.

"You're pretty casual with that plastique stuff."

"Without a blasting cap, C-Four is stable." He pinched a tiny gob and lit it with a cigarette lighter.

I stepped back. "Holy shit."

The C-4 burned like a candle with a blue flame.

"Burns like sterno." He put a piece in his mouth. "Tastes like peanut butter."

"Now I know why you guys drink a quart of whiskey every night. You're washing the C-Four taste out of your mouth."

"We drink to relax." Laughing, he reeled the det cord to the edge of the clearing. Along the way he wrapped the cord around a leaking can of napalm, and twice around a five-inch tree trunk. "Det cord burns at a rate of twenty-five-thousand-feet per second. Check what it does to that tree."

"I'd call that rate an explosion."

Conley nodded and connected the cord to a device that, in turn, was connected to a long powder fuse. He cut a second powder fuse the same length. "When I light this thing, you'll have five minutes to make your announcements. We'll take the second one with us." He lit both fuses.

Walking briskly to keep up, I broadcast my warning on tower frequency.

Conley carried the smoking cord that would tell us when to cover our ears.

I made two more announcements, warning all aircraft to stay clear. Then I crouched behind the truck with Conley.

With one minute to go, a Lao H-34 helicopter approached.

I yelled and screamed on the radio.

My watch showed thirty seconds left.

The helicopter passed over the blast site.

"He's not on the frequency," I said. "Nothing we can do now."

Conley put his fingers in his ears as smoke reached the last half-inch of the fuse suspended from his hand.

I put the radio down and covered my ears.

BOOM.

The ground shook. A flash accompanied the loudest noise I'd ever heard.

"Stay down," Conley warned.

Pieces of metal rained around us.

I could hear the helicopter engine now over the airfield. "What's the saying? God protects fools and Englishmen?"

After a minute passed, Conley led me to the site, marked by a huge gray mushroom cloud.

We stopped at the edge of a seventy-foot crater. Huge rocks lay exposed on the bottom. The earth groaned, as if protesting injuries from the blast. Napalm crackled and sent up a wisp of black smoke from the bisected canister. The wrapped cord had chopped off the tree like a dull saw. Shredded vegetation floated down like green snow.

"Mission accomplished." Conley folded his arms and surveyed the scene.

"Awesome."

"Big party tonight," Bill said. "It's for a good cause."

"Oh, yeah?" I pushed my chair back after a roast beef dinner.

"The local RLAF headquarters is raising money for widows and orphans of the men lost in combat in Military Region One."

"When and where?"

"Right now. Location is diagonally across from the Bungalow, on the corner of the main drag and the little street that drops down to the Mekong."

"Without referring to my social calendar," I said, "I could probably squeeze in some local color, especially if the cause is just."

"Let's do it."

I followed Bill to the jeep.

He pulled into the dark, muddy street and drove to the Bungalow Bar.

I spotted the party scene from a block away.

Next to a restaurant on the corner, a courtyard had been draped with white and orange parachute canopies. A stage and low bleachers had been set up around the sides, and Chinese lanterns were strung across the middle.

Bill parked at the Bungalow. "The jeep'll be more secure here."

We paid a small fee to enter the restaurant. A young woman sold bottles of booze at a stand near the door.

"What the hell," Bill said, handing her cash. "It's for a good cause."

T-28 pilots owned the first table by the door. They yelled and motioned us over.

We bowed and joined them.

"I've been here before," I said, throwing a capful of White Horse Scotch down my throat. I filled the cap, passed it on, then grabbed a few peanuts from a tray in the center of the round table.

A large general--the king's half-brother and M.R. 1 commander--entered, bought several bottles of scotch, and placed one on our table. His Lao words sounded kind.

We stood and shook hands.

Relentlessly, the bottle cap circled the table.

The Lao Air Force Wing commander entered and plopped a third bottle on our table, earning an ovation. Other military officers and a few civilians entered and did the same.

Like Poe's pendulum, the bottle cap came again and again to deliver its stinging edge. My stomach churned and burned.

Scooping a handful of peanuts, I inadvertently grasped a small pepper. When I discovered its fiery nature, I surmised it had used its own energy to jump into the peanuts from an adjacent dish. I stood as the ember burned slowly down my throat, like a fuse growing shorter and shorter. I ran from the tilting room.

Outside I stopped by the edge of the klong that oozed down to the river. After emptying my stomach, I used a napkin to wipe my face. My evening had peaked.

A new T-28 wingman, Bouathong, stepped up beside me, smiled, and vomited.

Vowing to avoid alcohol for the remainder of the evening, I slipped back to the party. In the courtyard I sipped a large cup of water.

The band struck up a Laotian tune with a repetitious melody and a driving rhythm. A crowd circled the dance floor, telling the story behind the song with waving arms, turning wrists, and curling fingers.

The delicate arm movements of the dance were best suited to petite females. I noticed Swick stumbling like a dazed linebacker among the dancers.

I sat down in the bleachers, trying to fade into the background.

A perfumed lady sitting nearby asked, "Do you know Henry?"

I laughed and shook my head. "Henry went home last month."

From time to time AIRA folks stopped to chat. Some danced.

When Swick climbed on stage and started to sing, I stood up to leave. I walked to Bill, who was talking to a senior Lao officer. "Ready to go?"

"Hell, no." He turned angrily. Then he smiled and put his arm around the general's shoulders. "The general is only starting to have fun."

"You have the jeep." I saluted. "I'm walking. Adios." I spent my remaining useful consciousness avoiding the deeper mudholes as I trudged home.

I awoke at six.

Bill's bed at the other end of our long room had not been touched.

I showered and went to breakfast. When everyone but Bill showed up, I asked, "Has anyone seen Mr. Bill?"

I was answered with blank stares and shaking heads.

"Before we go to the airfield, before we turn one wheel, we have to find him. I'll go the scene of the party. Chief, organize the troops. Ask around. Let's meet right here in one hour."

"Roger." The chief formed search parties and departed.

I went to the radio room and spoke to Swick. "Not a word about Bill being missing goes on the radio. Not a breath, unless you want a downtowner supervising your bowel movements for the rest of a short but quite miserable life." I exaggerated but only a little.

He smiled and nodded. "Not to worry."

With an extra set of keys in hand, I walked to the restaurant and found the jeep intact. Debris from the party lay in piles, and the restaurant was locked. I drove down to the Mekong and searched side streets and klongs for most of an hour.

Back at the house the chief pulled me aside. "I saw some little guys--friends of mine--downtown. They said Bill was in the monkey house."

"Thanks, Chief." I felt relief and shock, simultaneously. "I'll handle things from here. Press on to the airfield. I plan to fly as soon as possible this morning."

No one spoke English at the small military prison. My Lao proficiency was sufficient for a guided trip around back, where I found Bill in handcuffs washing his face in a smelly creek.

A soldier with an A.K.-47 guarded him.

"Are you okay?" I didn't know what else to say.

"No." Bill sounded hoarse. "Nobody speaks English. This is all a mistake. Get a senior officer over here."

"Sure. I'll be right back."

I drove to the home of Colonel Khongsovana, the Lao wing commander, and explained the situation.

He smiled. "Follow me."

At the prison, he went inside for about five minutes and returned with Bill.

I shook the colonel's hand and thanked him.

"I think the general's bodyguards do not know what to do with Beel last night. They take him here to be safe, you know?"

I nodded, and the colonel departed with a wave.

"Let's go home. Are you okay?" I helped Bill into the jeep.

Dirt splotched Bill's clothes. He looked like he hadn't slept. "I woke up around six a.m. in a tiny cell. Rats woke me--running around on the floor. A tiny window ten feet above sent a beam of light through the dust. I couldn't see anything. I thought I was in Hanoi. No shit, until I saw you, I had no idea what the hell was happening."

I started the engine and headed for the AIRA house. "The colonel said the general's bodyguards put you in the lockup for safekeeping."

"Oh shit, the general." Bill shook his head. "We took off in a jeep around midnight. Next thing I know, I'm locked up. Where were you?"

"I threw up early. Went home at ten."

"I'm through drinking. No more booze. That's it."

"Probably a good idea, Bill. Get some rest. I'm going to fly."

That evening after the movie, Swick brought a message out to me. "FAC assignments are in. Looks like you're all going to Air Training Command."

Bill was still sleeping.

I read the messages. Ernie and I would go to Craig Air Force Base in Selma, Alabama. Bill was ordered to Vance A.F.B., in Oklahoma. "I asked for a fighter, back to the war. A Tweet to Alabama is as close as the system could take me."

"Coulda been worse," Swick said. "You could be haulin' trash." He grinned.

I shook my head. I could enjoy the pure aeronautics of flying a trainer. I'd have to learn to deal with the chickenshit. I presumed enough warriors had preceded me in the command that most of the inanity had been cycled into the background. "Nobody in the training business will understand any of this crazy stuff I've seen here."

"Seen and done." Swick corrected me.

I laughed. "I suppose I should tell Bill." I went to our room and tried to wake him.

He grumbled and rolled away.

After flying a morning mission and eating lunch, I decided that Bill had slept long enough. I rousted him.

"What? Leave me alone."

"You've been in bed for twenty-eight hours. Get up. Eat. Drink water."

"Okay." He sat up in bed and started to light a cigarette. Then he put it down.

"We received our assignments. Are you ready for Oklahoma?"

He shook his head and walked into the bathroom.

I walked to the main house and met Swick coming from the radio room.

"Vientiane wants pictures of the top of the sleeping elephant." He handed me a sheet of paper from the printer.

"They want to put a TACAN station up there," I said. "Great idea."

"But they want us to put a roll of film on today's Courier flight."

"That's the downtowner mentality." My temperature rose a couple of degrees. "They sit on a project for years. When they finally pull it out into the light of day, they give operators an hour to respond."

Swick asked, "Are you going to try to take the pictures?"

"If this message wasn't about something that could save lives, I'd toss it in the trash and make 'em send another one." I shook my head. "I'll give it a shot."

I put a fresh roll of Tri-X film in my camera, drove to the airfield and parked.

Ramon pulled pins and covers from the O-1.

"I'll only fly for half an hour," I said. "I have to take a few pictures."

"Can I go, too?"

"Why not?" I couldn't think of a better way to thank Ramon for his excellent work and inspire him to continue than to give him a little ride.

We took off under scattered clouds. Level at fifteen hundred feet above the ground, I pulled out my camera and took a heading to the sleeping elephant, offset optimally for picture-taking. I asked Ramon, "Can you fly, please?"

He smiled and took control.

I began to snap pictures. I figured if the shots obviously progressed from large to small, the downtowners would have fewer questions. I took twenty pictures and reserved the final four for close-ups of the peak itself. I set up a pass, then asked Ramon to fly again.

I raised the 200-millimeter lens and took aim as we approached at fifty feet. I clicked and rewound three times. A thin wispy cloud blocked the view on my last shot. The peak had been clear of clouds only seconds before.

I looked north, toward the runway. "Uh-oh. We need to land."

A huge black bulldozer of cumulus crossed the Mekong. In front of the churning storm, clear air changed into a surreal layer of tiny clouds--wisps that reminded me of small animals running from a fire. Lightning flashed inside boiling clouds, and rain gushed from the bottom.

I figured I had about two minutes, aiming the O-1 at the runway. Three minutes later I turned and lined up at a quarter of a mile. "I think I'll leave the flaps up. Lots of runway."

As I approached, the runway disappeared in a blinding white sheet of rain.

I added power and turned left, climbing away from the storm. "We'll go to the Sayabouri valley and wait. The storm's moving fast. We'll try again in a half hour."

No longer smiling, Ramon looked pale.

I crossed the Mekong westbound and told him, "You fly for a while. Fly big circles around the runway in the middle of this valley." I figured flying would distract him from his fear.

He nodded, but his face showed despair.

"If the weather stays poor at Luang Prabang, we can land here. Many friendly people live here." I reassured my friend.

Ramon continued to look like he had lost all connection with friends and family, although he flew well for thirty minutes.

"Let's try to go home. We'll be fine."

I took control and turned east. Over the Mekong I dropped to a few hundred feet and turned north. I didn't want to traumatize my passenger by going any lower. I glanced over my shoulder.

Ramon still looked like he was feeling the initial stages of a cardiac infarction.

I followed the river around a wide bend to the city, then to the runway.

The storm had moved south, leaving clear skies and wet terrain behind.

I landed gently, taxied to the revetments, and shut down.

Ramon leaped out and chocked the airplane.

I rewound the film and pulled out the cartridge. I slipped it in an addressed envelope I had brought for that purpose. "Want to go fly a real mission now?"

"No." Ramon giggled, apparently euphoric to be alive.

Ernie arrived and spent a few days packing. He and Bill enjoyed a small non-alcoholic farewell party. They left on the same airplane that delivered Doc Russell.

Chapter 24
Color Me Gone

September 1971

The shoulder-holstered 9mm Beretta identified Doctor Charles Russell, our dentist cum senior Raven FAC. With blond hair and a disarming smile, he liked blue jeans, dark tee shirts, and cowboy boots, but he loved the Beretta. He left the shirt of his walking suits unzipped to allow quick access to his pistol.

I liked Doc from the beginning. I met him on the Air America ramp and drove him to the house shortly after noon on his first day in Luang Prabang.

He dropped his bag in Ernie's former bedroom.

I handed him Bill's maps. "When would you like to begin your local checkout?"

"How about right now?"

"Let's go." I drove him to meet Major Oum Peng, then we toured the local area in the O-1. From the backseat, I pointed out all friendly positions around the city and the places where we had destroyed larger enemy formations. "I recommend you always take a better interpreter than I am when you fly the local area."

A ground unit called and passed targets to us.

I copied strings of coordinates. I had mastered Lao numbers at a Bungalow Bar bingo game early in my tour. "If they see you, they'll ask for help. A Lao backseater can ask for more details about these air requests. Right now I'd prioritize the units near Pa Theung."

The afternoon T-28 flow began. Doc struck several targets.

After landing, I introduced the new guy to the Royal Lao Air Force leadership and the Company representative at the four o'clock meeting.

Over a can of beer after dinner, I told him, "Unless you have questions, I consider you checked out in the local area. Tomorrow we'll do the Nam Ou in the morning and Ban Houei Sai in the afternoon."

"Okay, but I feel like I'm sipping a firehose," Doc said. "This place doesn't have an A.O.C. Commander, so I'm doing both jobs."

"You have to prioritize." I shrugged and decided not to reveal my smart-ass tendencies. "The area you worked today is critical. To sleep well at night, keep a tight handle on the N.V.A. between here and Pa Theung. Talk to Major Oum Peng every day."

At eight the next morning, after checking the local area, we flew past Pa Theung and turned north up the Nam Ou.

I piloted the U-17.

"I hate this airplane," Doc said. "Not enough visibility, compared to any other FAC machine."

"I agree, but you'll need the fuel endurance to wait for the fighters and do damage on the north end of this river." Passing the W, I swooped down a few times to point out hidden boats.

"As much as possible," Doc said, "I'll work the local area, doing CAS in the Oscar Ace. I'll make one of the new guys an interdiction specialist."

"Do you know who's inbound?"

"We're getting a new kid named Skip in a day or two," Doc said. "Then, your replacement will be Craig Bradford, a friend of mine from Alternate."

I had pointed out dozens of boats and caves by the time we passed between the sheer cliffs at Muang Ngoi. At the big river bend to the west, I turned around. "I don't routinely go past this point. The N.V.A. radar coverage is excellent, starting here. If you find yourself over that airfield," I pointed northeast, "then you're in North Vietnam, and you'll need the President in your backseat for target approval. That's Dien Bien Phu."

Doc laughed.

"The North Vietnamese seem to think they own this part of Laos." I showed him hidden trails in the Nam Bac valley, then we flew home for lunch.

A few hours later I flew the left seat again, cruising the U-17 westward a thousand feet above the Mekong. "The situation out west is different. If you're interested in details of the ground war, ask the Company guys on scene."

"What do you mean?"

"The friendlies are Thai, for one thing, not Lao, not mountain people. And I don't fully grasp the strategic significance of the fighting. The Chinese are aiming a major highway at Thailand. The area is famous for opium and semi-precious stones. And the combatants out here fight vicious hill-to-hill battles." I shook my head.

Have you considered extending? I'm starting to feel overwhelmed."

"I've thought about it. I love this job, for the most part. I can't honestly picture myself leaving."

Doc nodded. "What's this outpost?" He pointed to a mountaintop on the north bank of the Mekong and east across a small river from the tiny village of Pak Beng.

"An elusive target--the southernmost vestige of the China Road. Five miles north you'll find an all-weather highway defended by the heaviest concentrations of thirty-seven-millimeter guns in Southeast Asia."

"I see trenches with a bunker at this end." We flew abeam the position, remaining about five hundred feet above the peak.

"Rog. They try to hide their radio antennas on the back side."

"Look. I see soldiers in the trenches. They're shooting at us."

I leaned over and squinted. "You have excellent vision. Damn." I saw muzzle flashes. Two soldiers fired short automatic bursts at us.

I stomped left rudder and pulled back on the controls.

Turning away, the nose came up into the sun. The airspeed slowed, approaching a stall.

I armed a rocket and kept my hand on the arming switches. Then, I stomped right rudder and released back pressure.

The nose fell, and we rolled, gently at first, in the direction of the shooters. The airspeed climbed to 200 knots as the trenches grew larger in the windscreen.

BAM . . .BAM . . . BAM.

I fired three rockets that hit the red dirt behind the fleeing troops. "Look at those bastards run."

The soldiers disappeared into the bunker.

I pulled up and rolled to a westward course.

"We should blow this mountain away." Doc seemed amazed at the audacity of the shooters.

"We've used T-Twenty-eights here in the past. Let me tell you two little secrets."

Doc looked back at the smoking mountain.

"First, one of our backseaters has family in the village of Pak Beng. Be careful when striking this place."

"Okay."

"Second, the assholes who shot at us are Chinese."

"What?"

"Watch this." I switched my microphone switch to V.H.F. "Cricket, Raven One-two. I have trenches and a large bunker. We are taking fire from this location." I passed coordinates and continued westbound.

"Cricket copies, Raven One-two."

Five minutes later, Cricket called. "Raven One-two, Painter advises you will not, repeat, not strike those coordinates. Acknowledge."

"Roger."

Doc's eyebrows shot up. He made notes in his little green book. "Painter is the embassy callsign. They're overriding your judgment?"

"Something strange is going on with China . . . probably at a high level. But I don't call what we're doing warfare when you can't shoot back. I call it a political situation."

"Those fuckers shot at me, too. They'll pay."

I nodded. "Crap like this reminds me of Vietnam--makes going home easier. I leave politics to politicians. They should leave war-fighting to us."

"Those fuckers'll pay. Period." Doc pounded the glare shield.

I smiled. The region would be in good hands. "I'll take your new FACs up to a remote Lima Site near the Chinese border--One-eighteen-alpha. You can get lunch and fuel there. Not sure about rockets."

Doc unfolded his map. "Looks like it's about thirty minutes due north, surrounded on three sides by China."

"Yep. We can stop in today, if you wish. The runway is steep and one-way, like Alternate, but not as busy."

"Nah. I'll visit later."

I flew on to L-25, Ban Houei Sai, and landed on the three-tiered airstrip.

Doc smiled as we bounced onto the uphill roller coaster of a runway.

A Company man named Smith welcomed us and gave Doc a detailed briefing.

We launched again an hour later.

I flew south and crossed the Mekong. "We're over the contested area. Come to this spot when you receive calls for help."

Doc surveyed the green mountains below. "Who makes those calls?"

"When chopper pilots show up at the AIRA movie, you'll know something's up." I circled, called Mo on F.M., and asked his situation.

"Raven One-two, this is Mo. Sawadee, krop. Maybe you can bring T-Twenty-eights for my targets?"

"Soon. We'll talk to the Air Force."

"Okay. Kop kuhn, krop." Mo thanked me in Thai.

Smiling, Doc studied the terrain below. "I caught the accent."

I gave the aircraft gentle and frequent turns. "Keep your nose moving in this area. The bad guys here shoot at airplanes more than most."

"Audacious bastards. Are they Chinese, too?"

"I don't know. The briefer said the N.V.A. and Chinese cooperate up here. The runway on the nose is Lima-Sixty-nine. Helicopter support stages out of there. The tiny strip in the hill to the west is Alpha. Would you care to visit some interesting characters?"

"Not now." Doc laughed and jotted more notes. "After Bradford arrives, we'll bring the O-One out here and spend a day or two. You have a lot of shit going on in this region."

I nodded. "A lot of shit, including U.F.O.s. They're probably Chinese, too."

"What?"

I told Doc my U.F.O. story as we drove home.

Tall with short curly hair and serious green eyes, Skip arrived the next morning. After lunch, we all drove down to the airfield.

Doc took the O-1.

Skip and I walked over to the U-17.

"Would you like the left seat?" I asked.

"No, you go ahead."

I gave Skip an overview of the local order of battle as we headed for the Nam Ou. "Don't be shy. Ask me anything while you can."

I found boats north of the W and requested T-28s.

A flight of two arrived within ten minutes.

"You want to control this strike?" I asked.

"No, thanks," Skip answered.

"Okay. Don't be reluctant. I'll help you any way I can. In a week or so, color me gone."

"The truth is," Skip said, "I didn't direct many airstrikes in Vietnam. My Army unit was pulling out, so I mostly did visual recon."

"How did you get into the program without experience?"

"I pulled strings. Maybe the volunteer list was short. I don't know. I'll watch you for now and figure things out."

"The only way I know to get experience is to plunge in with both feet," I said. "Your ass is sure to follow."

Skip laughed.

I wasted the boats, found more and struck them before directing the T-28 flow back to Doc.

Skip looked at his watch. "You directed seven airplanes on five targets in fifteen minutes. And the wings haven't been level since we took off."

"Roger. Things can happen fast. But I've survived doing this every day for six months. Let's slide over to the Nam Bac valley and hunt along N.V.A. trails."

After a few hours of reconnaissance we returned to Luang Prabang.

I flew a normal approach and, as usual, leveled off with three wheels a few inches above the pavement. Using the ground effect phenomenon, I floated to the opposite end of the runway.

Skip put his hand on the top of the instrument panel and smiled at me. "That had to be the smoothest touchdown I've ever seen."

"Oh, I'm good," I said, muffling a laugh. "But we haven't touched down yet." With three hundred feet of runway to go, I pulled the throttle to idle, and we squeaked on.

Skip's jaw dropped. "I have a lot to learn."

I spent the next day in the local area and on the Nam Ou with Skip. I flew the U-17 left seat with Somnuck in back.

I told Skip, "Lieutenant Somnuck has come a long way in managing his airsickness."

Skip raised his eyebrows.

I looked at Somnuck. "Remember the good ol' days?"

He smiled and passed thumbs up.

"Are you familiar with the term barfstorm?"

Skip opened his window.

After dinner Doc pulled me aside. "How's Skip doing?"

"I like him a lot. He's an intelligent guy, but I haven't done much evaluation. He told me he's short on experience, and it shows. He's been happy to ride along and evaluate me, I guess."

As we spoke, three Air America helicopter pilots arrived for the movie.

Doc and I looked at each other.

"Why don't I take Skip out west tomorrow and show him around?"

"Great idea." Doc began to laugh. "I'll try to shake loose a flight of Mustangs."

We enjoyed the movie, then set up close air support for a MEDEVAC--a helicopter medical evacuation of a friendly position near Ban Houei Sai at ten a.m.

At nine a.m. I cruised west along the Mekong with Skip in the right seat and Seo in back. At Pak Beng I made a low pass, daring the enemy troops to start something.

No one came out of the bunker.

I called Mo at nine-thirty. "Do you have a target for me this morning?"

"Affirmative, Raven One-two. Enemy has strong position on a hill about two kilometers west."

I put my binoculars on that location, then handed them to my rightseater. "Here, Skip. Tell me what you see."

He studied the ground as I circled. "Under a single layer of jungle cover, I see a dozen bunkers in a circle around the hilltop. I see movement."

"Roger that."

Skip passed the glasses to Seo.

I asked, "Would you like to do the honors?"

"No, go ahead."

I was surprised he didn't seize this opportunity. But I felt happy to proceed. I'd kick Commie butt and help save friendly lives. I knew of no better mission. "You have to remember, Skip. These guys would cut your fucking throat if they could."

Seo gave me a knowing smile.

The poorly camouflaged enemy had nowhere to go. The mission would start with a duck-shoot.

"I'll brief the Mustangs when they arrive at nine-fifty-five," I told Skip. "When the choppers call airborne from Lima-Sixty-nine, I'll hit those bunkers below us."

"Sounds like a plan," Skip said.

Seo nodded.

"Always have the Mustangs drop bombs first. Then they become light and maneuverable enough to hang around for half an hour with rockets and strafe."

Skip nodded as the Mustangs checked in.

Since we were away from the local area, I briefed Mustang Red, flight of four, in detail. I showed them the friendly position and passed the elevation of the enemy hilltop. "When I mark the target, please drop one bomb at a time around the smoke. Aim at the bunkers under the smoke."

"Roger, one bomb."

"Raven, Hotel Six-four's airborne." The choppers called on U.H.F.

"Roger." I switched to the ground troops' F.M. frequency. "Mo, tell your people to get down. Confirm my smoke is on target."

BAM.

"Good smoke, Raven One-two," Mo said.

On V.H.F. I said, "That's a good mark, Mustang Red. Hit the bunkers." Then I turned to Skip. "Help me give the choppers our total attention when they get here."

"Roger." He looked for the inbound choppers.

"Raven One-two. I see bunkers. Mustang Red is in hot."

"Cleared hot."

The T-28s attacked viciously. Sixteen times, fireballs and clouds of gray smoke boiled on the dug-in foe. "Raven One-two, Mustang Red is winchester bombs."

"Roger," I said. "Hold high and dry, please."

"Roger, high and dry."

"Hotel Six-four is inbound."

I watched the string of choppers approaching. "Skip, I can't overemphasize keeping your eyes on the choppers when they're in harm's way. They can disappear between heartbeats." I remembered how quickly Jolly 54 had crashed.

He and Seo watched.

I circled a thousand feet below the T-28s. As the first chopper approached and landed, I continued straight ahead, offset to one side.

Pop-pop-pop-pop-pop-pop.

"Oh shit," I yelled on intercom. "Can you hear that?"

Pop-pop-pop-pop-pop.

"No," Skip said. "Hear what?"

"Damn." I jammed left rudder and pulled back as hard as I could.

The airplane snapped up and rolled away from the enemy position I had crossed at five hundred feet.

I armed a smoke and rolled in carefully from the south.

BAM.

"Mustang Red," I called. "Hit my smoke with rockets. Work north-to-south."

Another chopper landed on the friendly position.

Roger." Mustang Red pounced on the enemy with seven high explosive rockets.

I monitored the attack, clearing seven more rocket passes.

The MEDEVAC continued on the adjacent ridge.

"What was that jinking all about?" Skip asked while Mustang Red attacked.

"Groundfire is hard to hear in the U-Seventeen. We just took a ton of it. I should have reacted sooner, rather than trying to teach you something only time can do. I'm sorry. I gave 'em a free shot."

Skip looked skeptical. "I heard nothing."

"Raven, Hotel-Six-four's clear. Thanks so much."

"My pleasure." I switched from U.H.F. to V.H.F.

"Mustang Red, please strafe the enemy position. North-to-south."

The flight leader, Chin, spoke Lao to his wingmen, then said, "Roger."

The Mustangs came down with guns blazing.

The entire hill sparkled and smoked under the fifty-caliber bashing.

"Excellent job today, Mustang Red. Cleared R.T.B. Thank you."

"Roger, Raven One-two." The T-28s departed.

"Thank you very much, Raven One-two," Mo called on F.M.

"Pope-gan, krop. See you later." I turned and followed the T-28s.

On the way home, I explained to Skip how we had taken fire. "Hearing popping below the aircraft is a life-saving skill. With the windows closed, the sound is muffled, and it blends with the purr of the engine."

"I didn't hear a thing." Skip sounded defensive.

"At first, you'll sense something is wrong. After you're used to the engine drone, you'll hear popcorn quite clearly." I asked, "Do you still think I'm kidding?"

"No. I feel frustrated." Skip folded his arms. "I don't know what to think."

I flew my standard approach to a few inches above the runway and floated.

Skip looked outside and confirmed the right wheel wasn't turning.

I pulled the throttle, and we landed. I taxied into the FAC revetment, swung the tail around, and pulled the mixture lever all the way back.

The propeller slowed gradually then stopped.

Our crewchief, Ramon, kicked a yellow wooden chock in front and one behind the right tire. He looked up and laughed.

We climbed out.

Ramon pointed to the flap.

Two bullet holes were lined up ten inches from where Skip's head had been during the strike.

Seo laughed.

Skip turned pale and said nothing.

"A.K.-forty-seven," I said. "I guess we turned just in time."

At lunch, I confessed my foolish act to Doc. "Ban Houei Sai's a nasty place. I should have kept the nose moving, and I should have reacted sooner."

"You just gave me another reason to hate that airplane. I'm glad you're back and the mission's accomplished," Doc said. "Why don't you take the afternoon off?"

"I'd love to. Thanks." I figured I'd walk around and take tourist pictures. I secured my gear in my bedroom and picked up my camera. When I pushed an extra roll of film into my pocket, I noticed my rabbit's foot was missing. I had touched it as my final pre-flight inspection item earlier that morning.

The charm passed on by Larry Ratts and former Covey FACs had disappeared.

I drove to the airfield and searched the U-17. Then I returned and searched my room. I wondered if the charm had used its last powers deflecting bullet trajectories during the morning mission.

Was Buddha telling me to go home?

I enjoyed an afternoon downtown, capturing the local culture on film. At the open-air market Hmoung women clustered in black dresses covered with red and yellow embroidery like wild flowers. Their silver jewelry could be measured in pounds, not ounces. I captured the texture of weathered wooden boats tied along the Mekong. I took images of laughing school children. What better evidence to show the folks back home why we fought?

After a couple of hours, I came home and took a nap on the sofa.

When Doc came through the door at five-thirty, I awoke. "Where's Skip?"

Doc looked at his watch. "Probably in Udorn. I sent him home this afternoon."

"Really?" I was shocked.

"I took him up the Nam Ou and found boats. I asked him to blow them away. He had trouble with the radios, and he flew into a cloud at the worst possible moment."

"I'm sorry. I liked Skip a lot. Maybe I should have insisted he work more strikes."

"He needed more experience than you could have given him in a few days. People's lives depend on us. We don't run a basic FAC school here."

"You have tough calls to make. Skip was a decent kid."

"I agree. He took the news well. Said to thank you for the help and support."

I nodded absently. I had nearly gotten him killed this morning.

"Bradford will be here tomorrow. Your replacement shows in a week or so."

Handsome Craig Bradford arrived early the next morning. Except for his shoulder holster, he looked like he had stepped from a movie poster.

I immediately showed him the local area and the Nam Ou. We spent a long afternoon visiting all the Lima sites west and north of Luang Prabang.

At dinner I told Doc, "Craig's checked out in M.R.-One. Can I go home now?"

Doc laughed. "He's done? After only one day?"

"Craig has a lot of energy. I think he was ready before he got here."

Craig flashed a Hollywood smile.

A few days later the courier delivered Gene Hamner, my replacement.

I took him up the Nam Ou on his first afternoon in town.

He flew the left seat, found boats, and blew them away. On the way home he told me, "I heard Luang Prabang is run like a tight ship. I like things that way."

The next morning I showed Gene the wild west. We talked to Mo and had lunch at Lima Sixty-nine-alpha. Like Bradford, Gene fit in like he was born to the task.

When we approached Luang Prabang, he flew down the runway in ground effect.

After landing I shook his hand. "Help yourself to my callsign. Be careful with it."

After dinner, several guests arrived to wish me farewell. The AIRA gang, my Luang Prabang family, presented me a knife with an ivory handle and an elaborate silver case. The Mustangs offered a Lao flag inscribed with their thoughts and opinions about my experience. Most were warrior words. Some pilots hinted I'd be back.

Somnuck represented the backseaters and gave me a bamboo commander's stick, silver-tipped and inscribed with a calendar that would allow me to sort my good Phi days from the rest of time. Major Oum Peng presented me a sparkling silver dish.

I sipped scotch and allowed the moment to overwhelm me. Had Doc presented extension papers, I'd have signed them.

"You have to stop in Vientiane." Sipping breakfast coffee, Doc was laughing.

"I don't want to stop in Vientiane." I was serious.

"You have to pick up important personnel records."

"I don't want to see Raven Zero-one or any other downtowners again. Ever."

"We can have the documents waiting at the A.O.C. trailer."

"Deal."

Several airplane hops later, I arrived at Udorn with all my records for several days of out-processing. I began at the officer's club. Strolling into the main lounge, I saw Bill, who seemed to be enjoying himself immensely.

With a walking suit and an Air Force captain's hat on, he was dancing on top of the bar. According to tradition, wearing a hat in the bar earned him the privilege of buying a round of drinks for everyone. After several weeks of rest and debriefing, Bill was leaving in style.

I strolled over and intercepted my friend as he climbed down onto a barstool. "Are you still here?"

"I'm leavin' in the morning." He gave me a small bear hug.

"I thought you took a vow of abstinence."

"That was Laos." Bill looked around the room. "This is Thailand."

"I'm leaving, too, in a couple of days."

"Bartender! Whiskey for my friend."

I spent the next morning packing my belongings, which primarily consisted of brand new stereo equipment. I completed a checklist for the bureaucrats on base, reducing my obligation to a bag drag the following afternoon.

When I entered the officer's club for the last time, I spotted a familiar face.

A sturdy major in a flight suit looked at me. He turned, and I saw Robbins on his name tag and a Jolly Green Giant patch on his shoulder.

I smiled. "Jolly Five-four. I'm glad you're alive."

He grinned and walked over. He lifted me off the ground in a huge bear hug. "My favorite Raven FAC. You aren't spending one dime at the bar tonight."

We shook hands and walked over to the Jolly Green table.

"I was in shock when we met," Robbins said. "I didn't have a clue what was going on. Damn. You guys saved our asses."

"I invited you to stay for a beer in Luang Prabang."

"I remember. We should have, too." Robbins grinned, re-living his crash from the perspective of knowing the happy ending. "Bartender!"

A few hours later, Leo Thomas walked over from the adjacent Nickel table.

I shook his hand and introduced him to my Jolly pals.

"I hit a great target today," Leo said, "way up north where you worked. We dropped snake and nape on trenches and a big bunker on the north bank of the Mekong."

"Pak Beng?"

"That's the place. Way up north. We were outa gas when we got there."

"Doc Russell must've done some fancy tap-dancin' to get F-Fours up there."

"I was number two, doin' a flight lead upgrade ride. Raven One-one marked the target. We dropped snakeye first and missed. Blew up on the backside."

"They had radio antennas back there." In my mind I saw the high-drag fins opening and five-hundred-pound bombs raining down on the Chinese outpost.

"Leader rolled in and missed with his napalm, leaving the bunker sitting there for my last pass." Leo's loud Kentucky twang attracted a small crowd.

"I realized we'd been flyin' around with one eye on the fuel gauge. Hell with that. I armed six cans o' nape and rolled in. Scraped those babies off on the bunker."

"Four crispy critters." Craig Bradford had walked up behind us.

"Exactly," Leo said. "Who are you?"

"Meet your FAC today." I introduced Craig, then asked him, "What are you doing here, and how'd you get approval for the strike?"

Bradford grinned. "I'm here to swap out the U-Bird. I got approval by playing their own stupid game. I told Cricket I had a command and control bunker complex. They asked me the source of my information. I told 'em that was classified--the truth. Ten minutes later they sent F-Fours."

The crowd howled.

Leo asked me, "When are you going back to the real world?"

"I go back to the States tomorrow." I looked around and sucked in the raw intensity and legitimacy of this scene. "But what could possibly be more real than right here, right now?

Epilogue

2001

Doc Russell died at Luang Prabang in a midair collision. North Vietnamese gunners killed Leo Thomas near the Plain of Jars. Dick Defer died in action.

Since 1970 not a day has passed in which I do not remember them, plus Mike Vrablick, Jerry Bevan, Pete Landry, Tom Duckett, Denny Morgan, Ed Troxel, Andy Capp--and the nameless American voices that fell silent in the dark Laotian jungles in Prairie Fire.

The N.V.A. shot down and captured Lieutenant Colonel Joe Kittinger and Captain Jim Latham. Dugan earned a purple heart, hit by metal fragments at his going-away party during a rocket attack on the firebase he had supported for a year near Danang. Roger Locher bailed out and spent three weeks on the ground evading the North Vietnamese before a daring rescue.

My friends' continuing trials after I was safe in Selma, Alabama, inspired me to volunteer to go back to Asia in 1973.

I returned while diplomats signed a peace accord that evicted Ravens from Laos. Ten of us stayed in Udorn and trained Khmer Air Force FAC pilots under Project Flycatcher, the Tactical Air Improvement Program, Cambodia. We tried with some success to build up a KAF FAC force from scratch.

After a year I went to Phnom Penh, Cambodia, and stayed until April 1975, when Congress quit paying the bills and the Khmer Rouge ran us out of town. Two million innocent victims then died in Cambodia at the hands of Maoist Communist butchers.

I returned to the United States with huge questions that seemed irrelevant to the American population at large. Most civilians who would talk about the war spoke negatively and from ignorance. They seemed fed up with television reporting that had brought the war home to America like a dark soap opera. They felt pain, but for most, only a dull pain.

For years I confined my circle of close friends to the military community. They may not have had better answers than civilians, but at least this group had faced the beast. I drew support from peers with whom I had shared the SEA experience of trying to survive the day, three hundred and sixty five times.

The vast majority of FAC characters seemed ready to forget and move on. Most resigned from the military and disappeared into civilian pursuits. Ravens who stayed for a career generally retired with eagles on their shoulders. Ed Eberhart, who ran Covey Pleiku operations as a lieutenant, eventually pinned on four stars.

I reached my career goal--mostly by timing and good fortune--and commanded the 493rd Tactical Fighter Squadron, flying the F-111F at Lakenheath, England. I supplied the warrior attitude and priorities, then stepped aside for young troops who were true volunteers and seemed better trained than my generation. I fought anything that resembled a stupid rule.

In another memorable assignment I resolved most of my differences with the Army as an Air Liaison Officer with the First Ranger Battalion. I learned herding soldiers through the gates of hell justified a different service culture. My friends teased me about jumping out of perfectly good airplanes, and I replied that Military Airlift Command didn't own any. I jumped from the first aircraft into Grenada with the Rangers in 1983, but that's another story.

Raven FACs maintained strong ties over the years as the Edgar Allen Poe Literary Society, EAPLS (www.ravens.org), under the leadership of D. Craig Morrison, II. His death in a T-6 crash in 1995 reminded me of the fragility of life and inspired me to finish this book.

Before I retired in 1994 from the faculty of the Air War College, we analyzed the lack of strategy in the Vietnam conflict. We recognized sound military advice did not regularly reach political leaders.

The other huge factor in the debacle was service parochialism, which surfaced as bitter subculture rivalries in Vietnam. We were our own worst enemy.

Many of the senior players in the Vietnam drama paraded across the war college stage to give their perspectives, yet I never felt pleased or satisfied. When asked why they didn't resign when they were denied access to the President or when their advice was ignored, most said they thought they could do more good from the inside.

Besides, they argued, they would only be replaced by yes-men.

I always had the feeling I had heard it all before . . ..

NEVERMORE

Jroper3531@aol.com

Glossary

I have used the convention that letters with periods are pronounced as letters. Without periods, pronounce acronyms phonetically.

AAA- Triple A, Antiaircraft artillery

ABCCC- A.B.,triple C., Airborne Command and Control Center, a unit in the back of a C-130 that assigned targets to airborne fighter-bombers. Callsigns were Hillsboro (day) and Moonbeam (night) in the Steel Tiger (panhandle) portion of Laos, and Cricket (day) and Alleycat (night) over the Barrel Roll.

A.F.B.- Air Force Base

A.F.V.N.- Armed Forces Vietnam Network provided radio and television service

A.O.C.- Air Operations Center where the Royal Laotian Air Force exercised control and tasking of fighters and gunships. A.O.C. was also the Air Operations Commander assigned to command sites in Laos on temporary duty in Project 404.

ARVN- Army of the Republic Of Vietnam (South Vietnamese Army)

Barrel Roll- Northern Laos, above the panhandle

B.D.A.- Bomb Damage Assessment

B.K.-37- A rack suspended from a wing pylon that carried four target markers

BUF- Big Ugly Fucker- a term used to describe the B-52 aircraft

C.C.C.- Command and Control Central- the area of interest of the 5th Special Forces Group (Green Berets) assigned to Kontum

D.M.E.- Distance Measuring Equipment- A digital readout of the nautical mileage from a selected ground station

FAC- Forward Air Controller

F.M.- Frequency Modulation, the radio commonly used by ground forces

F.N.G.- Fucking New Guy

F.O.B.- Forward Operating Base, which the Army called its forces at Kontum

G.C.A.- Ground Controlled Approach- An instrument landing approach using ground radar

G.C.I.- Ground Controlled Intercept- A surveillance radar used here for radar separation of air traffic

GIB- Guy In Back- the occupant of the rear seat of a two-seat tandem aircraft

I.D.P.- Interdiction Point

I.F.R.- Instrument Flight Rules- Flying rules required when weather does not permit visual separation of traffic

I.P.- Instructor Pilot

Lau-68- A tube suspended from a wing pylon used to carry and launch seven 2.75 inch diameter rockets

Life Support- A subordinate unit of a flying organization responsible for aircrew support and survival equipment, such as parachutes, survival vests, helmets, weapons

LRRP- Long Range Reconnaissance Patrol

L.Z.- Landing Zone

MAC- Military Airlift Command, the Air Force major command responsible for airlift

MARS- Military Affiliate Radio Station

N.C.O.- Non-Commissioned Officer

N.V.A.- North Vietnamese Army

OOM- Officers' Open Mess, or Officers' Club

O.T.S.- Officer Training School

PIF- Pilot Information File

P.S.P.- Pierced Steel Planks, which hooked together to form temporary runways, helipads

R.& R.- Rest and Relaxation

RAPCON- Radar Approach Control

Recce- Reconnaissance

REMF- Rear Echelon Mother Fuckers

R.O.E.- Rules Of Engagement

R.T.B.- Return To Base

SAC- Strategic Air Command- The Air Force major command responsible for nuclear war

Steel Tiger- An area of the southern Laotian panhandle where the Trail was interdicted

TAC- Tactical Air Command- The Air Force major command responsible for fighter training

Tacan- Tactical Air Navigation- A radio navigation beacon that provides cockpit bearing and distance to selected ground stations

T.I.C.- Troops In Contact, a firefight that required the most precise application of airpower

U.H.F.- Ultra High Frequency- A voice radio primarily used by air force aircraft

U.P.T.- Undergraduate Pilot Training, a one year course of instruction where air force officers earn pilot wings

V.C.- Viet Cong

V.F.R.- Visual Flight Rules- Flight operations based on the principle of "see and avoid"

V.H.F.- A voice radio used primarily by aircraft

VNAF- Vietnamese Air Force

W.P.- White Phosphorous, also called willie pete